Acclaim for Cara Lynn James

"A charming peek inside life during the Gilded era. Highly recommended."
—COLLEEN COBLE, BEST-SELLING AUTHOR OF THE
MERCY FALLS SERIES, REGARDING *LOVE ON ASSIGNMENT*

"Cara Lynn James brings the early 1900s alive with this tender inspirational love story. Her cast of delightful characters will warm your heart and stay with you long after you've turned the last page."
—MARGARET BROWNLEY, AUTHOR OF THE ROCKY CREEK
ROMANCE SERIES, REGARDING *LOVE ON ASSIGNMENT*

"James' debut novel is filled with romance, laughter and secrets, which will delight fans of historical romance. Four stars."
—*ROMANTIC TIMES* REVIEW OF *LOVE ON A DIME*

"*Love on a Dime* is a touching, well-written novel whispering the theme that all things are possible with God."
—*CBA RETAILERS AND RESOURCES*

"Her growing fan base won't be disappointed."
—*PUBLISHERS WEEKLY* REVIEW OF *LOVE BY THE BOOK*

"James is a wonderful author who writes her characters as though they were real people, with their flaws and weaknesses laid bare for the reader to see."
—*ROMANTIC TIMES* 4-STAR REVIEW OF *LOVE ON ASSIGNMENT*

A Path
Toward Love

Also by
Cara Lynn James

The Ladies of Summerhill Novels

Love on a Dime

Love on Assignment

Love by the Book

A Path
Toward Love

CARA LYNN JAMES

THOMAS NELSON
Since 1798

NASHVILLE   DALLAS   MEXICO CITY   RIO DE JANEIRO

Published in Nashville, Tennessee, by Thomas Nelson. Thomas Nelson is a registered trademark of Thomas Nelson, Inc.

Thomas Nelson, Inc., titles may be purchased in bulk for educational, business, fund-raising, or sales promotional use. For information, please e-mail SpecialMarkets@ThomasNelson.com.

Scripture quotations are taken from KING JAMES VERSION of the Bible.

Publisher's note: This novel is a work of fiction. Names, characters, places, and incidents are either products of the author's imagination or used fictitiously. All characters are fictional, and any similarity to people, living or dead, is purely coincidental.

Library of Congress Cataloging-in-Publication Data

James, Cara Lynn, 1949-
    A path toward love / Cara Lynn James.
        p. cm.
    ISBN 978-1-4016-8517-1 (trade paper)
    1. Widows--Fiction. 2. Life change events--Fiction. 3. Choice (Psychology)--Fiction. 4. Citrus fruit industry--Fiction. 5. Hernando County (Fla.)--Fiction. 6. Adirondack Mountains (N.Y.)--Fiction. I. Title.
    PS3610.A4284P38 2012
    813'.6--dc22

                        2012016580

Printed in the United States of America

12 13 14 15 16 17 QG 6 5 4 3 2 1

I'd like to dedicate *A Path Toward Love* to Jase Slaughter, my youngest grandson, who brings such warmth and joy to my heart.

Chapter One

HERNANDO COUNTY, FLORIDA

July 1905

Katherine Osborne couldn't escape the numbers. She dragged her gaze from the lush orange groves right outside her office window to the ledger open on her desk. Why had she ever believed she could run a business with little experience and less capital? The numbers screamed bankruptcy and the end of her dream—unless she quickly obtained a loan to tide her over. She hoped an answer would come in the afternoon post. All she needed was a little more time . . . surely business would improve.

For a few moments she gave in to her mounting fears and buried her head in her hands, allowing the warmth and stillness of the afternoon to wash through her. But at the sound of footsteps, Katherine glanced up and smiled at her maid. Etta Mae, young and pretty, strode through the doorway holding out a stack of mail. "For you, Miz Osborne." She grinned and her teeth glistened white against her dark skin.

"Is there a letter from the bank?" Etta Mae always riffled through the mail before she turned it over to Katherine.

The maid shook her head. "Sorry, ma'am."

Katherine nodded. No word from the loan officer killed her hopes, but only for the day. Perhaps tomorrow she'd finally receive her response.

"There *is* a letter from New York," Etta Mae said, holding out the envelope.

Katherine ripped it open and scanned the creamy page filled with her mother's spidery script.

My dearest Katherine,

Papa is on his way to Florida to visit you at Buena Vista. I expect he'll stay for a week or so, possibly longer. He's scheduled to arrive late afternoon on Monday. I do hope this letter precedes his arrival so that you can give him a proper welcome.

Today! Katherine's heart sputtered at the thought of Papa coming to Buena Vista. She missed him terribly, though a pinch of anxiety tempered her joy. Why was he traveling all the way from New York in the heat of the summer? Her family always spent the season at their camp on Raquette Lake tucked into the rugged Adirondack Mountains. The air was cool and fresh—nothing like Florida. Only something important would drive Papa from Camp Birchwood in July. She'd wager it involved her mounting problems with keeping the citrus groves operating.

Katherine glanced at her pocket watch pinned on her plain cotton shirtwaist. Papa's train would probably arrive within an hour or two. She needed to tidy up her appearance, and above all, calm her nerves. She continued to read Mama's letter.

I do so wish I could join Papa, but I'm afraid my social obligations prevent me from traveling so far.

Aunt Letty is with me at Camp Birchwood for the summer. Our weather is delightful. That's such a blessing since we have a houseful of guests to entertain. I do wish you could be here to vacation with us. Try to join us whenever you can, my dear.

Katherine placed the letter on her lap. How she wished she could visit her family. She hadn't seen any of them in eight years, ever since she'd eloped with Charles against her parents' wishes. They'd never extended invitations to spend summers in the Adirondacks when he was still alive. They detested him—with good reason, as she discovered too late. With a deep sigh rising from the depth of her lungs, Katherine lowered her gaze and read the next few pages of the chatty letter. At the bottom of the last page she found a postscript.

P.S. I neglected to mention that your old friend, Andrew Townsend, will accompany Papa to Florida. I'm sure you'll be anxious to see them both.

The letter fluttered to the floor in a humid breeze that blew through the window. *Why was Andrew coming too?* She couldn't begin to imagine. A picture of her tall, blond neighbor flashed across her mind. They'd been the best of friends for most of their youth. But when she married Charles, he ceased communication. There'd only been one brief note from him when her husband died.

She rose and went to the window, staring outside at the acres of lawn edged with flowering bushes. Her heart squeezed painfully at the memory of arguing with Andrew in the parlor of her parents' Fifth Avenue home right before her marriage. Red faced, her usually mild-mannered friend succumbed to his frustration as he paced the length of the parlor.

"Please don't marry him, Katherine. You'll live to regret it."

"You're maligning a wonderful man," she countered. Anger swirled through her, and she exploded with the hurt of Andrew's criticism. But at eighteen, how could she know Charles was not the gentleman he seemed to be? His suave manners and dashing clothing had swept her off her feet. Why hadn't she seen the real man beneath the facade of wealth and good looks? She thought he loved her deeply. In her naive mind, she imagined she'd become the center of his universe. How could she have been so wrong?

Her romantic notions had all been in her young and foolish mind. She'd rejected Andrew's sage advice and run off with Charles the very next day. Now here she was: a widow with little money, a business in shambles, and bitter memories of a marriage gone bad.

Would Andrew remind her of his warning? Katherine shuddered to think what he'd say about her life now. She had little to show for her endless work except a business teetering on the edge of extinction.

Katherine tucked the letter back in its envelope and locked it in her rolltop desk. She slapped the ledger shut and retreated to the kitchen for a glass of ginger ale to calm her jittery stomach, then upstairs to find something appropriate to wear.

Etta Mae, who doubled as her personal maid, helped her into a plain, plum-colored frock with a lace collar and cuffs, the most festive of all her drab garments. It was odd that she'd never before noticed how worn and faded her dresses looked. But day in, day out she donned the same frocks, skirts, and shirtwaists without a thought to their condition or style. Two years after Charles's death, she'd finished mourning. But even if she'd found the time or money to order a new wardrobe, she wouldn't have bothered. There were too many other things to think about. Pressing things.

Perched at her dressing table, Katherine glanced into the

oval mirror. Her eyes stared back at her like hollow holes encircled by dark shadows. Her mouth turned downward in a frown. Was this weary expression her permanent look? She seldom scrutinized her appearance for more than a moment, and then only to ensure she looked neat and presentable. The carefully groomed debutante of another time and place had faded into a gaunt businesswoman with more on her mind than fashion.

Etta Mae brushed her hair and carefully arranged it in a full pompadour, using silver clips to secure it in place. Katherine brushed powder across her nose and pinched her cheeks for a bit of color. Satisfied, she thanked the girl. Etta Mae disappeared downstairs.

Five minutes later the maid reappeared. "Excuse me, ma'am. Mr. Herne is waiting for you in the parlor."

Nodding, Katherine smoothed her skirt and hurried downstairs. She entered the parlor, the largest and airiest room of the Queen Anne house, to meet Mr. Herne, the manager of her citrus groves. The parlor boasted delicate furniture old Mr. Osborne had bought for his wife in Paris years before and a carved wooden mantelpiece with silver candelabra on each side. The tall windows were raised to the height of a door, letting in a mild breeze and a flood of light.

"Good morning, Mr. Herne."

He paced in front of the unlit fireplace, hands clasped behind his back. His long frame matched his long face, and his chin drooped into a scrawny neck. He averted his eyes for several long seconds and then focused them directly on her. She flinched at his sorrowful look.

"I have something to tell you, Miz Osborne, and I'm not sure how to say it."

Her throat clenched with apprehension. "Say it quickly," she urged. "It's easier that way."

He jerked a nod. "You're right, ma'am." Just the same, he paused again. Katherine held her breath. "I'm afraid I have bad news. I—I'll be leaving here soon."

Startled, Katherine struggled to control her shock. "But why?"

Of course, she knew deep down. They hadn't turned a profit in seven years, ever since old Mr. Osborne passed on. A severe frost in '95 devastated Florida's citrus crop, and their orange and grapefruit trees were wiped out. Charles's father replanted. The trees slowly grew and produced good fruit, but production was not yet back to previous numbers. It was tough to make it even when her father-in-law lived, but under Charles's neglect and mismanagement, the business spiraled downward toward insolvency.

During the past two years, she and Mr. Herne had fought to revive the groves but with only marginal success. So far. But they'd improved, little by little. Had he given up? Or had he merely accepted reality? A chill slithered down her spine.

"I got another job. It's in Georgia, closer to my kin. I'm sorry, Miz Osborne. You've been the best employer a man could ever want, but I got to think of my wife and kids. So I'll be moving on by the end of the week. I hope you understand it's not personal. I just hate doing this to you."

Katherine grabbed the back of a chair to steady herself. "I do understand." He had no choice. Loyalty to his family came first. Given the small crops, she hadn't been able to pay him what he needed to adequately support his family. Who could blame him? She forced a weary smile. "We tried hard, and we were a good team. I'm sorry to see you go." Indeed, Michael Herne labored with all the enthusiasm and competence of an owner, not an employee. But the time had come; practicality ruled. "I shall miss you very much."

Tears pooled in his eyes. "You've been good to me and my family. I hate to leave you high and dry. Can you find someone to take my place?"

Her mouth twisted in a wry smile. "No one can really take your place, Mr. Herne. You must know that. But I'll put out the word I need a new manager. I'm certain someone will come along."

Katherine wasn't sure at all, but she wouldn't allow this hardworking man to feel guilty about his decision. She had so little to offer him anymore. They needed more workers to plant trees and another manager to supervise. But would anyone work for the meager salary she'd been paying Mr. Herne? And who would want to work for a business on the verge of bankruptcy? A headache began to mushroom.

With leaden feet, Katherine walked toward her office, Mr. Herne at her heels. "Let me give you your pay, and then you can leave whenever you're ready to go."

"Thank you, ma'am. I appreciate your thoughtfulness."

She forced a confident smile. She tamped down the terror slowly swelling in her chest with a prayer.

Lord, I haven't prayed in such a long time, but please hear me anyway. Please. I need Your strength right now, or I'll start blubbering all over poor Mr. Herne, and he'll feel like such a cad for leaving me in the lurch. Help me to act strong and capable, even though I'm neither. And help Mr. Herne with his new job. Amen.

With shaky hands, Katherine opened the wall safe, counted out the correct bills and added a few extra. "Here you go. God be with you."

His eyes widened and his voice crackled. "Thank you kindly. I know you don't have money to spare."

She raised her palm. "I wish I could offer you more to properly thank you for sticking by me through such hard times." Clearing her throat, she continued, "Thank you so very much."

He nodded and hurried out the door, Etta Mae peering after him.

Katherine sank into the parlor settee and buried her head in her hands. If she could only arrange for that bank loan, she'd have enough cash to pay the workers and bring in the harvest. She sat up straight and pounded her fist into the palm of her other hand. She'd make the groves show a profit even if she had to work morning, noon, and night. The laborers depended upon Buena Vista for their livelihood. How could she turn them out and still live with herself? She'd fight for them, and for herself.

Thoughts of meeting Charles's loan, as well as a new one, dimmed Katherine's hopes. She already scrimped on every household expense possible; where would she find the cash to meet another bill? She couldn't surrender. Not yet. Not when every year the harvest edged the groves back toward profitability . . .

She'd failed at her marriage to Charles, but she refused to fail in the business he'd left her.

———·+·———

Later, Katherine moved out to the front porch and watched for a carriage to turn up her long driveway lined with crepe myrtle trees bursting with pink blooms. Several oaks dripping with strands of Spanish moss dotted the lawn. When she finally spotted a buggy with three men and a pile of luggage, she sprang to her feet and waved. Tears welled in her eyes, but she quickly wiped them away. The carriage halted in front of the house and Papa carefully descended, followed by his ancient valet, Royce. And then came Andrew, from the far side, smiling broadly.

Katherine rushed toward her father, her arms outstretched. "Oh, Papa, how grand to see you again!"

He looked nearly the same—tall, rugged, and a bit too robust— though wavy, gray hair now receded from his tanned hairline. He still sported a distinguished, well-trimmed, salt-and-pepper mustache and beard. But Katherine noticed there was more salt than pepper these days as she flew into his arms and nestled against his silk vest. A bubble of joy blocked her throat and tears spilled down her cheeks. With an embarrassed laugh, she dabbed them with a handkerchief he whipped from his pocket. His infectious grin was a balm to her heart.

"My little princess. Lovely to see you again. It's been far too long." Papa encircled her in a tight hug, and for a few moments, all was well in her world.

He stepped back and his affectionate gaze swept her from head to toe. "Let me look at you, honey. My goodness, you're all grown up." His smile faded a little and then veered toward a frown. "But you're so thin. You need some meat on your bones. Have you been working too hard?"

"Perhaps I have. A little," she said, trying to brush off his concern. "But I promise to slow down while you're here. And eat more."

"Good. But not *just* while I'm visiting, I hope."

Katherine nodded obediently. But inside, she wondered just where she'd find the time to eat, let alone rest.

Andrew stood beside Mr. Wainwright, satchel in hand. His eyes widened and his breath caught in his throat. Katherine was even lovelier than when he'd last seen her as an eighteen-year-old, long legged and girlish. Her expressive blue eyes contained a new depth; her honey-colored hair had darkened to a pleasing blend of shades of gold. She was still as slender as a willow branch. But as her father had noted, her frame seemed too thin, even beneath the full skirt of her purple dress. Her waist looked no bigger than a hand span. But he still found her very attractive. Too attractive.

When she turned toward him, a wide smile on her lips, his heart started bouncing in his chest like a Ping-Pong ball. But then he noted her hollow cheeks in place of the round, rosy ones he remembered, and her heart-shaped face now came to a sharper point at her chin.

Was the job of managing citrus groves too overwhelming for her? He'd find out over the course of the next week while he stayed at Buena Vista with Mr. Wainwright.

"Andrew," she called in her soft voice, "I can't believe you're here! I'm so happy to see you." Her genuine joy warmed him.

He swallowed hard. "It's wonderful to see you too, Katherine."

They chatted for a few minutes before a maid opened the front door and Mr. Wainwright lumbered over the threshold. "If you wouldn't mind, my princess, I'd like to go directly to my room, unpack, and take a short nap. It's a strenuous journey down the East Coast, even in my own railcar." He removed his bowler and waited for Etta Mae and Royce to bring in the trunks and valises. Together they hauled the luggage up the stairs. Katherine's father followed more slowly.

Once he made his way past the bend in the staircase, Katherine took Andrew's hands and pressed them tightly. She flashed an amused smile. "If you could only see your face. You look as if I'm going to bite. Truly, I'm not."

He gave her a sheepish grin and shifted from one booted foot to the other. "I can see that now. But I wasn't sure of my reception. After the way we left things, I didn't know if you'd forgiven me."

Sadness flickered across her face and then vanished. "Andrew, I forgave you long ago."

Her eyes were as welcoming as the sunshine, and his anxiety slid away. "I was wrong to interfere in your life, Katherine, giving you unwanted advice about Charles." He knew he had to apologize, but under similar circumstances, he'd probably repeat the offense. After all, how could he, in good conscience, let her run off with his disreputable college classmate without trying to warn her? "I'm sorry we parted on such a sour note."

Katherine nodded. "I'm sorry we didn't part on friendlier terms too, but that's water under the bridge. I accept your apology, of course. You should know I could never stay angry with you. We were best friends for too long."

He'd never quite forgiven himself for causing a breach between them. "Thank you. I'm relieved." Certainly he should've employed more tact instead of spurting out the unvarnished truth. For the entire trip south, he'd feared a chilly welcome. He cleared his throat. "I'm sorry about your loss—of Charles. That must've been a terrible blow."

"It was a dreadful shock," she said.

When she didn't elaborate further, he suspected Charles's death hurt too much to discuss—unless the marriage had turned out as horribly as he feared. He knew from society gossip that Charles had died within a week of contracting yellow fever.

She turned back to him wearing a bright smile that shut down further conversation about her deceased husband. "You must be famished. Would you care to join me for a snack and a cup of tea?" she asked.

"I'd like that." He strolled beside her as they entered her cozy home styled with gingerbread trim, open porches, dormers, and half a dozen gables painted white. She rang for sweets from the kitchen along with afternoon tea. They wandered through sunny rooms until they arrived at the back veranda filled with potted plants and blooming red and yellow hibiscus. They dropped into wicker chairs set around a small table and waited only a few minutes for the cook to appear with an abundance of sponge cake, raspberry tarts, éclairs, and a silver pot of hot black tea.

"Would you mind if I took off my suit coat?" he asked as perspiration seeped around the edges of his tight collar.

"Go right ahead. Florida is dreadfully hot during the summer. It takes some getting used to."

He hung the jacket over the back of the chair and loosened his tie. "I doubt if I'd ever get acclimated to the heat." He lifted off his bowler and placed it on his lap.

Katherine tilted her head. "Of course you would. After a while even the unbearable seems normal."

He stared at her, slowly nodding.

He was so happy to see Katherine again he couldn't pull his gaze from her stunning face, even shadowed as it was with weariness. Obviously she hadn't taken proper care of herself. But her smile was a beam of light. "Tell me, Andrew, what have you been doing since I left New York?" Katherine nibbled at the raspberry tart drizzled with melted chocolate.

"Me? Exactly as you might expect. I'm an attorney. About four years ago I started working for your father at his railroad. It's a challenging job, but very rewarding."

"Mama never mentioned you worked for Papa." Her delicate brow furrowed in confusion and she shook her head. "How odd."

Not truly odd, Andrew surmised. Best friends since girlhood, Katherine's mother and his Aunt Georgia Clarke lived next door to each other in limestone mansions across the avenue from New York's Central Park. After his parents died of influenza twenty years before, Andrew had moved in with his aunt, uncle, and cousin Randy. But the older women had always conspired to bring Katherine and Randy together, hoping to build on their friendship.

Steepling his fingers, Andrew hesitated for a moment. "Katherine, if you don't mind my curiosity, may I ask you a personal question?"

"Of course, you can ask anything you wish." But she didn't sound quite as positive as her words indicated. "What would you like to know?" The wicker chair squeaked as she shifted her weight.

"I often wondered why you didn't come home after Charles passed away."

Her answer came so fast he wondered if she'd prepared it earlier. "Mama wanted me to move back to New York, but I decided to stay and see the groves thrive once again, just as they had in Charles's father's day. Unfortunately, Charles didn't tend to business as well as he should have, so we've had some significant hurdles to cross. I wanted to restore the groves, and the business. It's as simple as that."

Nothing was as simple as it appeared, and Andrew suspected Katherine's explanation was only part of the story. Mr. Wainwright had heard from his Florida contacts that Charles Osborne had destroyed his business through poor stewardship, and he'd left Katherine with little money and a company in disarray.

He cocked an eyebrow, unable to hide a sardonic grin. "Do you enjoy managing the citrus groves? Or doesn't business suit you?"

She flicked a dry smile. "I was trained to become a wife, a mother, and a hostess. I can put together a menu and organize a ball. But I quickly discovered I could do much more, here at Osborne Citrus Groves. I'm still learning more every day. I love much of it."

Andrew couldn't help but admire such pluck. "But you don't need to work."

Katherine smiled. "Not if I'd turn tail and head home to Mama. I suspect no one in my family wants me to do *a man's job*. But I truly like to grow and harvest our fruit. I love working with people and selling a good product." She laughed self-consciously at her enthusiasm. "Actually, it's much more than that. When I first came to Buena Vista, Charles's father was so welcoming, I loved him instantly. He passed on a year later, but I'll always remember his zeal for the groves and his desire to bring them back to health. I'm partly doing this for him, at least as a memorial to him. Do you think me sentimental?"

"Not at all." Yet her answer left Andrew with a few questions. Katherine enjoyed the work and wanted to make the groves prosperous for Charles's father. Why didn't she want to do it in memory of Charles as well? Maybe his assumption about their marriage was correct.

Katherine leaned across the table and took his hands. The warmth of her palms shot up and down his arms, and in consternation, he felt a fiery flush to his cheeks. Even a cool breeze didn't lower the heat rising from his neck into his face. But Katherine didn't seem to notice. Her eyes glistened as her glance swept across the lawn to the orange groves.

"I'm hopeful we're on the verge of making a real comeback, Andrew." She dropped his hands and took a sip of tea. She tilted her head, her eyes sparkling, although not in the least flirtatious. "I'm doing this for the workers too. Those here in the house as well as in the groves. Even those who come for the harvest. They're like family to me, and they depend on this business to survive."

Andrew nodded. "I see." He looked away, out toward the trees, so his eyes wouldn't betray him. Her love of the land and the business would make her father's task that much more difficult. Undoubtedly, they were in for a battle.

Chapter Two

S itting this close to Andrew was surprisingly hard. Even with the tiny table between them, she could still smell the scent of bay rum. Not long after Charles had died, she remembered walking through the marketplace. There in the narrow aisles of one of the shops, a man passed by and his cologne wafted around her. She'd stopped, held her breath, and let the scent flood her heart with memories of home and of Andrew.

Today, as she listened to Andrew, she remembered how thoughts of him had invaded her mind many times throughout the two years since Charles had died. Maybe he was there only because she was lonely and he was someone who'd been a good friend to her, someone who understood her. Or maybe he filled her mind because she knew she'd missed the opportunity to allow their friendship to grow into something more serious.

Pushing aside that silly notion, she ate her sweets, slipping into easy conversation with him as they had done in their early years, and let the worries of the citrus groves and finances and possible financial ruin slide off her shoulders. Andrew always eased her concerns.

She wondered how she looked in his eyes. Did he merely see her as tired and part of whatever task her father had assigned him—or did he see her as the companion she'd been years ago?

He looked older now, more distinguished than she remembered. His mouth lifted slightly at one corner as if he were enjoying an amusing thought he seemed reticent to share. His eyes sometimes sparked and sometimes sparkled, hinting at opinions locked inside an active mind. When they were young she'd tried to probe his thoughts to see what made him so intriguing, but he seldom revealed himself. He was warm and aloof at the same time.

———————

After Andrew retired to his bedroom for the night, Katherine led Papa out to the side terrace. Since Andrew had remained stubbornly close-mouthed about it, perhaps she could discover why Papa had come to Florida now. As she gently rocked on the porch swing, he lit a Cuban cigar and sipped his brandy in the dusky light.

"You've got a beautiful place here," he conceded. "It's a shame you're so far from us. We miss you."

She reached over and patted his hand. "I've missed you too, Papa."

As the sun slipped toward the treetops planted in even rows up the hillside, she waited for him to end the small talk and broach the subject he'd come here to discuss. Her shoulders stiffened. She couldn't relax until they talked over the purpose of his visit and she convinced him she belonged here.

A smoke ring curled around his head. He mopped perspiration from his brow. "I suppose your mama and I are selfish, but we want you to come home. That doesn't surprise you, does it? It was one thing for you to live more than fifteen hundred miles away when you were married. But now that you're a widow, we don't understand what's keeping you in Florida. Your real home is in New York with your family." His eyes pleaded with her.

Now she understood. He came here to escort her home to her former life. In her parents' eyes, she could resume her role as pampered daughter and a widow in search of a suitable husband.

Sadness and elation collided within her. Could she ever return to her place in society, and did she even wish to? Would she be accepted for who she was or would she be ridiculed for marrying a disreputable man?

She glanced toward the groves that had become her life. Could she leave Buena Vista, the land she'd grown to love? And more importantly, could she once again become the obedient daughter after living independently for so long?

"Katherine," her father said, gently, nudging her for a response.

"If only I could be in two places at once," she said softly. "But I can't, so I have to choose where I'm truly meant to be."

"And?"

The apprehension in his tone made her flinch. "I'm so sorry to disappoint you, but I have to stay here. My heart is here now, as much as I long for you and Mama. Buena Vista is my home and I have a responsibility toward the people who work here. Surely you must appreciate that."

Papa nodded. "I do. I have hundreds, even thousands of railroad workers who rely on me. So I know what you feel for them." He swirled the brandy in the snifter. "You have a tender heart, Katherine, and that's something special. But perhaps we could find someone else who'd love to make a go of it here, someone with more experience. Maybe a local."

She sent him a wry smile. "You mean a man, don't you?"

He had the grace to look flustered. "I think a man is better suited to run a large operation, although I'm sure you do the best you can."

"I've been doing the best I can for two years, Papa."

He shifted. "And you learned the business from scratch?"

"I did. Mr. Herne, my foreman, is an excellent teacher, and he taught me everything I needed to know. We're on the verge of turning a profit and I'm very optimistic about the future." She looked away, embarrassed at her exaggeration. "Naturally I don't really know what lies ahead, but I'm certainly hopeful our situation will improve. Soon."

She ought to confess that Mr. Herne had quit and her situation was dire. But she couldn't quite bring herself to reveal the entire, brutal truth, at least not yet. She would before he and Andrew left. "Papa, it would break my heart to sell."

"Yes, but I daresay, after a while you'd recover. You'd have plenty of distractions in New York."

Just the idea of selling the business stole her breath away. Katherine shook her head. "No, Papa. I don't want to sell my business."

Papa cocked his head. "It's obvious you love running this place." He looked toward the green groves dotted with small, developing oranges. "I understand your attraction to having a company of your own, but surely you can come home for a good, long visit and see how much you've missed."

Katherine knew a *good, long visit* in her father's mind could mean six months or more. "I'm sorry, Papa, but I can't. We begin harvesting the navel oranges and grapefruit in the fall and continue until the winter freezes. And then in March we begin again, harvesting the Valencias and finishing in June. It's crucial that I'm here most of the year. You wouldn't be able to walk away from your railroads for six months, would you?"

For a second Papa was taken aback, but then he smiled. "No, I couldn't. But this is different. You don't need to work to support a family. I do."

Katherine nodded slowly. "I have a family of my own to support, in a sense—the workers. They depend on me. But I also have another reason for staying."

Her father's eyebrows lifted. "And what's that?"

"I want to restore the orange groves to the way they were before the Great Freeze. Mr. Osborne was devastated, but he stuck with it and started over. He was a determined but very kind man and I admired his tenacity. I feel—I feel I owe it to him."

Her father peered outward. "That was a devastating time. Perhaps this area isn't best suited to avoid another such disaster, though."

"Many of the growers left or moved farther south. But Mr. Osborne replanted. I'd like to make his citrus groves prosper again."

"But you haven't yet recovered," he said, gently probing for the truth.

"No, but in another five years we should be producing as much fruit as before the freeze. It takes about fifteen years for new trees to grow to full maturity. Every year we make gains. I'd like to plant even more trees and in a few years open a citrus packing plant near the railroad depot. We already ship most of our fruit up north."

Papa reached over and squeezed her hand. "I hear the enthusiasm in your voice. But, princess, will you be happy ten or twenty years from now when all you have is a citrus company? Don't you want to marry and have a family? Family can bring great joy, you know."

She'd already thought this through long and hard, and she knew her mind. "Papa, I plan on staying a widow for the rest of my life." She'd ruined her one opportunity for marriage by choosing unwisely. It pained her to accept that she'd never have children. It created a gaping emptiness she'd have to fill with something else. But she'd never risk love again. "I'm content, here in Florida."

Her father drew out a sigh. Like Mama, he wasn't used to any opposition and didn't seem to know quite how to handle it. Katherine's heart contracted. How she hated to let her beloved papa down, the parent who'd spoiled her and loved her with his every breath. But she was an adult now, and this was her home. Nothing he said would convince her to leave the place she loved and had made into a home for herself.

"If you change your mind, I'd be glad to help you find a buyer for your groves. I have plenty of contacts in Florida."

"Thank you, Papa. But no. I love my independence and the satisfaction of working hard every day."

He nodded grudgingly. Papa understood, though she knew he wouldn't change his position or give up his quest of taking her back north. He tried again. "Maybe you could direct your energy toward society."

Katherine chuckled. "I hardly think presiding over tea and gossip would fulfill me. It suits Mama, but society life never interested me. You know that."

"I understand." He smiled. "Nevertheless, working such long hours isn't good for you. You look exhausted."

Katherine shrugged. She couldn't disagree with the truth.

"Couldn't you at least consider coming home for a spell, before fall harvest? Perhaps Mr. Herne could manage things on his own. Or maybe you could hire someone else. Then you'd be free to visit Camp Birchwood for the summer and decide if you'd like to stay on."

A summer vacation at the family camp deep in the mountains did indeed tempt her after such a long stint of ceaseless work. "I'm afraid Mr. Herne couldn't help out," she hedged. "And I don't know of anyone else who'd manage the groves short-term."

Papa's crestfallen face saddened her. "Well, I would love to see Camp Birchwood again . . . But it's highly unlikely a competent manager will just come along."

Papa heaved himself from the wicker chair with a quiet groan. "Thank you, Katherine. Would you like me to make some inquiries?"

She shook her head. "Thank you for the offer, but I can see to it."

He said good night, kissed her on the forehead, and sauntered into Buena Vista, quietly closing the door behind him.

Katherine gently rocked back and forth on the swing, inhaling the fragrance of nearby roses mixed with the earthy smell of approaching nightfall. A grand summer on the shores of Raquette Lake appealed to her far more than remaining here in the blazing heat of summer. But what if her formidable mother pressured her to move home permanently and ruined the season with incessant nagging? Mama could be incredibly irritating.

Her mind skipped from Mama to Andrew, a much more pleasant subject. She imagined him settling into the guest room beside Papa's. She still wasn't sure why Papa had brought Andrew to Florida unless it was for companionship, or . . . maybe her parents expected she'd be willing to sell the citrus groves and return home without a fuss. Perhaps Andrew accompanied her father in order to do all the necessary legal work concerning the sale of the property.

Regardless of the reason for his visit, a frisson of happiness raced through her. Andrew and Papa were here at her home, the only friends and family who'd come to visit in eight years. A little of the loneliness that clung to her like a second skin fell away.

———

After breakfast the next morning, Katherine led Andrew and Mr. Wainwright through the orange groves. Andrew heard the pride in her voice as they strolled down the rows of bushy trees with tiny, green oranges clinging to the branches. They were planted on a rise, the best location.

"During February and March the orange blossoms cover the trees and smell heavenly. You must come back this winter to see for yourselves," she said. "It's quite lovely. And I'll even give you some fresh squeezed orange juice from our Valencias."

Andrew bit the inside of his mouth to keep from grinning at Katherine's enthusiasm and constant chatter, despite her apparent fatigue. Was she trying to prove to her father—and possibly to herself—that she could manage these groves with little assistance?

Two years of work and instruction by her foreman had undoubtedly given her a burst of confidence in her own management skills, but was this enough training for her to succeed?

"These are the trees Charles's father replanted after the frost wiped out the groves. It takes years for trees to grow to full size." She gestured toward the rows. "But they're producing *good* fruit, and that's the most important thing."

Andrew glanced around and noted empty acreage. He pointed to the fallow hillside. "Are you going to plant more over there?"

She nodded. "Just as soon as I get more money to buy the plantings. Charles left me enough land to eventually make this one of the largest citrus groves in Florida."

That she could forge ahead with optimism impressed him. If her breadth of knowledge also impressed her father, he'd never admit it. Mr. Wainwright was bound and determined to take Katherine back to New York and her mother.

"Our navel oranges are seedless and delicious to eat," she went on, "but not very good for juice."

Andrew couldn't pull his gaze from her smile. She almost glowed beneath the sunshine and clear blue sky. She deserved to spend the rest of her life living on her land, regardless of what her parents thought about women working, without a husband or father's supervision. Anyone with her dedication ought to be allowed to live where she was most happy.

But did he dare share his opinion with Mr. Wainwright? Judging from his frown, he didn't understand—or wish to understand—the extent of his daughter's love and commitment.

They turned around and started strolling back toward the white clapboard house.

"I must admit you're doing a remarkable job. I could never imagine you'd take to business so well," her father said, his smile brimming with pride. "But running orange groves is just too massive an undertaking for a woman without a partner to share the burden."

She halted and turned toward her father, her expression serious. "No, Papa. I can handle it by myself."

He shook his head, unconvinced. "By the way, I haven't seen your Mr. Herne. I'd like to speak to him, if he's available."

Katherine blanched and then flicked a tight smile. "I'm afraid he's taken a job up north. He's packing his things, so I imagine he'll be too busy to talk to you today." She spun around and hurried toward Buena Vista.

Mr. Wainwright narrowed his eyes. "Do you have a replacement for him?" he called after her.

Katherine shook her head and increased her pace. "No, he only gave me the news yesterday, so I haven't had a chance to look for anyone else."

Her father murmured, "I see." He hastened to catch up with her and asked, "Can I help you with the business in some way? I like to keep busy, even on vacation."

"No, Papa, but thank you all the same. If you'll excuse me, I have to get back to my office. I'll see you at luncheon. Enjoy the morning." With that, Katherine hurried off for her office, while Andrew and her father stood in her dust.

Mr. Wainwright stared after her and then shook his head. "My daughter worries me, Andrew. She won't admit she's fighting a losing battle. Anyone can see she needs a lot of money to make improvements. I'm afraid the gossip I heard about the groves is all true. They're going under."

He looked genuinely distressed and sorry for Katherine's plight. But Andrew knew enough not to suggest Mr. Wainwright loan her money or just give her the funds as a gift. Her father loved her, but he didn't intend to prolong a dying dream.

He reached up and touched a thick limb of the nearest tree, laden with fruit, then turned back to the lady of the orchard, hurrying away from them. Katherine Wainwright Osborne wasn't the same girl Andrew remembered. And yet she was more intriguing than ever.

———

As the sun started its slow descent toward dusk, Katherine strolled through the orange groves to escape the pressures weighing her down. Her father's obvious disapproval and the ever-present worry over cash for operating expenses rattled through her mind like loose marbles. But wandering through the groves brought tranquility she sorely needed. The peace of approaching nightfall washed through her and strengthened her resolve.

She hoped she could live through her father's visit with grace and optimism. Like Mama, he meant well. He wanted what he believed was best for her. But he didn't understand how keeping occupied with the groves helped her to forget Charles and her wretched, lost years.

At the sound of footsteps, Katherine glanced over her shoulder. Andrew was striding toward her, smiling. Her heart fluttered, as it hadn't in years.

"I thought I'd find you out here," he called.

She turned and waited for him to catch up. "It's a grand place to think. There aren't many interruptions."

Andrew laughed. "Except for me." A sheepish grin spread across his uncommonly handsome face. Her eyes lingered there, adjusting to the man she'd left when he was twenty, hardly older than a boy. He had a strong, square jaw with a small cleft in his chin, a straight nose, and eyes the blue-green color of the Gulf of Mexico.

"You're not an interruption. More like a distraction, but a welcome one."

"Thank you. I came to tell you that Stuart Osborne is in the drawing room waiting to see you."

She closed her eyes for a moment. "Oh dear. I completely forgot he asked to stop by this evening. Stuart is Charles's younger brother. He bought the citrus groves next to mine a few months ago. He's been living out west for the last ten years, but just moved back."

With her father prodding her to sell, this was a most inopportune time for Stuart to visit. Katherine's stomach twisted as she slowly headed toward Buena Vista. If she were fortunate, maybe Papa would be in his bedroom or the library. If the two met and started talking about the adjoining groves, his visit could turn into a disaster for her.

"What's wrong, Katherine?" Andrew glanced at her sideways, frowning. "You look grim."

She hesitated to explain. Andrew was still the best friend she'd ever had. She trusted him, but they hadn't talked in so long, and to complicate matters, he now worked for Papa. If she confided in him, would he tell her father? She didn't know where his loyalty lay, but certainly he must feel torn between the two of them and their opposing goals.

"Stuart and I have our disagreements." Katherine squared her shoulders and increased her pace, anxious to get the meeting over and done with as soon as possible. *Dear Lord, help me to be gracious, or at least civil, to Stuart. And please, Lord, don't let him stay more than a few minutes.* Together, they climbed the front stairs to the veranda.

"Would you like me to attend your meeting?" Andrew asked, a tentative note in his voice.

She shook her head and bit back a smile at his kind offer. "No need, but thank you all the same. This is something I have to settle on my own. I'm used to relying on myself. And the Lord, of course."

Andrew nodded, paused at the closed drawing room door, and lightly touched her sleeve. "If you want anyone to talk to later, remember I'm here."

"Thank you. I'll remember." She breathed deeply and entered the parlor. Closing the pocket doors she smiled cordially, she hoped, at the large, lumpy man waiting by the mantel, his lip curled in annoyance. He relaxed his scowl as soon as he saw it was she. "It's nice to see you again, Katherine."

"Good evening, Stuart. It's lovely outside, so I took a long walk. I lost track of the time, I'm afraid. Did I keep you waiting long?"

"It's all right." But his right eye twitched.

They settled across from each other on stiff wing chairs upholstered in cream brocade. "May I offer you something to eat or drink?"

"No, thank you. I can't stay long. But I'm hoping you've changed your mind about selling me your citrus groves."

She braced herself. "I'm sorry, Stuart, but they're too important to me to sell. If I ever change my mind, and I'm certain I won't, I'll speak to you first. I quite understand why you'd like them back in your family, but remember I'm an Osborne too, at least by marriage."

The muscles in his pasty face tightened. "I made you a reasonable offer two weeks ago. I'm now prepared to raise my offer by ten thousand dollars."

Suppressing a gasp, she hid her surprise behind a mild smile. "That's very generous of you. But I still won't sell."

He quirked a thick, dark brow. "Are you sure it's not a matter of money? If you're holding out for more, then I'm afraid you've overplayed your cards. I've offered more than the groves are worth because it's my family business, and I want it back."

She tried not to bristle at his menacing tone and forced herself to be calm. "No, it's not a matter of money. I enjoy what I'm doing, and I intend to stay put."

"My brother should've left them to me, not you, Katherine. By all rights they should be mine."

Taken aback, she didn't know how to respond to her brother-in-law without insulting him and starting a quarrel. He'd never been so overt in his claim. She steadied her heartbeat by taking a series of shallow, rhythmic breaths. "Perhaps you're right, but Charles willed them to me. I'm building the business, slowly but surely."

He snorted. "You don't know the first thing about managing Osborne Citrus Groves. You've only made insignificant gains since Charles's death. And now with Herne leaving . . ." He paused, seemed to gather himself, and leaned forward. "Katherine, I'm much better prepared to make a go of it, and I have the funds to do it. My groves in California are turning in cash crops. Given my resources, I'll turn the company around within a matter of months. It'll take years for you to see any real improvements."

His eyes bore into hers, but she returned his glare with a direct gaze. "You need extra cash to bring in the harvest this fall. Do you have it?"

"Truly, that is no business of yours."

He studied her. "Katherine, just give in to the inevitable. You'll struggle year after year . . . Aren't you weary of it by now?"

She fought to stay calm as her chest constricted. Angry words rose in her throat, but she swallowed them down. "You're wrong, Stuart. I'll find my way."

He stood up, towering over her. "You'll be bankrupt within a year and the company will go under. The next time I make an offer it won't be for nearly as much as I'm ready to give you now. If you were a shrewd businessman instead of a stubborn woman, you'd gratefully accept my offer. Don't wait until it's too late."

She rose on shaky legs. With a soft, calm voice, she answered him, "No one knows the future, Stuart, but I do hope your prediction doesn't come true. I've worked hard, and I know with the Lord's blessing these groves will flourish, and I'll find a way to bring in the harvest." If she were given more time and enough funds for the harvest and a few key improvements, she stood a good chance of success. But without time and money, she reluctantly acknowledged that Stuart was right. But she wouldn't let discouragement rob her of hope.

She led Stuart to the closed door, relieved that his harangue had ended. She hoped he'd never come to her home again. He paused at the door and attempted a smile. It emerged as a pained grimace, but Katherine gave him the benefit of the doubt. He looked toward the high ceiling, as if searching for a few final words. The taut lines of his face smoothed and his voice softened. "Look, Katherine, if you're doing this for Charles—"

"I'm doing it for your father. He was a good man, a man who loved me from the start. I want to see his dream realized."

Stuart studied her. "If you really want to honor Dad's dream, you'll sell to me. Let me bring it to fruition. We're after the same thing."

Flinching, she lowered her gaze for a moment. "I can't quite explain it, Stuart. Only that I know I'm to stay here. To see it through."

With an exasperated groan, Stuart pushed open the parlor door. "Let me know when you change your mind."

Katherine followed him out to the front hallway, her throat dry with the dust of unspoken words. She shouldn't lose her temper and spout off at Stuart, even if he deserved it. She heard a creak and glanced toward the staircase. Her father stood on the bottom step, his mouth agape, his eyes staring in distress at her and Stuart. And right behind him was Andrew.

Chapter Three

Katherine introduced everyone briefly in an awkward attempt at proper etiquette.

Accepting his fedora from the maid, Stuart bowed slightly. "I've made Katherine an excellent offer for the Osborne groves, but as you might have heard, she refused. Perhaps you can talk some sense into her, Mr. Wainwright."

Papa nodded. "I shall try."

"If you'll all excuse me, I'll be on my way." Stuart took his hat in hand and left.

When the front door closed and the maid disappeared, Katherine spun toward her father and Andrew. She was in no mood to rehash the unpleasantness, but couldn't find a way to change the subject.

Her father cleared his throat and broke the silence. "Why don't you sell to him? Wouldn't you like the company to stay in the Osborne family?"

"It's difficult, Papa. Complicated." She didn't like Stuart. He'd come home after his father died, furious that the old gentleman had willed nearly everything to Charles. And then there was the letter he'd sent to her right after Charles's passing, reinforcing her opinion. Incensed his brother had left the family business to her, Stuart badgered her to sell to him, and even threatened to contest the will if she didn't. He'd never followed through, but he'd caused her to worry for several months.

The neglected groves were all Charles had to leave her. He'd gambled away his own inheritance, and then the funds she'd received from her grandfather. This was her one and only chance to earn her own living and maintain her independence from her family, especially her mother. How could she explain to her father that she dreaded returning to Mama's tight control? If she went back to New York, neither of her parents would allow her the freedom to live in her own home and lead her own life. That just wasn't done in their social circles.

Katherine breathed deeply and averted her glower from Papa. Tears stung her eyes, but if she let them fall, he'd consider her weak and incapable of handling the pressures of the business world. Determination gripped her. "It might be logical to accept his offer, but I'm not going to. My life is here. There's no need to speak of this again. Good night to both of you. Sleep well."

———

After a restless night, Katherine rose before sunup. She turned up the gaslight and nestled into a softly cushioned chair by her fireplace. Opening her dusty Bible, she began to read John. The words were familiar. She'd read them often enough during her younger years, but from the time she'd fallen blindly in love with Charles, she'd gradually given up studying the Word and praying. When she again sought out the Lord's quiet voice in her heart, she didn't like what He had to say. He pricked her conscience.

Katherine shouldn't have turned against her parents' wishes and especially their wise advice, but she loved Charles—or who she thought he was—and she wouldn't abide any criticism of him.

She'd take care not to drift away from the Lord again. He provided strength when her own failed. And she felt hers slipping away little by little. She rubbed her face and turned to the window, staring over the straight rows of treetops. Perhaps news of the bank loan would come today and bring relief. She pushed down a wave of rising panic and headed out to the orange groves.

After a short walk in the cool of early morning, Katherine went to her office, located in a whitewashed outbuilding a short distance from Buena Vista. She worked until luncheon. When she returned to the office, she found the mail had been delivered and piled on her desk. Swallowing hard, Katherine glanced through the pile of letters, her hand trembling. Quickly she scanned the return addresses on each envelope. When she found the letter on the bottom of the stack, she stared at it for several long moments, afraid to tear it open. Savoring the hope that it would announce good news, she let several seconds tick by before she slit the crease of the envelope and pulled out the single sheet of paper.

Dear Mrs. Osborne:

    We're sorry to inform you that your request for a loan has been denied.

Her knees wobbled. She sank into her desk chair and read the rest of the letter, then the first line again, wishing that different words would somehow appear on the page. But, of course, they stayed exactly as the banker had written them. *Denied.* Why was she so shocked?

As soon as she'd talked to the bank officer, she'd known he had no intention of loaning money to a woman with no business credentials and minimal experience. She'd shown him the evidence that over the last year their production had improved. Modestly. But he'd declared Osborne Citrus Groves a shaky enterprise, destined for failure.

What had ever given her such unfounded optimism? Her wishful thinking had erased all her common sense and good judgment. She'd rushed headlong into a disastrous marriage and regretted it. Maybe her stab at operating the citrus groves was no more than another ill-advised attempt doomed for failure.

Katherine rested her head in her hands and let disappointment surge through her. What could she do now except sell her property to Stuart, pack her bags, and leave? She had no other alternative.

Unless . . .

Light on her feet, she raced to Buena Vista and shot through the empty rooms of the house in search of her father. He was so good to her she hated to ask him for a favor, but who else could she approach? Her heart thumped, not from running in a tightly laced corset, but from anxiety that mounted with every step. What if he refused her?

She finally spotted him on the back terrace, reading a newspaper and sipping lemonade with Andrew. They both looked up and grinned. "Can you join us for a glass of tea or lemonade?" Papa asked, gesturing toward the vacant chair next to him.

As a concession to the steamy July weather, he'd rolled up the sleeves of his white shirt and forsaken his tie.

"Papa, I have something important to ask you. Please consider it carefully before you answer." She knew his first reaction would be to reject her request out of deference to her mother. He'd list a dozen reasons why he couldn't possibly provide her with the funds she needed.

Andrew stood. "Excuse me. I'll leave you two alone."

"No," Katherine said. "Please stay. This a business matter, so you should hear what I have to say."

Mr. Wainwright nodded. "I agree. Go ahead, Katherine." But as his smile faded and he became solemn, her confidence wilted. He seemed to anticipate what she was going to ask.

She disliked placing her father in such an awkward position, but with no other choice, she had to control her anxiety and forge ahead. Katherine looked Papa directly in the eye so he'd understand the seriousness of the situation. "I would appreciate a business loan. As you can see, I need to plant trees and make repairs and improvements right away. But the biggest challenge directly ahead of me is that I need to hire extra help to bring in the fall harvest, and I'm afraid I'm short of cash. Five thousand dollars would certainly eliminate many of our problems. I realize that's a great amount of money, but I can assure you I'll put it to good use." Somehow she kept panic out of her voice. She thought she sounded reasonable, not at all desperate. But he knew her so well he wouldn't be fooled by her calm facade.

Papa shook his head, a mournful frown molding his expression. "Katherine, why do you want to keep this business going when you have the luxury of never working another day in your life? Oh," he said, lifting his hands to shush her retort, "I understand the satisfaction of working hard and bringing a crop to market. You've done a wonderful job, and I'm so proud of what you've accomplished, and against all odds too. But I know that this current challenge, Katherine, is only one of numerous difficulties you've encountered. I've also learned you've entertained offers beyond Stuart's to purchase the groves, but you turned them all down."

She wasn't surprised he knew so much about the state of her finances. News traveled fast around the financial world. She tried to gather her thoughts, wanting to sound reasonable, not desperate. "I know I can improve our production, even this year, if I can find the funds to make improvements. I'd reimburse you as soon as possible." Her father wouldn't miss the money, but of course that wasn't the point. She'd never take advantage of him.

"Have you gone to your bank?" he asked.

Katherine blew out a sigh. "Yes, and they rejected me. I received their letter in this morning's post. But I—"

He put up a hand to stop her. "You can't win, sweetheart. No one will give you an opportunity to prove yourself because—all right, because you're a woman. That's how the world works, and I'm afraid you can't change the way things are."

What argument could she possibly make to convince her father otherwise?

He squirmed, one of the few times she'd ever seen him uncomfortable. "Your mother and I want you to return home. Claim what's rightfully yours. Find your way to happiness and contentment again. We miss you, and we worry about you all alone and so very far away. Please come home with me." He was pleading with her, and her resolve weakened. How could she harden her heart to Papa?

But frustration swelled in her chest once again. "You're pulling on my heartstrings, Papa. It's not fair, not when you know how much I want to stay." The early afternoon sunshine beat down and formed rivulets of perspiration down her neck and forehead. She swiped at her brow with the back of her hand.

He leaned across the small round table and put his hand over hers. "I do understand why you want to stay. Yet the problems and frustrations are enormous for anyone, but especially for an inexperienced woman. Please believe me when I say the odds are stacked against you. It's unlikely you'll ever make a success of Osborne Citrus Groves."

"But I *know* I can. All I need is more time and capital."

"Katherine, if I had a nickel for every time I heard a man say that . . ."

She lowered her gaze and bit her lip. Only an easily defeated businesswoman would complain or weep over a setback. Yet she'd exhausted all her ideas.

Would the Lord give her a plan she'd never considered? What if He expected her to go home? Maybe He was leading her in a different direction than she wanted to go. *Lord, please don't lead me away from here.*

Her father cocked his head. "Your beloved Great Aunt Letty moved in with us awhile back. She's a dear old lady, but sometimes she can be a handful, even for a woman as formidable as your mother. Mama could use some help caring for her. And you said that you might get away for a bit this summer . . . Why not try? Come home, for just a time? Return come fall, if you must."

Katherine smiled at the thought of her favorite aunt and her adventurous stories.

Aunt Letty made the prospect of a visit to Camp Birchwood all the more enticing, but there were countless details that needed her undivided attention, even in the relative calm of summer.

Katherine shook her head. "I'm sorry, Papa, but I'm afraid I can't help. Especially with Mr. Herne gone . . . Perhaps when the orange groves are thriving, I'll make a visit home. I do miss summers in the Adirondacks." Sometimes she longed for her family so much she wanted to board the next train for New York. But she never let the nagging pain of homesickness get the better of her. "I'm afraid I can't leave now. Perhaps next year I can visit for a few weeks."

Papa met her gaze with his usual intensity. "Perhaps you need a visit home to remember all you left behind, and all that still awaits you." He studied her for a long moment. "What if we came to an agreement?"

Katherine frowned. "What kind of an agreement?"

"I'll lend you the money to make modest improvements and bring in the fall harvest—which, if you're right, should increase the value of the property—in exchange for one month of your time at home following whatever social agenda your mother has planned."

Andrew shifted uncomfortably in his chair, and Katherine's eyes flicked in his direction, then back to her father.

"But mind, you must not tell her about this arrangement, Katherine. She'd be madder than a wet hen if she discovered I gave you a loan."

"That's very generous of you, Papa," Katherine said, pausing. His steady gaze indicated he expected an answer, now. But she wouldn't jump at the arrangement until she thought through all its ramifications. A shrewd businessman, Papa never made deals that didn't serve his own ends. Or in this case, Mama's.

"I'd certainly appreciate a loan and a short vacation at Birchwood. But please, Papa, let me mull this over before I accept. All right?"

"Why do you hesitate, my dear? I'm offering you exactly what you want." His face showed frustration mingled with hope.

She nodded. "Yes, I know. But I don't want to make an impulsive decision." *As I normally do*, hung suspended in the air. She glanced at Andrew, hoping to gauge his response, but he kept his expression carefully neutral.

Papa flashed her a wry smile. "Of course." He and Mama had always accused her of acting first and thinking later. Well, for once she'd take her time and hopefully not make a mistake she'd later regret.

"May I join you for your walk?" Andrew asked as Katherine headed across the terrace after dinner.

The temperature had dropped a few degrees and a warm breeze blew across the rolling hills. But the heat still hung heavy over the land like a soggy wool blanket. He hoped Mr. Wainwright would decide to head north before they both melted like scoops of vanilla ice cream. The humidity sapped his boss's strength and shortened his normally even temper. Andrew couldn't imagine how Katherine kept her energy level so high and her disposition so sweet. Maybe after all these years she'd adjusted.

Yet how could she resist her father's invitation to vacation at Camp Birchwood where thick stands of trees shaded the land and the lake glistened with refreshing waters? The green, rolling hills of central Florida had a beauty of their own, but the humidity nearly suffocated him. And the bugs were even worse. If he lived here, he'd have to escape every summer.

"Have you given any more thought to coming home with your father and me?" Andrew asked in a mild voice. He didn't want to raise her ire, but he'd prayed she'd see reason and decide to return.

Katherine sighed. "That's all I can think about. I need Papa's loan to keep the business running, but I feel it's my responsibility to stay here to see that everything goes smoothly."

He admired her dedication and tenacity. No one, not even her beloved father, would easily manipulate her. Andrew swallowed hard as they strolled through the garden of colorful crepe myrtle trees, bougainvillea, and hibiscus. Her silky hair shone in the last golden rays of daylight, and her sculptured profile became even prettier in the descending shadows. He hadn't realized until now how very much he wanted her to return to New York to spend the rest of the summer at Camp Birchwood with her family. And with him.

"Katherine, come home for a month. A little rest and relaxation will give you a new lease on life. The mountain air will do you so much good." He was pressing harder than he meant to, but she'd be better able to decide about her future after a few weeks away from the stress of work. "I'm sorry. I shouldn't push you. It's really between you and your father."

She smiled ruefully. "Yes, but you heard him. A whole month of doing exactly as my mother asks?" She shook her head. "That's bound to only dissolve into more of our legendary arguments, even if I'm bound and determined to see through my part of the bargain."

His mouth slanted in a grin. "I remember those."

"I'm sure you do. Mama was mortified I didn't keep our disagreements private. But you and your aunt and uncle were always practically family."

"Your mother might insist you attend a few dances and dinner parties, but is that really so terrible? Think of all the benefits a summer at Birchwood would bring. There's swimming and boating, and tennis and—"

Katherine lifted her palm. "You're right, of course. But I'm afraid I'd feel idle and restless."

"I understand. I thrive on work too."

"Still, I'm seriously considering Papa's offer."

Andrew nodded as they dropped onto a stone bench. "Did you help with the business while Charles was alive?"

"No, not really. He didn't want me to have anything to do with the company. And actually, he wasn't very interested either. He was gone a lot. Most of the time, in fact."

"On business?"

She shrugged. "Charles never said where he was going or what he was doing. I assume he went off to find more markets for our fruit, but he never explained. After the first few years we practically led separate lives."

"I'm sorry." His heart clutched. Ever since the surprising elopement, he'd worried Charles would eventually desert

Katherine, at least emotionally. Charles never stuck with anything for long in college either. Always discontent, he quickly tired of his studies and his friends and moved on to new interests. But how shameful to leave Katherine nearly alone in the countryside of rural Florida.

He glanced toward the groves. The limbs hung so heavy with tiny oranges they reminded him of Chinese lanterns. Even though he'd never been involved with agriculture, he was fascinated with the neatly rowed trees and new fruit. He understood why Katherine loved this place. Even if it was ungodly hot and humid, it was a blessing to be so far removed from the hustle and bustle of New York. At least for a time.

"What kept you occupied while Charles was gone—on business?" Andrew suspected something besides business had lured Charles away from Buena Vista and his wife.

Katherine winced at the way he said *on business*, and Andrew regretted not taking more care with his tone.

"At first I decorated the house and retrimmed my hats. Then I visited neighbors, though we only have a few. I ordered books from New York. I read several classics during that time. Eventually, out of sheer desperation, I developed an interest in growing and selling our citrus fruit. Learning about the business from my manager, Mr. Herne, gave me a real sense of accomplishment. And it helped to prepare me for taking over after Charles's death." She hesitated and looked away before she continued in a softer voice. "I was so busy my loneliness faded away. Or maybe I grew too numb to care."

Andrew grimaced at the pain she'd endured. Katherine looked so vulnerable with her sad eyes and quivering lower lip. He wanted to pull her close and erase all the sorrow that came from being married to Charles. But he knew better than to act on his impulse. Katherine had only let down her guard for a moment.

"You must have been unhappy. Why didn't you go home to your family?" he asked gently.

She looked away. "Because I couldn't bear Mama gloating about how headstrong I was to marry Charles. She'd never let me forget it. And worst of all, she'd take charge of me as if I were a child again. I'd rather stay here than have that. At least I have some freedom in Florida." She met his gaze. "This is why it's so difficult to accept Papa's proposal."

He'd never realized how deeply she resented her mother's intrusion into her life. "I understand, but you have all the headaches of running a company. Surely that must weigh heavily on you."

"Sometimes. All right, all the time." She laughed without mirth. "Right now I'm sorely tempted to forget all about orange and grapefruit groves and go straight home with you and Papa, regardless of what I face with Mama. I'm tired, so tired . . ."

His heart thudding, Andrew tried to keep his voice calm. "Then why don't you?" He shouldn't care so much, but God help him, he did.

"Andrew, I failed at my marriage. If I also fall short in business, then I'll be a complete failure at everything I've ever tried to do. I'm not willing to accept defeat. Somehow, with the Lord's guidance, I'll find a solution." She sighed. "But right now, I can't imagine what it would be."

"Perhaps the Lord's solution is for you to follow your father's advice. A month isn't too long to be away from your business. Even an important railroad man like your father takes part of the summer off."

"Yes, but Papa has staff to carry on during his absence. I'm afraid I don't."

If he weren't Mr. Wainwright's employee, he'd wrap his arm around her shoulders and show his affection and support. He so admired her pluck. But if Mr. Wainwright caught him touching his daughter, he'd fire him before he had a chance to explain. Katherine's parents expected their daughter to marry well—someone like his cousin, Randy Clarke. The bitter taste of pure jealousy filled his mouth; he'd have to conquer that before it conquered him.

He owed so much to the Clarkes. He'd be forever grateful to his mother's sister, Aunt Georgia Clarke, who'd taken him in after his parents died and brought him up with Randy, treated him kindly, and paid for his education at Columbia. She and her husband, Clarence, had a fortune nearly as immense as the Wainwrights', while Andrew's father had earned only a modest salary as an attorney and later as a judge. Andrew wouldn't have fared well without his aunt and uncle. With no other relatives, he could've ended up in an orphanage. But despite the Clarkes' generosity and fondness for him, Aunt Georgia would never allow him to interfere with her marriage plans for her only son. Andrew didn't blame her. Katherine was a fine woman. A little battered and bruised, but fine to the core.

He stared at her, as inexplicably drawn to her now as he had been eight years prior. She looked lost and forlorn. Against his better judgment, Andrew eased his fingers around Katherine's hand. Immediately, feelings he'd suppressed for so long shot through his body.

Shifting her gaze toward him, Katherine smiled and squeezed his hand. Hers felt soft and silky, and he relished the touch of her warm flesh curved against his own.

"Katherine, if you really want to go home, then pray about it. The Lord will show you a way. I'll help you too."

"Thank you, Andrew. You've always been my white knight, and I don't think I've ever thanked you for your kindness. You tried so hard to lead me away from Charles, but I wouldn't listen."

He just wished he'd done more to prevent her marriage. But

maybe now he could support her. He resisted the urge to tip her head back and kiss her with all the love he'd stored up over the years. It took great willpower to steady his racing heart and pretend to care for her only as an old friend.

"Sometimes I'm unsure about my future. Usually I forge ahead convinced I know what's best, but every once in a while I feel lost and alone."

Katherine sounded so uncertain that he longed to reassure her. "The Lord will show you the road He wants you to take, but sometimes it's not the way you may want to go."

When she tightened her lips and lowered her gaze, he knew she still struggled with her willfulness. It was one thing to rail against her mother, but quite another to battle with the Lord. She'd face a long and difficult walk if this was the path the Lord had laid out for her, and if Andrew could do one thing, it'd be to stay beside her every step of the way.

Chapter Four

Andrew waited for the best time to speak to Mr. Wainwright privately, but he didn't find him alone or in the right mood until after breakfast the next morning. The temperature and humidity hadn't yet risen to unbearable, but they still headed for the library, the coolest room in Buena Vista. A giant oak just outside the window blocked the sunshine from streaming into the room and heating it to oven temperature.

They were both reading over business contracts when Andrew laid his papers down. "I'm sorry to interrupt you, sir, but I'd like to speak to you about Katherine."

Apparently surprised, his employer cocked a bushy gray eyebrow. "Of course."

Andrew hesitated, unsure where to begin. He should've planned exactly what to say before he'd disturbed his boss. "Katherine told me last evening she still hasn't decided about whether or not she can come to Camp Birchwood."

"I hope we persuade her soon, because I can't tolerate much more of this infernal heat." Mr. Wainwright mopped his brow, as if to emphasize his point.

Andrew nodded with sympathy. "She obviously needs the loan, but with Mr. Herne gone, she feels she ought to stay here to run the groves herself. She's in a real quandary."

Mr. Wainwright grunted. "She's out of options, but that's a good thing, Andrew. Does she ever look in the mirror? She's a rack of bones, the poor girl. Whatever happened to my beautiful, high-spirited daughter who took New York by storm? This business is crushing her."

"I think she's aware of the toll it's taking," Andrew said. "It's partly why coming home for a visit entices her."

"Listen, I realize she's disappointed that I won't hand her the money without strings. A father wants to give his daughter everything she needs and wants. But in this case, I can't." He narrowed his eyes. "What she wants isn't good for her. These misguided efforts will ruin her health and eat up her years. Her mother and I won't allow it."

"There is the fact that managing the groves makes her so happy," Andrew said lightly. "And she is of age to make her own decisions . . ."

"You know as well as I that Katherine has often made impulsive and ill-conceived decisions. Staying here and struggling against all the odds is just another mistake in a long series. Can you deny it?"

Andrew couldn't. "That remains to be seen, doesn't it? Unfortunately, it will take years to find out. But . . ." Andrew pretended to pick lint from his trousers and then dared to meet his boss's gaze. "I've found that Katherine's matured, sir."

Mr. Wainwright let out a huff. "Perhaps. We'll be better able to assess that when we all return to New York."

"You won't reconsider, then? Helping her out financially, but allowing her to remain here?" Andrew couldn't believe he had the audacity to ask his boss such a personal question. Yet he had to support his friend.

Mr. Wainwright shook his head and gave him a hard stare. "Absolutely not."

Andrew's mouth went dry as hay. An apology caught in the back of his constricted throat, and he couldn't push out the words. So he had to stick by them. He might have jeopardized his position at the Trans American Railroad, but at least he'd stood up for Katherine.

Mr. Wainwright rose and jammed his book back onto the shelf. "I understand your concern for my daughter, but you must understand her mother has plans for her future. My wife wants Katherine to marry—and marry well this time. No more running off with someone unsuitable. Who knows who she might run across here?" He shook his head at the thought. "All we want is for her to have a brilliant marriage with a society gentleman who'll make her happy."

"But if she doesn't want that, sir? What then?" Andrew asked.

Mr. Wainwright glowered. "Her mother will convince her we have her best interests at heart and she must listen to us."

For once in her life, Andrew finished silently.

———

Katherine climbed the stairs to the attic before the sun transformed it into an inferno. She rifled through several steamer trunks lined with cedar in search of a few more lightweight summer frocks. The year before he died, she thought she remembered Charles storing some up here for her as autumn arrived. She'd just about given up when she spotted a dusty trunk in the corner that she hadn't opened. It was worth a look.

But instead of a pile of clothes, she discovered old letters tied with string. Glancing through the small stack, she found notes she'd penned while Charles was courting her. She cringed at how she'd poured out her soul on paper. Obviously, he saved everything. It probably took too much effort to sort through old keepsakes and discard. Or had he truly cared about her? Once?

She climbed down the stairs and directed Etta Mae to bring the trunk down to the front veranda. Five minutes later Katherine continued sifting through the old chest. Without rereading any of the silly *billets-doux*, she ripped them in two and tossed them into a trash basket. *Good riddance.*

From the bottom she pulled out a packet with handwriting she didn't recognize. Who would've written in such a feminine hand? Her breath caught deep in her lungs. Were her suspicions about Charles's infidelity true? During the last years of her marriage she'd wondered if he kept a mistress, though she seldom allowed her mind to wander in such a dangerous direction. Long periods of time away from home, no interest in their marriage, no love. All the warning signs were there.

For several seconds she held the heavy packet and stared at the dark blue ink. She ought to rip them up without a second thought—and without reading them first. As she had with her own. But wasn't it better to read them now and spare herself the agony of imagining the worst?

With trembling hands, Katherine untied the string and removed a sheet of inexpensive paper.

My dearest Charles,

I've missed you so, my darling. My life without you is empty and meaningless. I try to stay busy and distract myself, but I'm just so terribly lonely. Please hurry back to me. I count the days.

All my love,
Harriet

The letter was dated a few years after Katherine's marriage to Charles. Why were there so many letters? Her heart squeezed so tight it hurt. Who was Harriet?

Katherine pulled open the next note and then the next until she'd skimmed all but a half dozen of them. Tossing them aside, she glared at a blizzard of paper spread across the beige seat cushion.

Reluctantly, she fished out one of the earlier letters to reread it.

I don't understand why your father dislikes me so. Is it because I'm not of your social set? You say you don't care about his opinion, but I fear very much that you do. If only I came from a prosperous and respectable background we could marry soon, as we both wish. But I don't, and I can't change that unfortunate fact. I hope he softens his attitude toward me when he realizes we are meant to be together. I couldn't bear to lose you, my love.

Katherine sat perfectly still while white-hot anger burned through her chest like flames to the skin. Gradually, she pieced together what had probably happened. Charles had met Harriet a few years before he'd met Katherine. Old Mr. Osborne had unyielding control over his family. He must've forbidden Charles to marry Harriet, so Charles obeyed. He'd never mustered the gumption to confront anyone. He'd drown his cowardice in whiskey and gambling instead.

But after the elderly Mr. Osborne died, Charles might have felt free to indulge his passions without any repercussion. He must've taken up with Harriet once again.

It would explain Charles's neglect. Katherine had ignored his frequent absences and chose to believe they involved business dealings, though if she'd used her God-given common sense, she'd have realized that couldn't possibly be the case. He seldom set foot in the office or groves. Their bank account dwindled, yet he refused to explain why. Katherine moaned quietly. How could she have closed her eyes to what was right in front of her?

She knew the reason. To admit her marriage had failed would compel her to take some sort of action. Either she'd have to return home to her parents and confess her mistake or stay at Buena Vista and suffer in silence. She chose to ignore the problems and hope their marriage would someday improve. But it didn't.

Katherine heard the front door open and footsteps on the gray painted floor. Glancing up, she saw Andrew approach, a look of concern etched in his face. She sniffed back a sob and blinked away tears, embarrassed to be found in such a state. Hastily she searched her pockets for a handkerchief, but they were empty.

He pulled one from his own pocket and offered it to her. "Thank you," she murmured, her voice trembling. He dropped into a nearby rocking chair and focused his attention on her. His beautiful blue eyes radiated an ocean full of sympathy. He didn't ask for an explanation, but she fought the urge to tell him.

"I was reading old letters. I let my emotions take over." She gave him a pathetic imitation of a smile and wondered if Andrew would accept her explanation. Even though she'd told him a little about her unhappy marriage, she didn't want to burden him with the ugly details.

He glanced toward the door as if ready to leave her alone with her grief. "I'm sure your pain must still be raw. One doesn't get over a marriage quickly, I assume."

She warmed to his kindness. "It's difficult to overcome the past and look toward the future. But I'm trying." She bowed her head and a torrent of tears wracked her body. Her shoulders heaved and her sobs grew louder and more desolate. "I'm so sorry for making a scene. I should learn to handle my feelings."

Andrew pushed the letters on the swing to one side and sat close beside her. Hesitantly, he touched her hand. "Do you want to talk about it, Katherine? It might make you feel a little better. I don't know a lot about love or marriage, but I'm a good listener."

She stiffened. If she weren't more careful he'd offer so much empathy she'd let her entire story slip out. She didn't want to share her humiliation with anyone, even Andrew. She'd said enough already.

Katherine touched his hand. "You're a true friend and I love you for that." Embarrassment scorched her face. "You know what I mean, don't you? We're the truest of friends. Our affection goes far beyond romance." She sputtered a nervous laugh. "I'm not saying this correctly . . ."

His crooked smile seemed to be covering up an amused grin. "That's all right. I believe I understand."

She wasn't encouraging him in a romantic way, was she? She'd never forgive herself for misleading him. After Charles, she vowed never to wade into those poisonous waters again. Andrew was the dearest friend she ever had, and she'd never intentionally hurt him with false hopes—in case he had any.

Katherine felt the tears burn again. More than anything she wanted to lose herself in Andrew's kindness and tell him what she'd learned about Charles. Andrew would understand, but should she burden him with her husband's infidelities and her sorrow?

She only had to look into his eyes to know she couldn't. He was a friend, possibly a bit more than a mere friend, and she'd never do that to him. Yet it was probably her weakness that drew her to him right now and not anything else.

She pushed that thought away.

Andrew looked down at the letters and then up at her. Did he want her to explain what was written on the scattered pages? Of course, he'd never ask.

He waited a few moments and then rose. "I'll give you your privacy, Katherine. I feel as if I'm intruding."

She didn't stop him, even though his departure left her feeling torn. When his footsteps died away, Katherine stared at the closed door a long time before she opened another envelope, her hands shaking, her pulse still racing. She wasn't sure why she tortured herself by perusing these hurtful letters. But perhaps she could completely rid her mind of Charles if she faced the brutal truth. Then, not one shred of emotion for him would remain to torment her.

For the last several years she'd combed the memories of their marriage trying to understand what exactly went wrong between them. She'd believed it was her fault he'd lost his passion for her. Shortly after old Mr. Osborne passed, open hostility had replaced Charles's love. He blamed her for their alienation and she'd believed him.

She believed she was at fault because her own mother had said nearly the same thing. Mama claimed she was outspoken and stubborn and willful. So the problem lay only with her—though now, when she scrutinized her married life, she couldn't recall when she'd acted in a headstrong manner as she had so often as a child and young woman. With Charles she'd never fought for her way or defended herself. She'd given in to his wishes at every turn.

Now she knew the cause; Charles longed for Harriet and saw Katherine as the only remaining obstacle. Katherine glanced through the next letter, and then another. The illicit words of lust twisted her stomach until she thought she'd vomit. There was just one letter left, the envelope blank. She steeled herself to read it; then she'd be through with Charles forever.

After ripping the letter open, she started reading, expecting more sickeningly sentimental words. But this was different. It was from Charles to Harriet, and it had never been posted.

My darling Harriet,

I'm so sorry you are suffering because I'm still living with Katherine. You know my heart is with you, and I yearn to join you soon. I can't tell you how agonizing it is for me to remain with my wife in a loveless marriage when I only wish to share my love with you and our little son.

Son? Katherine let the letter fall to her lap. She'd never suspected Charles had a child. Her hands trembled as she tried to absorb this new revelation. She'd wanted to give him a child, but that dream hadn't come to pass. Swallowing the bitterness rising in her throat, she picked up the note and resumed reading.

I shan't stay here at Buena Vista much longer. I can't abide the tension. At present, I'm trying to put my affairs in order so we can be together. As soon as possible I shall ask Katherine for a divorce. We make each other miserable, and I regret the day my father convinced me to marry her. But I shall soon rectify that sad part of my life and join you, my darling, the one I should have taken in holy matrimony.

I am desolate, my dearest Harriet, and I long for your sweet touch. Do be patient with me, my love. We shall soon be together, forever.

Katherine gasped. The date read only a day before Charles fell ill, and merely a week before his untimely death. He'd caught a fever and died quickly. Never once had he mentioned Harriet or their son, nor had he asked for an end to their marriage. But he'd been too sick and weak to think of anything except getting well.

Katherine had nursed him, stayed by his side, and worn herself out praying unceasingly for his recovery. He was probably yearning for his mistress and their son while she cared for him night and day.

But God help her, she hadn't felt any grief when he died, only relief. Her heart swelled with anger and humiliation. He'd been the most despicable of hypocrites.

Katherine shredded the letter and tossed it into the trash basket. Gathering the rest of the notes, she tore each one in strips and threw them away too. Finally, when the porch swing was bare once again, she arose, dabbed at her stinging tears, and strode into the house.

She found her father and Andrew in the seldom-used office next to the library. Whether Papa was at home or not, he needed to keep abreast of his railroads, and from Andrew's look of eager concentration, he reveled in work as well.

"I have something to announce," she said, clutching the back of a chair. "I've made a decision. One you'll like, Papa." Her voice sounded thin and reedy, as if it came from far away.

Papa smiled in anticipation.

"I've considered my circumstances and I've decided I shall return with you to New York for the rest of the summer."

Andrew's jaw dropped open, and her father beamed a grin as bright as a lightbulb.

She put up a palm. "I can't agree to move home permanently. I still love these citrus groves and my work here, and I hope this fall's harvest brings us closer to profitability. But I believe a change of scene is just what I need."

"I'm so pleased," her father said, obviously overcome with relief. "You won't regret your decision."

"If I'm to leave, then I'll need someone reliable to take care of the groves and run the business for the summer. I'm not sure I can find a good manager, but I shall try."

Papa placed the cap on his fountain pen and stood. "Leave it to me. I shall contact Stuart Osborne. I imagine he'll take over the company on a temporary basis."

With the hope I'll eventually sell. Papa would pay him hand-somely for his trouble. She preferred to leave the day-to-day operation to someone other than Charles's brother, but she didn't know anyone else who could fill in for her on short notice. And the idea of trying to find the right person wearied her further. "All right, Papa. Thank you."

"I'll get on it right away." Her father dropped his pen and papers on the desk and headed into the hall for his bowler and walking stick.

"Do you wish for me to accompany you?" Andrew asked.

"No, thank you, Andrew," her father said. "I'll only be gone an hour, I imagine." The big man propelled himself forward with a burst of energy that Katherine had never imagined possible.

When the front door closed, she turned toward Andrew. "I do hope I'm not making a big mistake." Once she left Florida, her parents would use every weapon in their arsenal to keep her from returning in the fall for the harvest. But she would return, if she really wished to. No one would physically stop her, but the reality of a business barely limping along, on top of these new revela-tions about her marriage, had seemed to rob her of any meager wind she'd had left in her sails.

She turned away to the staircase before Andrew could see what was happening in her heart. Charles had deceived her right here, in this house, under her sightless eyes. Remaining in a home filled with such sad memories was far more than she could bear. She pictured Charles clattering down the staircase, valise in hand, as he had so often, calling out that he'd be gone on business for a while. A while usually stretched into days and sometimes weeks.

Andrew cleared his throat and she met his puzzled gaze. "Katherine, one of those letters convinced you to leave here, didn't it?"

She nodded. Collapsing into a soft chair, Katherine closed

her eyes for a few moments. What point was a secret between them? "Yes. I've just discovered Charles had a mistress and a child I knew nothing about. He planned to leave me, but he fell ill and died before he had the chance."

Her voice faltered. Blinking back tears, she said, "I'll have to make a list of all the chores I'll have to do before we leave—assuming Papa can convince Stuart to oversee the property in my absence."

Andrew took the seat beside her. "I'm so sorry about Charles. Is there something I can do to help?" he asked.

She shook her head. "No, but thank you all the same." She looked up at him. "I was a fool not to listen to you about Charles. Forgive me, Andrew."

He nodded. "You were young."

She tossed her head back and groaned. "And headstrong and stubborn. I should've listened to my head, not my heart. You can be sure I'll not make that mistake again."

His gaze captured hers with a seriousness she hadn't seen before. "Remember to look for God's path for you. To listen to His still, small voice."

"More good advice, my friend," she said.

But what if she couldn't discern what the Lord had to tell her?

Chapter Five

A week later they waited in the carriage, ready to leave Osborne Citrus Groves. Glancing back at Buena Vista, Katherine felt a twinge of sadness. Would she regret abandoning the dreams she'd invested in the business, even temporarily? Memories of earlier hopes for a happy life flooded her mind. None of her expectations had worked out. Buena Vista was a beautiful home, but filled with memories of her loneliness.

Numbness froze her heart, and she doubted it would ever thaw. Yet somehow a few hot tears escaped and rolled down her cheeks.

Her father patted her hand. "You'll get over this, princess. Once we're back at Birchwood you'll forget all about Florida and your citrus groves. You'll have a grand time at camp. Did your mother tell you I added a bowling alley last year, and a new game room?"

She smiled and ignored his unintended jibe about her dreams. Papa was still trying to promise her joy, something he couldn't deliver. Raising her gaze, her eyes met Andrew's, and his sent a message of concern. He seemed to read her mind and discern emotions she'd never admit. It was most disconcerting.

———

They soon boarded Mr. Wainwright's private railcar attached to the back of the northbound train. The varnish was custom-built by George Pullman to Mrs. Wainwright's exact specifications. Andrew had heard that his boss had paid seventy-five thousand dollars for the *Isabelle*, named after Mrs. Wainwright.

Andrew settled into his stateroom, a compact area with everything he needed—a double bed with brass headboard, a desk, washstand, and wardrobe. Like the parlor, the walls of his stateroom were paneled in mahogany and trimmed with a design in gold leaf.

Surrounded by wealth since the age of ten, Andrew had never quite adjusted to extravagance. Like the millionaires' servants, he lived among someone else's treasures, without owning any of them himself. Yet, unlike the servants, he had luxuries to indulge in because he was part of the family. A cherished nephew, but on the periphery.

He held the best of both worlds in the palm of his hand. With the Clarkes' connections, he received countless opportunities for success in the law—yet he hadn't enough funds to become lazy or even vaguely dissatisfied, chronic conditions plaguing so many sons of privilege.

Andrew unpacked and then wandered into the parlor. His boss glanced up from a stack of papers piled beside him on the plush green sofa.

"Just the man I want to see." Mr. Wainwright gestured for him to sit in the nearest chair.

Andrew sank into a coordinating seat, overstuffed with the softest of cushions.

"You remember that trunk line for sale in California? Well, I might buy it, especially if I can get it at a lower price. I've made inquiries. I hear they might be ready to sell this fall, for much less than their asking price."

Andrew nodded. The line from San Francisco down to San Diego was already profitable and worth a lot of money. "It's a good opportunity."

"The owner is returning from abroad in September. I'd like to go to California to negotiate, but it seems Mrs. Wainwright has other plans. There's a wedding of some cousin of hers in Boston the same month. It's a nuisance, but she has her mind set on attending, and I don't have the heart to turn her down."

Andrew kept his amusement from invading his smile. He doubted Mr. Wainwright had ever turned down that domineering wife of his.

The big man leaned forward, holding out a sheet of paper. "I'd like you to go to California in my place. I anticipate you'll only be there for a week or two. The entire trip should take less than a month."

Accepting the paper, Andrew glanced at the details of his itinerary. "Thank you, sir. I'll look forward to it." As Mr. Wainwright's private legal counsel, this assignment was the most important given him to date. "I'm most grateful for the opportunity. Thank you."

Mr. Wainwright nodded, apparently satisfied. "Good. I know you'll do an excellent job."

Together they reviewed Mr. Wainwright's potential offer and all his detailed instructions over cups of coffee and a mid-morning snack of Danish pastries made within the *Isabelle*'s well-equipped galley. When Mr. Wainwright adjourned to his stateroom, Andrew cupped the back of his head in his hands and let a grin spread across his face.

"Why do you look so self-satisfied?" Katherine swept into the parlor, a partially refurbished hat and a bag of feathers and flowers in hand. She took her father's spot on the sofa. She wore a gray-green traveling suit, appropriate for a widow but hardly a flattering color. Yet she flashed the first truly relaxed smile he'd seen since his arrival in Florida, and she looked young and beautiful again.

He pulled his attention back to her question. "Your father just gave me a big assignment. I'll be heading west this September."

"Why, good for you! No wonder you look so pleased."

"I'm thrilled," he admitted.

"I have no doubt you deserve the assignment," she said, examining the plain straw hat. She glanced up at him. "My father doesn't lend his trust readily; I'm glad you've conquered that hurdle."

Deep pleasure from her secondary praise rose in waves of heat and probably stained his face tomato red.

"Do you enjoy working for my father? He's a dear man to his family, but I don't know how he treats his employees."

"He's a stickler for detail and getting things exactly right. We work hard, and he rewards us with fairness and respect. What else could a man ask for?"

Katherine nodded, then riffled through her small bag and pulled out pieces of pink ribbon, rose tulle, and clusters of silk roses interspersed with something small and white, maybe baby's breath.

"That'll look lovely on you," he said, envisioning Katherine topped with the wide-brimmed hat boasting as many flowers as a garden. It might threaten to overwhelm her delicate face, but those luminous blue eyes would still dominate.

A smile turned up the corners of her lips. "Oh no, this isn't for me. It's for my maid Etta Mae. She loves pretty things. I want to finish it so she can have it before we reach New York." She leaned closer and lowered her voice. "I have a feeling she'll quit once we stop in the City."

"Why would she do that?"

She shrugged her narrow shoulders. "Because she wants to experience New York. She's lived in the country all her life, and she's tired of it. Who would blame her, with the opportunity so literally at hand?"

"Not you, I take it."

Katherine laughed. "Of course not. I love the citrus groves and the sounds of crickets and tree frogs, but she doesn't. She thinks there's more to do in the evening than just catch fireflies in a jar. I'll miss her, but if she's happy, then I'll be glad to let her go."

"That's very generous of you." Most ladies would show at least displeasure at the departure of an efficient servant. But Katherine had always helped others without even realizing it. "And I'm sure a new hat will be a kind send-off."

"Well, thank you, Andrew, but I'm not doing anything special. Decorating hats is no chore. It's my favorite way to relax." She tilted her head and gauged the top of his. "I can make over one of your straw boaters, if you'd like. Should I add a handful of daisies or would you prefer pink carnations?"

He smiled back at her. "I think I ought to stick with a plain, black band," he said.

"Ah, well. I'm hoping to spruce up many more hats once I'm at Birchwood. It'll fill up some of the hours I might idle away otherwise. I can't imagine being content just making social rounds with my mother. Not after growing accustomed to the constant demands on my time."

"If you're looking for a way to keep busy, decorating hats could be a useful summer project. Maybe you could turn your hobby into something more meaningful."

"What a splendid idea, Andrew. I could design hats for a few of my friends. If they were lovely enough, they might even pay me. I'd donate any profits to charity, of course." Then she sighed and shook her head. "But my mother would never approve."

"Approve of what, Katherine?" Mr. Wainwright asked as he entered the parlor. "Here's more information about that trunk line." He handed Andrew a sheaf of papers.

Hesitating for a moment, Katherine quickly regained her confidence. "I believe I might try my hand as an amateur milliner. Just for the season, of course. I'd donate any proceeds to that orphanage you support in New York."

Her father's jaw dropped. "You're quite right, your mother would never approve. Besides, you need not work at all. This summer is about rest for you, recuperation after all your trials in Florida. I'll gladly give you whatever you want."

She lifted her chin. "Papa, if you wish to please me, then convince Mama to let me do something constructive over the summer."

Mr. Wainwright sent her a mild frown as he settled into a sofa. "I meant that I'd gladly *buy* you anything. But I can't allow you to start any sort of business, even for a worthy cause. You know that, Katherine. It'd be unseemly."

She shrugged, apparently undeterred. "Then I suppose I'll have to persuade Mama myself." She gave a mischievous laugh, but Andrew knew she was seriously considering the idea.

Andrew widened his eyes, but held his tongue. How amazing that a slip of a girl could speak to the great William Wainwright in such a tone and receive a smile instead of a rebuke. Such impertinence in the office would land a man on the streets.

Mr. Wainwright groaned. "Surely you can find something more appropriate to occupy your time."

Katherine smiled as she rose. "Mama will find all kinds of tedious activities if I let her—which I won't." She planted a kiss on her father's high forehead. "Papa, please don't get upset.

Truly, it was only a passing thought. Please excuse me. I must get ready for luncheon."

When she disappeared down the passageway, Mr. Wainwright lifted a brow at Andrew. "Discourage her, if you can. I'll not have my daughter making hats while she should be enjoying herself. Doesn't she understand I work from dawn to dusk so she won't have to?"

Andrew nodded and mumbled, "I see your point, sir. But turning a hobby into a modest summer job might give her great satisfaction." He paused and swallowed the discomfort clogging his throat. "In fact, I suggested she make hats." He held his breath.

Mr. Wainwright's eyes narrowed. "That wasn't a good idea, Andrew." Then his gaze shifted toward the curved ceiling. "My father laid track before the War. As a young man he rose from a fisherman in Maine to the owner of one of the largest railroads in these United States. By golly, I won't allow my family to slip backward. We fought too hard to get where we are for Katherine to throw it all away on a silly whim."

Andrew gathered every shred of his courage. "Mr. Wainwright, Katherine also needs to feel useful. She—"

His employer raised his palm to silence him. "Her mother will make sure she feels useful. But this isn't the proper way to go about it. Do speak to Katherine about dropping her idea. You'll do that, won't you?"

"Of course, sir," Andrew reluctantly agreed.

———

As the train chugged northward, Katherine grew more and more apprehensive. With little to do but read and glance at scenery flying by, her mind replayed her father's disapproval of the millinery project she proposed yesterday. If he objected to creating hats for society ladies, then he'd certainly continue to discourage her from returning to her citrus groves at the end of summer.

The train swayed gently as it clattered down the track. Rain splashed against the wide windows, splitting into rivulets as it dripped down the glass. She sipped her afternoon cup of tea across the dining room table from Andrew. He devoured a rich Sacher torte with whipped cream on the side and strong black coffee as the day's dreariness seeped through the window and dampened her spirits.

Katherine placed her fork on the china plate next to the untouched chocolate cake. "Andrew, do you think I'm making a mistake going home? I keep fighting the urge to leave the train and head back to Buena Vista. I know I need to get away from the memories of Charles and Harriet, but what if they haunt me wherever I am? Maybe I should've stayed in Florida and faced them head-on."

Last night she'd dreamed of discovering Charles embracing his mistress in the parlor of Buena Vista. When they finally noticed her standing in the archway, they'd lunged toward her, demanding she give him a divorce. She'd cried and tried to flee, but her feet stuck to the floor. Charles raised his arm as if to strike her. Or push her. And then she'd awakened in a sweat, her heartbeat thundering in her ears.

"It'll take time to recover, but you will. I think Camp Birchwood is a perfect place to heal your hurts and begin to discover what might be next for you."

She shrugged, unconvinced. "I do hope so, yet I'm not sure. Maybe I'm just uneasy about mixing with society again."

"Or perhaps you're already restless and bored, being stuck in a railcar. You're used to your long walks among the groves." He finished the last crumb of his torte and pushed his plate to the side. A steward refilled his cup with fresh, piping hot coffee.

"No, it's more than boredom. I'm concerned about my company."

Hands folded, he leaned across the table. "What's there to worry about? Stuart will give his best to the groves, hoping they'll one day be his, right? And your father gave you the funds to harvest your crop."

She dragged out a sigh. "Yes, but unfortunately, Charles mortgaged Osborne Citrus Groves so he'd have working capital. At least, that's what he told the bank."

"Oh, I see. But that wasn't the truth?"

She shook her head. "Partially. We did need capital, but after Charles's death, my attorney discovered the money wasn't put into the business." She bit down on her lower lip. "He said Charles spent it gambling . . . but now I think that he might have used some of the funds to support his . . . other family." Her voice cracked as she glanced out the wide window and struggled to rein in her emotions.

"I assume you're meeting payments on that loan," Andrew said gently.

Katherine paused before she nodded. "Well, I'm trying, but it's difficult. No matter how hard I work, I never have quite enough to repay Charles's loan and run the business. It's a constant battle to balance both." There was more to the story, yet she couldn't bring herself to explain the deeper problem, at least not now.

"I see why you're concerned. Have you told your father about this other issue?"

She shook her head and her brow lowered in fear. "No, and I do hope you won't tell him either. I know you owe Papa loyalty, but that doesn't mean you should repeat what I tell you in confidence."

"Calm down, Katherine. I promise I won't say a word. This is between you and your father. But I urge you to mention it to him." Andrew rubbed his chin. "Your father can offer better advice than I can about managing a business. Why didn't you ask him for a bit more money so that you have enough to meet that loan's payments this summer too? It's a legitimate business loan. At least it was meant to be."

Katherine shook her head. "But it's *become* more of a personal loan. I won't ask Papa to repay money owed by a man he despised."

"I understand, but he might do it. For you."

"No. That wouldn't be right. The thought of him covering a loan that went to support my husband's . . ." Her words faded and she appeared pale.

"So the loan from your father only solves part of your problem this summer."

She nodded. "I'm afraid so. It'll pay for repairing some equipment and harvesting my fall crop. The profit will enable me to repay Papa. But I still have Charles's loan to negotiate." She smiled faintly and tilted her head. "Are you sure you can't recommend something? You used to advise me all the time."

Compassion and reticence collided in his heart as he stammered over his reply. As her father's employee, Andrew wasn't allowed to give an opinion that differed from his. And now, he was just as beholden to her father—and in turn, her mother—as she was.

He'd always prided himself for rising above the scramble toward power and riches. But had he, too, sold his soul for a chance at advancement?

Chapter Six

S everal days later the *Isabelle* pulled into the small depot by the edge of Raquette Lake, New York, without Katherine's maid. She'd left with a profuse apology, a big grin, and a new hat on her head.

With her father's assistance, Katherine stepped from the Raquette Lake steamer onto the Birchwood pier, parasol and reticule gripped in her hands. After the long journey from central Florida, every nerve in her body tingled with anticipation and anxiety.

She gulped a deep breath of fresh mountain air and glanced up at Birchwood Lodge, her family's summer retreat designed in the style of a Swiss chalet. Tucked into the Adirondacks, the chalet and all its cabins and outbuildings overlooked the shores of the crystal-blue Raquette Lake. Purple and yellow petunias— her mother's favorite colors—still sprang from window boxes painted cranberry to match the trim of the paned windows.

Her home of countless childhood memories had often echoed through her mind these last several years, and now it was as if she couldn't quite believe she was really back.

At long last she was home. It was time to reunite with her mother. Would Mama welcome her with as much love and enthusiasm as her letters always suggested? Or, as Katherine suspected, would she dwell on the hurts caused by her rebellious elopement? Well, she wouldn't know her mother's reaction until she faced it. Expelling a pent-up breath from deep within her lungs, Katherine waved good-bye to the captain and her fellow passengers, all neighbors heading to their lakeshore camps.

A trio of footmen waiting on the Wainwrights' dock retrieved the mountain of steamer trunks and bowed slightly. The older one, apparently in charge, greeted them. "Good afternoon, Mrs. Osborne, Mr. Wainwright, Mr. Townsend. Welcome home."

Katherine smiled. "Good day. It's grand to be home again." She followed the men across the lawn and to the back porch where the footmen placed her trunks near an empty rocking chair. Her luggage contained all the private mementos of her entire married life—pitifully little for six years of marriage and two more of widowhood. If all went well, she'd take her belongings back to Florida in a few months, but probably leave photographs of Charles at Camp Birchwood. *Or I might burn them*, she thought with a shiver of fury. The trunks, suitcases, and valises belonging to Andrew and her father were carried through the back door of the lodge.

As Katherine climbed the shallow porch stairs, her mother whipped around the corner of the chalet, watering can in hand. Mama's mouth tipped upward in a broad smile that stretched across her pale, square-jawed face. She stripped off her gardener's gloves, set her watering can upon the rough planked decking, and rushed forward with arms open wide. Mama smothered her in a hug so tight Katherine could scarcely breathe. But she melted into the warmth of Mama's small, wiry body pressed against her own and inhaled the faint but familiar smell of potting soil mixed with the scent of Mama's lily of the valley perfume.

"Welcome home, Katherine," Mama whispered, her voice choked. She stepped back, took a handkerchief from the pocket of her skirt, and dabbed at her light blue eyes. An embarrassed laugh bubbled up. "Pardon me, please. I'm just so happy to see you again."

"And I you, Mama." Her mother's enthusiastic welcome allayed her fears, at least for the time being. Katherine let her rigid shoulders relax.

Mama stuffed the lace-trimmed handkerchief back in her pocket and sniffed. "I've missed you so. It's been far too long."

Mrs. Clarke, Mama's dearest friend from their school days—and Andrew's aunt—trudged several paces behind. Tall and large framed, she dwarfed Katherine's spry little mother but could never cast her into the shadows.

"Katherine, my dear," Mrs. Clarke said, "it's so good to see you. We were so anxious that you'd listen to reason and return home with your papa and Andrew. Welcome home!" She leaned down and kissed Katherine on the cheek.

"Of course she'd listen to reason! I'm sure it's a relief to escape that awful Florida heat," Mama added, her eyes roving over Katherine's elbow-length sleeves. "You must remember to cover your skin, my dear, or you'll look like a foreigner."

Her mother's clipped, New England accent sounded exactly as Katherine remembered. Firm and definitive, yet honey-coated. Still thin and ramrod straight, Mama looked much the same. But the web of fine lines that fanned out from the corners of her eyes had deepened to crevices. Those intervening years had added wrinkles to her forehead and gray to her chestnut brown hair coifed in a stylish, yet rather messy, pompadour. Even her formidable mother couldn't escape the ravages of middle age.

"Martin, take Mrs. Osborne's trunks to the cabin nearest the lake." Mama glanced around and frowned. "Where's the rest of your luggage, my dear?"

Katherine swallowed hard. "That's all I have. I didn't need anything more than a few frocks for working in a citrus company."

Mama's mouth opened wide. "Only a few frocks? I've never heard of such a preposterous thing."

"Well, I've been in mourning for the last two years," she hedged, "so I haven't needed anything fancy."

"I suppose." Mama's voice held doubt. "But where's your maid? Don't tell me you haven't got one." Glancing toward the boat now steaming away toward the next camp, she looked to Katherine for an explanation.

"As soon as the train pulled into New York, Etta Mae quit. She said factory work paid more. But no worries. I'm quite capable of seeing to myself."

Mama shook her head and sighed. "I don't understand servants these days. You give them a good position, pay them handsomely, and then they leave without warning or any consideration for their employers." She shrugged, not one to dwell on matters outside her control. "Well, no matter. Aunt Letty's maid will help you." Mama bent over to water two clay pots frothing with red geraniums before she strode after the footman, her head held high with the confidence of the great society matron she was. "Come along, my dear."

Katherine stepped briskly to keep apace as Mrs. Clarke dropped into a wicker chair with a deep sigh and a copy of *Ladies' Home Journal* magazine. Katherine followed her mother across a small patch of lawn studded with evergreens and several leafy sugar maples, and then headed down the covered walkway connecting many of the camp's outbuildings. Late afternoon sunshine spilled through the tangle of pine, black spruce, and white birch trees and splashed across the boards of the walkway. Katherine inhaled the aroma of fresh-scented fir trees and rich, dark earth.

They passed the laundry with servants' quarters above, and several new guest cabins, some sheathed in birch bark and others built of logs cut right on the Wainwright property. Her father owned hundreds of acres of wilderness and some of the most beautiful and rugged terrain in northern New York State.

Mama leaned toward her. She lowered her voice, though the footman was well out of earshot. "We have so much to catch up on. You must tell me everything, Katherine. I've worried about you—that perhaps your life in Florida hadn't lived up to your dreams. Your letters were rather vague, to say the least." She reached over and grasped Katherine's hand as they walked past a guest cabin. "Do tell me I'm wrong and I'll feel so much better."

Katherine suppressed a grimace. "Oh, Mama, we have the whole summer to catch up." Although she loved her mother, as any daughter should, she had no intention of ever blurting out the horrendous details of her marriage. Her relationship with Charles was out of bounds, especially with her bloodhound of a mother. "My life . . . there are some aspects that are difficult to talk about."

Her mother's face puckered. "I understand. To be a widow at your age must be heartbreaking." She reached over and gave Katherine's arm a squeeze.

"Yes, in many ways."

Yet Mama had detested Charles right from the start. She'd called him a rogue and a reprobate and tried everything in her bag of tricks to prevent the marriage.

Her mother continued, "I've arranged all sorts of activities for you. It'll take your mind off your sadness. You'll have a busy summer ahead. I know you'll enjoy every moment."

Katherine kept her voice steady and steeled herself for a protest. "I need some time to readjust before I step back into society." Holding her breath, she glanced sideways at Mama and hoped she'd let her comment pass. Perhaps she'd mellowed with age.

Her mother's eyebrow arched. "Readjust? To your own home? That seems quite unnecessary. Ludicrous, in fact." A scowl slid across her face. She wasn't used to having her plans questioned.

Katherine cleared her throat, clogged with fear. She might eventually have to concede defeat, but not yet. "Losing Charles and then running the groves for two years on my own—it was an ordeal. I'm hoping my time here can help me recover, in part."

Mama looked askance for several long moments. "You can't mourn forever, dear." Then she grasped Katherine's hand in an unexpected gesture of love and understanding. "I don't mean to sound harsh. You've been through a dreadful time. But you must get on with your life. The sooner the better."

"Don't fret, Mama. I'm looking ahead, not back. But I need awhile to rest. Managing the business has left me tense and exhausted."

Mama nodded. "I daresay, I'll never understand why you even tried. When Charles passed away you should've come straight home where you belong. We would have taken good care of you." Mama drew out a resigned sigh and then swept Katherine with a long, critical look. "My dear, you do look drawn and so thin! We'll order up some hearty, nourishing food from Cook."

"I promise I'll eat like a horse."

Mama brightened, visibly encouraged by her responsiveness. "Excellent. Once you regain your health, you'll feel so much better."

Katherine bit back a smile. Her health was fine. But the last thing she needed was to run from morning until night with social obligations.

"Now remember, being out and about will drive away your sadness. Brooding won't do you a bit of good." Mama's hooded eyes widened. "By the way, Randy Clarke is visiting for the summer. He can't wait to see you again." Her voice was much too nonchalant.

Katherine resisted a groan even as she smiled at the thought of seeing dear Randy again. Mama must be up to something, and it didn't take a genius to figure out what. "I'm surprised he doesn't have a wife and children by now."

Mama laughed slyly. "No, my dear Katherine. His mother believes he's waiting for you. Truth be told, Georgia and I have always hoped you two would marry someday."

The hairs on the back of Katherine's neck prickled. A few seconds passed before she managed to find any appropriate words. "Mama, I've only just gotten home." *Keep your voice light, Katherine, and don't quarrel.* "You must realize I'm not here to catch a beau. I'm here to be with you and Papa and Aunt Letty. And to rest."

"Yes, I know, dear. I'm only talking, not pushing. I simply hope that when the time comes, you'll choose a gentleman from our circles. Someone we know." Katherine could practically hear her unspoken words. *Someone we approve of.*

When they'd wed, Charles's father had owned hundreds of acres of citrus groves, but the Osborne family hadn't the lineage her mother—the great social leader, Isabelle Wainwright—insisted upon for any potential beau intent on courting her daughter. The Osbornes weren't part of the New York set, and therefore they were out-of-bounds. Katherine had met Charles when he'd visited Randy during a weekend away from college. His charm and good looks immediately attracted her.

Katherine sweetened her voice. She'd not be dragged into a disagreement with Mama on the first day back at Camp Birchwood. Arguing with her would surely not be abiding by her agreement with Papa. But she'd never agreed to entertaining prospective suitors! "I'm mostly here because Papa said Aunt Letty needed a companion," she said. What would happen if

Mama knew she'd received a loan in exchange for agreeing to come? "I plan to keep company with Aunt Letty and lead a quiet life this summer. But you should know . . ." She paused, dreading the outburst sure to follow. "I've made up my mind to remain a widow." Much to her horror, she sounded strident when she hoped to sound cool and rational—and above all, pleasant.

Mama blanched. "My dear! That's utter foolishness. You're still young and beautiful. But if you delay too long there won't be any appropriate suitors left. Not even Randy will wait forever."

Katherine swallowed. "Mama, I don't wish to *ever* remarry. I know that upsets you, and I'm sorry. But I've made up my mind." The Lord had given her one opportunity at love and she wouldn't ask for another. She didn't *want* another.

Mama halted and pinned Katherine to the railing with her disbelieving gaze. "Surely you'll change your mind. You can't bury yourself in the past. No matter how difficult, you have to accept Charles's death. You must go on and face the future."

"You make it sound so easy, Mama. But it's not." She didn't know how she'd ever get past Charles's infidelity, to trust again.

All Mama's energy drained into one long sigh. "I've not experienced the pain you have. But I'm sympathetic, so I won't press you now."

"Thank you," Katherine murmured. Obviously, Mama wouldn't approve of staying a widow indefinitely, but they needn't argue about it, not while she was home. When she returned to Florida, her decision would speak for itself.

They continued down the walkway. The heels of their buttoned boots tapped against the wood, the only sounds competing with the chirp of birds nesting in the tree branches. They passed a game room, the dining hall, and the icehouse. From the kitchen floated the aroma of baking bread and roasting meat. Her mouth watered in anticipation of dinner.

"There's one more thing, Mama. You do know that I'll be returning to Florida at the end of the summer, don't you? I have to get back for harvest."

Mama's jaw dropped, and Katherine's heart sank. Had Papa manipulated them both? "You look shocked. Didn't Papa mention I'm only here for vacation?"

"Indeed, he did not," her mother said, tight-lipped. "I trust your time here at Birchwood will change your mind. In more ways than one." Mama had always seen any wall as an obstacle to be conquered. Katherine supposed it was that tenacity that had fueled her own dreams at the citrus groves over the years.

When they came to a small structure overlooking the lake, Mama pushed open the door and stepped inside. The coachman had placed her trunks on the rag rug in front of the wardrobe. A young maid with coppery hair and curly bangs bent over it and carefully removed the clothing. She wore her afternoon uniform, a black dress, frilly white apron, and doily cap with streamers. Life at Birchwood was far more casual for family and friends than in the City, but her mother maintained high standards for the staff.

By habit, Mama wiped her finger along the top of the maple bureau, checking for dust. Local craftsmen had made most of the camp furniture in an artistic but rustic Adirondack style. They used logs and twigs in their creative designs, making one-of-a-kind bed frames, headboards, and chairs.

Apparently satisfied with the maid's work, Mama turned her attention back to Katherine. "If you don't mind, you'll share the cabin with Aunt Letty until some of the guests leave the Lodge. I miscalculated and invited a few more people than we really have room for. But the more the merrier, I always say. We have thirty-four visiting for another week or two."

"That's fine. I'll enjoy the privacy." It'd keep her clear of the chalet and Mama's well-meaning, but intrusive, questions.

"If Aunt Letty drives you to distraction, let me know and I'll speak to her." Mama chuckled and raised an eyebrow. "Not that I can do anything about her chatter. She's still irrepressible."

"She won't be a problem," Katherine said as she walked across the floor of the combined bedroom and sitting room. "I'll enjoy watching over her. She's always been such fun."

Katherine glanced around the pine-paneled room. Kerosene lanterns and a tall jar of daisies, lavender blue chicory, and Queen Anne's lace topped a fieldstone fireplace with a simple wooden mantel. It stood across from twin beds. Colorful quilts covered the white iron bedsteads along with knitted afghans, one blue and one red, hanging over the foot rails. A yellow one fell across the back of the sofa near the fireplace. She remembered how the nights chilled when cool breezes blew over the lake. But now, bathed in the gold of late afternoon, the room felt as cozy as a cocoon.

"Where *is* Aunt Letty?" Katherine asked.

"Out for a boat ride with some of my guests." Mama glanced toward the mantel clock. "They should be back soon. Let's see if we can spot them on the lake."

Together they strolled outside and lingered by the deck railing that overlooked the small patch of lawn edging the water. Katherine watched the sailboats dip in the breeze and noted a few canoes and guide boats riding through the rippling waves. She spotted Papa's yacht steaming around Loon Island and heading toward the pier with a group of women on deck chairs. Aunt Letty might've been among them, but Katherine couldn't distinguish her from the others partially hidden under wide-brimmed hats.

As she waited for the yacht to draw closer, Katherine looked toward the garden and noted a gardener bending over bright yellow and red nasturtiums and black-eyed Susans. He pulled up a few weeds and tossed them in a pile. No doubt she'd often see her mother out there early in the morning tending to the blooms and humming one of her favorite Broadway show tunes.

It was good to see her mother after such a long separation, and she hoped their relationship would improve as time went by. But why did communicating with Mama always end up in a struggle? And why couldn't she herself be more like other young women who followed docilely in their mothers' footsteps, marrying their parents' choice of a partner and making their families proud? Instead, she'd run off and embarrassed her family without thinking twice. If Charles hadn't died, she'd still be trapped in a dreadful marriage of her own making. Had God brought her here to finally concede to their will? To acknowledge their wisdom, no matter how it grated?

She had the summer to find out.

The yacht pulled into the pier and the passengers disembarked and started toward Birchwood Lodge. Aunt Letty glanced in Katherine's direction and waved her handkerchief. "Woo hoo!" she called.

A sudden gust of wind pulled a few strands of snow-white hair from her bun and blew them around her pudgy neck encased in a tight collar. As she pinned back her hair, she chugged up the path that skirted the yard. She wore a fussy maroon frock with a bustle at least fifteen years out-of-date. It puffed out in the back, adding yards and yards of extra fabric to the skirt. From the looks of Aunt Letty's thick waist, Katherine suspected she didn't wear a corset. *Good for her.*

Katherine bent down to hug her great aunt and brush her withered face with a kiss. "It's so grand to see you, Auntie. You're looking remarkably fit."

"For an old lady, you mean. Yes, I'm in fine form, thank the good Lord. No aches and pains to complain about. I hear you've agreed to come and keep me company. Thank you for your kindness. I know we'll have a lovely time together."

Aunt Letty headed toward the cabin door. "Come inside and tell me all about your journey north. I do so love railcars, and your parents' varnish is the nicest one I've ever ridden on. We'll see you in a little while, Isabelle. I'm sure Katherine would like to freshen up now."

Katherine held back a giggle at Mama's indignant expression over her obvious dismissal. She hurried inside after Aunt Letty and closed the door before Mama could see her smile.

Chapter Seven

Andrew passed through the lounge of Birchwood Lodge where the guests normally gathered at night for entertainment. He headed upstairs and then quickly settled into the bedroom he shared with his cousin Randy.

"I'm glad you're back. It's been boring without you around." Randy thumped his cousin between his shoulder blades. Tall and thin, Randy had a luxuriant mustache he kept waxed at the tips and a pair of slightly slanted eyes as dark as hot coffee. The ladies all made a fuss over his thick eyelashes. "How was Florida?"

"Muggy. Though I wouldn't mind escaping the snow to return to it, come winter."

"I'd like that too." Randy nodded as he ambled over to his three-legged chair in the corner and picked up his mandolin. "I heard Mr. Flagler built a grand hotel in Palm Beach. It's called the Breakers, I think. It's right on the ocean. Or maybe we should go farther south. Come January, we could take the Florida East Coast Railway all the way down to Biscayne Bay and stay at the Royal Palm. What do you say?" Randy strummed a few chords.

Andrew opened his valise and unpacked his clothing and toiletries. "I say you must be dreaming. I have to work for a living."

Randy wrinkled his nose. "That sounds boring. Surely you can finagle a few weeks off. Mr. Wainwright likes you. I'd say he even admires your work ethic. So I'm sure you can convince him; a hard worker such as yourself deserves a vacation."

Andrew knew he'd need too much time off for a trip to Florida. He'd waste several days just traveling. But that was beside the point. He'd never be able to save enough money to stay in a fancy hotel frequented by the idle rich. Randy received a generous allowance from his father, but Andrew had to earn his keep.

"By the way, where's Katherine?" Randy asked.

"She went off with her mother to her cabin. I assume she'll unpack and settle in."

"How does she look? As pretty as ever?"

"Certainly pretty," Andrew said carefully. "But . . . changed. The years have been hard on her."

"Then she's exactly where she ought to be. Keeping company with us at Camp Birchwood will surely bring her back 'round." Randy sang "Wait 'Till the Sun Shines Nellie," so popular this year. His rich tenor voice could catapult him to Broadway stardom, if he had the inclination. Of course, his social set would never approve, and Randy was far from a rebel.

Andrew changed into old clothes and pulled on a pair of worn hiking boots. "Care to join me for a walk?"

Randy shrugged and then put down his mandolin. "I suppose a bit of sunshine and exercise won't hurt—unless you mean one of your infamous ten-mile hikes up and down mountainsides."

"Not at all."

An hour later they were tromping through the woods beneath a leafy canopy as thick as a thatched roof. Only a few flashes of sunlight penetrated the cool shade.

Leading Randy, Andrew crashed through the brush until they came to the dirt trail that wound through the deep forest and would lead them back to Birchwood Lodge. He trod over twigs and loose pebbles, and kicked through crumbled leaves and half-crushed pinecones. A wild rabbit skittered across the path a few yards ahead and disappeared among the brambles and bushes.

Randy halted and stared at his bare arms below his rolled-up shirtsleeves. "Look at this." He held out his arms, enflamed with ugly red bumps.

"Poison ivy," Andrew pronounced with a grimace. "Better use some calamine lotion or Burow's solution."

"You shouldn't have prodded me to go on *a nature walk* today. Clearly, too much fresh air and exercise isn't good for anything but a nasty rash."

They continued on, this time with Randy in the lead.

"Don't scratch so hard. It'll only make it worse," Andrew warned as he watched his cousin rake his skin with his fingernails.

The usually congenial Randy glared over his shoulder. "From now on I'll confine my exercise to the dance floor. Hurry up. If I don't lather myself in something soothing, the itch will drive me crazy." He turned and strode down the path, scratching and muttering.

Andrew laughed. "Don't get testy, cousin."

Finally they emerged from the darkness of the woods into bright light. Blinking, Andrew's eyes rapidly adjusted to the late afternoon sunshine. They hastened across the lawn toward the lodge. Andrew glanced at the cabins strung behind it and connected by the covered walkways.

He spotted Katherine leaning over the railing of the deck, staring at the lake. Even though he'd spent the last couple of weeks near her, his breath still snagged at the sight of her loveliness. The sun made her hair shine and bathed her in a warm glow like a Rembrandt painting.

"Look. Katherine's outside," Andrew called, shielding his eyes from the sun.

"Why don't you go tell her I'll be there shortly? I'd better get this rash taken care of first." Randy's mouth raised in a crooked smile. "You downplayed her comeliness, Andrew. She's more beautiful than ever."

"I believe you're right." Filled with as much admiration as his cousin, Andrew couldn't hold back his appreciation of the vision of her. "She's the prettiest girl I've ever seen," he whispered. Even to his own ears, he sounded like a besotted boy barely mature enough to shave a few, sparse whiskers.

Randy focused suspicious brown eyes on Andrew. "Well, don't get any ideas. She's all mine, you know. Our mothers decided our fate ages ago. Not that I mind."

In an effort to accept reality with a modicum of grace, Andrew swallowed hard to keep from spewing his true feelings. "Right," Andrew said. The most he could aspire to was friendship with Katherine. Without a fortune attached to his name, he'd never be in the running at all.

"Good man," Randy said, clamping him on the shoulder. "I wouldn't want you poaching on my territory." He gave a wolfish grin that reminded Andrew of the animal heads mounted on the walls of Birchwood Lodge and recreation hall.

Andrew composed himself. "Never fear. I wouldn't dare compete with you."

"But you'd like to, wouldn't you?" Randy jammed his hands on his hips and narrowed his dark eyes. "No matter how much you protest, I think you like Katherine Osborne. You were totally bewitched when we were young, and these last weeks with her have obviously done nothing to change that."

Andrew shrugged, unwilling to out and out lie. "Of course I still like her, but I hold no illusions."

Randy pounded him on his shoulder. "Excellent. I'd hate for us to vie for the same woman." He chuckled. "You'd be sure to lose."

"You think?" Andrew muttered jokingly, then got serious. He touched his cousin on his upper arm. "Randy, Katherine isn't the same young woman who left us years ago. She's been through a lot. Don't expect the carefree girl whom we used to know. During the time I spent with her in Florida, I realized how much she's changed."

Randy shrugged. "It's been two years since Osborne died. I'll bet I can bring that outstanding girl we once knew back around."

Andrew hesitated. "I'd love to see our old Katherine again, but truly, we've all changed. We're not the same boys we used to be either."

"Speak for yourself, my man." With that, Randy laughed, turned, and marched toward the chalet, scratching his arm.

Andrew watched him go, agitated that Randy wasn't willing to see Katherine as anything but a conquest, revisited. *He doesn't deserve her,* Andrew thought as he strode across the grass toward Katherine's cabin, annoyed he'd so easily given himself away. When it came to Katherine, it was difficult to hide his feelings.

At the sound of his approach, she partially turned. Her wide smile sped up his heartbeat. "Randy will come over to see you as soon as he douses himself in calamine lotion. He's got an awful case of poison ivy."

"The poor man," she said. "Some things never change, do

they? He always managed to find the nearest poison ivy patch when we were kids romping through the woods."

Andrew nodded and smiled. Leaning against the deck railing close beside her, he watched a group of her parents' friends dock the guide boats and pile out. The ladies in their plain shirtwaists and skirts held parasols above their heads while the gentlemen wore straw boaters and shirts with sleeves rolled up to their elbows. "Are you glad to be back, Katherine?"

"Yes, but it seems a bit strange after being away for such a long time. So many things are the same, yet they seem different somehow. Maybe it's because I'm different." She hesitated. "I'm not sure I'll ever fit in again."

He glanced at her sideways. "Is it your mother?"

"Oh, I can manage my mother. I'm up to the challenge." Her eyes twinkled. "After all, I inherited her determination, didn't I?"

Andrew allowed a sly grin. "Yes, indeed."

Katherine grew serious. "If you think of it, please say a prayer that I'll adjust to Birchwood and my family again. It's so peaceful here, and I have such happy memories, but . . . I don't feel as if I belong anymore."

"I already pray for you, Katherine, and have for as long as I can remember. Maybe after you're here for a while you'll feel more comfortable. You'll find new ways you can fit."

Hope curved her lips into a smile. "Yes, I'd like that." She studied the lake and then looked back toward him. "I love your optimism, Andrew. I wish I had some of it."

He wished he had more of it himself. His spirits had plummeted with Randy's cavalier announcement about his claim on her. "Katherine, may I speak frankly?"

She nodded. "Yes, of course."

"I know I shouldn't give you advice about marriage, but I

want you to be happy. So . . . contrary to what everyone says, I don't think a common background or a lifelong friendship is enough to make a marriage work. I mean—"

"I know exactly what you mean, and I agree. But please don't worry I'll make another mistake. Believe me, marriage is the furthest thing from my mind."

Relief rushed through him. Andrew felt in the deepest, most honest place in his heart that Randy and Katherine weren't meant for each other.

He'd have to fight for her. But did she have any romantic feelings for him? He couldn't tell. He suspected she considered him merely an old, reliable friend just like Randy, not a possible suitor. If he pursued her, he'd most definitely lose his position at her father's railroad and the approval of the Clarkes, the only family he had left. It gave him pause.

His personal life and fledgling career rested on making the right decision. They stood by the railing for a long while gazing at the sailboats skimming through the waves. He felt content to stand by her side, absorbing the warmth of the sun on his hands and face, and inhaling the sweetness of her perfume.

"Katherine, my dear, you are a vision of beauty." At the sound of Randy's voice, Andrew and Katherine both turned. Randy extended his arm, and with a flourish, presented her with a bouquet of red roses. Dressed in an informal sack suit and crisp white shirt, Randy looked every inch the eligible bachelor ready to court.

"Randy, it's wonderful to see you again." She accepted the bouquet and pecked him on the cheek. "Thank you for the beautiful flowers."

His mouth curled in a raffish grin. "They're not half as lovely as you." He stepped away from her, perusing her from head to toe. "Florida has agreed with you, Kat. You're thin, but more comely than ever."

"You're still the flatterer. How is your poison ivy? Any better?"

"The itch is driving me mad. But shall we go for a canoe ride anyway? I need a distraction."

"I'd love to," she answered. "Let me put these flowers in water, then change."

Andrew watched Katherine emerge five minutes later wearing a faded, violet print dress she might have borrowed from her maid. But in the Adirondacks the ladies wore old, casual clothes, except to dinner. Not that she needed a Parisian outfit to showcase her beauty or catch a beau. After a gust of wind threatened to send her straw hat over the deck railing, she squashed it onto her upswept hair and repinned it, wincing as she stuck the long pin against her scalp.

"Shall we go?" she asked, already striding the length of the walkway, with Randy following close behind.

Andrew hung back as the couple sauntered down the walkway toward the tree-studded back lawn. The desire to win her heart bloomed in his own, but he hesitated. No true gentleman would tag along and insert himself where he wasn't wanted. Still, he'd not be left behind unless he was sure she wished it. He was just about to call out when she turned and looked his way, her brow furrowing in confusion.

"Aren't you coming, Andrew?"

He noted a scowl from Randy behind her, but ignored it. "I'd love a jaunt out on the lake." Andrew took long strides to catch up, unable to hide his pleasure.

They descended the steps to the small patch of back lawn, wound their way through the rock garden, and passed the gardener. Katherine strolled between Randy and Andrew, following the dirt path to the fieldstone boathouse. Randy's mouth twisted in a petulant and persistent glower. He might be the most confident of suitors, but he still hated competition of any sort. It gave Andrew a curious sort of pleasure to be the source of his agitation.

Two small sailboats and several other small craft rested on the shore. Andrew helped Katherine into one of the long wooden guide boats painted forest green on the hull. Its interior shone with a fresh coat of shiny varnish. "Would you mind rowing?" Randy asked Andrew.

"Not at all," Andrew said. Although a guide boat resembled a canoe, it was rowed, not paddled. He climbed in the center and settled between the long, graceful oars.

Refusing assistance, Katherine scrambled into the stern. Randy took the seat in the bow.

Andrew steered the boat through the water toward Loon Island, a small dollop of land covered with tangled trees and brush, and edged with a strip of golden brown sand. The oars dipped into the clear lake and they glided into deep water. The waves rippled from the breeze and slapped lightly against the hull.

Katherine leaned forward on the cane-backed chair. "Do you remember when we all came to the island as kids? We called ourselves the Three Musketeers. We brought a picnic lunch and you two ate almost all of it. My mother thought I was quite fast, stepping out with two boys without a chaperone." Her laugh nearly drowned the cry of a gull swooping down on a small fish. "I was all of twelve years old, but she was already worried about how everything appeared."

Andrew nodded, smiling with her. "I don't think I've ever

had more fun. Or ate more delicious food. Fried chicken, fresh bread, chocolate cupcakes with white icing . . ."

She tried unsuccessfully to hide a sardonic smile by glancing down and shielding her face with her hat brim. "You two finished all the really good food and left me with only a few sour pickles."

Andrew recalled the memory of Katherine's outrage when she found they'd left her only a dill pickle and half a cucumber sandwich. "We still need to make it up to you."

"Yes, you should. I'm sure you two gentlemen are far more gallant now than you were all those years ago."

"Sorry, I can't vouch for Randy, but I shall certainly try to be more polite."

Katherine threw back her head and laughed heartily. "You always were such a dear friend, Andrew."

Heat blasted through his skin. She met his eyes and tilted her head, as if she just now realized his great fondness for her. As they drew closer to the island, his face cooled and he felt better—more in control. He hated how she affected him. Yet he loved it as well. His insides shook with delight and discomfort at the same time.

He rowed the guide boat to a narrow strip of coarse sand just as the sun slid behind a mass of gathering clouds. He helped Katherine off the boat and then pulled it up and onto the pebble-strewn beach.

"Shall we hike to the other side of the island?" Her gaze slid from him to Randy.

"That sounds like a fine idea. Let's go," Andrew agreed.

Randy put up a hand. "Wait a second. No hiking for me. This island's covered in poison ivy. I don't want any more than I already have. Why don't you stay down here with me?"

"We could keep to the paths," Andrew said. "But it's up to Katherine." He glanced her way, hoping she would choose to take a walk and leave Randy behind.

"Come on, Katherine, don't wear yourself out hiking." Randy dropped onto a large, smooth rock and patted the space beside him.

She shook her head. "No, I'd like to walk up the trail for a bit, stretch my legs. After all those days on the train, I'd welcome the exercise. But please, go ahead and rest." She planted her hands on her hips and grinned at his expression. "Don't pout. I promise we won't be gone long."

Staring upward, Randy frowned. "Look at the sky. It's going to rain soon. Perhaps we ought to just head back to camp now."

"We'll hurry." Katherine turned and followed Andrew, who quickly hid his smile.

Andrew led the way up a path that skirted the edge of the island. After they'd turned a corner, he grabbed her hand under the pretense that she needed help as the terrain had steepened and grown rough with roots and stones. Overhanging branches dipped in the freshening breeze and brushed their faces and arms.

"Stay on the inside of the path," he warned as they continued to climb. "We don't want to run across any of Randy's dreaded ivy. And that's a sheer drop to the lake."

She squeezed his hand. "I'll be very careful. But I don't remember this path being quite so treacherous. Do you think I'm losing my nerve now that I'm older?"

"I doubt it."

They finished their climb in silence until they came to a clearing on the far side of the island. Stepping back from the path onto an open spot, they watched canoes rock and sailboats tip in the mounting breeze.

"I'd forgotten," she said, panting, "how breathtaking it is."

He looked across the lake to the large, rustic camps surrounded by acres of woodlands and rounded mountains dotted with evergreens and hardwoods.

Some of the New York millionaires had purchased enormous tracks of Adirondack wilderness for their summer retreats, far from the noise and pollution of the city. And then they built railroads for easy transport of their families, friends, and goods. He'd never own such a great camp himself, but he felt thankful he could enjoy the Wainwrights'. How many young men with only moderate incomes and modest inheritances even got to see places like this, let alone stay for an extended amount of time? He was a fortunate fellow. Andrew removed his cap and felt a light wind brush through his hair.

"I missed this place," Katherine admitted as she gazed at the royal blue water. "I didn't realize how very much." She spoke like a pensive old lady who reveled in her most treasured memories of times long past. He smiled.

"I'm glad my father came for me. I didn't understand I was more than ready to come home. I hope I'll feel the same way a month from now."

"Just relax, Katherine. Give yourself time to adjust." *Heal. Find hope again.*

"I shall. If my mother will allow me that time." She held her straw hat on her head so the stiff breeze wouldn't lift it off. "Mama and your aunt Georgia expect me to marry Randy."

"I've always known that. Didn't you?" Andrew held his breath, waiting for more from her. Did she welcome that plan?

Katherine shrugged. "I suppose I knew, but I didn't know they were still holding out hope until Mama hinted at it today."

"Katherine, before you decide who you want to marry—"

"As I told you, there's no need to worry, Andrew. I don't want to marry anyone," she said, staring at him with a quizzical expression that drew her brows together. "I'm returning home to Florida."

Andrew frowned. "Nevertheless, your parents might press you. But before you pick a husband, you should pray about the Lord's plan for your life. And then ask for the courage to follow it." He looked away before she read too much in his expression. He knew exactly what he'd like God's plan to be, but that was more likely a pipe dream than a reflection of the Lord's will.

"I'm not sure what you mean."

"Do you pray?"

"Of course I pray!"

"But what do you pray for?"

Obviously befuddled, she paused. "Well, I pray for everyone's well-being, for happiness, for guidance that I'll do the right thing. What else *would* I pray for?"

"You could also ask the Lord to show you what He has in mind for you to do with your life."

Katherine looked skeptical. "You don't think He wants me to become a missionary, do you? I can't imagine traipsing off to Africa or China. It's a splendid ministry, but certainly not for me. I'm quite sure of that."

Andrew laughed. "I agree. I can't quite imagine you're meant for the mission field."

She tilted her head and smiled. "Some would say the wilds of Florida are practically a mission field."

He smiled with her. "The Lord wants each of us to listen for His voice."

"Then I'll have to listen better, because I'm afraid I don't hear Him very clearly. But tell me, Andrew, what does He have in mind for you?"

Taken aback, he hesitated for a few moments. "Right now

it's to work for your father. But I don't know what the future holds. The Lord may send me off in an entirely different direction."

"And you believe He'll tell you which road you should take?" She sounded more doubtful than he would've liked.

"Yes, I do, although it might not be the one I'd choose for myself." He was open to a change in plans, though he hadn't received any hint he'd be sent down a new road.

"Hmm. Well, you've given me a lot to think about, and pray about."

Andrew pointed toward the fat clouds rapidly turning from pearl gray to charcoal. The wind stiffened and clouds began to thicken. "Look at the sky. We'd better start home. We'll have to hurry before the rain starts." A distant boom of thunder quickened his step.

She followed close behind. "I agree. I'd hate to look like a drowned rat on my first day home."

They picked their way back down the path and ignored the few raindrops slapping their noses. Andrew glanced over his shoulder. Even with her arms wrapped across her chest, she was shivering. He pulled off his lightweight jacket and tossed it over her shoulders.

"Thank you. It's getting a bit chilly." Katherine slipped her arms into the long sleeves. The jacket swallowed her, but she seemed grateful for the warmth.

Glancing toward the lake, he noticed darker clouds pouring over the mountaintop like an attacking army. Thunderstorms sometimes invaded from the west without warning. "Come on. We need to hurry." He led her forward as the trail darkened.

She tripped over an embedded root hidden by a scattering of crumbled leaves, lost her balance, and pushed into him. Twisting around, he grabbed her before her knees slammed into the ground. "How clumsy of me," she muttered, quickly straightening.

The urge to pull her close almost erased his good sense, just as it had nearly overcome him in the orange grove. *What is the matter with me?* He had to maintain control; he couldn't rush her, push their relationship, not if he hoped to keep her near. He struggled to drop his hands while fat raindrops fell in earnest.

"Let's hurry," she said, looking at him strangely. Did she feel the pull too? Or merely wonder over his odd pause?

Back at the beach, they found Randy huddled under the limbs of a swaying tree.

"Shall we try to make it back to camp?" Andrew gauged the distance between the island and Birchwood. The camp looked a long way off, but it might be possible to make it back before the storm unleashed its full fury. He glanced up at the tall trees above them, already swaying in the wind, and felt a renewed urgency to get Katherine to safety.

She nodded without hesitation. "Let's try. These trees don't make a good shelter." A crash of thunder, followed several seconds later by lightning, hurried her along. "The heart of the storm's still a few miles off yet. I think we can make it."

"Don't be ridiculous," Randy said with a scowl and stared at the sky. "We'll capsize."

"We're going to get wet either way," Andrew pressed. "Either on our way home, where we can dry out and nestle by the fire, or here on the island where we might catch our death from the cold."

"Go on, then," Randy said. "You can come back and retrieve me as soon as the storm ends."

Andrew stared at him. He couldn't very well leave his cousin behind. And the waves were growing rapidly. "All right, then. We'll wait it out, together. Come on!" Hand in hand, he and Katherine ran toward a clump of swaying, short, scrubby trees.

Leaves pulled loose and scattered across the beach. Once beneath the sheltering limbs, they leaned against the rough bark and lifted his jacket over them both to try and maintain some cover. *We might be stuck here for hours,* he thought, glancing back at his cousin. Not that he'd really mind. Because Katherine was with him.

A jolt of thunder sounded and a brilliant flash of lightning seared the dark sky. But it was a second loud crack that caught their attention. Andrew looked toward the noise. Forty feet away, a tree tore from its roots and began to fall directly in their path.

Chapter Eight

Katherine's heart tightened, and for a split second she froze, staring as the tree hurtled down upon them. Andrew grabbed her wrist and yanked her to the side just as the trunk smashed to the ground behind them. Branches snapped and broke and brushed against her skirt as they fell, and the heady scent of wintergreen arose from the severed twigs. Rising to her feet, Katherine turned away from Andrew and examined her knee, scraped and bloody.

"I'm so sorry, Katherine. It's all my fault." Rain pelted down upon them, running in streams down his face now, as well as hers.

She blinked and smiled up at him. "It's your fault that you saved me from being crushed? My knee will be fine." She ripped the bottom of her cotton petticoat, balled it up, and dabbed at her scrapes and cuts, careful to keep her back to Andrew and an old, disfiguring scar on her leg out of view. She tied the improvised bandage around her knee, trying to ignore the steady throb.

Randy hurried over to them. "Are you two all right?" His eyes ran up and down her, clearly horrified at her disheveled state.

Katherine glanced downward. She was a sodden mess, now as dirty from her fall as she was wet. She accepted Randy's arm and they followed Andrew to another stand of trees, sheltering them from the worst of the wind and driving rain. Her throat gurgled with nervous laughter and she couldn't stop staring at her two old friends. "So much for not arriving back at camp looking like a drowned rat. Aren't we a sorry sight? Just look at us."

They nodded, glancing down ruefully at their clothes and wiping their faces of rain.

"Mama won't find my appearance at all funny, but it really is—unless I'm just a bit hysterical." Her straw boater caught the wind and tilted over her forehead at an angle and covered one eye.

She reached up to rearrange it, but it blew off and skittered across the beach and out over the roiling lake. Andrew raced after it before she could stop him. "No, don't bother! I can buy another!" she cupped her hands and called over the wailing wind.

"There's a good man," Randy cheered as Andrew plunged knee-deep into the water and caught the hat riding a wave. "Well done!" he called.

She noticed he edged closer to her in his cousin's absence.

Andrew waded back in with the soggy piece of millinery. "Here you go." Looking sheepish, he handed her the remains of the hat with a filthy, ripped band and streamer. "I'm afraid it's ruined."

She giggled as she accepted it. "Don't worry. I can dry it out and make it look as good as new. Thank you for retrieving it."

They settled under swaying branches of a red maple, its leaves silver-white on the underside, as the men talked about storms of this magnitude from their youth. Strands of damp hair whipped around her face and into her mouth as she stared across the angry waters, as impassible as a stormy sea at the moment. "I think we'll be late for dinner," she said benignly.

"I don't think we should stay under these trees," Andrew said, looking upward. They all heard the thunder, rumbling ever closer. Lightning flashed.

"There's that old lean-to on the other side of the beach," Randy said doubtfully. He pointed to a broken-down shelter, open on one side. "Want to make a run for it?"

Both men offered their hands, and together they dashed across the wet sand and into the hut. Katherine collapsed onto the floor littered with leaves and branches and hugged her hurting knees to her chin. Her sodden skirt clung to her legs. "This reminds me of my childhood," she panted. "Our childhood."

"You're remembering the last time we got caught out here," Randy said, shaking rain from his hat brim and then taking a seat beside her. Andrew sat down on her other side.

"We couldn't get home for hours and Mama had a fit," Katherine said.

"Not a memory I like to revisit," Randy winced.

But Katherine gave a nostalgic sigh. "We had such fun together. Such adventures!"

Andrew's mouth twisted in a wry smile. "Until you turned sixteen or seventeen." He was closer than before, and Katherine decided to not ease away as she should. It felt good to be close to the two of them. Truly like old times.

"I'm afraid I dropped the two of you because you were my chums, not my beaux. That was a dreadful mistake, and I'm sorry." She looked at each of them, remembering those fateful years. She'd wanted to explore the world of adults and indulge in new experiences and turn strangers into friends. Randy and Andrew lost their allure. To her great shame, she hadn't appreciated their loyalty until a few years later, when she'd looked back at the friends she'd left behind and compared them to Charles. Only then did she begin to appreciate them.

Randy smiled sadly. "We never lost interest in you."

"Well, I regret that I took you both for granted. I was so absorbed in myself I never noticed you still wanted to be chums." Katherine reached for their damp hands and pressed them tightly. "Can you two ever forgive me?"

Andrew squeezed back. "Of course. I suppose we were like a pair of comfortable old shoes and you wanted a brand-new pair."

She chuckled. "Not a very flattering description of you. Or of me, I'm afraid. But you're right. I wanted excitement and charm, so I turned to Charles."

She stopped, afraid she'd reveal more about her marriage than she wished. Andrew was a most sympathetic man, but she wasn't sure about Randy.

Another clap of thunder disrupted her reverie. She slapped her hands over her ears. "My, that was deafening."

"We're in the thick of it now," Andrew said.

"It'll be all right, Kat," Randy said. He reached for her hand without hesitating. It was a proprietary gesture, and she wasn't quite sure she liked it. Andrew tightened his mouth and looked away. Were they each silently struggling to lay claim to her? She shivered, this time not from the cold and damp. She needed old friends to laugh with and confide in, not suitors vying for her attention.

"Shall we go home?" she asked, as soon as the wind died down and the rain slowed to a drizzle.

Together the trio rose and watched as the water calmed and

the sky lightened to pewter. By the time they pulled the guide boat to shore in front of Camp Birchwood, the storm had entirely blown past, leaving cooler air. Mama, Aunt Georgia, and a handful of her mother's other guests were gathered on the beach, awaiting them.

Mama came forward and gripped Katherine's hands. "I'm so relieved to see you're all right. But what were you thinking? Why did you not return as soon as you saw the storm brewing? Really, Katherine, I should think you'd be more prudent at your age."

Katherine winced, but she wasn't willing to disagree with Mama in front of her friends. She wouldn't defend herself and cause a beehive of gossip that might be repeated and enjoyed for weeks to come. "You're right, Mama. I should've paid more attention to the weather."

Randy brushed a thin layer of mud from the bottom of his trousers and muttered, "If they hadn't gone hiking, we could've returned before the rain started."

Mama blanched and focused her disapproval on Katherine, opening her mouth to speak, but then apparently thinking better of it. Several seconds passed in silence.

Apparently Randy realized his mistake, because he tried to backtrack. "Actually it wasn't their fault. No one knew it would rain." But Katherine knew he couldn't undo the damage.

In a voice as hard and cold as an iceberg, Mama directed the threesome as if they were children once again. "All of you should change out of your wet clothes before you catch your death of cold."

Katherine strode toward her cabin, her head down. Once inside, she washed off the dirt with a quick sponge bath and donned a dry, moss green skirt and tailored shirtwaist, adding a cameo at the neck. Right when she thought she was free from threat of her mother's wrath, Mama entered the cabin. She stood by the bed until Bridget—Aunt Letty's maid—finished fashioning her damp hair into a simple chignon. The maid left quietly.

"I'm very sorry to say you haven't acquired a bit of common sense, my dear," Mama said. "You're as headstrong as ever. You still leap before you look."

Annoyance rose in Katherine's chest. She stood up from the dressing table and faced her mother. "Really, Mama, anyone could get caught in a storm. But I'm sorry if I worried you."

"Yes, dear, you did worry me. But I'm even more concerned about you going for a hike with Andrew and leaving poor Randy behind. What's gotten into you? If you're going to entertain a gentleman, shouldn't it be Randy Clarke? He *is* the most eligible and suitable gentleman you'll ever meet."

"Oh, Mama. Andrew is only a friend! Randy did not wish to hike with us. We made it quite clear he was invited." But her mother's words echoed in her mind. If he were truly the most eligible bachelor in her life, then why couldn't she think of Randy as a beau?

He was an amiable fellow, but rather moody, either glowering or jolly—something that didn't measure up to her vision of an ideal suitor, and especially not a husband. She'd lived with a man who could be either the center of every party or so depressed and angry she was afraid to be around him.

"But Randy—" her mother began.

"Mama, please. I just can't think of Randy as a suitor. I know that displeases you . . . But how could I lead on such a dear friend when I know that it will only end, come fall?" She shook her head and stared out the window.

Her mother sighed and then came over to rest her palm on Katherine's shoulder. "I'm sorry, my dear. I'm so eager for you to find yourself again, now that your mourning is over."

My mourning is over . . . Then why did she feel so raw, like it had just begun again? *Harriet* . . .

Mama raised a thin eyebrow. "Please remember my friends are watching everything you do. Impetuous behavior reflects poorly on you—and also on your papa and me."

Keep a civil tongue, Katherine. She'd not start any more arguments to drive a wedge between her and her mother. They'd fought mightily during her youth, and some of those harsh words still echoed through her mind. "Maybe you're right, Mama. I'll be more mindful of my reputation in the future." It was much better to agree with Mama than argue with her, and she'd promised her father that she'd do as her mother asked this summer. But the conciliatory words nearly clogged Katherine's throat, making her gag. She certainly sounded less sweet and compliant than she wanted.

"Pay attention to my advice, dear. Guard your reputation." Her mother's words flowed like cream turned sour. "Pay more attention to Randy and a little less to Andrew." She raised her small hands, shushing Katherine's retort. "Andrew's here to work for your father, not to play. So mind, don't be a distraction to him."

Katherine nodded and held her breath, hoping the conversation was finished. But Mama was opening her mouth to say something more when Great Aunt Letty burst through the door.

"Good afternoon, children." Her head bobbed from Mama to Katherine, and her eyes sparkled.

Katherine chomped down on her lower lip to keep from laughing. To Aunt Letty, she and Mama were both youngsters, and always would be.

"My, it's chilly," Aunt Letty said, rubbing her arms. "That storm brought some cold air our way." Letty threw a shawl around her rounded shoulders and scampered across the floor to light a fire. "That'll feel better."

After she had the fire roaring, she tugged at Katherine's sleeve with one blue-veined hand. "Katherine, if you're not busy, perhaps you'd be so kind as to help me sort through some of my treasures. I simply must get rid of a few." She sighed. "But it's so hard to throw away my memories. Isabelle, would you mind if I steal some of Katherine's time?"

Mama flashed a disingenuous smile. "Actually, I was about to ask her to help entertain our guests. Perhaps later, Aunt."

Katherine shook her head and pushed back a giggle over Letty's conspiratorial glance. "But, Mama, I thought you told Papa I should come and keep Aunt Letty company and assist her in any way I can. Might I not visit with your friends tomorrow?"

Mama bristled, then excused herself and swept out the door.

A gust of wind puffed through the screens. Aunt Letty hustled around the cabin and pulled down the windows, chattering every step of the way.

"There. That's so much cozier." The fire crackled in the hearth. The yellow and orange flames leaped, sparks shooting upward. The smell of smoky wood assailed Katherine's nostrils, reminding her of bonfires on the beach.

Great Aunt Letty plopped in a wing chair by the fireplace and halfheartedly glanced through a box of loose photographs, yellowed from age and slightly faded. "Organizing all of these will be quite a task. Are you sure you're up to it after your *adventure*?"

"I am. If you'll hand me a stack, I'll sort them out."

They worked for the next half hour regrouping the photographs and adding them to a new album. Katherine recounted her escapade with Andrew and Randy, and how much she'd enjoyed herself, despite the incident with the falling tree.

"Quite a close call, but how exciting." Letty put the rest of the photographs in a large envelope. "There. We've accomplished quite a lot today, though it's only a start. I think I'd like to embroider for a while. I find needlework very relaxing." Aunt Letty reached down by the side of her chair and removed a white linen pillowcase. Despite a touch of arthritis, her fingers worked nimbly on a garland of butterflies, dragonflies, and ladybugs.

"I must say, it feels so grand to be with you again, Aunt Letty. I looked forward to this time with you most of all." Katherine took a seat on the overstuffed chair across from her and picked up an unadorned hat she'd bought during the stopover in New York yesterday. On the last leg of the journey north through the mountains, she began to decorate it for Aunt Letty. It was a small surprise gift Katherine hoped would nudge the dear old lady into the twentieth century. Perhaps it'd even convince her to give up her ancient bonnets, lined up in their shared dressing room on wire hat stands.

Katherine sifted through the basket of silk marigolds, carnations, and daisies, along with ribbons, feathers, and beads that Bridget had unpacked. She selected sprigs of greenery, a few daisies, and a yellow ribbon to attach to the brim of the white straw hat. The bright colors would suit Aunt Letty well.

"That's lovely, Katherine. You have a real artistic flair." Aunt Letty reached over and ran her fingers over the silk flowers.

"Thank you. I love giving new life to my old hats. Sometimes I even buy new ones and decorate them myself."

"It's splendid to have a hobby or two. I've always worked on my needlepoint and embroidery wherever I've traveled. Even when I didn't enjoy the countries we visited, they seemed so much better when I had my needlework to keep me busy." Aunt Letty peered over her rimless spectacles.

"What places didn't you like?" Katherine asked, with some surprise. Over the years, Aunt Letty always told tales of places she'd loved, countries she longed to return to. She didn't remember any negative stories.

"Let me see. When my husband took me down the Amazon River for our wedding trip, I thought I'd melt from the heat or much worse, I'd fall overboard and a caiman would eat me for dinner. All those snakes and mosquitoes! Oh, my dear, I was terrified."

Katherine glanced up from her daisies. "Why ever did he choose the Amazon?" Letty had spent most of her adult life traveling with her husband, who'd passed on a few years ago. The family considered her a harmless eccentric, but Katherine always looked forward to her visits, eager to hear her stories.

Letty's rheumy blue-gray eyes glistened. "We honeymooned in the Amazon because Norman wanted to. All those exotic birds and monkeys thrilled him. And I wanted him to think I was brave, so I pretended to be fearless. I couldn't bear to see his disappointment if I asked to go home."

Katherine shook her head. "I'm afraid I couldn't martyr myself."

Aunt Letty laughed. "After a while I adapted to the weather and the inconveniences so much that I *almost* enjoyed myself. At least I appreciated seeing an entirely new world. It was quite an experience for a girl of nineteen."

"I imagine so," Katherine said.

"Oh yes. Norman could have stuck me in a parlor serving tea and cake. But instead, I viewed the sphinx and the pyramids, and rode on a camel in Egypt. Once we traveled to India to visit the Taj Mahal. Thanks to Norman, I've had a most exciting life. I'm grateful for every moment of it."

"You are a fortunate woman," Katherine admitted, feeling a pang of envy.

"Yes, indeed. Sometimes places or trips that sound dreadful turn out to be magnificent, marvelous journeys we'll always remember. Don't ever be afraid of the unknown, dear girl, regardless of what the road looks like behind you."

Katherine bit back a grimace. She'd ventured into the unknown with Charles and it had proven the worst mistake in her life. "You know I've never dodged adventures, but I've found some territories are more dangerous than you can ever envision," Katherine blurted.

Letty searched Katherine's face. "Whatever do you mean, my dear?"

Katherine knew she shouldn't make cryptic remarks that she didn't wish to explain. "I'm only trying to be a bit more prudent than I used to be, to keep the peace with Mama, if nothing else."

The old lady laughed easily. "Your mother will appreciate that. But don't lose your spirit or you'll dry up way before your time."

Katherine rested her hat in her lap. "Do you think it's a mistake to try to follow society's standards?"

"Follow the Lord's guidance, not society's." Aunt Letty lowered her needlework to her lap and leaned forward. Her spectacles slid to the bottom of her nose, and she pushed them back. "I suspect the Lord wants you to dare to love, Katherine. Begin with that. It's His desire for all of us."

Love. What did that mean? Katherine spoke slowly, her throat suddenly dry and dusty. "Love . . . as in marriage?" Was not her mother enough to handle on this front? She had to bear it from Aunt Letty too?

"You're so young and passionate I can't imagine He wants you to remain a widow. But you'll have to wait and see for yourself. All in good time. But do keep an open mind and an open heart."

"I'm afraid I wouldn't recognize love if it slapped me in the face." The words slipped out, and she couldn't snatch them back.

"Ah, so there's the crux of it." From the look in Aunt Letty's eyes, she understood exactly what Katherine meant. "You'll have to begin anew. Learn what it means to love," Letty said gently. "That man you married clearly didn't know what he had in you," she added, shaking her finger at Katherine. "But true love of any kind involves giving. Without giving love yourself, you won't recognize the genuine emotion when you receive it. You have to know the difference so you can avoid the counterfeit variety. I'm afraid there's a lot of that around."

Katherine winced. With Charles, she'd encountered ardor without love, but she hadn't discerned the difference until much too late. "You've given me a lot to consider."

Aunt Letty raised her crooked index finger. "And one more thing. We can learn about real love from the Lord—His unquenchable love for us. But to have a relationship with Him, we have to forgive our enemies. Forgive our hurts. We mustn't hold grudges, though I'll admit, it's hard not to."

Nodding, Katherine couldn't think of anyone she considered an enemy. Except Charles, long dead and gone, and Harriet. Guilt skittered across Katherine's heart. She couldn't forgive the woman who stole her husband and bore the son who should've been hers. *Lord, help me to try.*

"Another thing—if you've offended anyone, ask for their forgiveness."

Katherine stifled a groan, wishing Aunt Letty would stop now. But her words brought Mama and Papa to mind. She'd hurt them terribly when she'd run off with Charles. To ask Mama for forgiveness would place her mother in a powerful position that she'd no doubt use to her advantage. Could she really bear to do that? Should she?

"Take care of those things, then soak in God's love, get down deep with it, and then you'll be ready to understand the love between a man and a woman."

Putting the hat in her basket, Katherine nodded. "Andrew talked to me about the Lord when we hiked this afternoon, and God's plan for my life."

Aunt Letty's eyes sparkled. "Did he? Andrew is a good man to speak of spiritual things. Most gentlemen are only interested in parties and sports. You're fortunate to have him as a close friend."

"I am, indeed."

Chapter Nine

Katherine didn't want to admit Aunt Letty was right about apologizing. Humbling herself might be biblical, but it would certainly hurt. The next day she braced herself as she scoured Birchwood Lodge for Mama and Papa. She could endure a blow to her pride to ensure peace, or at least a truce, between herself and her mother. It was the right thing to do. Wandering down the hallway near the main lounge, Katherine discovered them in Papa's cramped office pouring over the household accounts. Mama stood behind him at his desk, glancing over his shoulder.

A photograph of Papa proudly holding up a prize fish still hung on the pine-paneled wall beside an image of him as a young man toting a hunting rifle. Silver framed photographs of the family graced the desk crowded with papers, New York newspapers, magazines, and writing supplies needed by a businessman who brought his work wherever he went. All the things were in the same places as she remembered. Her parents glanced up and smiled.

"Do come in and have a seat." Papa waved her toward a hard wooden chair on the other side of the desk. "Can we help you with something or did you come to visit for a while?" He closed his ledger and leaned back in his swivel chair, ready to pay attention.

Katherine swallowed her reluctance and forced herself to speak the necessary words. "I want to thank you both for forgiving me after I eloped with Charles. I knew you distrusted him. But I thought you didn't accept him because he wasn't of New York society and you didn't know his family." Katherine gave a wry smile. "As it turns out, his father was a delightful gentleman who treated me as if I were a queen. Unfortunately, his son did not." Her voice snagged over the last few words.

She paused and glanced from Papa to Mama. Mama's fleeting look of triumph was clear and expected.

But Papa's brows furrowed. He obviously found no satisfaction in having been right. She knew he'd feel only sympathy for her. "I'm so sorry, princess. I'd hoped—we both hoped—that we'd misjudged Charles. We wanted your happiness more than anything."

Katherine nodded. "You and Mama saw through his facade to his true character. I didn't. His charm blinded me." Sucking in a deep breath, she glanced from one parent to the other. "I'm very sorry I put you through so much anxiety and embarrassment. In the future I promise to act with far more caution."

Light on his feet for a heavyset man, Papa rounded the desk and pulled Katherine into a tight embrace. "You know we forgave you years ago."

"Yes, but I'd never apologized. I wanted you to know I'm terribly sorry, and I love you both with all my heart."

Tears glistened in the corners of Mama's eyes, but she sniffed them back, reluctant to show sentimentality. "It's so gratifying to hear you admit your mistake. Now that you're a grown woman I hope you've learned that listening to us will keep you out of trouble. We'll never lead you astray." She patted her daughter's hand.

Katherine forced a nod. Mama meant well, but would she try to lead her down the wrong road? This time she'd continue to pray for guidance and keep Him at the center of her life. Until she understood exactly what He had in mind, she wouldn't cross Mama. But if His will clashed with her mother's, then Katherine knew Whom she'd have to follow.

Mama squeezed her arm. "I can spot a scoundrel from miles away, even when you can't. I also know who's likely to bring you happiness. You can trust my judgment."

Gulping down her objections, Katherine stepped back and stared at her mother's smug expression. A frisson of disappointment and self-doubt twirled around Katherine's spine. Maybe Mama was right; maybe her judgment hadn't improved over the years. Maybe she'd always make impulsive mistakes unless she heeded her mother's counsel.

Oh Lord, please guide me in a way I can't possibly misinterpret. Her gaze shifted from Mama to Papa. She had listened to Mama long enough. "Please excuse me. I promised Aunt Letty I'd help sort through her old magazines today. She has so many."

Mama rolled her eyes. "She keeps everything. You're doing her a great favor by helping her part with her paraphernalia."

Heading toward the door, Katherine heard Mama's warning. "I want you to always remember this moment, Katherine—before you're tempted to act, do speak with me first. We can talk about it, and I'll help you in any way I can."

Looking over her shoulder, Katherine mumbled, "Yes, of course, Mama. Thank you."

But as she turned away, she couldn't quite imagine doing so.

Talking over a problem with her mother meant Mama did all the advising and Katherine did all the listening and agreeing.

She found Aunt Letty playing croquet with the Clarkes. When the game ended, Aunt Letty took her by the hand and led her down the covered walkway toward the kitchen building. "How would like to pick raspberries with me? I thought I'd ask Cook to bake a raspberry tart with whipped cream on top."

"I'd be delighted. But what about throwing out your ancient magazines?"

The old lady shrugged. "Well, I'm not sure tossing them was such a good idea when there's nothing wrong with any of them except they're old. You might find the stories entertaining and get a real laugh from the out-of-date fashions." She held out the enormous leg-of-mutton sleeve of her shirtwaist. "Like this, for instance. It hasn't been popular in ten years, but I still love the puffiness."

"It might not be stylish, but the blouse looks lovely on you."

Aunt Letty laughed until her eyes watered. "You're quite the diplomat, Katherine."

"Nobody's ever called me diplomatic before. Mama often says I'm too outspoken and direct."

Aunt Letty nodded. "Don't you buckle under Isabelle's weight when you think she's wrong. She believes she has a monopoly on insight and wisdom, but sometimes her wisdom is a bit self-serving."

Katherine laughed. "I've noticed."

Once at their cabin, they changed into their most service-able frocks and pulled on boots and donned plain straw hats. They located tin pails in the kitchen and set off across the lawn toward the woods. Birds chirped in the thick tangle of bushes and skinny pines and white birch trees that reached high for the sun.

Katherine tilted her head. "I took your advice and I apologized to Mama and Papa this morning. It wasn't as hard as I expected. Of course they accepted it graciously. But Mama feels more convinced than ever that she knows best and I ought to follow wherever she leads. I was afraid she'd feel that way."

Aunt Letty sighed. "You'll have to accept your mother as she is. I'm afraid she won't change, unless the Lord Himself works a transformation. Listen to what she says, but follow your own conscience." Letty's sideways gaze perked with curiosity. "Tell me, how do you feel now that you've apologized? Relieved?"

"I do. I've felt guilty for all the grief and worry I caused them. It's not easy to admit blame, but now I think I can leave my mistake in the past."

"Splendid. I'm so proud of you for not allowing your pride to stand in your way. It's hard to ask for forgiveness, but it's good for the soul, isn't it?"

Katherine smiled. "Yes, it is. I've learned a lesson. I'll ask for forgiveness when I should and I'll forgive those who've hurt me." But the moment she spoke she realized her anger toward Charles and Harriet still burned like acid, and she had no charity in her heart for them. "I need to pardon others, but it's so very difficult. Will you pray for me?"

Her aunt nodded. "Indeed, I shall."

Katherine and Aunt Letty walked for a quarter of a mile before they came across a narrow trail that forked to the right. They followed the trial until it ended at an open vista with a pond directly ahead. Spiky evergreens ringed it on three sides and gave off a balsam fragrance that reminded her of Christmas.

They stopped at the side of the path where some of the wild raspberry brambles shot up a few feet above their heads, though most were shorter than eye level. Aunt Letty drew a whistle from her pocket and blew it with one mighty breath. A flock of birds flapped their wings and leaped into the bright blue sky.

Katherine covered her ears until Aunt Letty tucked the whistle back in her skirt pocket.

"There. That should scare away any bears. They love raspberries too, you know."

"It's been awhile since I've had to worry about bears. In Florida, it's the alligators."

"Well, you won't find any of *those* around here, thankfully. All right, now, let's pick." Aunt Letty gingerly pulled the small, round berries and plunked them into her pail.

Katherine pulled apart a red berry, examined it, and then popped it into her mouth. Before long her bucket held an abundance of red, purple, and black berries. The hot sunshine seeped through their long sleeves and high collars.

Aunt Letty put down her pail and smiled up at the sun. She tipped her hat back and let the golden rays heat her face. "This feels wonderful. I think I'll rest for a minute or two."

Katherine finished filling hers to the brim. "We have enough for several pies. Should we go back now so you can rest at the cabin?"

"A grand idea. We'll be back in time for a brief nap before luncheon." Aunt Letty cocked her head and wrapped her hand through the loop of Katherine's arm. "While we walk, would you mind if I ask you a personal question? If you think I'm far too nosy, I understand perfectly."

"Go right ahead." Buckets in hand, they headed back through the cool, shaded woods.

"All right then. When you mentioned it's hard to forgive some of the people who've caused you pain, I wondered if you meant Charles."

Pausing, Katherine noticed the hum of insects and tree frogs took the edge off the quiet. "Yes, I most definitely meant Charles. And Harriet. She was his mistress."

Aunt Letty's eyes widened with shock and then sympathy. "Oh, my dear, I'm truly sorry." She pressed Katherine's hand.

"I'd like to tell you the story, if you don't mind listening."

"If you feel it will help, go right ahead."

Katherine briefly explained how she discovered Charles's infidelity through the letters between him and Harriet, and how her marriage had died long before Charles's passing. Unburdening herself seemed to lighten the weight she'd been carrying for far too long.

"No wonder you're sad, and if I might say so, a bit unforgiving. Am I wrong about that? Nurturing the pain is quite understandable, my dear. But as more time passes, you'll learn to forgive them. Let the bad memories fade. Don't let this keep you from future happiness. You'll be blessed with a second chance at love. I can feel it in my old, creaky bones."

Katherine smiled, but doubted Aunt Letty's prediction. Who was set aside for her? Randy? She shook her head. Even if the Lord sent her another man to love, she probably wouldn't have the judgment to recognize him. *If that's in Your plan, Lord,* she prayed silently, *make it clear. Please make it very clear.*

———

Midafternoon the following day Katherine wrote a note to Stuart Osborne asking for news about her citrus groves. When she heard a rap on her cabin door, she cracked it open and Mama stepped over the threshold flashing a resolute smile. "Some of the ladies are out on the back veranda waiting to see you, dear. So do come, and bring your needlework or that pretty little hat you're fixing up."

If she hesitated, Mama would pounce. She'd put her off as long as she could. But the possibility of an afternoon by herself was at least worth a try. "I'm sorry, Mama, but I was planning to take a short nap. I have a bit of a headache. I'd be awfully dull company until I feel better." All of which was true, if slightly exaggerated.

"Nonsense, my dear. You mustn't indulge yourself. I have just the thing for headaches. I'll have Bridget get it for you." She glanced around for the maid, who immediately emerged from the dressing room with a dress draped over her arm. "Bridget, go fetch my headache medicine. And be quick about it."

The maid bobbed a curtsy and disappeared.

Mama scrutinized Katherine from top to bottom. "Surely you have a light-colored frock somewhere. Do put on something less drab. Honestly, you dress as if you're as old as Aunt Letty." She marched to Katherine's wardrobe, scanned the meager assortment of tired dresses and plain, gored skirts. "Hmm. Not much to choose from, I see."

Mama pulled out a light gray skirt and paired it with an old white shirtwaist in need of bluing, but the best of the lot. "At least it has a few tucks down the front and a row of pearl buttons. With your cameo at the neck, it might be pretty, or at least not as shabby as most of your clothes. I shall see you on the veranda in five minutes." With that, Mama turned on her heel and left.

Unlike Newport and Bar Harbor, Mama's guests at Birchwood shared a love of nature's rugged beauty and eagerly shed the majority of their pretentions along with their elegant wardrobes. They eschewed silks and satins in favor of lawn and muslin, and took to calling vacations in the Adirondacks "roughing it." But despite their rustic furniture housed in log cabins and a simple, though spacious, lodge, they maintained their high standards of ease—indoor plumbing, a fleet of boats, and a staff of servants to cater to their every whim.

Katherine changed her clothes, swallowed a small dose of aspirin, and strolled down the walkway leading to the chalet's back veranda. Ladies of various ages gathered on wicker chairs in a semicircle facing the lake. Mrs. Clarke motioned Katherine to the seat beside her. Mama was potting marigolds from the top step of the veranda only a few feet away from the group.

Katherine tried not to squirm as several sets of curious eyes focused upon her. She flashed her most polite smile at each lady and waited for the genteel inquisition to begin. Oddly, they hesitated. Her hands fidgeted in her lap, so she busied her fingers with her half-finished boater. The steady *click-clack* of knitting needles filled the quiet. A bumblebee buzzed around the plain straw hats and the ladies swatted it away.

"It's wonderful to see all of you again. I'm delighted to be home," Katherine began, unable to bear the silence. "Florida is lovely, but Raquette Lake holds my heart. I've always loved the Adirondacks. They're so wild and primitive."

Mrs. Porter arched a brow. "I'm not surprised that wild and primitive would appeal to you, Katherine," she said in a measured voice laced with censure.

She could play Mrs. Porter's cutting little game too, but she'd not embarrass herself, or anyone else. "Perhaps when I was younger, but no longer. My youth has fled and I'm content to live out my days as a widow."

She gazed down at her hands and then glanced toward Mrs. Clarke, whose face cracked with disbelief. "Katherine will no doubt change her mind about remarriage once she rejoins society," she explained in her chilliest tone. "And that will take place in the fall, as soon as we return to the city. Isn't that right, Isabelle?"

Mama looked up from her flowers. "Yes, indeed. Everyone

misses you, Katherine dear. They'll not allow you to keep to yourself for long. Mark my words." Mama glanced around for reinforcement.

Katherine peered at Mama in confusion. She'd made it very clear she was only home for the summer. Was this evidence that her mother didn't believe her?

"You're so right, Isabelle. We're all so glad to have you back," pretty Mrs. Lessman said. "And you mustn't dwell upon the past or you'll make yourself miserable. You're much too young to shut yourself away. Do try to overcome your grief and sadness. You must be strong."

Mrs. Porter smirked. "If you'll pardon my boldness, Katherine, too much grieving is just plain self-indulgent. Listen to Mrs. Lessman. You mustn't give in to your weakest emotions."

Katherine's impulse to refute these ladies wobbled on the tip of her tongue. *Lord, help me smile politely and stay in this chair. Don't allow me to throw down my hat and storm off. Please keep me from embarrassing Mama.* "I see your point, Mrs. Porter," Katherine murmured through clenched teeth.

Mrs. Porter nodded, apparently mollified. "I do hope when you do decide to marry again, you'll favor us with a proper wedding. We were so *deflated* when you eloped with Mr. Osborne and deprived us of a grand celebration."

"This time will be different, Pamela," Mama insisted as she shoved her trowel in the clay pot. "When Katherine remarries, her wedding will be a lovely affair, I assure you."

This time? When Katherine remarries? Had Mama not heard a word that Katherine had said?

Mrs. Porter persisted, "But why did you run off the first time, Katherine? You knew your mother's dearest wish was to give you a lavish celebration."

Poor Mrs. Porter didn't know when to retreat. If only she had noticed Mama's red, puckered face. Katherine saw her mother mentally scratching Mrs. Porter off her list of friends to invite back to camp, let alone any future wedding. Echoing Mama's sentiments and opinions was expected, but badgering her daughter was solely Mama's prerogative, not anyone else's.

Katherine expelled a puff of air. "I didn't wish to put Mama to so much trouble." That was such a lame excuse her cheeks flamed. From the widening of eyes, no one believed a word of it. Hastily she added, "And Charles wanted to get back to Florida as soon as possible. His father was ill. In fact, he passed on about a year later."

Mumbled condolences followed. They sounded sincere, and she decided to give the ladies the benefit of the doubt.

"Where did you marry?" tiny Mrs. Bruce piped up. "I don't believe I read about it on the society page."

"In New York. I couldn't travel with a gentleman without being married, now could I?" Katherine coated her voice with a dab of honey. At least she'd done something right.

"No, indeed, you could not." Mrs. Clarke's steely gaze slid from lady to lady. "Katherine would never do anything improper. She's a woman of impeccable character."

Flustered, Mrs. Bruce nodded. "Naturally. I'd never imply otherwise, Georgia."

Birds twittered, leaves rustled, and the sunlight glinted through the branches. The lake gleamed like a silver tray. Everything seemed so normal and so beautiful, except for the turmoil that boiled in Katherine's chest. She tried to focus on the project in her hand and hoped the ladies would change the subject.

After a short pause in the conversation, Mrs. Lessman said, "Your hat is lovely, Katherine. You have quite a knack for decoration."

Relieved that the topic of marriage was being replaced,

Katherine flashed a sunny smile. "Mama's maid taught me how when I was young, and I really enjoy it. I've salvaged several of my hats. They're like new."

Of course none of these ladies needed to economize by refurbishing anything, so they nodded, eyes vacant.

"It's an enjoyable hobby." Katherine hesitated for a few seconds, eager to keep the subject off her future relationships. "I've toyed with turning my hobby into something meaningful and worthwhile. What would you all think of me creating some unique hats for my friends and donating the proceeds to charity?" She held her breath and waited for remarks. Perhaps Papa had been wrong.

But all their eyes widened at once. Mrs. Porter gasped. "You don't mean you'd *sell* your hats, do you?"

Katherine mustered all her courage. "Perhaps, if someone wishes to buy one. As I said, all the funds would go to a good cause. A charity."

Mama clapped the dirt off her gloved hands and then tore off the dirty gloves and tossed them aside. "Impossible, my dear. Women are not meant to be entrepreneurs. What a ridiculous notion." Mama's gaze cut her with a sharp warning.

Mrs. Clarke huffed. "You're clever, Katherine, but not practical. Just be satisfied with redoing hats for yourself. All is innocent until one enters the world of commerce, for charity or otherwise. That's a realm best reserved for the men."

Aunt Letty, who'd just joined the group, spoke up. "I, for one, think it's a brilliant idea, Katherine, and if it tickles your fancy, you ought to pursue it."

Mama groaned. "Really, Aunt, you mustn't encourage such a silly idea."

Katherine buried her head in her work so no one would notice how her face was heating up. When would she learn to keep her own counsel like the rest of these ladies and conform to their standards? Yet it seemed impossible to curb her impulses.

Mama piped up. "I hear Rowena Howard is home from England." She lowered her voice to a conspiratorial whisper. The ladies leaned into the circle, obviously eager to hear the latest gossip. "Rumor says she's *divorced* from the earl. How dreadful. Her dear mother is distraught, as you might well imagine."

"A divorce, not just a separation?" Mrs. Lessman's jaw dropped open. The poor woman was easily scandalized. What would she do if she found out about Charles? "She'll never get away with it. No one will receive her."

Mama nodded. "Just because Alva Vanderbilt divorced and survived it, doesn't mean anyone else can. You'd have to be as rich as the Vanderbilts to even try."

"Or Caroline Astor's daughter, Charlotte Drayton. Remember she ran off to Europe with a *man*," Mrs. Wyatt purred.

"And to make matters worse, they were both married, but not to each other," Mrs. Porter agreed.

Katherine bit her lip. Less than two years into her marriage, she'd considered fleeing to New York and back to the arms of her family. But she couldn't dredge up the courage. As much as Mama disliked and distrusted Charles, she'd never countenance a separation, let alone a divorce. Old-fashioned and convinced that divorce violated God's will as well as society's, Mama believed in lifelong commitment. Katherine did too. So she'd waited and prayed for some improvement in her situation. Only it had to arrive through Charles's death.

Before she realized it, Katherine found herself talking. "I, for one, shall welcome Rowena. We were fast friends at school and I'll not desert her." Katherine lifted her chin, but softened her expression with a slight upturn of her lips. "The Lord requires us to forgive. Not that Rowena's done a thing to any of us. The problems in her marriage are between her and her husband. And the Lord."

Mrs. Porter looked askance. "My dear Katherine, you're much too tolerant. It's your youth, no doubt. When you grow older and wiser, you'll learn that society's rules are made for good reason. To flaunt them is to invite disaster."

Mrs. Bruce nodded. "Your elders know best."

Katherine's fingers flew as she attached silk ribbon to the crown of her hat. Their judgmental attitudes appalled her. How could they relish ostracizing a young woman they'd all known for years? Had they no mercy for someone probably no worse than they? Poor Rowena sinned, but so did everyone. She didn't deserve to be singled out merely because her transgression embarrassed society.

The ladies continued to gossip, but Katherine, head bent over the boater, concentrated on the silk daisies and yellow ribbon and ignored the chatter. Could she ever fit in with this self-righteous group and accept their prejudices and ridiculously strict standards without a whimper of protest? Did she truly want to?

Chastising others for failing to forgive was far easier than extending forgiveness herself. Katherine sighed inwardly. She'd tried to absolve Charles and Harriet, but her grievances still burned deep in her chest like an unquenchable fire. *Lord, please soften my heart. It's as cold and hard as a rock. I have no right to condemn these smug ladies when I also fail to forgive.*

That evening she mulled over her own hypocrisy. Her dinner of venison stew sat like an indigestible lump in her queasy stomach. Under Mama's scrutiny, she smiled and chatted and acted as charming as she possibly could. But she yearned to lie down on her chaise longue and be alone with her thoughts.

"I think I'll retire early." Katherine leaned into her mother on their way out of the dining hall. "I'm not feeling very well," she said, touching her stomach.

Mama pursed her lips. "Oh, my dear! I was counting on you to help Randy entertain tonight. He's going to sing and play the mandolin. I thought you might join him in a few duets. Perhaps a bit of ginger ale will settle your stomach?"

Katherine suppressed a sigh, knowing that any argument was futile. And she had promised she'd cooperate with Mama; she ought to at least take a stab at it. "Perhaps ginger ale would do the trick." She followed her family and Mama's guests into the lounge. Andrew was among them, but he remained curiously apart, choosing a chair in the far corner. She'd hardly seen him over the last day—presumably, he'd been hard at work on her father's business. But it was good to see him, even from afar. His eyes met her glance and they both smiled. Unexpectedly, she felt heat sear her cheeks and she quickly looked away before their gazes locked again.

For the next few hours she accompanied Randy on the piano and together they sang several popular songs they both knew well. And her mother had been right—a glass of ginger ale gradually settled her stomach. As she relaxed, she started to enjoy herself, much to her surprise.

Singing had always brought her joy and peace, and tonight she sang along with Randy with a lighthearted lilt to her voice. Several times she glanced in the direction of her mother and felt glad to see that she smiled and nodded her approval. Finally, somehow, she was doing something right in her mother's eyes.

Chapter Ten

Between songs, Mr. Wainwright slid into the empty chair beside Andrew. With his eyes fixed on Katherine and Randy, Andrew's boss leaned sideways and said softly, "They make splendid music together, don't they?"

"Yes, sir, they both have beautiful voices."

"I'd say they blend in perfect harmony, as if they were meant for each other."

Andrew glanced at Mr. Wainwright then. From the older man's expression, he understood the meaning behind the statement. Had Mrs. Wainwright put her husband up to this? It mattered little. If it was what his boss wanted, who was he to argue? "I hear what you're saying, sir. As pretty as the music is, I think I'll retire for the evening. It's getting late and you know how I like to start work early."

Katherine's father nodded with satisfaction. "An excellent idea, Andrew. I'll see you in the morning."

Vaguely dispirited, Andrew left the lounge without a last glimpse toward Katherine. But her voice, mingled with Randy's, echoed in his mind as he climbed the stairs to the second floor and disappeared into his bedroom.

Settling into a chair by the window, Andrew felt the night air cool his burning face. Apparently his affection for Katherine hadn't gone unnoticed. From now on he'd take care not to look like a lovelorn suitor, or else he'd find himself back in a hot, stuffy New York office for the remainder of the summer. Or even worse, without a job.

Andrew opened his Bible, but he couldn't concentrate. He lowered the book and let his mind wander. And then he prayed. *Lord, You know all about this dilemma I'm in. Please guide me to do the right thing for everyone concerned, not just for me. I have such a strong feeling that You mean for Katherine and me to be together, but could I be mistaken? Am I blinded to Your will, Lord? Speak to me. I'm listening.*

When Katherine looked for Andrew again, he'd vanished. The discovery left her feeling oddly bereft. The glow from the evening dimmed.

Mrs. Lessman warbled a sweet, slightly off-key song, followed by a surprisingly good duet from Mr. and Mrs. Porter. Later in the evening, footmen served refreshments, but Katherine passed them up, afraid to upset her sensitive stomach.

After the guests dispersed to their bedrooms, Randy lingered in the lounge, shuffling around his sheet music. "Thanks for joining me, Katherine. Wasn't that great fun? Let's sing together again soon."

"I'd like to. But now I'm tired. If you'll excuse me, I'll be on my way."

"Please, Katherine, stay awhile longer. Only five or ten more minutes. We should practice the songs for the sing-along your mother is planning. She'd like us to perform a few duets."

Katherine looked around the deserted room, practically expecting her mother and Mrs. Clarke to peer around the corner, hoping a meeting exactly like this was occurring. The grandfather clock chimed midnight, but Katherine summoned the last bit of her strength. "All right. Just awhile longer. Then I simply must be off."

They practiced a few more songs, all Gilbert and Sullivan tunes from their comic operas. Randy eased a few inches closer as she played the piano, but Katherine ignored his movement. When they finished the song, he folded the sheet music and placed it in the piano bench.

"Did you enjoy tonight?" he asked, taking her hand.

Her impulse was to slip her fingers out of his grasp, but instead she smiled. "Yes, I did." His hand felt almost too soft and smooth.

"It's grand seeing you smile for a change. You were much too glum when you first arrived. But now you seem happier and ready to rejoin society. Am I right?"

In the dim gaslight, his chiseled features softened. His straight black hair, usually parted in the middle and controlled with macassar oil, fell across his high forehead. She smelled the pleasant scent of coconut from his hair tonic and mustache wax. For a moment she thought she'd push the stray lock back in place, but that was much too intimate a gesture toward a man she considered just a friend. He might think she was falling in love—or at least falling into line—and she wasn't anywhere near ready for their fledgling relationship to accelerate.

She slid her hand away from his. "I *am* happier, Randy. And I had a delightful evening. Thank you for that."

He smiled at her. "You're exhausted. Let me walk you to your cabin."

She nodded, relieved to be moving, even if he was coming along. He offered his arm, and together they strolled down the dark walkway, lit only by the lights still burning in the lodge.

"Maybe tomorrow we can play tennis or Ping-Pong. Or go for a swim. The water is cold, but that never used to bother you."

"We'll see. Thank you for asking."

Frowning, Randy tilted his head. "Katherine, why are you acting so formal? So, uh, *removed*? We've known each other all our lives. And yet you act as if you hardly know me."

They halted at her door. Gazing into his bewildered eyes, she felt a twinge of pity for him. "Eight years has changed us all, Randy. I'm not the same girl I was. Even though we're good friends, we must get acquainted all over again." *I didn't have the same impulse with Andrew*, she thought. *With him, it was like nothing had changed, even after all these years . . .*

The twist in his mouth signaled he didn't agree. "I'm the same fellow I've always been. You already know just about everything there is to know about me." Then he raised his boyish grin that never failed to melt the hardest of hearts. "My life is an open book."

She straightened her crooked smile. "Yes, I can see that. But I'm afraid *I'm* different, Randy. Give it time, will you? Give me some time."

They couldn't force love to happen merely because their families expected it. And she couldn't pretend a grand and glorious romance if it didn't truly exist. Yet she'd neither dismiss his interest out of hand nor would she rush into a relationship before she was ready. Regardless of what their mothers desired.

Andrew strolled toward the dining hall early the next morning and took a deep breath of crisp mountain air. His mood seesawed from joy to depression and back again. Maybe it was because Katherine had dominated his dreams last night. Watching her sing had lifted his spirits, regardless of her father's warning shot across his bow. Her bright smile reminded him of the young girl he'd fallen in love with years ago, and nothing could dim that. Except for the fact that most of those smiles had been directed toward his cousin, Randy. Yet once or twice she'd caught his eye, tilted her head, and flashed a grin, but then let her gaze flit across the rest of the group.

Andrew had felt something that probably no one else saw. The old Katherine was emerging from her web of sorrow. He could tell, even if no one else could. He wondered if she felt anything beyond friendship when their eyes met last night. Was there an inkling of love in her eyes? Or was he merely wishing so hard that he'd imagined it?

It doesn't matter, he told himself. Katherine seemed happy, and even though he might never have her love, her good spirits had lifted his own. His fate, and Katherine's, was in the Lord's hands. If it were to be, it would be, despite her father's veiled warning. Was he merely an incurable optimist when it came to Katherine? Or would "fool" more aptly describe him?

"Good morning, Andrew." Katherine's voice brought him out of his thoughts of last night, and he glanced up in gleeful surprise. She met him on the walkway leading to the dining hall. "Are you on your way to breakfast?"

"I am. Care to join me?" he asked.

She nodded. As they entered the building they found it nearly deserted, typical at this hour. "Do you always rise at this time?"

"I like to get to work at the crack of dawn so I can have part of the afternoon to myself." He couldn't imagine an employer nicer or more considerate than Mr. Wainwright, allowing him a flexible schedule here at camp. "How about you? You're to be on vacation. Why up so early?"

She shrugged. "I'm used to business hours, up with the sun and dead-asleep by moonrise."

They served themselves sausage and eggs, toast and blueberry muffins from the sideboard. A maid delivered cups of steaming coffee and a small pitcher of fresh cream.

"If you have the afternoon off, maybe we could play tennis together. I haven't played in years, and I'd like to try again," Katherine said.

Andrew hesitated. As much as he wanted to jump at the chance of being with her, he knew he shouldn't. He didn't wish to annoy his hostess, his aunt, or more importantly, his boss. And playing tennis would be awfully . . . public. "That would be wonderful, but let's wait and see how the day progresses. I might have more work than I expect."

From her frown, he could tell she didn't believe a word he said. "All right. But you're not trying to avoid me, are you?" She seemed genuinely puzzled, though she shouldn't be.

"No, but judging from last night, things are unfolding nicely for you and Randy. I shouldn't interfere." He tossed it out, disliking his own petulant tone. But he couldn't stop himself. He'd been enraptured by the return of her girlhood smile last night, as well as eviscerated by her attention toward Randy.

Irritation flickered across her face. "Randy is Mama's idea, not mine. We're nothing but dear friends."

He glanced at her, considering her words. Did that mean she might consider Andrew her own idea? He couldn't risk everything before he knew for sure. And yet, what if she felt the same way about him? Only friendship? His appetite gone, he excused himself just as Mrs. Wainwright, Aunt Georgia, and Randy entered the dining hall. He greeted the three, falsely cheerful. "Please excuse me. Time to get to work."

That afternoon Katherine helped Aunt Letty arrange photographs in her leather album as she listened to her rambling but fascinating tales of days long gone. They emptied two more boxes of loose photographs on the sofa and discarded a few blurry and faded ones before Mama burst through the door.

Without pausing for pleasantries, she came straight to the point. "Katherine, I'm glad to see you assisting Aunt Letty, but you mustn't stay cooped up all day. Randy is resting in the hammock by the lake, and I thought you might join him. Make sure you wear your hat to shield your face from the sun."

Katherine understood an order when she heard one, though she had already spent a considerable amount of her time in the outdoors, canoeing. *But I promised Papa . . .* "Yes, of course, Mama, if you'd like." It took every ounce of her strength to smile, to rise, and to obey. Regardless of her agreement with Papa, if Mama decided she didn't show enough interest in Randy, she'd leave Katherine with no measure of peace.

Mama pursed her thin lips, not fooled. "I do so wish you'd show more enthusiasm for socializing. Randy can be great fun."

Katherine beat down the anger flaring in her chest. "I don't know why you're agitated, Mama. I'm off to see Randy, as you've suggested." She turned hopefully to her aunt. "Unless you mind my absence?"

But the elderly lady was so engrossed in her pile of photos of Norman that she merely lifted a hand. "Go right ahead, my dear. I have to decide which of these to get rid of, though I doubt I can part with any. I'm a sentimental old fool, you know." Her eyes glistened with a teary smile. She belatedly looked from Isabelle to Katherine, understanding too late. But Katherine's mother was already on the move, opening the porch door and waiting for her to pass. Aunt Letty gave her a little shrug of apology.

Katherine sighed and headed out to the backyard studded with white birch, quaking aspen, white pines, and several full-skirted sugar maples as Mama returned to the lodge, a self-satisfied prance to her step. Sunshine had chased away the chill and gray skies of morning and filtered through the canopy of greenery arching above the yard.

She thought back to her breakfast with Andrew. She wished he'd agreed to her suggestion of a tennis match. He wasn't working this afternoon—she could see him on the beach, launching a small sailboat into the water. So why had he dodged her? Her eyes moved to Randy, and she remembered how Andrew had hung back last night, and then disappeared as they went on singing. Might he be . . . jealous? Or was her father warning Andrew to stay away from her?

Letting the clear air sweep away thoughts of Andrew helped her focus on her mother's request. Stretched out on the canvas hammock, Randy let his straw hat slip down and cover most of his face. She shoved down a wave of irritation, wishing he'd read a book, for once, rather than while away the hours napping. *Focus on the good things,* she reminded herself. *The fine things about him.* He wore dark trousers, a soft collared white shirt open at the neck with sleeves rolled up to his elbows. The rash on his arms looked more pink than red, a sure sign the calamine lotion was working.

At her approach, he lifted his hat. "Well, good afternoon, Katherine." He made a move to arise, but she motioned him to stay still.

"Don't let me disturb you. You look quite comfortable."

"Come sit beside me." He patted the canvas as he righted himself.

She tilted her head. "I hardly think so. We'd slide to the middle and I'd end up in your lap."

"That wouldn't be so bad, would it?"

She had to grin at the twinkle in his dark eyes. "Hardly proper," she answered with a crooked smile. "I'll just stand here by the tree, if you don't mind." She leaned against the trunk and stared out at the lake, trying to keep her eyes from a small sailboat bobbing in the waves.

But Randy did the gentlemanly thing and got out of the hammock, edging near her. He pulled the hat off his head and twisted it in his hands, rolling his foot idly over a tree root. "You know, Katherine, I'm really glad you're back. Nothing's been the same since you married and left the rest of us behind."

She raised her eyebrows. "That's certainly an exaggeration."

"Well, for me it's true. You broke my heart when you ran off with one of my best friends. I never quite recovered from your defection." He shot her a wide, friendly grin. "What? Must I prove it to you?" he said dramatically. He staggered backward and then to the side, one hand clutching his heart, the other hand to his head. "See? Still I yearn so for my sweet Katherine, 'tis as if I ail! 'Tis as if I still bear an arrow through my heart!"

Katherine shook her head at his melodrama and giggled. "Even though I said earlier we hardly know each other anymore, you're really just the same, Randy. You can still make me smile."

He dipped his head. "My pleasure."

"Tell me, what have you been doing in the last eight years?"

Randy shrugged and then scrunched his face in a wince. "If you mean 'what have I accomplished,' I'm afraid if I tell you, you'll think less of me. If you ask my father, he'll say nothing at all. But I've enjoyed myself, so in my own mind I've achieved everything I set out to do."

Randy was very much like Charles when it came to work.

But Randy didn't have a mean side or fearsome temper. And his fortune was so vast, it'd be difficult to gamble away. He merely wanted life to swirl around him in an endless party. Not a very ambitious goal, to be sure, but at least he was honest about it. Many young men of their generation seemed at loose ends, she mused. Their fathers or grandfathers had made the family fortunes, and now there was little for them to do except spend the spoils.

He gently kicked away a twig and then dug the heels of his shiny boots into the dirt. "While I was learning the intricacies of bridge and idling away my time, you were running a company. I can hardly believe the girl I dreamed about all these years managed citrus groves. It's astonishing, what you've had to bear."

She doubted Randy ever pined away for her, or ever would. He was merely being charming. A gust of wind lifted her skirt a few inches. She held it down as best she could while Randy's gaze strayed toward her ankles and lingered.

"I miss working and the feeling of accomplishment at the end of the day," she said, making him look her in the eye again. "You should try it sometime. It truly is a fulfilling sort of life."

He shook his head, clearly bewildered. "My goodness, Katherine. I can't believe you actually *enjoy* working. I can tell you, your mother certainly disapproves. Most mothers would, of course. No woman of status should have to go through such things." He let out a laugh. "Few men of status should do so either."

Katherine fought back a frown. "So you disapprove as well?" She pulled off a maple leaf and slowly shredded it.

He shrugged, peering at her, clearly gauging her reaction. "I've never considered a woman working before, except for those who haven't a choice. But whoever heard of a society girl *wanting* to work? No one, I'll wager."

Katherine breathed deeply to relax the tightness building in her chest. "Perhaps I don't belong in society anymore."

His eyebrows raised. "Nonsense! You did once and you will again. Just forget about your groves and concentrate on having fun with me. I'll show you the way back. I know the path well." He cocked a brow and gave her a flirtatious grin.

"Randy, I think you misunderstand. I truly enjoy working. As much as I love it here, I miss my business."

"And you are not understanding me. You had another life, a different life, in Florida. But you've returned, to the life you were born to." He reached out and placed a gentle hand on hers. "Undoubtedly, you're confused. A bit lost, really. But take heart, Kat. You're not alone. I'll show you the way. Shall we begin with a boat ride? This time without a tragic, stormy culmination?"

She forced a smile and took his arm. But his words rolled around in her head. Was she truly missing her life in Florida? Or was she merely lost, a boat without an anchor? She owed it to Randy, and her parents, to at least give this life a chance again. He was right—she'd been born into it. God never made mistakes. But after the boat ride, she decided to slip in a telegram to Stuart, to find out just how the groves were faring in Florida without her. The letter she'd sent him might not receive a response for a week or more. If she were to concentrate on her life here in New York, she had to know all was well in Florida. Until that day, she'd simply rock back and forth between them in her heart and mind.

Chapter Eleven

~∾~

Late the next morning Andrew completed his work for Mr. Wainwright, and his boss dismissed him for the day. Given the gathering clouds, he couldn't head out in a sailboat as he had done the day before. The perfect solution was a hot cup of tea, a crackling fire, an overstuffed chair, and his copy of *The Adventures of Sherlock Holmes*.

Andrew slid his book out of a lower desk drawer and headed toward the lodge library. But when he arrived, he found Katherine and her great-aunt already settled in. He paused, considering other places he liked to read, but Katherine caught sight of him and smiled. She put her finger to her lips, gesturing toward Letty. Asleep in the corner, snoring softly, Mrs. Benham still held a magazine in her hand.

To leave now would be awkward, he decided, so he tiptoed over to the chair by the fire and settled in. At least with Letty sleeping, he could be near Katherine, but it appeared entirely innocent. He opened his book and attempted to focus on the words, not on the pretty young woman so close to him on the leather sofa. She was working at attaching a feather to the brim of another hat. Who was that one for? Another for Letty? A friend? Herself?

Andrew bit back a whispered question and tried to find his place in his book, but he couldn't keep from taking surreptitious glances at Katherine and Letty. For a moment he allowed himself to relish the quiet scene, wishing the three of them sat in the house he hoped to have someday, albeit a small place with less expensive furniture and fewer servants. Both those things wouldn't matter as long as Katherine sat beside him . . .

He watched her adjust the frills on the hat and then smile with obvious satisfaction at her handiwork. He let out a long breath and returned to his book. Reality was impossible to ignore. This was Mr. Wainwright's lodge, he was a guest, and Katherine had been declared out-of-bounds, at least for the time being. If he waited, another opportunity might present itself. At least, he hoped it would.

The butler entered the library with mail for Katherine a short time later. He bowed slightly and extended the silver salver. She glanced at each envelope, frowned at one for several seconds, and then accepted the letter opener. With a slight tremble in her hand, she slit the crease and stood to read it with the aid of the light seeping through the window. Her color faded. Two sheets of paper fell to the bearskin rug.

"What's the matter?" Andrew jumped up, retrieved the letter, and placed it in her hand again.

She dropped into one of the wooden chairs, gripping the papers so tightly they crumpled. He knelt down in front of her chair, wanting more than anything to pull her into his arms and comfort her. For a long while she sat silently, without moving. "Katherine?" He waited helplessly, glancing over to Letty to see if she might be of assistance, but the old lady snored on.

"Can I get you something? A glass of water? Or perhaps tea?"

She shook her head, responding as if she wasn't quite aware of his presence.

"Katherine, I don't wish to interfere. But if you need something, I'm here to help."

She lifted a grateful smile. "You're most considerate, Andrew. Please stay. I don't want to be alone."

Her words struck deep. More than anything, he wanted her to need him.

Gradually she emerged from her shock, still pale, and handed him the letter. "Please read this. I think I may need your legal opinion." Her eyes rapidly blinked back unshed tears.

Andrew glanced at the envelope addressed to Katherine before he looked through the sheets of paper. He read the feminine looking script and felt a twinge of anxiety.

Dear Mrs. Osborne,

I'm sorry I must write to you because I fear it will cause you great distress. I'm afraid there's no easy way to say this, so I'll just begin and hope you'll try to understand. Forgiveness is more than I can possibly wish for.

Charles Osborne and I had a son together several years ago. Although we didn't marry, we continued to love each other until Charles's death. If you didn't know about us or even suspect, I'm truly sorry to bring you news that you'll most likely find painful.

Charles protected me from vicious gossip in Florida, but after he passed on, I was ostracized and penniless. So I returned to my family in New York City and found a job. I wouldn't write except that I've lost my position and have no prospects for employment. I need support for my child or we will soon be without food and shelter since my relations can no longer provide for us.

If you are a good Christian woman, I pray you will take pity and send us funds so Charles's son won't suffer. Please believe me, I wouldn't ask if I weren't desperate.

I have letters from Charles expressing his love for me and acknowledging the paternity of my child, whom we named Zeke. I'm enclosing one of the notes so you'll see for yourself I'm telling the truth. You'll recognize his handwriting, I'm sure. I'd like to settle this with you in a civilized way, so please write back at the below address as soon as possible.

Sincerely,

Harriet Roles

Andrew glanced at the next sheet of paper penned in a bold, masculine writing. Beginning with "My dearest Harriet," it was signed "Your loving Charles." *Our little boy* stood out on the paper. Anger flared in Andrew's chest as he scanned the note. He glanced at Katherine. As he expected, her face glowed red with humiliation as she sat clutching her hands on her lap.

"I'm so sorry, Katherine. This must be a terrible blow, her coming after you for anything. Not after . . ."

She shook her head without glancing up. "I should have known I couldn't escape the past."

"If you'd like, I can contact a friend who's an investigator in the City. He can check on Harriet Roles." Andrew fought the urge to offer anything but formal empathy. "Do you believe what she says is true? About the child being Charles's, as well as her present circumstances?"

"Yes, I'm sure it's all true. He mentioned their son in another letter too. And it is Charles's handwriting." Her head still bowed, she rose and paced the length of the bookshelves. "You told me he was a cad and I should run from him as fast as

I could. But I didn't believe you. I loved him so much I couldn't see the truth, even though it was staring me right in the face. I should've listened to you, Andrew, but I wanted Charles so badly. I—I adored him. But I was completely mistaken about his character."

Andrew stepped toward her. "I'll help you in any way I can."

"Thank you."

He cleared his throat. "I suppose Charles didn't provide for the boy in his will."

"No, of course not." Katherine's voice faltered, and she swallowed hard. "He never could see anything through to completion in any part of his life." She stopped and leaned back against a bookcase, as if her spirit had drained out of her. For a moment she seemed to wobble and he thought she might collapse. But instead, she gripped the back of a nearby chair and steadied herself.

Andrew drew closer. "Maybe he didn't want you to find out about the affair. Maybe he hoped to spare your feelings." Andrew didn't believe a word he said, but possibly Katherine would.

She snorted, her anger spurting to the surface. "If he hadn't died, he would have left me, gone to live with Harriet and the boy. He probably assumed he had time enough to get his affairs—*all* his affairs—in order. And then he didn't."

She looked so stricken that he searched for words to lessen her pain, but all that came to mind were platitudes so trite they'd be far worse than sympathetic silence.

"I need some air. I'm going for a walk. Would you come with me?" she asked, already headed for the hallway.

"I'll be glad to." He glanced around, making sure none of the other Wainwrights were around, and then followed her down the paneled hallway and out the side door.

The clouds had blown away and the sky had brightened to deep blue. They strode around the grounds and then across the gently sloping lawn toward the bridge that led to a gazebo jutting into the glistening lake. Katherine sat down on a bench beneath the branches of a red maple and stared out at the lake. Andrew unbuttoned his coat and then dropped down to the bench beside her, unsure of what to say.

Katherine buried her head in her hands. When she looked up, she tried gamely to keep her emotions under control. "I didn't expect Harriet would ask for money. She must be very worried." Glancing at the blue water lapping the shore, Katherine bit her trembling lower lip. "I don't feel a personal responsibility for Charles's child, but as a Christian, I won't let them starve. I can't blame a child for the sins of his parents."

A dragonfly flitted by. She looked out over the glassy lake smoothed by the still air, her lips compressed as she turned his way. "But Harriet stole my husband, and I can't forget that." She breathed deeply, obviously trying to stave off her tears.

He couldn't deny it or even downplay Charles's despicable behavior. What could he say to ease the raw pain in her voice? She pitied Harriet and her son but hated the woman's adultery.

Pausing for what seemed like hours, she finally looked up at him. "During the first year of our marriage, Charles and I were happy. But then for some reason I never understood, he didn't want me anymore. When his father died, he obviously went back to her. He loved her, not me. Maybe he never loved me, not really."

Fury swelled in Andrew's chest. He could only imagine the hurt she must feel. But if she didn't forgive Harriet and Charles, the pain might linger for years.

"I wanted to be wrong about him, you know," he said at last. "I always hoped you'd live happily ever after."

At least after she'd eloped. Before then he'd prayed she'd see Charles for the scoundrel he was. But the Lord had failed to answer his prayer, at least in the way he expected. How could a kind, loving God let Katherine make such a horrible mistake? He still didn't know the reason, but he'd learned to live with unanswered questions. It was part of trusting the Lord.

Katherine sighed. "I was so sure Charles loved me. I wouldn't listen to anyone who said otherwise. But apparently, I am to continue to pay a heavy price for my foolishness." She grimaced. "Andrew, would you write to Harriet for me? I couldn't bear to contact her myself."

"Yes, of course. As I've said, I have a friend in New York, Marston Voyles, who can track down information about Harriet Roles, just to make sure everything she claims is actually true. Don't contact her until we hear from Marston."

"All right. If you think that's the wisest course of action. Thank you."

Andrew fought off the desire to touch her. "Are you going to talk to your parents about Charles's affair? Your mother might understand why you're so reluctant to rush into another marriage if you shared it with them. And perhaps she'd let you alone, at least for the time being."

He waited while she apparently mulled over his suggestion.

Her words rushed out. "I already told both my parents that I was mistaken about Charles, and I don't want them to have to bear this burden too. Besides, Mama still thinks I lack good judgment, and I should rely upon her to make any future choices; this would only strengthen her resolve to see me married off as soon as possible."

He fought a sardonic grin. Katherine's judgment wasn't so bad; she definitely understood her mother.

"Is she truly pressuring you to marry again?" He could scarcely breathe in the warm, stifling air.

Katherine gazed deep into his eyes and for a long moment he knew his heart had stopped beating. Her calm voice prickled the hairs on his arm. "She says she's not trying to rush me. But unless

I want Papa to call my loan on the groves, I must do as she asks during my time here. And that means keeping company with Randy."

His heart thudded painfully in his chest. "If she insists, will you marry him?" He had to know the answer, no matter how awful.

Katherine shook her head. "My plan is to stay a widow, despite Mama's badgering."

He could see that she and Randy made a lukewarm match at best. But would she also reject a man she truly loved because she feared another failure? Her defenses were too strong for love to crack open her heart. Poor Katherine was sentencing herself to a lonely life she might regret someday.

He folded her small hands into his own and was pleased when she didn't pull them away. "Katherine, hear me out. I think you're making a terrible mistake shutting yourself off from genuine love. You'll get through this if you open yourself to what the Lord has in store for you. You're a warm, caring woman. Don't settle for the appearance of love when you can have the real thing." Blood rushed to his face. He hadn't meant to divulge his feelings. Yet he couldn't stay silent.

She shot him a searching look. Then, clearly panicked, her eyes pleaded for understanding. "Please, Andrew, it's all too much. Let's not speak of this again."

He drew out a frustrated sigh. "All right, as you wish."

"I'm sorry, Andrew. I need your friendship most of all. Will you kindly pray for me?"

"Of course I will." A lump the size of a rock wedged in his throat. Pray for her? That was easy. He'd do anything she asked. The problem was that she seemed unready to do the one thing he needed from her—love him in return.

Chapter Twelve

～

S tartled, she stood, and Andrew rose with her. It was as
she feared; Andrew had developed true feelings for
her, beyond friendship. Much as she cherished him as a
friend—her dearest friend—she couldn't offer him love, at least
not the kind he apparently wanted.

In Andrew's eyes she found genuine passion, unlike the selfish lust she'd often seen in Charles's face. In Andrew she saw real
affection and kindness. No half-curled, mocking lips. No anger
sizzling just beneath the surface. But acknowledging the stark
differences between them terrified her.

She'd never love anyone again, even a man as thoughtful and
deserving as Andrew. No matter how much the romantic yearnings still smoldering deep inside threatened to flare up. No matter
how much she desired him now. She shouldn't indulge herself by
offering a kiss, even a platonic one. Her heart, rubbed raw from
Charles's treachery, would never completely heal. No one else
should suffer because of it. Harriet's emergence was merely the

latest rap of the judge's gavel, wasn't it? She'd made her decision long ago. And she'd need to learn to live with the consequences.

Dear Lord, don't let me do this to Andrew. He deserves better. Give me strength to resist.

Charles had deprived her of love for so long, she craved heartfelt intimacy. But she shouldn't use Andrew's interest for her own selfish benefit. *This isn't fair to him; this is wrong.* Numbly, she stepped back from him and took a deep breath. Her heart continued to slam against her ribs. Years had passed since she'd experienced such emotion.

"I should go, Andrew," she whispered, glancing up at him. "I needed you . . . and you were there for me. You're a dear friend."

His smile slipped at the word *friend.* Her heart ached for him. He didn't want friendship anymore, and who could blame him? He wasn't a flirtatious boy enjoying the antics of a precocious schoolgirl.

He was a grown man falling in love. Unfortunately, with a woman left with little more than a shriveled heart. Andrew deserved love in his life. A kind, generous, wide love. And that just wasn't something she could offer.

Andrew excused himself and headed across the lawn. He shouldn't have pressed her, especially at such a vulnerable moment. He couldn't berate himself. What was done was done. Yet from now on he'd behave properly and not endanger their friendship—or his career—any further. That would please the Wainwrights and his Aunt Georgia. And Randy, of course.

Andrew sighed. He hoped Katherine wouldn't feel awkward about this, or even worse, avoid him. He returned to his bedroom, still reeling, and wrote a short letter to Marston Voyles.

Marston had opened his detective agency a few years before and sent notices to his classmates advertising his services. Andrew thought it odd a fellow graduate of Columbia from a prominent family would settle on police type work. But Marston had laughed when Andrew mentioned his surprise.

"Now that so many society people are getting divorced, they need evidence of the more sordid variety to use against their spouses. I'm here to oblige. My business is booming."

Marston would uncover the true facts about Harriet Roles and her son, Zeke. He'd heard his old schoolmate was discreet, professional, and thorough. Maybe Marston could set up a meeting with Harriet. If Katherine didn't want to go herself—and he felt sure she wouldn't—he'd take her place and discover exactly what it would take to make Harriet go away, forever.

He gave his letter to the butler to post, and in the sanctuary of his bedroom, he opened his Bible. He flipped to Jeremiah 6:16, a verse he thought fitting. "Thus saith the Lord, Stand ye in the ways, and see, and ask for the old paths, where is the good way, and walk therein, and ye shall find rest for your souls."

As soon as Katherine turned around, she spotted Mama picking black-eyed Susans in her rock garden at the foot of the bridge. From behind the bouquet of bright yellow flowers, Mama scowled and then slowly ambled toward her. Katherine checked her first impulse to run. Trying to escape Mama was a futile notion because she'd follow right behind. But maybe she hadn't seen her with Andrew.

As Mama drew closer, Katherine painted on a smile and hoped for the best. "Lovely afternoon, isn't it?"

"Yes, indeed." Mama's pale blue eyes glared like sun rays

striking ice. "I saw you sharing intimacies with Andrew Townsend. What was the meaning of that?"

Mama moved so close, Katherine had to step away. Her backside slammed against a rough tree trunk. "It was merely conversation, Mama. Andrew is like a brother to me. He always has been. You know that."

Her mother shook her head. "I know nothing of the sort. Don't try to pull the wool over my eyes, young lady, because you can't. I saw you two holding hands." Mama's usually soft voice gathered strength and rose.

Katherine edged away. "If you'll excuse me, I must be going."

"Wait a minute. I'm not finished. You must understand that I can't allow your shocking behavior to continue. If it does, I shall have to ask your father to send Andrew back to the City, even though from what I could see, you were as much to blame as he was. Is that understood?"

Anger welled up and blocked Katherine's throat. But also fear for Andrew. Had she put his job in danger? "Yes," she sputtered. "I understand."

"Good. I hope we'll never need to speak of this again. It's unseemly."

Spinning around, Katherine strode off toward her cabin, where she could safely escape Mama's prying eyes and acid tongue.

Two days later Katherine fidgeted in her mother's dressing room as Bridget pinned and tucked, altering a new gown Mama had ordered for her without asking. Apparently, Isabelle wanted her looking just right for tonight's festivities at Camp Birchwood.

Katherine wanted to skip the dance, but there was no chance of that. Mama had hired a local band and invited dozens of their neighbors and their neighbors' guests from nearby camps. She expected Katherine to reacquaint with her old friends and blend back into society. Starting tonight.

"Are you quite through with her, Bridget? We have yet to see to her hair! Let's try a new style and see how it looks."

"I'm almost finished, Mrs. Osborne," Bridget said, still pinning.

Mama circled the pair, scrutinizing the length of the gown. "It's long on the right side. Do take it up a little."

"Yes, ma'am."

Katherine grew claustrophobic as she waited in Mama's cluttered dressing room. Well-pressed clothes hung from hangers all about and deep drawers burst with odds and ends. Hatboxes rested on shelves and a few dozen pairs of shoes were lined up in neat rows. Even with the informality of camp, Mama insisted upon all the proper accessories for the occasional dance.

Katherine fidgeted as Bridget pinned a torn ruffle on the skirt of her violet, watered silk gown. On her hands and knees, the maid continued to work quickly. But then Katherine sneezed and Bridget's hand slipped. The pin jabbed Katherine in the leg, piercing her skin. She let out a yelp.

"I'm so sorry, ma'am," the young maid mumbled, horror in her eyes.

"Oh, Bridget!" Mama exclaimed. "I believe there's a spot of blood on the fabric now!"

Nervously, Bridget bent down to examine the tiny stain. "It won't take much to get the blood out, if I see to it immediately." Flustered, she whisked the gown off Katherine, leaving her in her chemise and corset.

Katherine tried to hide the bloody speck on her sheer stocking, but the movement drew Mama's sharp eyes to her leg. As soon as Bridget left for the laundry, Mama came closer. "Katherine, let me look at your leg. Roll down your stocking, please."

"There's no need, Mama." Katherine yanked her petticoat over her legs and turned away. Mama straightened up, but with less agility than she used to have. "What happened, Katherine? I can see your right leg is severely scarred. Goodness gracious."

Heat seared Katherine's neck and face. She'd planned to keep her scar hidden from everyone.

"Please tell me how this happened," Mama repeated, her voice softer.

Katherine took a ragged breath, giving in. "Several years ago when Charles and I were hiking in the Blue Ridge Mountains, I tripped and fell down a cliff. I was badly injured, and my leg required quite a few stitches." Her voice snagged and her shoulders heaved. *Dear Lord, please don't let me break down in front of Mama.* Thankfully, she was able to sniff back tears that threatened to spill. Why did she always react with such emotion?

"Katherine, my dear," Mama asked, grasping her hand, "you look as if you're ready to cry." Mama's touch felt cold and dry, not in the least bit comforting, but her voice sounded kind.

"My mind wandered. I'm sorry."

"No need to apologize, dear. But are you all right? Weeping for no reason isn't at all like you. Is it your leg?" Mama motioned Katherine down on an easy chair. Her mother removed the garter and rolled down the stocking. Gasping, her hand slammed over her mouth, her eyes wide. "Oh my goodness. My poor, dear Katherine. Your leg is—"

"Hideous. I know. My scar never healed. In fact, as time passed it got uglier and more painful." Katherine bit her lip hard so she wouldn't burst into a flood of noisy tears. She hated the scar and could hardly bear to look at the angry, thick, red line. It was just another way she'd emerged disfigured from her marriage, both on the outside and deep within.

She'd hoped Mama would never see this awful souvenir of

her marriage. The "accident" happened during the early days of her marriage.

Pity and compassion radiated from Mama's eyes. She was now *poor Katherine, a woman scarred*. A girl in need of her mother, in so many ways. For a second she wanted to blurt out everything, open her heart, and lay her head in her mama's lap as she had occasionally during childhood. But the moment slid by before she uttered a word.

"We should have a physician take a look at this. Maybe he could do something."

Katherine shook her head. "No, it's not necessary. I'm sure I saw every doctor in Florida, and no one could help. It's all right, Mama, I can live with it." She feigned a reassuring smile. "It's only a scar and no one sees it." It was another reason never to marry again; a husband would certainly notice the ugly reminder of her accident and recoil at the sight of her.

But everyone has scars of one sort or another, she told herself. This was just one of the many she bore that she'd yet become accustomed to.

"Why didn't you write and tell me you were injured?" Mama dropped into a nearby chair.

Katherine yanked up her stocking and covered her legs with her petticoat. "Because there was nothing you could do from so far away. I didn't want you to worry. And I recovered. So please don't fret about this. I'm fine now."

Mama drew out a sad, weary sigh. "As you wish. I'm just so sorry you didn't tell Papa and me."

"It happened when we were estranged." During her first two years of marriage, her parents, led by her mother, no doubt, refused to correspond.

Mama pursed her lips. "I . . . I see. But I hope in the future you won't keep anything so important from me. An injury like that . . ."

She shuddered in fear. "You ought to know I'm here to help in any way I can. You're my only child. My dear, precious daughter."

"I know, Mama," Katherine said with a sigh.

A knock sounded on Mama's door. "I'll be right back," she said.

Katherine closed her eyes, trying to block out the memory that suddenly swelled in her mind. But as usual, she couldn't. Once again she was hiking beside Charles on a mountain path, and they argued. She halted, jammed her hands on her hips, and faced him, shaking, not caring who heard her down the trail.

Her voice vibrated with outrage. "You squandered the year's profit from the orange groves. In one short weekend you gambled everything and lost. We'll have little to live on until the next harvest, and barely enough to keep the groves producing. You must stop at once."

"Well, I don't intend to," he said, swaying. "And stop your nagging, Katherine. It's unbecoming for a lady to scream at her husband." He glared at her as they slowly climbed the path that edged a sharp drop. He turned mean when he had been drinking, and lately he'd taken to doing it more often.

"I can't live like this, Charles. We'll have nothing left if you continue playing poker. You lost my grandmother's inheritance in a couple of games. What will you gamble away next? Buena Vista? The Osborne Citrus Groves?"

His gambling was a more than a vice—it was a disease consuming him like a cancer.

"I've heard enough from you, woman."

They strode on in silence. From the corner of her eye, she watched him steal a gulp of whiskey. She smelled the stink in his breath. He'd destroy them both if he didn't quit drinking spirits. She increased her pace, not looking where she was going. Her ankle twisted on the rough, deeply rutted path, and she felt herself swaying. Arms flailing, she fought to right herself. His hand reached out to her, and for a split second she thought he'd help her avert a terrible fall. But instead of pulling her back to safety, he either missed her flailing hand or thought better of it. She was never sure.

She tumbled down, down, down, through brush, over sharp rocks, all of it scratching and cutting as she rolled. Her breath came in gasps, and she thought she might suffocate. She rolled so fast she could only glimpse the approaching terrain. Then the rough earth gave way to a cliff. Dropping over the edge like a rag doll, Katherine felt nothing beneath her. She fell and fell until the hard earth again rose to meet her. Seconds later she smashed into a tree trunk and came to a dead stop. It stole her breath, and every part of her body screamed in pain. And then her world faded and she blacked out. Mercifully.

When she awoke the next day she found herself in her bed at the inn where they were staying, bandaged and in such excruciating pain she wanted to die on the spot. Every muscle and bone flared like fire burning out of control. Charles sat by her bedside, his head in his hands, sobbing.

"I'm so, so sorry, Katie." He coughed up jagged shards of words, and she barely understood what he said. Her usually debonair husband's face had been so puffy, as red as stewed tomatoes, that it startled her. He blinked away tears, frightening her more. "I didn't mean for you to fall."

The day before returned in a haze of memories; she couldn't quite remember everything that happened. But she did recall he missed her when she needed his steadying hand.

"I'm sorry to tell you this," he whispered, shuddering. "But you lost the baby."

She barely comprehended his words. "Oh God, no." Her mouth was so cut and bruised, she could only whimper.

"I tried to grab you, Katherine, but I only fell with you." He thrust out his arms. She squinted to distinguish a few superficial scratches and a tiny bruise on his hand. Charles's fresh sobs reeked of remorse and self-pity.

Later, after she'd recovered, the wound on her leg worsened and Charles found the resulting scar repulsive. And in spite of her injuries and grief, Katherine found the strength to stand against him. She wouldn't allow him to ruin his business and their marriage without a fight.

He never came to her bed after that. Not that she missed him. He took to sleeping down the hall in his own room, and his distance came as somewhat of a relief. She heard him coming and going at all hours of the night, but she never questioned it, content to believe he was with friends or business associates.

Katherine blinked repeatedly, trying to disengage from the awful memories. But at least now she knew why she'd lost Charles during those dark days.

It was about the time of her accident that he'd gone back to Harriet.

Chapter Thirteen

At eight o'clock that evening Katherine donned the altered gown for the dance. Bridget swept her hair into a pompadour, without the need for concealed rats and rolls to provide extra fullness. She added diamond hair clips that sparkled even in the mellow kerosene light and a fragrant white gardenia in place of a feather. Katherine slipped her feet into borrowed satin shoes embroidered with silver thread and sighed with relief when they fit perfectly. An amethyst necklace from Mama graced her long neck.

Katherine and Aunt Letty strolled the short distance between their cabin and the lodge as boats docked at the pier. Katherine entered the converted ballroom and inhaled the fragrance of roses freshly picked from the garden. Yet even the delicate blooms and pretty tablecloths couldn't fully transform the country atmosphere of antlers, deer, and moose heads staring down at the guests. She walked across the shiny wooden floor, devoid of the Oriental rugs that footmen had rolled up and cleared away early in the afternoon. The sofas and chairs lined the walls. They'd added a few wicker chairs from the back veranda so all the ladies would have comfortable seating.

Katherine passed the band tuning their instruments in soft disharmony. At the other end of the spacious room, a fire roared within the stone fireplace, crackling and spitting sparks up the chimney. It diminished the slight evening chill so common in the mountains. The smoky aroma mingled with the scent of flowers and the ladies' French perfume.

Katherine greeted stodgy Mrs. Porter, who was decked out in a wine-colored gown hugging her plump form, and Randy's mother, who looked like an Amazon next to her stick of a husband. She spotted Andrew among the gathering crowd and immediately her spirits lifted for a moment before she realized that things were not as they once were between them. Steeling herself, she headed toward him, hoping she could find the words to bridge the gap.

Spellbound, Andrew watched Katherine gracefully weave through the crowd, drawing several men's lingering looks. A vision in violet, she held her head high, displaying a flash of jewels at her neck and wrist. Mrs. Wainwright intercepted her before she reached him and guided her over to a group of friends centered around Randy. Before long, his cousin led her to the dance floor, and they joined the couples swirling about to the music of a Viennese waltz. Then they danced a reel, another waltz, and a schottische. When they moved on to a polka, Andrew had had enough. He moved outside, perspiring as if he'd been dancing with them.

He leaned over a railing, staring at the lake glittering under the moonlight, trying to forget how well Katherine looked in Randy's arms. How they looked so right together. He shook his head. *I'm beginning to think like my aunt and Mrs. Wainwright.* Regardless of how right they appeared on the *outside*, there was something so incredibly wrong *within*, he couldn't imagine how Katherine could tolerate it. Randy either, for that matter.

Not that his cousin cared for anything but his own entertainment . . .

Katherine's laughter tickled the back of his neck. He dared to glance over his shoulder. She was chatting with an old friend, fanning herself, and drinking from a crystal goblet. "My, I'd forgotten how hot a dance floor could get!"

After a moment, her friend returned inside. Andrew thought she would follow, but she joined him instead. "It's beautiful, isn't it?" she asked softly.

He nodded. But he was thinking, *Not half as beautiful as you* . . . Moonlight peeked through the dark tree branches that rustled in the breeze. Katherine folded her arms across her bodice shimmering with glass beads.

"Why so gloomy, Andrew? Why aren't you dancing?"

Andrew took a sip from his own goblet. "The girl I wanted to dance with was taken."

She was silent for a moment. "We can dance, Andrew," she said gently. "At least once."

He turned to stare at her and then gave her a sad smile. "No. No we can't." He straightened. "Listen, I should be going. You're having fun, and I'm only intruding now. Confusing you." He glanced over her shoulder, and through the glass doors he saw Mrs. Wainwright systematically searching the crowd for her daughter. He slipped his hand around hers and looked into her eyes. "I want you to enjoy yourself, Katherine. You deserve to have nothing but fun, after all your heartache, and all your hard work . . ."

He turned to go, but she held on to his hand and gave him a pleading look. "Please stay, Andrew." She fingered the necklace, drawing his eyes to the creamy skin between her long neck and her modestly cut gown. "Is it because I confided in you about Harriet's letter? I was so grateful for your understanding and your help. I can't imagine what I'd do without your friendship."

"I want us to stay friends too, but we should keep our distance. Especially in public. I don't want people to gossip about you. About us."

He saw a blush rise up her cheeks.

"When we were out at the gazebo, Mama saw us together and gave me a terrible scolding. Andrew, if I embarrassed you, or endangered your position with my father's company—or worse, threatened our friendship—I'm dreadfully sorry. I promise it won't happen again."

"Actually, I hope it does," he murmured.

———

Had she heard him correctly?

But with one look into his eyes, she knew she had. He stood there, his eyes holding hers, begging her to reconsider and disregard caution.

"Andrew, you shouldn't put yourself in an awkward position with my father because of me. Don't endanger your career." Swallowing hard, Katherine tried to turn her head away, but his gaze still captured her. Her heart flipped over. It wasn't safe to think of Andrew in a romantic way, but she couldn't deny the heat she felt warming her insides . . .

Trying to turn the conversation to a safer topic, she heard her voice sounding unnatural and shaky. "I'm seeking the Lord's path, Andrew. I'm waiting for His answer. About everything in my life."

He edged closer. "Just don't make any important decisions without being sure they're the right ones." He didn't dare say, "About us?" But he wanted to know if he figured in her plans or if he was merely deluding himself.

Katherine nodded. "Please say a prayer that I'll recognize His voice."

"I will." Through the French doors, Andrew spotted Mrs. Wainwright striding across the lounge in their direction. Katherine followed his gaze. "I believe your mother is on her way out here to pay us a visit." He reluctantly took a step away from Katherine and picked up his goblet again. "You'd better return inside now."

Mama threw open the glass doors and joined them on the veranda. "Good evening, Andrew. Would you mind, terribly, if I borrowed my daughter? Randy is waiting to dance with her."

Katherine frowned. "Mama, we were simply sharing a brief conversation."

Mrs. Wainwright pursed her lips as she gripped her daughter's wrist. "What were you talking about that was so important?"

"The Lord." Katherine lifted her head and stared directly at her mother.

Andrew could barely keep from chuckling as Mrs. Wainwright sputtered, "The Lord is for Sunday mornings."

"He's for every day, Mama, and you ought to know that."

"I must say religion is an odd topic of conversation for a dance." Mrs. Wainwright tugged her daughter's arm almost out of its socket as she steered her farther from Andrew's side. But as Katherine followed, she glanced over her sloping shoulder and grinned.

———

But Katherine's smile sagged as Mrs. Wainwright led her through the doors. Once she'd been safely deposited inside, the formidable older woman glanced over her shoulder at Andrew. "I'm quite sure Katherine's monopolized enough of your time. So many of the other ladies are dying to dance with you, Andrew. You wouldn't wish to disappoint them, I'm sure."

"Certainly not," he said, his tongue planted firmly in his cheek. But he made no move to follow her inside.

Andrew lingered on the veranda until the night chill penetrated his starched shirt and tailcoat. He refused to watch Randy court Katherine, but it was too early to retreat to his bedroom without raising eyebrows. So he wandered back inside, accepted another glass of punch from the maid at the refreshment table, and tried to summon the interest to ask anyone but Katherine to dance. After a casual glance around the floor, he took his drink over to a deserted corner of the room where the dancers were less likely to ram his elbow and spill the liquid down the front of his silk waistcoat.

When he'd drained the glass and returned it to a waiter passing by, his Aunt Georgia appeared and pinned him to the wall right beneath a black bear's head. The poor, dead creature gazed down at him and seemed to empathize with sad, glassy eyes.

His aunt rose to her full height of five feet ten inches. Unlike most women, she only had to raise her chin slightly to meet his gaze almost eye to eye. In her high-heeled dance slippers she stood only a few inches shorter than he, and despite his own large frame, she must've outweighed him by fifty pounds. Her contralto voice rose clearly over the music.

"I've been watching Katherine," she said in a guttural whisper. "Her gaze follows you wherever you go."

Shocked his aunt would notice, he tried to hide his grin. "You must be mistaken. You know we've been friends for ages. But never anything more."

Looking around, he saw Katherine across the room chatting with Randy. But, sure enough, she was glancing in his direction.

His aunt toyed with her long strand of pearls dangling over the bodice of her chocolate brown gown. "I'm wondering if you've given any thought to marrying? You're certainly at the right age."

His throat dried. "You don't mean to Katherine, do you?" His attempt at a joke fell flat. He shouldn't tease her about something so near and dear to her heart.

"Of course not. We all expect her to marry Randy. Eventually. There's no question about that. I'm talking about *you*, Andrew. Do you have an interest in anyone?"

He shifted his weight from one foot to another. As much as he appreciated his aunt, he'd never let her manage his life as she was attempting to manage Randy's. Why was she suddenly so interested in his future plans? Did she perceive him as a threat?

"Not yet. To be blunt, I'm not in a financial position to marry."

His parents had left him a small inheritance, but it was miniscule compared to the fortunes of the upper crust. He lived with Aunt Georgia and Uncle Clarence in their Fifth Avenue mansion, but if he married, he'd need a great deal of money to build a home and support a wife. The only ladies he knew came from the upper class. Yet no heiress would consider him a good catch. The only thing he had going in his favor was that his future at Mr. Wainwright's railroad appeared bright—that is, if he didn't lose his job over Katherine. His eyes returned to her. Right now he had a small nest egg, but it might take a decade to acquire a fortune large enough to be worthy of her interest. But could Katherine wait that long?

Aunt Georgia settled her gaze on a gaggle of young ladies across the dance floor giggling behind their fans. She gestured toward them. "Any one of those young ladies over there would certainly have you, regardless of your financial standing."

He knew better. His lack of financial resources kept him firmly off-limits for all but the lowest in their social set, none of whom were present at the dance. "Which one do you suggest, Aunt?" he asked idly.

She scanned the different groups of girls, scarcely nineteen or twenty years old. Not a spinster or poor relation among them. "Perhaps Gertrude Breen or Jane Van Horn. They're both beauties. Do you have a preference?"

"No, not between Gertrude and Jane."

"In that case why not ask Miss Van Horn to dance? She's so tall, she'll be thrilled with an even taller gentleman. They're hard to find, you know." Aunt Georgia smiled. She topped her short, slight husband by several inches but didn't seem to mind a bit.

"All right, if you wish." He bowed and made his way around the perimeter of the polished dance floor, weaving through knots of chattering friends. At least the decision had been made for him. He could dance with both Jane and Gertrude and then excuse himself for the evening.

When he asked Miss Van Horn to dance, her pinched smile vanished. "Yes, I'd be delighted."

They glided through a waltz and swirled between the lines of dancers in a Virginia reel. But when he returned her to her friends, Mrs. Van Horn appeared with Rodney Peck, one of New York's richest heirs with a taste for polo and his father's mistresses.

"Good evening, Mr. Townsend," Mamie Van Horn said between clenched teeth as she nudged closer to her daughter. "Jane dear, Rodney just mentioned he'd adore dancing with you. You don't want to disappoint him, do you?"

Andrew slipped away, his face hot from Mrs. Van Horn's intentional slight. He knew his aunt was wrong about his chances to marry well, and this proved it. Society daughters might find him acceptable, but their mothers didn't. He leaned against the rough wood of the wall, avoiding a crossed pair of snowshoes.

Dancers galloped to a catchy German polka and veered peril-ously close. Flying past him were Katherine and Randy again. Randy's face glowed, but Katherine appeared . . . delightfully distracted. Did he dare hope that she was still thinking about him? Them?

No one attracted him as much as she did, and no matter what anyone wanted, he wouldn't settle for second-best. But should he fight for Katherine when they both had so much to lose? He'd have to search his soul long and hard and pray for an answer. Because even if he were willing to give up his excellent position with Mr. Wainwright, he wasn't certain Katherine would thwart her family's desires for her future again.

———

After the dance, Randy offered Katherine his arm and together they strolled down the dark walkway. Other guests ambled toward the dining hall, where a midnight supper was in progress.

"Thank you for tonight, Randy," she said, glancing side-ways. "I didn't realize how much I missed dancing." During her mourning period, and for the months following, she'd seldom socialized with her neighbors. There just wasn't enough time.

"I'm glad you're enjoying yourself. Leisure time isn't so bad, now is it?"

She hesitated a moment too long. "No, of course not. Interspersed with good purpose."

He frowned. "You're not considering returning to Florida, are you? Don't tell me you like the heat and humidity in July and August, and all those awful bugs buzzing around and biting."

She laughed. "I much prefer Camp Birchwood in the sum-mer, but I do enjoy Florida during the rest of the year. And the groves . . . I so wish I could be there, just to make sure all is well, then return here to enjoy more of the summer. That's the difficulty, Randy. I want both." She shook her head. "Does that make me greedy?"

He stared at her. "Greedy? No. Torn, perhaps. Like you belong in two different worlds."

She looked up at him in wonder. That was exactly how she felt, in so many different ways. "You're right."

He reached over and tucked a tendril of hair behind her ear and she stilled, resisting the urge to move away. "The tearing away might hurt for a while, Kat. But then it'd be over. Sometimes difficult choices have to be made. You should come back to our world. This world. Where you belong."

She considered his words. "Maybe. Or maybe I belong there, not here."

He stopped and let a few couples pass by. "What can possibly compare to this?" His eyes narrowed with a serious look she'd seldom seen before. "Return home, Katherine, do as your mother desires, and you can run off to Florida on holiday whenever you wish. Why go against her? Why choose such a difficult path?"

Katherine shrugged. "Sometimes the harder path leads to the most rewarding vistas. I could choose the easier way, the path of least resistance, but just think what I might be missing."

He gripped her gloved fingers and pressed a little too tight. "Katherine, I'd be devastated if you left again. You belong with your family—and with me."

"Thank you," she managed to murmur. "You've been so kind in how you've welcomed me home, Randy. I'll always be grateful for that."

For a moment she feared he'd leap ahead and propose marriage right here on the dimly lit walkway, but instead, he swallowed hard and loosened his grasp. "You mean a lot to me,

Kat, and you always have. We've had such good times together in the past, and I hope we will in the future."

Lifting her lips in a stiff smile, she kept her voice non-committal. "I'm sure we will." Katherine waited a few more nerve-wracking seconds for Randy to continue and make his intentions clear, if indeed he had any.

Randy looked like a man in search of just the right words, but definitely not someone driven mad by love. He didn't incite a passion that smoldered beneath his light-hearted personality, but she didn't mind at all. In fact, relief loosened all the knots in her stomach. *He feels the same about me as I do for him.*

Randy's shoulders tensed. "Are you listening to me?"

Blushing, she shook her head and focused her gaze back on his blinking eyes. "Forgive me, my mind drifted for a second."

"I was saying we should spend more time really getting re-acquainted. Let's do all the things we used to do when we were young. If I can pry you out of your Aunt Letty's cabin."

Did he feel true affection for her or was he merely playing a role in a script written by their mothers?

She had to find out before Act Two began.

Chapter Fourteen

Hours after Andrew retired, Randy pushed open their bedroom door and sang a tune in his rich tenor voice. Andrew buried his head under the soft pillow and tried to ignore his cousin.

Randy fell silent for a moment. Then, "Katherine's going to marry me. I'm convinced of it," Randy crowed in the semi-darkness lit only by the flicker of a kerosene lamp between their twin beds.

Andrew forced himself to casually rise, his heart pounding in his ears. "Have you asked her?" He turned up the bedside lamp, despising the slight shake in his hand.

"No, not yet." Randy stood by his wardrobe, his hands jammed on his hips, his grin triumphant.

"Then how can you be so sure? Just because the mothers want it to happen doesn't mean Katherine does." He hadn't meant to sound so grumpy—and jealous. Fortunately, Randy was not prone to take offense.

"She seemed amenable to me." Randy kicked off his shoes

scuffed from dancing all evening. "Who can tell what a woman is really thinking?"

Shaking his head, Andrew said, "You ask her. But I predict you won't catch Katherine as easily as you think. She's not ready for another marriage, or even courtship, as far as I can tell. And she plans to return to Florida to see to her harvest."

"Or so she says. Maybe she's just playing hard to get. With my outrageous charm, combined with the pressure our mothers are exerting, I don't see how she can resist."

Andrew felt sure Randy couldn't fight them either. Always one to take the easy route, he'd undoubtedly fold like a bad hand of cards. "Don't you fear . . . growing tired of her? I mean, since you're merely friends?" He was taking a stab, hoping it was true.

Randy winced. He pulled off his formal jacket and bow tie and tossed both on a chair for his valet to pick up. "You're not giving me much credit, Andrew. I shall never tire of Katherine. We're dear friends and everyone says that makes for the finest of marriages. Mother says that once I forget my flirtatious ways and settle down, I'll make for quite a good husband. I wager she's right."

Andrew managed to make a sound that might pass as agreement. Over the course of the last several years he'd watched his cousin raise the hopes of many debutantes, and then drop them when he grew bored. He easily moved on to his next conquest without a backward glance. How would marriage change him? He doubted it would, regardless of what he said. He was merely parroting his mother. And if he fell into affair after affair, how would that affect Katherine, especially after Charles's infidelity?

Andrew groaned inwardly. If he weren't so envious, he wouldn't harbor such a mean spirit. His cousin deserved better than he was giving him. It wasn't fair to only dwell on Randy's weaknesses. And good fortune. "Are you in love with Katherine?" Andrew asked, not sure he wanted an answer.

Randy frowned and tugged at his mustache. "In love? I haven't really thought about love. It's enough that we're lifelong friends and well matched."

"Like a good team of horses," Andrew added with a wry smile. *Lord, help me to curb my tongue.*

"Not a flattering comparison, cousin." He squinted at him. "Why is it that everyone except you seems to think we're well suited?" His lifted his chin. "I suspect it's because you're jealous."

"Perhaps," Andrew admitted, rolling to his back and staring at the ceiling. While a match between his two friends struck him as another mistake for Katherine, no one would agree with him.

Still, he needed to control his envy before he made a fool of himself or ruined his career. Unless the Lord showed them another road . . .

———

Katherine fidgeted at her dressing table while Bridget took down her hair and brushed it for the required one hundred strokes. Randy's playful grin filled her mind with warmth. He was a delightful gentleman—or should she say boy? He'd never truly grown up. He'd grown tall and handsome, but not mature. Yet how could a woman not find him appealing? He had everything she'd been taught to want—a pleasing personality, good looks, an enormous bank account, an illustrious family background, and an excellent education.

All he lacked was seriousness of purpose and a deep intellect. But did those drawbacks really matter? If she gave in to the court-ship, at least she wouldn't have to worry about Randy ripping her feelings apart. He didn't hold that kind of power over her.

But was a courtship with him simply the easiest path? After a while would he fall short and bore her to tears? And how would he respond to the ups and downs, the trials and tragedies of life? Here in New York he was largely insulated, but struggle had a way of hunting everyone, missing not a one over time. When faced with adversity, would he crumble like Charles had and take up drinking or gambling—or womanizing? She didn't have the inner resources to relive that disaster again.

Only a man with integrity and firm convictions could satisfy her in the long run. If she ever left widowhood behind her, she wanted someone who cared enough to understand her spiritual yearnings, her need to place God at the center of her life. A man who'd help her to draw closer to Him and honor Him.

And as much as she wanted to respect Mama's wishes and her agreement with Papa, as much as she wanted to give Randy a fair chance to prove himself, her thoughts kept returning to another.

Andrew.

———————

A few days later Katherine and thirty of Mama's guests rode in Papa's steam yacht across the lake to Camp Algonquin. Once they arrived at the rustic camp hemmed in by hills and dense woods, Katherine made her way up the sloping yard for the informal lawn party. She headed toward the main house, a sprawling log cabin, by far the largest of many outbuildings within the compound. Every few steps, old friends whom she hadn't seen in many years waylaid her for a chat. More than a few were curious about Katherine's daring elopement, but she skirted around intrusive questions with smiles and vague answers.

She judged there were at least one hundred guests from neighboring camps milling around the lawn, the lodge, and the open porch. Small tables were set up under the spreading trees on rough ground littered with rocks of all sizes, twigs, and pine needles. Katherine inhaled the woodsy fragrance.

Campers with heaping plates of food from the buffet wandered around, searching for empty tables. The guests wore their casual clothes, but Katherine recognized the high quality of the fabrics and exquisite workmanship of the ladies' blouses and skirts. Most of the men were dressed alike in sack suits and caps or boaters, and they looked more comfortable than the ladies. Some of the older gentlemen leaned on canes as they made their way up from the boat dock to the sumptuous buffet spread across trestle tables on the porch.

Katherine followed behind a gaggle of gray-beards who were nattering about the War they'd fought in their youth. Off to the side, she spotted Aunt Letty with a plate heaping with lake trout, lyonnaise potatoes, and spinach salad. Giggling with another elderly lady, Aunt Letty wandered down to the lawn with her ancient friend trailing right behind.

Katherine took a china plate with hand-painted wildflowers, silverware, and a linen napkin from the end of the table laden with all kinds of tempting foods. She spooned creamed chicken, tomato aspic, and garden salad onto her plate and accepted a frosty glass of iced tea. The small round tables dotting the lawn all the way down to the edge of the lake were filling quickly. Maybe Aunt Letty wouldn't mind if the three of them shared a table.

Randy came up from behind and loomed over Katherine's shoulder. "Will you join me, Kat? I've saved us a place by the maple tree."

"Thank you. I'd be delighted." He'd chosen the smallest table with only two chairs. Eating by themselves wasn't what she had in mind, but she couldn't object now without sounding rude. Once they settled in their ladder-back chairs, Randy leaned toward her and drummed his fingers against the white damask tablecloth. Then he knotted his napkin. Katherine had never seen him quite so fidgety. She wouldn't ask him why he was acting nervous because she felt sure she already knew. Her mother and his were watching them from a short distance away and murmuring behind their open fans. Their eyes lit with expectation.

Randy made an effort to clear his throat. "Katherine, we're great friends, aren't we? I mean, we haven't seen each other in years until recently, but you can't ignore the past we shared. That's right, isn't it?" He leaned over his plate loaded with untouched roast beef, cold baked ham, and potato salad.

She'd find his insecurity amusing, and maybe even endearing, if she didn't know where his babbling was leading him in a roundabout way. "Of course we're great friends."

She needed to head him off before he mumbled words they'd both regret. His unease spread to her and she found she'd crumbled her napkin like a handkerchief. "And I hope we'll always remain friends no matter how our paths diverge in the future." She couldn't be any clearer, now could she?

His face clouded with confusion. He probably expected encouragement instead. So she forged ahead, hoping to derail his momentum.

"I'm afraid my destiny is in Florida. I'm quite determined to return."

From the tightening of his jaw, Randy understood all too well. His brow furrowed. "Of course. I understand that you must see things through there. But when you're ready, surely you'll return here to us . . ." His voice trailed off.

She patted his hand. "Thank you, Randy. We'll just have to wait and see what's in store for us." *If anything.* "I don't know where the Lord will lead me in the future, but I'll always cherish the childhood memories we've made. Do you remember playing in the tree house my father built by the meadow?" she asked. She took a sip of iced tea sweetened with sugar to moisten her dry throat.

Randy brightened. "Of course. You and I had a grand time. Along with Andrew. But I also recall falling off that tree house roof and dislocating my collarbone." His reached up and ran his fingers across it, as if it still hurt.

"Remember when you got lost in the woods and I rescued you?" Katherine laughed at Randy's chagrined expression. "And that winter's day we built a snow fort in Central Park and I knocked you over with a gigantic snowball?"

"I only pretended because I wanted to please you. *You* wanted to show all the boys how mighty you were."

They both laughed. "I *was* always trying to prove I was as brave and strong as you boys."

"You were, though your smaller size limited you. But you had the heart of a lion."

She cocked her head. "Even now I'm sure I can beat you in a tennis match. Would you like me to demonstrate after luncheon?"

"Perhaps later. It's too hot to overindulge in sports." His gaze gleamed like the afternoon sunshine. "It's good to see you returning to your old self. When you first came home I thought you were still mourning Charles. You looked so gloomy most of the time and kept to yourself. I didn't know what to make of it."

"I'm slowly recovering. The mountains and the lake have done wonders for me."

He sat back, apparently short on any other words to persuade her. Together, they stared in awkward silence at the other guests.

———

Along with a handful of young ladies and a few friends from his college days, Andrew lounged on one of the wicker chairs set in a semicircle at the end of the porch far from the buffet table. Smiling amiably, he'd said little while they all sipped lemonade and ginger beer from frosty tumblers. They were a privileged set that chatted about places in Africa and the Middle East he'd read about but hadn't visited. While he envied their leisure pursuits, he didn't envy the inevitable boredom that ensued in between.

Andrew spotted Randy leaving the table he'd shared with Katherine and ambling up the lawn in their direction. When he got closer, Andrew called to him, "How was your lunch?"

Randy shrugged. "Care for a short walk, cousin?" A frown knit his black eyebrows.

"All right." Andrew excused himself and followed his cousin across the lawn toward the deserted pier. "What's wrong?"

They strolled across sparse patches of grass interspersed with a thick carpet of pine needles. Tall aspen and white birch trees cast the yard in cool, deep shade. At the dock, small craft bobbed gently in sparkling blue waters. From here, Birchwood Lodge shrank to the size of a matchbox.

"So, what is it, Randy?" Andrew asked. They came to the pier lined with visitors' boats. Andrew leaned against the wall of the log boathouse and waited.

Randy's suntanned forehead creased with anxiety. "My mother has encouraged me—no, ordered me—to court Katherine. The sooner the better. Mother and Mrs. Wainwright insist upon an autumn engagement."

Andrew almost felt sorry for his cousin trapped in a situation he couldn't handle through his usual methods—good humor and the light touch of charm. But he'd gladly switch places with him. "And?"

"I don't want a fall engagement. And clearly, Kat is intent upon returning to Florida." He gave him a level stare. "I wished to visit the Breakers. I hold no desire to *live* in such godforsaken country."

Andrew shrugged. "So tell them. What's so difficult about that?" He shouldn't needle his cousin; he completely understood Randy's dilemma. But at the age of twenty-eight, Randy should have the gumption to disagree with his mother and take charge of his own future. Choosing a mate was one of the most important decisions in life, and to leave it to one's parent seemed not only ridiculous but also cowardly.

"It pains me to admit this, especially to you, Andrew, but I'm leery of defying my mother. I know I sound like a mama's boy—and maybe I am. The truth is, I'm just not anxious to settle down, even with a girl as grand as Kat. I have my entire life to marry. Fall is too soon. And so is next spring or next summer."

"So when would you want to settle down?" He had to choke out the words. Envy slithered through him and coiled around his ribs like a python. Shame over his jealousy soon followed.

Randy shrugged. "Oh, I don't know. Maybe I'll be ready for marriage sometime in five or six years. It's too soon to contemplate a date. She's just returned home, and to tell you the truth, we hardly know each other anymore. Any connection we seem to have is based on childhood memories. And she has this mad idea about returning to Florida to see to the harvest . . ." He threw out his hands. "Why can't she relinquish such tasks to a man? Why must she do it herself?"

Andrew leaned back against the wall of the boathouse. "So . . . you didn't bring up your mother's desire for an autumn announcement?"

Randy removed his boater and ran his fingers through his straight black hair parted in the middle. "I didn't bring up marriage specifically. All right—I hemmed and hawed. But I got the distinct impression Katherine is no more interested in marriage than I am, at least not right now. When I hinted at my intentions she sounded lukewarm. Cold, actually. I'm sure we'll settle down eventually and live happily ever after and all that. It's inevitable, really. And if I *must* marry, I certainly don't want to lose her."

Euphoria swelled inside Andrew's chest until he thought he might burst with renewed hope. But at his cousin's expense? That didn't seem right. And in reality, there was still little hope for Katherine and himself, even without Randy in the picture. "Then I don't see any problem," he managed. "Simply tell your mothers you two aren't ready."

Randy grunted. "They're insistent. They won't tolerate any defiance from either one of us."

"Stand up to them and assert yourself. You're a grown man. Your mother can't *make* you do anything."

Randy winced. "You know how formidable she and Mrs. Wainwright can be." Randy heaved a long, desolate sigh, and his entire face drooped like a pair of baggy trousers. "The best solution is to wait until Katherine and I are both enthusiastic. Perhaps through the summer love will blossom, and we can agree to a marriage . . . with a *long* engagement."

"Possibly. But is there something else bothering you?" Andrew asked. Why did Randy still look so glum?

Randy shoved his hands into his trouser pockets. "If we don't marry, Mother insists I go to work for Father. They'll exile me to the bowels of the Clarke Building. I'll be forced to learn the banking business from the ground up, literally. You know I have no head for finance and no interest either."

Andrew took a deep breath, understanding at last. So that was what drove him. They'd caught him in their web, but he could easily pull free with a small amount of effort. "Come now, Randy, a little work won't kill you. Try it. You might find you like it. I do."

Randy glowered. "You're not very helpful, you know. As for work, I'm not temperamentally suited for long, boring hours slaving over facts and figures."

"You mean you're suited for spending money, not making it." Andrew cocked a brow.

Randy brightened. "Exactly. But stop making light of this. I might be lazy, but I'm not fool enough to think I could ever adapt to an office routine."

Andrew knew he should stop chiding Randy and express more empathy, but he couldn't condone Randy's sheer indolence. "All right. Then what are you suited for? Let's consider it together. It has to be productive and satisfy your parents."

Randy's shrugged and even his mustache seemed to droop. "Nothing, really. Perhaps I could learn to sculpt or make clay pots. Who knows, I might sell a few. Or give them to friends as Christmas gifts. You'd like one, wouldn't you?"

"I would. But you know your parents will consider that a hobby, not a job." He thought of Katherine and her father's reaction to the idea of her selling hats.

Randy sighed and kicked the toe of his shoe into the pier. "The truth is I'm not suited for much of anything."

"But the beauty of being rich is you don't have to be. Go to work for a while, then convince your parents you're supposed to resume this life again and become a charming decoration."

"For goodness' sake, Andrew, stop mocking me. I'm in a bind. Do you have any *worthwhile* suggestions?"

Andrew shook his head, enjoying this far more than he should. "Truly, Randy. Call their bluff. Go and try working for a while. It will delay your mother's demands and give you more opportunity to get to know Katherine . . . and see if you truly belong together." *Or discover she's better suited to me.*

Randy drew out a melodramatic groan. "Maybe I should just bear down and convince Kat to marry me sooner rather than later."

Andrew's legs wobbled. "You mean, simply give in?" His faint hope for his own relationship with Katherine sank.

"What other choice do I have?"

"Work! Go to work!" Andrew said, barely able to keep from shouting.

Randy looked at him with chagrin and shook his head. "No, Andrew. I just can't see it. Father would be dreadfully disappointed with me if I tried and failed. I would fail, you know. And I've already experienced enough of *that* to last a lifetime."

His words brought Andrew up short. What had brought Randy to such a low place? Surely this wasn't God's plan for him. Could it be that Katherine could help Randy find his way? Was she truly meant to be Randy's wife, his helpmate? He put his hands on his head as if he could drive away the sudden pounding. Nothing, nothing seemed right, no matter which direction he turned.

Taking a deep breath, Randy cast a pleading gaze at Andrew. "Do you think you could convince my mother to give up her scheme?"

Andrew grunted. "You know as well as I do that your mother and Mrs. Wainwright won't be crossed. I'm afraid nothing will change their minds. So reconsider working at the bank. That would be far preferable to marrying before you're ready. Really, Randy, think of Katherine, if not yourself. Her marriage to Charles . . ." He shook his head. "She deserves love and loyalty if she marries again."

Randy frowned at him. "Of course I'd treat her well. And she'd have anything she desired!" His frown turned into a petulant sulk. "One thing I know for certain. I *will not* work for my father. That's a life sentence of dreariness." He pulled at the corners of his mustache. "I suppose I'll have to court her. No doubt her mother can persuade her to accept the idea, just as my mother did me. Sometimes, mothers truly do know best."

Randy hesitated before tilting his head and narrowing one eye. "Would you do me a favor, cousin?"

"Anything," Andrew said, before he really thought it through.

"Talk to Kat. See if she's interested in me, either now or in the future. See if this whole 'heading back to Florida' bit is merely a bluff."

Andrew considered him and then gave him a slow nod. "I'll do it," he said.

Because he'd like to know the answer to that question too.

Chapter Fifteen

From under the leafy sugar maple, Katherine watched Andrew and Randy huddle on the dock like a pair of conspirators. What were they cooking up? Not a plot involving her, she hoped. She'd ask Andrew later if she caught him alone. Her eyes settled on him, alternately smiling and frowning at his cousin. Andrew had grown to be so handsome . . .

She jerked her gaze back to Randy. Her earlier conversation with him had left her rattled. It took all her strength to keep from rushing down to the lake to insist he turn his romantic thoughts to someone else who'd truly make him happy. Someone who'd love and cherish him and appreciate his fortune and happily join him in his lackadaisical ways.

He couldn't truly be in love with her, could he? He didn't look at her with nearly the same intensity—and affection—that Andrew did.

The thought brought her up short. *Remember the groves, Katherine,* she told herself. But the more she repeated the phrase, the more her eyes wandered back to Andrew.

That evening at dinner Mama placed her next to Randy and consigned Andrew to the far end of the table, as usual. Randy chatted politely, but an unfamiliar awkwardness lay between them. To make matters worse, her mother listened to every word they said.

After the interminable dinner finally ended, the ladies adjourned to the lounge while the gentlemen remained in the dining hall for cigars and brandy. Later, at Mama's direction, Katherine played a few hands of bridge and then table tennis with a plump and pedantic young man, the son of one of her mother's old friends. She beat him handily in three games and then quit before humiliating him any further.

"I'm terribly tired. I believe I'll retire to my cabin and read for a while." Under Mama's disapproving eye, Katherine hurried away.

Although nightfall had blackened the sky, she dropped onto a wicker chair outside of her cabin. Inside, Aunt Letty was already slumbering, snoring steadily. Outside, crickets hummed, fish flopped in the smooth lake, and a few birds drew out the last notes of their evening song. She pulled her shawl around her shoulders against the breeze stirring the maple leaves and lifting the branches of fir trees and pines.

A canoe with the silhouettes of two men cut through the dark waters toward camp. Only the moon and stars sprinkled the lake with pale light to guide the pair. They soon landed the boat and dragged it onto the beach. The murmur of voices rose above the hoot of an owl and the distant bark of Papa's springer spaniel. The men walked up the gentle rise of the lawn.

Of course. Andrew and Randy.

Andrew glanced in her direction, but she couldn't tell if he spotted her. Probably not, since her royal blue frock blended into the descending night. The pair soon passed and their voices faded away. But then a few minutes later, she heard footsteps creak the boards of the covered walkway. She glanced toward the sound as Andrew's tall, broad-shouldered form emerged from the dusk.

"I came to wish you a good evening." He halted and then leaned back against the deck railing, his eyes riveted upon her as if he wanted to share something but didn't quite know how to begin.

"Good evening to you, Andrew. Come join me if you'd like."

He dropped into the wicker chair just inches from her own. Grasping his hands in his lap, he leaned forward. She caught a whiff of his aftershave, just as fragrant as the balsam trees. "Randy says you two might be getting serious."

"It is serious in no one's mind but my mother's and his."

He rubbed his chin. "But it's not a part of your thinking at all?"

"I daresay a woman should not share all that she thinks about with a man."

He smiled. "You don't need an endorsement from me, Katherine. You've known Randy since childhood, so you ought to know if you want to spend the rest of your life with him. He's kind and fun loving and rich." His voice flattened. "And it's expected." He flicked the last few words off his tongue as if they were bitter herbs.

For a moment she closed her eyes and let a deep breath escape from the depth of her lungs. "'Marry in haste, repent in leisure,'" she said slowly. "I'll not repeat that mistake again."

"But Randy may have other ideas . . ." Andrew sounded so tense she assumed he was sent here under duress. Was he here to warn her? Perhaps she'd evaded Randy's advances today, but for how long could she hold him off?

She shook her head. "No, I don't think Randy really wants to commit to me. If he does, why didn't he say so at the picnic?

For a few moments I thought he might . . . but then he didn't. He's very ambivalent."

Andrew swallowed. "He told me you weren't exactly encouraging."

She scoffed and stood up, pacing angrily back and forth. "And why should I be? I'm here to rest, not to find a husband. I agreed to do as Mama asked of me. But I did *not* agree to court again." She frowned at Andrew. Was he annoyed with her? For discouraging Randy? She brought her fingers to her temple. It was all so perplexing . . .

"I just thought you should know that Randy has it in mind that he ought to court you now and become engaged, sooner rather than later. Perhaps . . . perhaps it would be a relief to you too, Katherine." Was Andrew gritting his teeth or was she just imagining it in the dim light? From the anguish in his tone, she decided he was delivering a message he found disagreeable.

She sighed. In the end, if she couldn't save the citrus groves, she might have to acquiesce to Mama and return to New York for good. But it was far too early to give up hope; maybe the harvest would bring in far more than they even hoped for! It seemed so wrong to buckle without trying her best to succeed.

Regardless, she knew she shouldn't tarry out here in the dark with a man she liked very much but could never marry. "Perhaps I should go inside," she murmured.

"No. Please," he urged in a husky voice that thrilled her with its intensity. "Stay here for a while longer."

Katherine hesitated. "All right, but just for a short while. Let me get a light." She rose and quickly fetched an oil lamp from her cabin.

Andrew lit the wick and placed the flickering lamp on the deck railing. It gave off sufficient illumination to see her as a shadowy outline. He settled into the chair again. The wicker chair squeaked as he fidgeted. This closeness to Katherine sparked his heart like a match to a stick of dynamite.

He'd completed his task for Randy, though he'd done a half-hearted job and accomplished little. But how could he pretend enthusiasm when he yearned for the same woman? He'd lose the only family he had left and his position if he attempted to win her, and in the end he'd have no one and nothing if she didn't accept him. No, she had to find wholeness, healing first. Then and only then would he know if she was ready for anything but friendship with him.

"Katherine, may I be bold and give you a word of advice?"

She smiled crookedly. "If you think I need it."

Speaking too personally might end their friendship or at least sour it, but how could he watch her suffer and not try to help? "This isn't about a courtship with Randy. I think before you move on with your life you must forgive Charles. And Harriet as well. They don't deserve your forgiveness, but it'll help you get past what happened and move on with your life."

He wondered if the hoot of a nearby owl and the drone of crickets had drowned out his voice when she didn't answer right away.

"Of course, I've tried. And I believe I have forgiven them, although I don't *feel* very forgiving. But how can I *forget* their callousness?"

"I think . . . only time allows us to fully forget. And maybe *forget* is the wrong word for it. It's more like . . . the pain mellows, grows less sharp. Like a rock in a riverbed. It begins as a shard from a cliff, sharp enough to cut, but in the end, it's nothing but a rounded marble of a stone, smooth to the touch."

Katherine exhaled a long, weary breath. "So you believe I'll get through this?"

"Of course you will! A new love will cause you to forget all about Charles and Harriet." And her new love wouldn't be Randy. Andrew was quite sure of that.

"Perhaps that new love is already here." She murmured so softly, he wondered if his imagination was tricking him. Maybe he'd dreamed it, because he wanted to hear that so badly. But judging from her surprised expression, he knew her thoughts had escaped unwittingly.

He leaned away from her, stunned. "Katherine . . ."

She stood abruptly, and he rose as well. He stepped in front of her and opened his arms. "Please. Come here."

She paused and then wrapped her arms around him. He held her tight, closing his eyes, barely resisting the urge to kiss the top of her head and run his fingers through her sweet-smelling hair. "I hope Charles didn't turn you against marrying. I'm sure God will lead you to the right partner and a far happier marriage the next time around."

She gave her head a definitive shake. "I don't know, Andrew. I just don't know. It's very bewildering." Katherine didn't move a muscle for several seconds, but then she stepped away, forcing a smile as she wiped tears from the corners of her eyes. "How about you? Why haven't you married?"

He looked down at his feet, evading her gaze. "The right girl married someone else." He looked back at her and cleared his throat. "And until I save more money, I won't really be in a position to marry. I'm a man of modest means."

She stared at him for a long moment, lips parted. "What about your inheritance?" she stammered. "Surely you have something?"

Was that a note of hope in her voice?

He shook his head. "My father was a judge, not a millionaire. So my inheritance was small by society's standards. Very small. I'll have to make my own fortune. Thanks to my job, I've taken a significant step forward. But am I ready to propose to the right girl?" He shook his head gently and rubbed the back of his neck. "I'm afraid I have a long way to go first."

And further if I continue to dally with the boss's daughter.

Katherine nodded, her eyes falsely bright with encouragement. "I'm sure you'll do well. It's getting late and I really must go inside. See you tomorrow?" She glided toward her cabin door, then glanced over her shoulder and smiled. Her dimples deepened. "Thank you for coming over. And for listening. It means a great deal to me. You're such a comfort, Andrew. Truly."

He swallowed hard and then nodded. She was beginning to care for him. He felt it in his bones. But acting upon their feelings would undoubtedly bring disaster down upon them. Katherine knew it too. They both had much to consider.

———·—·———

Back in the lodge, outside his bedroom, Andrew braced himself before he walked inside and faced Randy.

Strumming on his mandolin in the corner, his cousin glanced up, eagerness written in every line of his face. "Well? What do you think? Is she more ready to marry than I imagined?"

Andrew winced and fell to his bed. He laid the back of his hand over his brow. "Not really."

"But do you think she's inclined to accept me, when the time is right?" Randy's desperation made Andrew feel a twinge of sympathy.

"I don't know. She's . . . Randy, she's still working through her grief over her past. How can you even think of pressing her?"

He sat up and pulled off his tie and tossed it toward the wardrobe. He didn't bother to ring for the valet.

Randy placed his mandolin in the corner beside his three-legged chair and sunk into his soft bed, propping his head with two fluffy pillows. "Why do I get the sense that this is more about you than me?" He stared hard at Andrew, silently challenging him.

"Stop." Andrew pulled off his shoes and placed them in the wardrobe and donned his night clothes. "It's morally unconscionable to marry for any other reason than love, dedication. Just bear down and go to work for a while, Randy. It's best for all of you." How could Randy disdain the easy work of pushing papers for a few hours a day when he'd never tried it? He'd advance soon enough, if he showed any initiative at all.

"Better for us? Or for you?" Randy asked, narrowing his eyes.

Andrew ignored him, but his chest tightened. "Listen, find your focus elsewhere. If you don't give Katherine more time, she'll turn you down."

"Then what am I to do?" Randy whined.

Andrew narrowly suppressed a shout of outrage. *Lord, give me strength. Give Randy wisdom. Help us!* "Think about it. Pray about it. Maybe the Lord has an answer you haven't thought of." *Or maybe I'm the answer.*

Randy rolled his eyes and shifted to his side. "I hardly think so. I'm not the praying kind."

"Maybe you should be." Andrew tried to cut the ice from his voice. "You might reconsider your relationship with God. He can definitely give you better direction than I can."

As far as Andrew knew, Randy hadn't opened a Bible or darkened the door of a church in many years. He'd prove a bad influence on Katherine's faith unless he shaped up and learned who granted all those blessings he accepted as his birthright.

Already in his nightshirt, Randy slid beneath the covers and turned off the kerosene light on the pine nightstand between their narrow beds. In the semi-darkness, Andrew pulled back the bed linens and dropped into the soft mattress. The sheets felt so cool and fresh he thought he'd have little trouble sleeping.

But tonight neither the gurgle of the lake nor the rustle of leaves outside his window lulled him to sleep. Still wide-awake at two o'clock, he let his thoughts meander until they rested on Katherine and Randy. Poor Katherine was determined to lead her own life without family interference. But if the groves failed, sometime soon she'd awaken to reality and the futility of struggling against her fate.

She'd have little choice but to sell her business and marry Randy unless something—or Someone—intervened.

Chapter Sixteen

Randy stopped Katherine on her way out of the dining hall after luncheon a few days later. "If you're not too busy, may I have a word with you?"

"Yes, of course." She noted the glances darting between Randy and his mother and shoved back a feeling of apprehension. Surely he'd taken the hint at the picnic. Katherine strolled beside him down the covered walkway leading to the gazebo, one of the few spots free of guests. Her heart thudded.

Randy blew out short huffs of breath that resembled sighs of resignation. His mouth twitched; he tugged on the corners of his mustache so hard she thought he might pull out all the bristly hairs. But when they settled on the gazebo bench, Katherine knew exactly what topic he wanted to broach . . . if he could work up his nerve.

She arranged her vanilla-colored dress over her legs and waited for the ordeal to begin. Her heartbeat sputtered and spun discomfort through her chest, but that was minimal compared to the distress on Randy's face. *Oh Lord, please let me do the best thing for both of us.*

Randy cleared his throat as he inched closer. Taking her hand, he closed his eyes for a few seconds, and then with a look of determination, he began to speak in a halting voice. "Kat, I've been thinking about us ever since you returned to Birchwood. And I'm hoping you're as fond of me as I am of you. So . . . " He hesitated for only a second. "Would you honor me by keeping company with me?" Relief swept the dark thundercloud from his face. "Nothing will make me happier than to court you, my dearest." He laid his other clammy hand atop hers.

"Randy, are you sure this is what you truly want? We've been friends forever, so please be honest."

He swallowed so hard his Adam's apple quivered. "Of course. I wouldn't want us to step out together if I didn't care for you. Deeply." Yet his voice lacked ardor, so she couldn't quite believe he felt more than mild affection for her. Definitely not passion or love.

"We mustn't act too quickly," she said, giving him a warm smile she hoped would soften his disappointment.

"We're not."

Her heart lay in her chest like a cold, dead trout. Surely she ought to feel something grand. Happiness, satisfaction, relief—a prick of something positive.

Courtship, then an engagement followed by marriage promised to please Mama and end her own financial difficulties. She could sell the Osborne Citrus Groves to Stuart and be freed from all her responsibilities. She'd never again have to fret over payroll, winter freezes, or loans and mortgages. The temptation to accept Randy's offer grew strong, almost irresistible. But the very notion of shedding her burdens should send her spirits soaring. Instead, her mood spiraled downward.

"I'm honored," she answered. "But I must take some time to think this through." She rose and squeezed his palm. The poor fellow's eyes widened to the size of dinner plates. He seemed to find all this quite awkward, just as she did. And he obviously faced the prospect of a possible engagement in the future with equal reluctance. But he expected her to accept his offer without delay.

Randy let out a soft groan. Annoyance pinched his mouth. "Why do you hesitate, Kat? You must have already given courtship some thought. Our mothers have been planning this for a long time."

That's the truth of it, she thought. "I know. I'd like to please them just as much as you would. But it's what we decide that matters, not what they want." Or *almost* as much. "Neither one of us should bow to pressure from our parents. We must decide on our own." Her words poured out like babble from a baby. "Courtship is a commitment of its own." The sunshine slanted through the open sides of the gazebo, and drops of perspiration erupted on her forehead. She dabbed at her brow with a lace-trimmed handkerchief.

"It's all rather sobering, but I'm not afraid of it." He gave her a lopsided smile. "You have never been intimidated by me before."

She smiled back at him. "I'm not intimidated by you, silly. You know that. It's what it might mean . . ."

He studied her a second. "When will you decide?"

"Soon, I promise." She lifted her most winning smile, but judging from his falling face, he didn't accept her evasion with even a hint of grace. Surely he wasn't really upset she'd put him off. Young ladies sidestepped these first steps toward marriage all the time. So why was he pacing across the gazebo floorboards? Bent over with his hands clasped behind his back, he resembled his dry-as-a-stick father. Would the dapper Randy *become* his father in another thirty years? Shuddering, she pushed the thought to the furthest corner of her mind.

Katherine met his petulant gaze. "You can't begrudge me a few days," she said in surprise. "After all, this is a momentous decision." *I should refuse him now and not wait a minute longer.* That was the right thing to do. She needed to consider this more carefully before setting her future in stone. She had to make sure no other avenues of escape were available.

He threw his head back and closed his eyes. She'd never seen him without an easy smile. "All right, Katherine. If you must have time, you shall have it. But you might find our mothers questioning why you're acting so stubborn."

She planted her hands firmly on her hips. Her temper flared. "I'm not stubborn, I'm prudent." Then she softened her voice almost to a whisper. "And you know I'm still recovering from Charles's death." *Lord, please forgive me for not telling the entire truth.* Was her face as red as a radish? "I never expected to remarry—at least not for many years."

"Surely you knew your mother would insist." Randy narrowed his eyes, tilted his head, and scrutinized her with a large dose of skepticism. "You're not *that* naive, Katherine." He sounded more incredulous than angry.

Where was her carefree friend with the cheerful disposition and amusing banter? His puckered brow and tight mouth registered frustration. As the only boy and youngest child in a family of many girls, the Clarkes' universe centered upon him. But how often in his life had anyone denied Randy what he wanted? Probably never. She recoiled from this side of his character lying just beneath the surface of his sunny personality.

"Perhaps I should talk this over with my mother. If you'll excuse me, I think I shall go find her."

"Katherine, wait a moment. Please. Forgive me for acting petulant, but I'm disappointed. I didn't expect you to rush into my arms, but I did expect you to accept. My mother said you would." His voice softened to almost a whisper. "It isn't Andrew who's stopping you, is it? Tell me you're not in love with him."

Katherine swallowed a confession and shook her head. Tears sprang to her eyes, but she blinked them back rapidly before he detected the truth.

"Well, that's good, because if Andrew came after you, your father would fire him in an instant. And we all know how important his career is to him." He smiled.

"Yes," she said numbly, "I'm sure you're right."

She'd never threaten Andrew's position at the railroad, and neither would he. It meant too much to him, and he'd worked hard to obtain it. Her father had reprimanded him for supporting her idea of designing hats. He'd certainly fire him for pursuing his only daughter without his blessing.

"So, Kat, tell me. If you know I'm right, why don't we forego all this and simply become engaged now? Why prolong your decision? It makes no sense."

She hesitated. "As I told you, I intend to return to Florida. The most I can offer you now are the remaining weeks of summer to get reacquainted, but not formally court. Then we might better see what is ahead of us."

He looked askance. "Surely you'll change your mind." He paced restlessly across the gazebo floor. "About returning to Florida." He shook his head. "Why sign on for more struggle? Why not give in to all this and enjoy it?" He waved around him.

She lowered her voice. "I'm sorry, Randy. I'm not ready to give it up. I can't."

He studied her, disapproval coming off him in waves. She stiffened. She'd endured enough of that with Charles.

"Might you give me your answer by tomorrow?"

Katherine stood and squared her shoulders. "No, I won't keep you in limbo a moment longer. I can answer you now." What was the point in delaying the inevitable? She couldn't continue to give him false hope. "I'm so sorry, but my mind is made up. I'll be going home to Florida in just a few weeks. Why make a commitment I know I likely won't keep? Thank you for your offer. You are most kind. But I believe it's best we remain nothing but dear friends."

His mouth dropped open and his eyes widened with disbelief. "If you come to your senses, please let me know." He briefly bowed, then spun on his heel and strode off.

———————

"Off for the afternoon, Andrew?"

He heard Aunt Letty's warbling, high-pitched voice from right behind him. He halted on the walkway leading down to the pier and watched as she approached at a fast pace. Tipping his straw boater, he grinned at the endearing widow with her merry eyes and funny button nose. "Good day, Mrs. Benham. My work is done for the day and I'm off on a boat ride. Care to join me?"

He'd spoken to her only a handful of times over the course of the summer. But he found her bubbly laughter and straight-forward remarks very refreshing.

She peered over the spectacles resting on the tip of her nose and smiled sweetly at him.

"I'd love some time on the water, if you don't mind taking along an old lady instead of a lovely young girl." Her eyes squinted with mirth.

He imagined she was quite the charmer and maybe even a beauty in her day. "Please," he said, offering his arm.

"Have you seen my dear Katherine? Perhaps she'd enjoy an outing too," she asked as they strolled toward the pier.

Shaking his head, Andrew sighed deeply. "Her parents have *suggested* we stay apart. We're both doing our best to honor their wishes."

"Well, you mustn't pay too much attention to them. They're well meaning, but Katherine knows what's best for her. Her parents can be quite overbearing at times."

He grunted his agreement. But then he caught sight of Randy stalking from the gazebo, shoulders hunched, eyes cast downward. A scowl tightened every muscle in his face.

"I wonder what's the matter with him," he mused, momentarily forgetting he wasn't alone.

"I'd wager it's Katherine," Letty said, a smug smile on her face. She squeezed his arm. "See? What did I tell you? She knows what's best for her."

A few moments later Katherine appeared on the bridge leading from the gazebo. Like Randy, her head was bowed and she looked troubled. But when she spotted them, she waved and headed across the yard in their direction.

"We were just heading out," he said when she was within earshot. "Care to join us?" He held his breath, not really thinking she'd accept.

She visibly brightened. "Oh yes, that would be just the ticket."

Only a few guide boats were left, so Andrew helped the ladies on board and then took the middle seat. Was Katherine going to explain her frown or was he going to have to guess?

Fortunately her aunt wasn't as reticent. "Do tell us why you and Randy both look so upset," she said from the backseat.

Katherine looked to the side. "Randy asked if we could keep company, and I turned him down. I'll be returning to Florida in early fall, so there's no point to it. Don't you agree?"

"Good for you, Katherine," Aunt Letty said. "I'd say it makes perfect sense. But undoubtedly it was difficult."

Relief welled in Andrew's chest and throat, and he didn't trust himself to speak; he merely nodded his approval. He felt so much more optimistic than the circumstances warranted, but he couldn't help reveling in a surge of hope.

Andrew found his voice. "How'd Randy take it?"

"He was shocked and more than a little irritated with me. But he'll understand, in time. I'm sure of it. We shall get to know each other again, but not court formally. I need to take it slowly." Katherine groaned. "But now I'll have to face Mama and Papa. They'll be furious."

Aunt Letty dismissed her apprehension with a wave of her hand. "Of course they will. But remember, they have no right to direct your life. Your mother can be a trial, but you can stand up to her."

"Thank you for your vote of confidence, Auntie. I'd rather confront a hungry bear than Mama."

"Never let her intimidate you, Katherine. She doesn't mean to be bossy, but she's convinced she always knows what's best. If she'd only been born a man, she would've made a great army general."

"I agree," Katherine said with a giggle.

Aunt Letty continued, "Nevertheless, she has a warm spot for her family that delves deep in her heart. The trick is to bring it out."

They all fell into companionable silence until they reached Loon Island. Aunt Letty clapped her hands with delight. "Yes, let's explore. I don't believe I've gone hiking in years."

Andrew wasn't sure the elderly lady was up to the physical challenge, but since Katherine seemed game, he was too. They walked up the path to the other side of the island and then paused to view the lake and the mountains on the opposite shore. Unlike the last time they'd come here, the sun shone in a clear, azure blue sky.

It was perfect, really. Being there, with them. Impulsively, he slid his arm around Katherine's tiny waist and smiled when she didn't edge away. She just smiled enigmatically and continued to gaze out over the lake beside him. What did it mean? He resolved to appreciate the moment and not rush ahead.

They returned to the boat at a more leisurely pace, not breaking their silence. Aunt Letty dragged a step or two behind, but her spirits seemed invigorated.

On the way down to the beach, Katherine turned her gaze on Andrew. "I'm a little puzzled by Randy. When I explained I was going back to Florida, he became quite agitated. I'm sure his mother pressured him to court me, but he normally doesn't let her opinions influence him. Do you think there's another reason why he was upset?"

Andrew swallowed the truth before he blurted it out. She had a right to know Randy was pursuing her in order to avoid working at the family bank. But since she'd turned him down, Andrew wouldn't betray his cousin's secret.

He shrugged. "You'd have to ask Randy."

"No, I think I'll just let it drop. I was merely curious."

They soon boarded the guide boat and shoved off. Andrew rowed back toward Camp Birchwood, feeling better than he had in a long time. But when they approached the dock, he noted Mr. and Mrs. Wainwright treading down the pier to meet them. Had Randy run directly to them? The weasel . . .

He heard a soft gasp from Katherine. "I knew this was coming. Thanks for granting me an hour's respite, you two."

"Stand your ground, Katherine. I have faith in you," Aunt Letty said.

"I'll do my best, Auntie."

Chapter Seventeen

"Hello, Mama, Papa," Katherine greeted them, a false cheer to her voice. "What brings you down to the pier? Are you going yachting today?"

"We had a delightful time over on Loon Island," Aunt Letty volunteered in a relaxed tone as Andrew helped her out of the boat.

"I'm so glad you enjoyed yourselves," Mama said dryly. "But I'm afraid we have bad news, Katherine."

Katherine stiffened, preparing herself for what might lie ahead. "What's the matter?"

Papa pulled a telegram out of his pocket. "This is from Stuart Osborne. 'Fire destroyed Buena Vista and all outbuildings. Complete loss. Crops fine. Letter to follow.'"

"Oh no," Katherine murmured, slamming her hand over her mouth. Her legs wobbled and her body weakened.

"I'm so sorry, princess," Papa said, folding her into his arms. "This must be devastating for you."

Buena Vista—burned to ashes. The loss was more than she could comprehend. She'd lived in the beautiful old home for eight years. Even though it held sad—even bitter—memories, its craftsmanship and beauty were rare. She loved the grand old house. And now all her memories had gone up in flames, both the good and the bad.

"How dreadful, my dear," Aunt Letty murmured.

With his hands clasped, Andrew murmured his condolences too. She wished she could take his arm and draw strength from him.

Seconds later Katherine found her voice. "The only thing to do is to rebuild." She took a big gulp of air. "I might need another loan from you, Papa, but under the circumstances, I hope you'll see the need."

Mama's eyes narrowed and she held up her palm, her fingers spread apart. "I'm sure Aunt Letty and Andrew will excuse us. This is hardly the forum for such a private discussion."

Abruptly chastened, Katherine nodded and followed her parents toward the lodge. She glanced over her shoulder to her great-aunt and friend, wishing they could be with her for what was to come. Katherine walked to the end of the dock, her knees still knocking against the thin fabric of her white skirt, and dropped onto a wooden bench across from her parents, who had settled in two chairs.

"Papa, is there a problem loaning me money to rebuild?" Katherine knew the funds weren't the real issue. It would be no more than pocket change to him.

"Your father and I have discussed this loan, Katherine, and he knows I am vehemently against it." She pursed her lips. "Nevertheless, we're very sorry about the loss of your home and buildings, and wish to give you our very best guidance. You've suffered a terrible shock, my dear." She hesitated for a moment. "But might this not be the perfect opportunity for you to sell the property to Stuart Osborne and be done with it? Papa told me Stuart seems eager to purchase it."

Katherine shook her head. "I cannot make such an important

decision when I'm so upset. My home and my outbuildings, gone. This is too much for me to absorb all at once."

"Please, take a day or two to think it over," Papa soothed.

Katherine sighed. "My first impulse is to return to Florida immediately and see to the rebuilding."

"But as you said, you'll need the funds to do so," Papa reminded her.

"Yes," she said, leaning forward and looking to him, her mother, then back to him again. "I'm depending upon you both. Don't you see what the citrus groves mean to me?"

Papa's face puckered, and his chin melded into his neck. Mama's lips pursed, and her forehead creased as if she was struggling with a knotty problem. Mama reached for her hands. "My dear, your distress is painfully obvious. You have my heartfelt sympathy. I know how horrid I'd feel if we lost Birchwood Lodge."

Katherine nodded, appreciating the rare moment of empathy from her mother. "Thank you."

"Papa and I spoke about the fire while you were out on the lake, dear. We want to offer you any assistance we can."

Tears burned in Katherine's eyes. "Oh! Thank you both so much." She'd hoped they'd come through, but she never expected her mother would show real generosity.

Papa cleared his throat. "I'll provide the funds so Stuart can supervise the construction of the outbuildings. If you're certain you want to return for the harvest, then I'll also have him put up a small house for you. You'll need a place to stay. We can talk about a larger home later on, if you decide to return to Florida permanently."

Katherine nodded, fearful of saying anything that might ruin this perfect answer to her dilemma.

Papa's mouth tightened. "How much fire insurance do you carry?"

"I'm afraid the buildings were underinsured. My resources are quite limited, so I had to set priorities. I spent most of my money covering the citrus groves." Her voice dwindled off.

He tapped his thick fingers against the armrest. "If you'll give me the information, I'll write to the insurance company for you."

"Thank you, Papa. I have the information in my cabin."

"Good. I'll handle all the details of rebuilding, all the financing, regardless of what the insurance company pays out."

"Thank you," she breathed, immensely relieved.

"There is one caveat."

Her eyes moved to meet his again. "We must insist you allow Randy to court you for the remainder of the summer."

Katherine glanced from one parent to the other. The shock of the fire had completely erased the problem of Randy. Katherine lifted her chin. "You must know by now I have no intention of stepping out with Randy—and I probably never will." She met her mother's stony gaze. "It's unfair to give him—or you—false hope."

Mama's jaw jutted and she shook her head. "Yes, Randy told his mother and me you turned him down."

Papa spoke softly and raised an eyebrow. "Remember, Katherine . . ."

The agreement. Yes, she remembered, and his willingness to cover the aftermath of the fire merely heaped more burning coals of guilt upon her head. But spending her life with Randy wasn't part of their original deal, at least in her mind. Getting along with Mama was one thing, attending social activities as she directed, spending time with Aunt Letty . . . but truly courting? With an eye toward an engagement? That was hardly what she had signed on for.

No one spoke for several long seconds, and it became gradually clear to Katherine her parents wouldn't fund the construction unless she agreed to this. Her heart squeezed shut and then pulled open, threatening to rip apart.

"All right. I need the rebuilding to begin as soon as possible. It seems I must let Randy court me, at least to the end of the summer. But I need a few days to get used to the idea before I speak to him about it."

"I don't suppose a few days will matter," Mama agreed with a resigned shrug. "Although I don't know why you're procrastinating. There's no point to it."

Papa's face eased into an affable smile. "That's fine, princess. Now, fetch me the insurance information and I'll get started. There's much work to be done."

Andrew kept an eye out for Katherine, but she withdrew to her cabin for the remainder of the day and evening. How much more could the poor woman endure? With loans, Harriet asking for money, growing indebtedness to her parents, pressure to be wooed by Randy, and now the fire, Katherine carried a heavy burden on her delicate shoulders. But he knew Aunt Letty would comfort her. He only wished he could as well.

As he worked at his desk the following morning, he waited for his boss to reprimand him for taking Katherine out on the guide boat the day before. After warning him to avoid her, Mr. Wainwright couldn't ignore his disobedience. But his boss was absorbed in the mail and undoubtedly had more weighty problems on his mind. Finally, Mr. Wainwright turned toward him. Andrew held his breath.

"I've just learned that the owners of the California trunk line will be returning to the States earlier than expected. I've also learned that another group is interested in buying. We cannot let a competitor slip in ahead of us. So I'm advancing the date of your departure to sometime in the next few weeks. Are you ready for a month-long sojourn, the moment I send you?"

Andrew hesitated for a split second. "Uh. Yes, sir. I think I have all I need."

"Andrew? What is it?" Mr. Wainwright peered at him over the rims of his spectacles. It was then that Andrew realized he'd remained awkwardly frozen in place.

"Nothing, sir." But this was the worst possible timing with Katherine on the verge of making such crucial decisions. "Thank you again for the opportunity," he managed to say.

Mr. Wainwright nodded vigorously. "I'm sure you'll make the most of it."

He hoped he wouldn't be leaving for California before Harriet got in touch. Surely the woman would arrive soon and contact Katherine with her demands. At least he could assist Katherine through that . . .

Andrew shuffled the papers in his stack, but had difficulty concentrating. As much as he wanted to leave for California and prove his worth to Mr. Wainwright, he might have to ask for a delay if Harriet didn't come forward soon or if she resisted a quick settlement. He'd have to talk it over with Katherine.

Mr. Wainwright pushed his reading spectacles back to the bridge of his nose and then returned to his mail. Before long he handed Andrew a sheet of paper. "This letter arrived in the morning mail. Stuart Osborne wrote it days before the fire." Mr. Wainwright laced his fingers and rested them on the green blotter while he waited for Andrew to read the letter.

Andrew's shoulders tensed as he scanned the text.

Dear Mr. Wainwright,

I'm writing to you, instead of Katherine, confident in the knowledge that you'll always act in her best interest. I'm quite sure you'll be as interested as Katherine to hear about our progress this summer. Everything is going well. I've located workers for the coming harvest, made arrangements for shipments, and seen to the construction of several temporary sorting sheds that will greatly enhance our processes come October.

As you probably know, I've made several offers to Katherine over the last few months, but she's turned all of them down. I can assure you I've offered to pay more than the groves are worth at the present time. I'm afraid my brother Charles was negligent and ignored his business to an alarming degree. Katherine toiled valiantly but was unable to produce enough fruit to make the company truly profitable. Fortunately, I have the means to invest in the groves and see them successful again.

Sir, I hope you'll attempt to convince Katherine to sell the groves to me as soon as possible. As per our agreement, I shall manage the operation until the end of the summer, but no longer. I strongly suggest she accept my generous offer before harvest begins.

Please convey my offer to Katherine once again, along with my deepest regards.

Sincerely,
Stuart Osborne

Andrew looked at the amount. "It's a handsome offer."

Stuart's offer was reasonable, and Katherine ought to accept. Between the specter of Charles's old loan, the loan from her father for cash, and now the cost to rebuild, she really didn't have another option. He pitied her for the mess she'd inherited.

Mr. Wainwright's shaggy gray brows drew together. "Osborne is likely motivated by legacy. He wants his father's old company. But he's not a sentimental fool. He wants them because he can clearly see profit on the horizon." He glanced toward the window and then back to Andrew. "Do you believe she should sell?"

Mr. Wainwright expected him to fall in line, but Andrew couldn't hold back his honest opinion. "Katherine's only options are to return to her groves and harvest the crop, or sell. I'm afraid I don't know which she'll choose. Practicality demands she accept his offer, even if he reduces it after the fire. But," he said, clearing his throat, "I do believe in following one's heart, sir. If she could persevere, find the way to make it through the next five years, she might enjoy some of that profitability that Osborne sees on the horizon." His mouth went as dry and gritty as sand. "As much as Osborne would like you to press Katherine to a decision, I don't think she'd react favorably to it. She already feels an exorbitant amount of pressure."

His boss nodded slowly, clearly agitated by his answer. "My daughter trusts you, Andrew. Could you not persuade her it's in her best interest to sell? I'd be beholden to you. In fact," he said, fiddling with his pen a moment, "I'd even be willing to consider you heading our legal department when Mr. Heisler retires at the end of the year."

Andrew stared hard at him, wondering if he'd heard correctly. Heading up the department? "I'm overwhelmed, sir, and very grateful." This would be a big promotion, one he was ready for. But to influence Katherine . . . he wasn't sure he could or should even try when running the groves meant so much to her. And yet, such a promotion, with the accompanying salary . . . Andrew's heart leaped. He'd become a man of respectable means. He might even be able to court Katherine himself! "I'll speak to her, if you wish."

Mr. Wainwright nodded. He knew he held him in his grip. "Excellent."

"Thank you, sir." Andrew returned the letter to his boss, his hand far from steady. He'd coveted a promotion for as long as he could remember. William Wainwright was a generous employer and a fair man, but in this case, it was clear he was employing all means available to him for his daughter's sake.

Andrew glanced at Mr. Wainwright's features, crinkled with age and weariness, as if the world's pain had finally wounded him and his family. Andrew knew for certain his own future depended upon his success with Katherine over this matter. His stomach tumbled with nausea.

Mr. Wainwright shook off his melancholy and snorted loudly. "She's a mulish girl, isn't she? Katherine makes reckless decisions and probably lives to regret the worst of them. But she has courage."

Andrew suppressed a dry smile. Mr. Wainwright understood his daughter far better than most fathers. "I admire her determination. I even respect her for trying her hand at running the company. I'm not one bit surprised it was more than she could handle, but by golly, she deserves credit for trying. It's astonishing for a girl to take on a large business."

A look of pride mingled with frustration played for dominance in Mr. Wainwright's jowly face. No doubt he saw Katherine as a chip off the old block. "I'm going out on my boat." He hefted himself up and walked toward the door, pausing there a moment. "You know, Andrew, it's harder to manage a family than a railroad."

Chapter Eighteen

Outside on the veranda, Andrew waited for Katherine to finish reading Stuart's letter. From the stony look in her eyes, he knew exactly what she thought of her brother-in-law's latest offer.

She stood and leaned against the porch railing. "Why won't Stuart give up?"

"It's a decent offer, Katherine. Especially with all you face, wouldn't it be wise to reconsider?"

Her eyes flashed an icy blue. "Not you too, Andrew! Stuart's gone to Papa because he knows my father will pressure me to sell. But I'm not interested." She pushed a long tendril of hair, loosened by the breeze, behind her ear.

Andrew nodded. "I understand your feelings. But consider how much easier your life would be if you didn't suffer any further financial strain. You could be free, Katherine." *Free to accept any suitor you wished.*

She grimaced. "You're right, but you've forgotten how much I enjoy the business. Even now, I long to be back among the citrus trees, watching as the oranges grow fat upon the limbs . . ." She closed her eyes, as if going there in her mind.

He remained silent while a group of guests passed by, wandering down toward the lake.

Katherine folded the letter and shoved it into her skirt pocket, sighed, and then leveled a stare in his direction. "Papa put you up to this, didn't he?"

"He asked me to speak to you, and I agreed."

She rolled her eyes. "Tell me your honest opinion, Andrew. If you were in my position, what would you do?"

He hesitated a moment. "I'd do what seemed right," he said. "Whatever made me happiest. Only you know the answer."

"Thank you for not pushing me." Her eyes narrowed as she appraised him. "What did Papa offer you, to attempt influence?"

Shame rose inside him and he suffered from deep regret. "A promotion, I'm afraid. Forgive me, Katherine."

She gave him a wry smile. "It's all right, Andrew. Don't look so embarrassed. I don't blame you for trying. No one crosses either one of my parents and gets away with it for long."

"Yet you're trying."

She snorted softly. "It helps that I'm their daughter, not an employee." She looked out to the water again. "My parents want a very different life for me than the one I envision for myself. I'm drawn to both. Yet I can only have one or the other."

He swallowed his reticence before he asked, "And what about Randy? How does he fit into your plans now?" Could he possibly manage to obtain the promotion and the girl? Convince her that he loved her far more than Randy ever might? He chastised himself for his wild imaginings.

Katherine took her time answering. "Most people settle for what's practical. But I still have romantic notions about what a marriage might look like, were I to ever venture into such territory again." She glanced at him guiltily and blushed. "But I'm afraid my parents are forcing me to give up my idealism. Oh, Andrew, I so hate to tell you this, but I can't keep it from you any longer." She breathed deeply. "Papa offered to reconstruct all the destroyed buildings if I agreed to a serious courtship with Randy."

His eyes widened. "No, Katherine. Please tell me you're joking."

"I had no choice. But it's not a formal engagement. We're only courting, getting to know each other better."

Andrew shook his head. "You already know everything there is to know about Randy. Your parents will expect to announce an engagement by fall. Katherine, I can't tell you how disappointed and sorry I am to hear this. But I understand the awkward position you're in." At the same time he fought the impulse to take her in his arms and protect her from the machinations of her family.

"I haven't told Randy yet and I won't until I get used to the idea."

"Katherine, please don't jump into marriage unless you're sure it's right. You must really be in love."

"I believe the same as you do," she returned steadily. "Marriage must be based on genuine love. And both people ought to be ready. I still have to completely recover from Charles's . . . infidelity . . . before I can go forward. I'm still learning to forgive and forget."

He nodded, hopeful she'd hold firm and not rush.

She stared at him, and several long seconds ticked by. "We're a lot alike."

Was it his imagination again, or had some hidden, inner door within her heart just swung open?

On Sunday morning, Katherine, Andrew, and several of the Camp Birchwood guests took the steam yacht to the Church of the Good Shepherd on St. Hubert's Isle. The small stick-style chapel had been built over twenty years ago for the summer people.

Katherine sidestepped into a pew between Andrew and Aunt Letty, even though Mama scowled at her from beneath the wide brim of her feathery hat. The rest of the family and some of her parents' friends filed in beside them. Katherine felt relief that the Clarkes hadn't come along. She flinched every time Randy greeted her with a quizzical glance. He'd no doubt heard she'd reconsidered his idea of courting and would be accepting soon. He must wonder why she was waiting.

But Katherine understood she couldn't delay much longer without fraying everyone's patience. Yet her heart didn't belong to Randy, and so far, nothing had convinced her that it should. Still, she kept seeking God's will for her life, her heart, her vocation, praying day and night. But the only thing she could sense was the desire to not make any decision at all. Could God be asking her to wait?

The warm morning and cozy little chapel seemed to ease away thoughts of the groves, of Randy, of her parents, and even of Harriet. But as the pastor droned on in his sermon, Katherine's mind drifted like a twig on a river. It wasn't until the pastor intoned Matthew's words that she paid attention again, startled. "I say unto you, Love your enemies, bless them that curse you, do good to them that hate you, and pray for them which despitefully use you, and persecute you." *Love your enemies.* Her chest prickled with guilt at the convicting words. How could she possibly *love* the woman who stole her husband and ruined her happiness? She didn't despise Harriet Roles any longer, but she was nowhere near loving her. Anger still burned inside, even though she yearned to be free of it. The Lord had much work to do in her heart to make forgiveness and love possible.

Andrew glanced sideways and Katherine feared he'd detect all her changes in emotion. His constant scrutiny unnerved her, yet gratitude rose from deep within. He steadied her with his common sense and wise counsel, his constant care. *Thank You, Lord, for sending me Andrew. I couldn't do without him.*

She closed her eyes. What was she thinking? After she committed to Randy, Andrew would have to fade from her life as Randy gradually assumed his role of confidant and best friend.

Only she couldn't picture Randy caring enough to fill Andrew's position.

So why did You bring Andrew back into my life, Lord?

The answer came immediately. Of course. The Lord sent him as a temporary helper for this very time. Then their lives would diverge, and they'd each go their separate ways.

But then, why did her heart flutter whenever they spoke alone? Why did his opinion matter so much? She loved to be around him, sharing her thoughts and listening to his. If only Andrew wasn't so attractive and helpful . . . it'd help her keep her mind and heart firmly on friendship, rather than darting to something more.

Everyone stood for the last hymn. Opening the thick hymnbook she shared with Aunt Letty, Katherine stole a glance at him. He sang with enthusiasm and looked so engrossed in the written words, she knew he believed them with all his being. And so did she. They had more in common than any other couple she knew.

Pity they couldn't draw any closer without endangering their hearts and throwing their futures into chaos.

Early the next morning Katherine and Aunt Letty arrived at the boathouse and found a dozen or more of the Birchwood guests already boarding canoes, rowboats, and Adirondack guide boats.

"I'm looking forward to catching some trout and walleye." Aunt Letty rubbed her palms in anticipation. "Thank you for taking me, Katherine. Cook always appreciates fresh fish for luncheon."

"My pleasure." Katherine shivered in the morning chill despite a shawl wrapped around her shoulders.

"It might've been better to fish for walleye at night, but maybe we'll be lucky," Aunt Letty said.

As the rest of the group shoved off, she picked up a box of bait and headed for the remaining boat with her great-aunt.

"Let's take a guide boat," Katherine suggested as she gathered fishing equipment from the boathouse.

They boarded the canoe-like boat that was light enough for hunters and fishermen to easily carry over land. Katherine rowed out into the calm gray-blue water.

In another hour or so the sun would rise high above the mountains and shower light and warmth over the lake and forest. But now the water reflected the mountains in a greenish distortion that reminded her of a Monet painting. Not one breath of air rippled the water's glassy surface or stirred the tree branches dipping over the shoreline. Everything was hushed except for the occasional twitter of robins and the sound of oars and paddles dipping into the water. Gradually each boat headed off in its own direction in pursuit of a leisurely sightseeing journey or a fishing expedition.

Katherine rowed in the opposite direction to a cove where she hoped the fish were biting. Aunt Letty baited the hooks with live minnows, and then they dropped their lines into the water and waited.

"The water's a little too clear for us to catch walleye, but maybe a trout will swim by," Katherine said as she relaxed.

Aunt Letty didn't relax at all. She cast her line, reeled it in slowly, and then cast it again. Katherine had to smile at her aunt's determination. As she maneuvered her rod back and forth, she looked at Katherine.

"Have you reached a decision about your citrus groves, my dear?" Her great-aunt's voice was as quiet as the morning stillness.

Katherine shook her head. "I'm going to return to Florida, but I'm afraid the combined debts might just put me under, Auntie."

"Oh dear. I don't suppose you'd want to ask your father."

Katherine shook her head. "My goodness, no. He's already helped me a great deal. But what remains . . . I don't even want him or Mama to know about it. It's too humiliating."

"Oh dear, this is quite a problem."

"I'm afraid so. There is the hope that I could catch up after the harvest on all the various debts. If the crop is good, I can at least catch up on the delinquent payments."

"Oh my dear, that sounds like such a tremendous burden!"

Katherine explained about the bank loan Charles had taken out for the business and had squandered on his own pleasures. "I'm feeling overwhelmed," she admitted. "In the end, I may have to sell, although I refuse to give up the fight yet. I keep hoping something miraculous will happen."

"I'm so sorry, my dear. I do wish I could help." Aunt Letty's frown added several years to her age.

Katherine forced a small smile. "Andrew wishes he could too. But there's really nothing to be done. If I sell, I can pay off the bank. But I won't have much money left to live on my own, at least not for long." She looked out to the water. "I'd end up returning to Mama and Papa. And they'd pressure me to marry Randy as soon as possible."

"No matter how much your parents badger you, the decision to marry is most important, dear one. Doubly so, after your terrible experience with Charles." Aunt Letty inhaled deeply, let her bait settle for a moment, and then leaned back in the cane chair. "You've said before you didn't have any desire to marry again. But I wonder if you're more opposed to *Randy* than to marriage itself." She raised her palm. "Not that you don't like him as a dear friend. You simply can't envision him as a husband. Am I right?"

Katherine shrugged. "Perhaps it's easiest if one doesn't love with such intensity. Perhaps the best kind of marriage for me would be one of convenience. Keep it simple. My marriage with Charles was so dreadfully complicated."

"Oh, Katherine, I know you don't believe that. You mustn't think in such a defeatist way! Don't fear the joys and sorrows of living. Believe me, they can't be completely avoided. You must have courage and understand you're not facing your troubles alone. The Lord helps us through the trials."

Katherine considered her words. "I do trust the Lord, and in His guidance. I only wish He would guide in a more *overt* way."

Aunt Letty grinned. "Are you certain He isn't?"

Katherine peered at her through narrowed eyes. "What do you mean?"

"Sometimes," the old woman said, casting her line again, "what seems obscure at the present, in hindsight seems so vivid we can't imagine how we missed it." Her eyes widened. "Oh my, I do believe I feel a bite." Aunt Letty sat up straight, and with fierce determination in her eyes, she started reeling in her line. At first the fish pulled hard, swimming away from the boat, but Aunt Letty gripped the rod, held the point high, and then reeled in on the downswing.

"You're quite adept with the rod, Auntie," Katherine said as she watched, eyes wide.

"Oh yes. My Norman made me learn the correct way. He said there was no use fishing if you were going to give the fish the advantage."

Aunt Letty pulled at the rod and reeled in once more. "Look. There it is," Katherine said as the fish swam near the surface. She leaned slightly over the side of the boat with a net to help Aunt Letty land the fish. Together they pulled in an olive and gold walleye.

Aunt Letty reached into the net and held the fish high. "This fish must be ten pounds. Not huge for a walleye, but a good size for this time of the day, don't you think?"

"Oh yes. You're quite the fisherman, Aunt Letty."

"Norman and I both were. How I miss that dear man. We enjoyed doing so many things together. I do hope you'll have many wonderful experiences with the man you love."

Katherine flinched. She felt her jaw tighten as she lowered her gaze. Aunt Letty meant well, but all her talk about love and happiness just brought on waves of sadness. She'd never have such a special relationship with Randy. It would be adequate at best, but certainly not bubbling with joy. Yet hardly anyone she knew experienced high peaks of emotion. With a sigh of resignation, Katherine baited her hook again and cast it into the lake next to her aunt's line.

"Aunt Letty, I understand that it's expected I remarry."

"Your mother is dreadfully pushy, but she understands you'll be far happier when you have a loving husband. Frankly, I believe the same. *With the right man*."

"And Randy isn't that man," she whispered. There. She'd finally admitted the truth. He was a good person, but he wasn't her choice for a husband.

Aunt Letty nodded sagely. "I can see that, my dear."

"But if not Randy, then who should I marry?"

The elderly lady lifted one white eyebrow and then let her smile broaden into a big grin. "Who, indeed?"

Katherine looked to the lake, hoping that in the bright sun, her aunt would not be able to see her furious blush.

———·———

Later, Katherine found a letter on her bureau. The return address caught her attention—her bank in Florida. She tore open the envelope and pulled out one sheet of paper.

Scanning the letter, the typewritten words slapped her in the face.

> We regret to inform you . . . property has been decreased in value due to the unfortunate fire . . . your loan has been recategorized as high risk, given that your loan exceeds market value . . . immediately make a payment to rectify by 1 September 1905 . . . or seek a loan from an alternate financial institution . . .

Her eyes returned to the amount they demanded by the first of the month. She gasped and closed her eyes. Could this really be happening to her? Her worst fears were coming true. She'd read the terms of the loan a hundred times after Charles died and she knew the bank was within its rights to demand repayment. But she knew the banker and didn't expect he'd ever be so harsh.

Aunt Letty touched her arm. "What's the matter, dear? Not more bad news, I hope."

"You remember what I told you about my financial woes this morning? Well, the bank is asking for full payment by the beginning of September. I certainly didn't expect that. I don't know where I'll find the funds."

Aunt Letty led her to the sofa. "Do sit down. I think we should turn to the Lord and pray hard about this. If there's one thing I know for sure, it's that difficult situations can never be thought out by man—or woman. They must be placed in His hands."

Chapter Nineteen

arly in the evening Andrew wandered down a dirt road toward the bowling alley Mr. Wainwright had installed a few years earlier. He thought he'd throw a few practice balls and enjoy the quiet of dusk.

"Mr. Townsend!" Letty called. "Andrew!"

He turned around at the sound of his name and spied Letty Benham hustling down the road, huffing and puffing. She clutched a small bag in her hand. He concealed a smile as he waited for the sweet old lady to catch up with him.

"Would you like to join me for a game of bowling?" he asked as they strolled toward the Birchwood alley.

She surveyed the long lane—covered by a steep roof and open at the sides—and looked at him askance. "To be honest, I've never seen a bowling alley before. But I'd be delighted. How do you play this game?"

"It's simple." Andrew explained while he picked up a ball to demonstrate his technique. He hurled it down the polished alley and watched it smash into the pins. "Nothing to it." He grinned at her tilted head and pursed lips.

"I'm not sure I can learn. It looks rather difficult."

As he reset the pins, Mrs. Benham held up the heavy ball with some difficulty, getting ready to step forward, swing her arm back, and then let the ball roll off her fingers. But her hand twisted, and the ball bounced partway down the alley and veered into the gutter. They chuckled together as she buried her head in her hands.

"I'm not starting off well. But I'll improve, you'll see. At least I'm hopeful. But in the meantime would you like some Saratoga chips?" She opened the bag wide and offered it to him.

"Thank you. They're one of my favorite snacks." First made locally in Saratoga Springs, he'd heard they were now being sold in New England where they were equally as popular. The thin and crispy potato chip crunched when he bit into it.

Mrs. Benham flung the ball down the alley again and this time knocked down all of the pins except one. It wobbled but didn't tumble. Clapping her hands, she bounced up and down on the toes of her shoes.

After they finished their game, Mrs. Benham plopped on a wooden bench. "Now that I've gotten the hang of it, I believe I'll try again, but not today. Next time I'll beat you, dear boy. Mark my words." She munched on several chips, then glanced up at him. He leaned against a nearby post.

"Andrew, I'd like to speak to you about a plan I have." She lowered her voice, even though they were alone.

"Yes, Mrs. Benham?"

"I'll get right to the point. Katherine received a letter today from her Florida bank. They're calling in a loan and appear to not be very forgiving."

His mouth pressed tight. Would her troubles never end? "If I could, I'd lend her the money, but as you probably know, I'm not from the prosperous side of the Clarke family."

Letty chuckled. "No, but you're from a very distinguished and honorable side. I knew your father well. He was a wise judge and exceptionally intelligent. You should be very proud of him."

"I certainly am." His father had the respect of everyone he encountered except, perhaps, from some of the great industrialists and financiers who esteemed money far more than personal integrity. He had wonderful memories of his parents, though with each passing year his recollections diminished a bit.

"It's very kind of you to want to help my niece. I can see how disappointed you are that you cannot."

It hurt and even humiliated him to acknowledge his lack of power and fortune, at least at times like these when most likely a relatively small amount would make all the difference in the world. The feeling of helplessness burned his insides. Maybe Mrs. Benham could give Katherine a loan.

"Unfortunately, I'm not rich either," she said.

His heart sank down to his boots.

"I have adequate means for my own needs, although most of my set considers me rather poor. Of course, I have the Lord in my life, and He makes me the richest one of all. I expect you understand what I'm saying."

"Yes, I do."

She nodded. "Good. I have an idea that might help Katherine. Would you like to hear about it?"

"Yes, of course." He'd consider any plan, even though he doubted anything would work.

She pulled on the gloves she'd removed to bowl. "You'll probably think I'm only a silly old lady without an ounce of business experience, and you'll be right. But since neither of us has managed to come up with a solution for Katherine, I thought we could join together to try to work something out."

"I'm ready to listen, Mrs. Benham." He couldn't imagine what she had in mind, but he didn't hold out much hope for a solution.

"Good. And please call me Aunt Letty. If we're going to become partners we should at least be on a first-name basis."

"I'd be honored to call you Aunt Letty, Aunt Letty," he said with a smile. He angled his head closer to hers and listened intently. "What is Katherine's most immediate financial need? What would keep the bank at bay?"

She chewed her lower lip. "Oh dear, I don't know. It seemed rude to ask. But we'll need to find out the amount or we won't know if we have enough."

"Let's return to the cabin and you can take a look."

Aunt Letty covered her mouth with her hands and giggled like a little girl. "This is rather clandestine, isn't it?"

They strode down the darkening path to the Birchwood complex and headed toward the walkway while a few dozen guests sauntered up from their boats. More entertainment in the lounge or recreation hall, Andrew expected.

"I do hope Katherine isn't in our cabin." Aunt Letty shoved her key in the lock and pushed open the door to a room lit only by a single oil lamp. Andrew lingered by the doorway.

The young maid, Bridget, emerged from the dressing room with an armful of skirts and shirtwaists. "Good evening, Mrs. Benham, Mr. Townsend. If you'll excuse me, I'm on my way to the laundry. I need to have some of your clothes pressed again, ma'am. They've gotten a bit wrinkled in the wardrobe."

As soon as she was off, Andrew came inside and followed Aunt Letty to the bureau. He glanced toward the doorway every few seconds to ensure Katherine wouldn't catch them in the act of reading her mail.

"Here it is," Letty whispered as she read the small print by the light of the lamp. "Forty thousand dollars! My, that's quite a large sum. I can understand why it's difficult for her to repay it. The poor girl. No wonder she's so distraught. But I can afford half. Can you come up with the other half?"

"Why, yes, I believe so." He'd have to turn over every penny he'd saved working for Mr. Wainwright, as well as the remains of his family inheritance. But Katherine certainly was worth it.

"Fine. We'll put our money together and offer it to meet this pressing need." Aunt Letty clapped her hands with glee. "Aren't we clever?" She chuckled.

He hesitated. "I don't think we should admit we're her backers, because I doubt she'd accept a loan from us. She'd think we ought to keep our money," he said.

Aunt Letty nodded. "True. And if William got wind of it, he'd dismiss you in a flash. He surely doesn't want you to work against him when he and Isabelle have tried so hard to get Katherine to come their way. We can't jeopardize your job. So let's just say you found an investor who wants to remain anonymous. We won't be fibbing, and that will keep our consciences clear. Well, clear enough."

Andrew nodded. "If she accepts our loan, I can send the funds to Katherine's bank in Florida. I do believe this will work. Thanks for coming up with a solution." He refused to consider what this would do to his career if they were caught.

Aunt Letty squeezed his hand. "I'm happy we can do this for her."

"As am I. Now I'll have to devise a plausible story that will answer all the questions she's bound to have. Katherine won't be easy to fool."

"No, indeed. Just be as truthful but as vague as possible and pray she doesn't pose too many questions."

Andrew nodded. "I'll begin thinking right away. There's

really no time to waste. Let's tell her together as soon as we can get her alone. I don't want anyone to overhear us."

Aunt Letty nodded enthusiastically. "Oh, Andrew, I know we're doing the right thing, helping her."

"We are." But what price would be extracted, should they be found out?

Katherine paced in front of the cabin's fireplace before breakfast the following morning. She couldn't continue to hide in her bedroom, nursing a headache just to avoid Randy. She despised herself for causing the bafflement she saw in his eyes. Understanding why she didn't immediately accept his offer of courtship seemed way beyond his comprehension. She doubted a girl had ever turned him down.

She couldn't procrastinate any longer. Her pounding heartbeat sounded in her ears as she swept out of her sitting room in search of Mama. Her mother had laid low these last few days. Katherine's methods of escape were gradually closing, and Mama understood it. She was winning, in a sense, but fortunately had enough tact not to gloat.

She discovered her mother watering her daylilies in the rock garden and humming a tune from *H.M.S. Pinafore*, one of her favorite operas from her younger years. A riot of bright orange, yellow, pink, and red blooms reached toward the blue sky. Birds drank from the birdbath set among the rocks and splashed in the small stone basin. A breeze gusted from the lake only a few yards away, but it wasn't nearly cool enough to lower the heat in Katherine's face. Mama glanced sideways, then straightened and placed the watering can on a small patch of grass.

"Good morning, Katherine. Lovely day, isn't it? Dear me,

you look distressed. Is anything the matter?" Clapping the dirt off her gardening gloves, she leveled a penetrating gaze. "Something I can help you with?"

Katherine took a deep breath and slowly exhaled. "Mama, I'd like to speak to you about Randy's intentions."

Her mother brightened, though she still had a wary look in her eyes. "Yes? Go right ahead."

"Why are you and Mrs. Clarke so set on a marriage between Randy and me? It seems we've never had a say in the matter. You and your best friend decided for us years ago."

Mama would normally reprimand her daughter for impertinence, but this time she resisted. Drawing out a weary sigh, Mama nodded. "We wanted you and Randy to see what we saw—dear friends complementing each other in every way . . . shared backgrounds, similar interests. We always saw you as such an ideal couple. We still do."

But they'd never been a couple except in their mothers' imaginations. The families wanted grandchildren who belonged to one big happy family, not two, and marriage was their perfect resolution.

"I understand, Mama. But why are you pushing us together right now? Why aren't you content to wait until we're both ready? I don't understand your impatience. It's obvious neither Randy nor I want to rush into things. And please don't disagree, because I can plainly see his reluctance."

"Perhaps he's just afraid you'll turn him down. For good."

"But if we're meant to be together, then waiting a year or two will help us be sure we're making the right decision."

Mama averted her gaze and returned to watering her flowers. Several seconds later she turned back to Katherine and jammed her hands on her hips. "All right. I'll explain why Mrs. Clarke and I are so anxious. We believe Randy is a safe choice for you, and you'll be a steadying influence on him. I don't wish you to make another horrible mistake. And Randy . . . well, he needs a good woman at his side."

Katherine couldn't believe Mama still didn't trust her judgment to choose well. And to see her as an anchor of some sort? "Mama, you don't honestly fear I'll run off with the first man I find dashing and romantic—"

"Why, yes, I do."

Katherine stared hard at her. "Do you believe me a simpleton? That I learned nothing from my marriage to Charles?"

Mama looked up at the sky. "I don't know *what* to expect from you, Katherine. You seem to specialize in the unexpected!" Her eyes snapped with all her mounting frustration.

"But who would I run off with? No one besides Randy is even interested in me. Do you think I'll elope with one of the footmen?"

Mama looked disgusted. "Stop talking nonsense. You know perfectly well whom I'm referring to."

Katherine paused. "A–Andrew?"

The creases in Mama's face deepened, especially around her narrowed eyes. "Of course I mean Andrew! You can't possibly pretend you haven't noticed he's mooning after you. And you seem eager enough to receive his advances. His Aunt Georgia and your father have warned him not to toy with your affections, but he won't listen."

Her mother continued, but her petulant words sounded like a bee buzzing in Katherine's ears. Of course others had noticed Andrew's attention. How could she have assumed otherwise? She'd disregarded Andrew's apparent fondness because love was too overwhelming to even contemplate. After all the disappointment she'd inflicted upon her parents, she'd not add another wound to the injury. "Andrew is a dear friend, but I have no inclination to marry him now or in the future."

Mama's skeptical stare caused Katherine to flinch. "Simply promise me you won't elope with him."

Katherine's throat dried. "Really, Mama. You're being ridiculous."

"If you don't promise, then I shall continue to worry. Andrew is unsuitable for you. He's a gentleman, but to put it bluntly, he's not of our social set. He's been dependent upon Georgia and Clarence since his parents passed away. If it weren't for the Clarkes' generosity, you wouldn't even know him. He was well brought up, but he has almost no money. What kind of life could you possibly have with him?" Mama's face looked as red as her crimson roses.

A fine life, she thought. *We might be poor, but we'd be happy.*

She didn't dare say it aloud to Mama, but in her heart, she knew it was true.

———————

Katherine scoured the chalet in search of her father and finally found him shooting targets at the sighting range he'd set up for himself and his friends. Set by a small, empty field near the edge of the woods, Papa's range boasted ten shooting positions. He stood beside Randy's father, Clarence Clarke. Papa was peering intently through his sight one hundred yards away from his target.

Katherine halted by her father's side. "Papa, I'm sorry to interrupt, but may I have a word with you?"

He nodded. "What can I do for you, sweetheart?" He placed his rifle on the bench rest with the barrel pointing downrange.

"It's private." They moved away from the shooters to an area where they couldn't possibly overhear. The crack of gunfire shattered the quiet.

When they stopped near a clump of evergreens, Papa cocked his head. "What's wrong, Katherine? You look pale."

"I just spoke to Mama about Randy. She practically ordered me to turn my affection toward him. She fears I'll revert to my old, impulsive self and run off with Andrew. Can you imagine?"

When Papa hesitated, Katherine felt the knot in her heart twist like a rope. "You don't agree with her, do you?"

Papa shifted his bulk from one booted foot to the other. He scrunched his face as if he didn't know how to answer without offending her. When he sighed, Katherine swallowed hard and steeled herself for a response she didn't wish to hear.

"Sometimes your mother exaggerates, and she's often an alarmist. Yet I do believe this time she's hit the mark. You may not have seen the look in Andrew's eyes, but we have. Without a doubt he's fallen in love with you. And your mother won't have it."

"Have you questioned Andrew, or are you merely guessing?"

Papa shook his head. "I'd never be rude enough to ask him directly. He's my employee, after all."

Katherine nodded.

"But I have to agree with your mother. I suspect he's always been half in love with you, whether he realized it or not." Papa narrowed one eye and stared at her with such skepticism, she glanced toward the woods. "I can't believe you haven't noticed, princess. Surely you must be well aware of his interest."

"I, uh . . . well, yes." Heat burned through her and scorched her cheeks. "Have people been gossiping?" She dreaded his answer.

"You know how our set is. Some people delight in gossip."

"Do you suppose Andrew and Randy have heard it?"

"Perhaps not, although I really can't say. But you ought to carefully guard your reputation."

"You don't think I've been inviting idle talk, do you?"

Papa winced and rolled back on his heels. "I don't know about such things. You'd have to ask your mother her opinion." He glanced toward the gun sighting range with longing in his eyes. He stepped toward it as if he wanted to excuse himself and bolt.

But she wouldn't allow him to go yet. "Papa, please tell Mama that if I marry, I don't want her to choose my husband for me."

Her father shook his head sadly. "I'm sorry to have to tell you this, but I can't put myself between you and your mother. You'll have to work out your own disagreements."

Katherine's jaw dropped and tears blurred her vision. "But, Papa, you've always stood between Mama and me." She stopped. No, she was mistaken. Papa always listened to her complaints and murmured his understanding, but he never once took her part against her mother. He was a mere sounding board, not an advocate.

Gazing down at her with deep regret, Papa gently touched her shoulder. "Your mama asked me to fire Andrew, not because he's doing a poor job, but because of his fondness for you. In her mind, he's interfering with her plans for your future with Randy."

Katherine gasped and gripped his arm. "You wouldn't dismiss him, would you?" She couldn't believe her beloved father would do such a terrible injustice to a loyal employee.

"No, but that's why I'm sending him to California, in all haste. It'll be better for all of us if he's gone for a while. While he's an excellent worker and I admire him greatly, there are hundreds qualified to take his place." He held up his hands to shush her retort. "You have to understand that I'd hate to lose him. I'd like to promote him, actually. But I've only got one wife and I intend to keep her happy. She's irreplaceable. I'm sorry if I'm disappointing you, Katherine."

Her breathing came in short gulps. "I was counting on you to help me with Mama." She shook her head in disappointment. "Just promise me you won't fire Andrew."

He shook his head too. "I'm sorry. I can't, princess. If he continues to pursue you, and if you encourage him in any way, I'll have no option but to let him go. Believe me, I won't want to, but I will do it."

"So you'd send Andrew packing simply because I enjoy socializing with him? Doesn't that seem a bit punitive?"

He studied her. "I shall not take any action if you keep your distance from Andrew and allow Randy to begin courting you now. You've put Randy off for too long. It's not good for a man's reputation."

"His reputation. My reputation. Do you ever feel as if all we consider are our reputations? What about passion? Direction? God's path?"

He opened his mouth and then clamped it shut. "I'm sorry about all this, but now you have a firm understanding about where your mother and I stand. I trust you will tell Randy he may begin to court you."

Mr. Clarke called out to Papa, and he glanced over his shoulder and then back to her. "Excuse me, Katherine. I must return to my shooting." He tipped his cap and strode back to the range, leaving her behind.

Katherine's legs weakened. She wrapped her arm around the thin white bark of the birch tree and struggled to regain her composure. What choice did she have except to follow Mama's wishes? She couldn't allow her stubborn ways to lead to Andrew's dismissal. *Lord, Lord, please help me see the path You've laid before me. Please.*

She strained to hear even a whisper from the Lord, but she only heard the call of a loon, flying toward the lake.

Chapter Twenty

On the way out of the dining hall that evening, Andrew brushed by Katherine and slipped a tightly folded paper into her hand. Her pulse quickening, she eased it into the folds of her skirt, excused herself, and made her way to her cabin.

Safely inside, she unfolded the paper and read the note.

> I've received important information from Marston Voyles. If you're able, take your swim tomorrow morning to reach Pine Point by 7 a.m. I'll be waiting.

With thoughts of her father's subtle threats about firing Andrew alive in her mind, she shredded the note and tossed the strips into the wastebasket.

Early the next morning Katherine waited for Aunt Letty to leave for breakfast before she donned her bathing costume, a black wool dress with a white sailor collar, big bow, stockings, and slippers. She assumed Andrew would walk to their meeting place, and given that she liked to take morning swims, no one would think twice about her heading west along the shore—nor would they consider she might be meeting up with Andrew at the thickly wooded, secluded peninsula.

As she rolled up one of her black stockings, a large rip down the front caught her eye. Apparently Bridget had forgotten to mend it. Katherine pulled it off and searched through her bureau drawers for another pair. But she couldn't find more thick black stockings of the type she wore for swimming.

The mantel clock struck six forty-five. If she was late, he might be gone by the time she arrived. He didn't dare arrive later than eight for work, especially now with her parents on edge about his interest in her. Katherine huffed. She'd have to go bare-legged and hope no one spotted her and reported back to Mama. No lady appeared without stockings in public, even garbed in a calf-length bathing dress and bloomers. She'd just have to chance it. She simply had to know what he'd heard from Marston Voyles. And truth be told, she was dying to see him. To verify a certain inkling in her heart . . .

She slipped out of her cabin and glanced around the yard, still deeply shaded and deserted. Rushing across the small patch of lawn to the beach, she glanced back and breathed easier when she didn't see anyone. Without tarrying a moment longer, she hastened to the narrow strip of beach.

Without wind to ruffle the water, the lake shone like a sheet of blue tinted glass. All around its edge, forested hills and mountains rose, one behind the other, into the distance. Birds twittered in the branches of yellow birch trees that hugged the shore, and bushy-tailed squirrels skittered across the lawn and scrambled up tree trunks.

Gingerly she stepped across the coarse strip of sand and into the crystal clear water, immediately invigorated by its chill. She hugged her chest as goose bumps broke out on her arms. She waded out into the chilly water and dived in. When she'd rounded the corner, she spotted Andrew in the distance, swimming toward Pine Point, and she began treading water, wondering if this was a mistake. She'd been certain he'd walked . . . What if someone saw him head out, and then her following?

She looked back over her shoulder, remembering the vacant yard, the guests likely to still be slumbering for some time yet. With luck, no one had seen either of them. Committing, she settled into her breaststroke, enjoying the feel of the water and the exercise—in her opinion, the perfect way to begin any day.

Ten minutes later she reached the peninsula. When she spotted Andrew resting in the sun on a giant boulder by the foot-wide strip of sandy dirt, she waved. Invigorated but shivering, she waded toward shore.

He came forward, took her hand, and helped her over the rocks and protruding tree roots. His arms and legs, usually covered by his shirt and trousers, displayed strong muscles and pale blond hair lightly covering his tanned skin. He wore a bathing costume with fashionable navy blue and white stripes, which exposed more flesh than she usually saw on a man. Although standards at camp were more relaxed, Mama would never approve of this secret rendezvous. Not that she'd approve of any rendezvous at all with him, so what option did she have?

She leaned against the sun-warmed boulder and noticed his brows were furrowed. "I'm glad you could come, Katherine. I looked for a few moments to speak to you alone last night, but you were always surrounded by a crowd."

She nodded. "I'm afraid I can't stay long, so we must be

quick. What did Marston say? I've been so worried I could hardly sleep last night."

"He sent me a telegram late yesterday. He says Harriet is on her way to Raquette Lake. She might even be here already."

Katherine lifted her hand to her chest and felt her heart racing.

He reached out and gently took her other hand. "You must be prepared to meet her—unless you'd like me to go in your place. I'd be glad to take care of all this for you."

She clasped his hand. "Thank you. I've been thinking about that a lot lately and trying to decide."

"And?"

She sighed. "I want to meet her in person. I'm curious about what she's like." Katherine pictured her as a scarlet woman, a femme fatale.

"Are you certain she won't upset you?" he asked, pressing her hand.

"No, I'm not at all sure. But I'm afraid if you went in my place, Papa would miss you. How would explain your absence?"

He shrugged off her concern. "Don't worry about me. I can take care of myself. It's you I'm worried about."

She smiled, not a bit surprised he placed her welfare above his own. "I just want this meeting with Harriet to be over and done with." Shuddering, she crossed her arms over the bodice of her wet bathing costume.

He pulled her toward him and wrapped her tightly in his embrace. She warmed in the comfort of his arms and nestled her head against the top of his damp swimming suit. Her mind spun, knowing that if they were caught, there'd be a steep price to pay. But her heart won out. *He cares for me. He truly cares.*

She forced herself to ease away, feeling their parting like a physical tear, and the tears came too fast to curb them. "Forgive me," she said, wiping them away in embarrassment. "My whole world is crashing down on me at once, and you're the only one who truly understands how I feel."

"I'm glad you know that." His eyes didn't leave hers, and he smiled with more fondness than she'd ever seen in anyone's gaze before. He wasn't bothered by her messy, dripping hair half concealed by a ruffled cap, or the soggy frock, or even her bare legs.

Her bare legs. She fought the desire to turn and hide them. In the moment, she'd completely forgotten that she was without stockings. Her scar, bright red and thick as dress cording, stood out against the white of her legs. But he didn't stare at her disfigurement.

Her tears stopped as suddenly as they had begun and she stared up at him in wonder. "Thank you for not caring," she murmured.

"What are you talking about? I *do* care, Katherine, very much." He looked puzzled.

"But not about my scar. You hardly noticed." She pointed toward it, silently daring him to look. His gaze traveled right to it, but he didn't flinch.

"Katherine, someday you'll tell me about how you got that. But you need to know—you're beautiful to me, every bit of you."

"Thank you." Tears blocked her throat again; she blinked them back. Her eyes lingered over his mouth and she yearned to press his lips against her own. She moved closer, but then her better judgment forced her to step away.

"I ought to go back before anyone catches us together." Glancing toward camp, she glimpsed two tiny figures standing at the edge of the pier. From the height of the two she guessed they were Mama and Mrs. Clarke, though they were too far away to be certain.

Andrew's gaze followed hers. "You'd best go now. I'll wait until you lead them away."

Katherine nodded. She tucked her hair into her mop cap and waded into the water. She took slow, easy strokes, but she arrived back at camp much too soon. Pasting on a smile, she trudged toward the beach and lifted her chin. But her heart still pounded with the powerful beat of what she'd nearly done.

"Hello, Mama, Mrs. Clarke." Katherine picked up a towel she'd left lying on a rock, dried her arms from her elbows to her wrists, and then patted her face and blotted her hair. As she dried off, she waited for them to explain why they'd come looking for her when they knew she'd soon join them for breakfast.

When she looked up, Katherine noticed her mother's jutting jaw and cool, appraising expression. Her eyes narrowed when she saw that Katherine had gone out without stockings. "We'd like a few words with you, dear," Mama said with a sniff.

"I assumed so, given that you could hardly wait for me to even return from my morning constitution."

Mrs. Clarke stretched up to her full height, towering over Mama. "Katherine, we'd like to encourage you to speak to Randy as soon as possible. You've delayed long enough that keeping company 'over the summer' only leaves several precious weeks. There really is no room for further delay. He's counting on you."

His pampered ego would take a dreadful beating, but Katherine felt sure if she rejected him, he'd regain his pride and optimism soon enough. He never seemed to care about anything intensely enough to stay dispirited for long.

When Katherine didn't reply quickly, Mama raised a warning brow. "What do you have to say for yourself, Katherine? You know the consequences of—"

"I spoke to Papa," she interrupted, "and he told me what would happen to Andrew if I refused. That's unconscionable, Mama."

Her mother's face flamed. "Be that as it may, you now understand the penalty for rebelling. And you're getting off the subject."

Katherine turned and walked up the hill, the women following behind her.

"We are only looking out for the happiness of our children," Mrs. Clarke said in a more conciliatory tone. "I deeply believe that once you allow Randy access to your heart, you'll see what a fine young man he is. He truly cares for you, my dear. And our Andrew . . . well, he will be fine. There is some other girl out there for him."

Katherine supposed Randy did care for her, in his own way. But she feared his affection lacked real depth. But so did her own. What a terrible situation their parents had forced upon them. Her impulse to challenge Mama grew stronger by the second. But she couldn't endanger Andrew's position at the railroad.

She cleared her throat and looked skyward. "I'll talk to Randy again. But I must speak to Andrew first. He deserves an explanation."

Mama nodded. "If you must, I suppose it's all right. But be brief. I'll not have camp tongues wagging about you two flirting. It's unseemly."

"I won't, Mama." They'd reached her cabin and she turned to face them.

"I'm relieved you've finally come to your senses." Mama managed a small smile and rubbed Katherine's arm. "I'm sorry you don't realize we're only encouraging you to make the right decision. Getting to know Randy in a more serious way will certainly bring you the most happiness."

Katherine fought the urge to pull away from her mother. "I do hope and pray you're right, because if you're not, you'll be ruining two lives." And Andrew's made three.

That evening Katherine followed the crowd to the beach where an enormous bonfire blazed and sent orange and red flames shooting upward into the blackening sky. The fire snapped and crackled and nearly drowned out the quiet wash of dark water gliding over rough sand and stones. She watched Andrew toss another log onto the pyre. He glanced her way as she wove through the tangle of guests gathered in the firelight and smiled at her longingly, just as Mama said. He didn't hide his feelings well, but she'd hardly noticed before.

Maybe she hadn't *wanted* to notice because Andrew's obvious affection complicated an already thorny situation. Because part of it felt deeply familiar.

Randy motioned for her to sit beside him on a Muskoka chair while he strummed his mandolin. Dropping down, she watched Andrew turn to tend the fire and keep busy. He helped the footmen and gentlemen carry several benches and chairs from the lodge and the grounds. They placed them around the bonfire for the ladies to sit in comfort while Randy entertained with his music. The guests took their seats and settled down once he began to sing. Mama and Mrs. Clarke walked around insuring all the campers had chairs.

Mama's friends sang familiar tunes to the accompaniment of Randy's mandolin. His rich tenor voice soothed like flowing honey. He led one song after another, his voice rising above the weak and reedy voices of several of the ladies. Some of the men's voices boomed off-key, though most sounded just plain loud.

Randy was as animated as Katherine had ever seen him. He sang well-known hymns and let the singers choose their favorites. He knew them all. Katherine wondered how he managed to remember at least four verses of every hymn since he seldom attended church. Or at least she thought he didn't. But in the eight years they'd been apart perhaps he'd developed an unexpected liking for church music.

Randy belted out "Rock of Ages" and "Shall We Gather at the River?" Everyone sang with gusto and some with obvious devotion. Later, the moon rose in a black velvet sky studded with twinkling stars. Katherine and Randy harmonized to several hymns they'd practiced earlier. After a while Randy stopped for a short break and drank down a tall glass of ginger beer to quench his thirst. The guests rose to mingle.

"Please excuse me," Katherine mumbled to Randy. She left before she heard his reply. Scanning the crowd for Andrew, she spotted him at the back of the circle. He grinned as she approached.

"Can we talk?" she asked him. He looked so hopeful she dreaded telling him she'd decided to accept Randy's attentions. But she needed to explain before he heard the news from someone else. He leaned closer. "But what about your parents?"

"They approved a brief conversation," she said.

Andrew squinted his eyes and nodded, a tiny smile at the corners of his lips. "Of course. I'd be delighted."

She knew he wouldn't be so pleased when she blurted out the reason for their tête-à-tête. They eased to the back of the group and then lowered onto a log near the border of the woods, well within sight of the bonfire and the crowd.

Katherine stretched out her legs and spread her skirt down over the tops of her black boots. They talked of the unusually balmy weather and a few other trivial topics before she mustered the courage to speak about the courtship.

"I need to talk to you about my future. This is hard for me, Andrew. I don't know where to begin." She'd never hint at her parents' threat to fire him because he might very well become angry enough to quit on the spot. And where would that get him?

If he overstepped, Papa would keep him from obtaining another legal position in New York, and probably anywhere else he applied. The tentacles of Papa's power spread across the country. If Mama nudged him, he wouldn't hesitate to use his influence. At first he might balk, but in the end he'd give in to Mama, just as he always did.

"Begin wherever you like, but please don't be afraid to tell me anything." Andrew dug the heel of his boot into the carpet of sparse grass and crumbled leaves. "You seem awfully hesitant. Is this some sort of bad news?"

"You might think so."

"Sometimes it's best to just come right out with what's on your mind." He cocked his head. "You'll feel better when you do."

Perhaps, but he certainly wouldn't. Katherine forced an unhappy smile.

When her gaze locked onto his, she felt such a rush of affection she couldn't bear to upset him. Her heart filled with—she couldn't say the word or even whisper it, but she knew what it was all the same. *Love.* The feelings washing through her couldn't possibly be anything less.

She'd never felt this way with Charles, who'd charmed her with his glib tongue and musical laugh. But his actions had never matched the selflessness of his silvery words. He talked a good story, but those words evaporated in the chill of reality. And she didn't have these warm—no, *sizzling*—feelings for Randy either.

Her mouth dropped open as she stared at him, any words leaving her head.

"What is it, Katherine?" Andrew asked as Randy began to sing "A Bicycle Built for Two." The rest of the crowd joined in the old favorite and several swayed to the beat of the music.

"I should go now," she said, but more than anything she wanted to stay.

"But you haven't told me what you brought me here to say," he said, leaning closer to her. From the hungry look in his eyes, she knew he fought his urge to take her in his arms and kiss her with the passion she craved. And so did she.

But she wouldn't deceive Andrew. They'd never be together and he mustn't believe they would. She'd not let her heart rule her, though she felt her resistance melting away. She wouldn't embarrass her parents again. And more importantly, she wouldn't jeopardize Andrew's career.

Andrew glanced over his shoulder at the bonfire. "May I walk you to your cabin?" he asked.

She nodded. Together they left the edge of the woods. Andrew guided her across the night-shaded lawn until they reached the front door of her cabin. Only the moon and a dusting of stars gave off dim illumination as they faced each other. The balmy air wrapped around her like satin streamers. She drank in the scent of cedar and fir trees and the pungent smoke wafting from the bonfire.

"It's a beautiful evening," she murmured. "But there's something I should say." *Or I'll let you kiss me and then everything will become infinitely more complicated.*

"Katherine, I—I'd like to say . . ." Andrew halted, grimaced, and shook his head. "I don't know the right words." Instead of continuing to stumble over his message, he moved quickly, bending forward and pressing his mouth against hers.

The kiss stole her breath. She answered his gentle force by reveling in the taste of his soft lips; his arms clasped her waist and gently urged her toward him. And when it ended, Katherine let a sigh escape. They moved so close, not even the mild breeze flowed between them.

Placing her palms on his broad chest, she glanced into his eyes, then around, making sure no one was about, then back to him. "We shouldn't do this." Her ragged voice sounded weak and unconvincing. She wanted to ignore her silly objections and return his kisses with the ardor overflowing her heart.

"There's nothing wrong with kissing if we're both in love." Then he stopped and gazed down at her with both hope and dread in his eyes. "*Are* we in love?"

Chapter Twenty-One

Andrew held his breath, waiting for Katherine's response. Her head dropped down, and in the dim light he couldn't see her features. But he noted her sagging shoulders and heard her sigh above the hum of the crickets.

"Andrew, I—how I wish . . ." She took a step away, putting her hands behind her back and tucking her chin.

"Ah." He held up his palm. "So that's what you had to tell me. There's no need to explain, Katherine. I understand." He fought to keep his feelings under control, but he burned with frustration and mounting anger. He hadn't misunderstood the passion between them, the yearning in her eyes. Why did she have to cave in to her parents' pressure? Now? After all these years? He understood the risks well—Mr. Wainwright had made his desires plain. And employees who did not support Mr. Wainwright's goals never lasted long in his company. But money and position meant nothing to Andrew, compared to having her.

He kissed the top of her head and inhaled the sweetness of her hair, struggling to control his feelings. He spoke softly, barely above a whisper. "I should be going. But I can't leave before I tell you something."

She nodded and then glanced toward her closed door, clearly anxious to get away.

"Katherine, I love you with all my heart and I always have. It seems nothing will come of it, but I need you to know. If there is any way we can be together . . ."

She opened her mouth to speak, but nothing emerged except a strangled moan. A moment later she gently touched his arm. "Andrew," she said, her voice choked. "I'm so sorry. For both of us."

He stared at her in confusion. "You're going to accept Randy's courtship," he said dully.

"You don't understand," she said.

"No," he said, shaking his head, "I don't."

Twin tears ran down her cheeks, glimmering in the moonlight. Had it been just this morning that she had cried, but with nothing but joy and love in her eyes? How could he have been so wrong?

"Good night, Andrew," she said. "I'll pray for you." With an unsteady hand, she unlocked the cabin door. As soon as she vanished inside, he strode off toward the lodge, his head lowered. A searing pain cut through his entire body. *You're a fool, Andrew Townsend.* After all, he'd always known her mother wouldn't allow her to choose him over any of the richer and more prominent men. But, somehow, he thought she'd stand up to her mother and answer the call they obviously both felt.

He had grasped for someone way out of his league. Well, he was human, wasn't he? He couldn't help who he found attractive. But he'd get over her, he hoped. He'd done so before and he'd do so again. He had no alternative. And he definitely wouldn't sulk about life's inequalities and unfairness. He had so much to be grateful for. Usually.

When he arrived at the deserted chalet, he knew he didn't want to return to his bedroom. The last person he wanted to run into right now was Randy. He turned on his heel and settled onto a path, hoping a walk would dispel some of the tension mounting in his chest. With only the moonlight to guide him, he hiked down the trail closest to the lodge, not caring that he could barely see a step ahead, a million questions in his head. Why hadn't he swept her up and kissed her until she admitted she loved him too? He sighed. *Because I can't ask her to give up everything for me.* He had so little to give in return, except love.

Had he acted cowardly by not letting her decide? But then, hadn't she really decided in that moment? He'd told her he loved her and all she could say in return was, "I'm so sorry . . ." Too many thoughts and emotions roiled through him. He needed to go back and put Katherine out of his mind for a while.

Maybe he should find Aunt Letty and together they could give Katherine the news about the money they'd cobbled together to pay off Charles's debt. Maybe then she'd decide to return to Florida instead of letting Randy court her. But he feared he and Aunt Letty were too late with their offer to make any difference. For some reason she felt cornered, unable to do anything but accept his cousin's pursuit. His eyes narrowed. Had it all simply become too much for her to battle? The combined loans? Harriet's impending arrival? Her parents' constant pressure?

He walked down the path toward the bonfire in search of Aunt Letty, but she was not among the group any longer. Perhaps she'd returned to the cabin. Desperate for diversion, he turned and moved back up to the lodge and entered the library.

The gaslights burned dimly in the darkened room. He yanked Verne's *Twenty Thousand Leagues Under the Sea* off the bookshelf. It should hold his interest well enough, at least for a while. Settling into a soft chair, he lit the kerosene lamp on the end table, rested his legs on the hassock, and opened to the first page. Footsteps by the door caught his attention.

"May I join you, Andrew?" Randy called as he stepped over the threshold and strolled across the bearskin rug, mandolin in hand.

"If you'd like." He didn't want company, and Randy was the last person he wished to see.

Randy plopped on a nearby sofa. "A book would put me to sleep in seconds."

"Hmm." Andrew waited for his cousin to get to the point.

"My mother says Katherine is close to letting me court her, but I'm not so sure. What do you think?" Randy paused and looked over to him.

Andrew's jaw clenched. "I don't know. But I suppose she's right."

"I don't know why she's stalling."

"Can't you think of any reason?" He must know Katherine didn't want to marry anyone, especially a fellow she didn't love. She might believe she wanted a safe, boring marriage, but obviously her hesitation suggested otherwise.

Randy shrugged. "Maybe she hasn't gotten over Charles. It's hard to compete with memories of the dearly departed. But it's time she moved on. With me."

"You told me only a short time ago that you yourself weren't ready for marriage."

"Actually, I'm not. But according to my parents, one never feels quite ready for such things, and I ought to take the plunge. And given that Katherine is their choice—and mine, of course— and our paths have once again converged, it seems rather fated. Can you think of a more perfect match?"

One or two . . .

"I take it you don't object."

Andrew stared hard at his cousin, fury building in his chest. Why was he pressing him so? "Why would I?"

"Because you might wish to marry her yourself." Randy raised black eyebrows over equally dark eyes.

"We all know she's going to marry you eventually. It's practically settled."

"But not quite settled. I saw you two leave the bonfire together and I wondered . . ." Randy stopped and sniffed. "Forgive me, cousin. It appears I actually am feeling some sort of jealousy. Imagine that." The crease in Randy's forehead smoothed into wide-eyed surprise and wonder. "It's getting late so I think I'll turn in. Good night."

Andrew nodded and watched his cousin depart. A hollow ache took over his heart. So it was done. He was a dreamer, a fool . . .

But then a thought made him sit up straight. *There was one more thing . . .*

Aunt Letty chugged into the cabin. "Wasn't that bonfire delightful? Randy Clarke has the loveliest singing voice." She placed her new straw hat rimmed with silk daisies and feathers on the hat stand in the dressing room. "I'd love a cup of hot milk. It'll help me sleep. And maybe a nice piece of lemon meringue pie or perhaps a dish of Cook's vanilla ice cream. Will you join me, dear?"

Katherine nodded. She glanced at the clock. It was only ten thirty, and given the way her emotions whirled within her heart, she wasn't ready for bed just yet. Sleeping was out of the question when all her conflicting thoughts and feelings bounced off the walls of her mind. "Of course. Shall we go?"

They strolled down the darkened walkways and entered the kitchen. Cook and her assistant were baking muffins for tomorrow's breakfast.

Aunt Letty placed her order. "We'll eat in the dining hall."

The young girl hurried ahead and lit a few gaslights to give off dim illumination. "Is this bright enough, ma'am?" she asked.

"It's fine," Aunt Letty replied. She and Katherine settled into wooden chairs at the long table with a country-style tablecloth of blue and white checks. The sugar bowl and salt and pepper shakers were laid out for breakfast.

The long, cavernous room had a cozy feel, despite its size. As soon as the maid served the hot milk and pie, Aunt Letty dug in with gusto. "My, this is delicious." She looked toward the young serving girl and grinned her angelic smile that must have once stolen the hearts of many beaux, including Uncle Norman. "Do tell Cook she outdid herself. Again."

Katherine sipped her cup of tea and watched her elderly aunt eat.

Aunt Letty lowered her fork after a few bites. "May I speak frankly, my dear?"

"Yes, please do."

Aunt Letty leaned across the table. "I think you've been mulling over your friendship with Randy and you can't make up your mind what to do." When Katherine didn't comment, Aunt Letty continued, "I know there are a fistful of obstacles standing between you and Andrew. Personally, I believe those are ridiculous barriers."

"Andrew?" Katherine's asked, surprised as how quickly Aunt Letty changed the subject.

"Yes, my dear. It's obvious you two are in love. Only you won't face your feelings."

Katherine lowered her gaze. "As you said, there would be many difficulties to overcome."

Aunt Letty shook her head sadly. "If you're not deter-mined, those obstacles are nearly insurmountable. But if there's a will, there's a way. That's what they say. And there's truth to it, I believe." Her sympathetic eyes narrowed. "I noticed Randy watched as you wandered off with Andrew Townsend."

Katherine blushed. "I should have stayed with the group, I know. But Mama and Papa knew I needed to speak to Andrew."

"Yes, if you're concerned with propriety, you should have. But you never were—were you?" Her face belonged to a merry elf, full of mischief.

"No. But I should've been. And I'm trying to conform more than I used to. No more childish lapses." Though it turned out marriage to Charles was far worse than a mere childish lapse.

Aunt Letty waved away Katherine's comment. "Nonsense. You must do as you see fit, not what your mother or society demand. Of course, since I'm a Christian woman, I always con-sult the good Lord first to see what He advises. And if He's clear enough, I follow His will without hesitation. He's never led me astray so far, and I'm well near eighty. You'd do well to listen to Him too." Letty ate another forkful of pie and looked up at Katherine.

She nodded. "I do listen, Aunt Letty."

She cocked her head. "And what does He tell you about Randy?"

Katherine paused, taken aback by her great-aunt's direct ques-tion. "Actually, He tells me absolutely nothing."

"Just as I thought. But I imagine He does say something about Andrew."

A flash of heat rushed to Katherine's cheeks. Squirming in the hard, ladder-back chair, she struggled for an answer. "The only message I can discern is to follow my heart. And Andrew is my heart. But of course, that's really out of the question."

Aunt Letty shook her head, "Oh no, my dear, it's really not. But you must have courage to claim the man God has for you. It won't be as easy as settling for someone else's choice, but much more satisfying in the long run."

Katherine rose. "Be that as it may, I'm not sure I have the strength to see it through."

Was it wrong to accept society's values when everyone except Aunt Letty and Andrew encouraged her to do so? She'd have to decide once and for all, although right now she felt drained from too many conflicting emotions.

Letty finished her pie and pushed aside the plate. She rose and took Katherine's arm. "You'll find your way, dear," she said, patting Katherine. "I have every confidence in you."

"I'm glad you do, Auntie," Katherine said. "I'm afraid you're the only one left who does." They moved to the dining hall door, and just before they reached it, Andrew stepped inside.

"I'm glad I finally found the two of you together. Would you sit a moment with me?" He gestured toward a table.

"Oh, it's so late. And we were about to leave, Andrew." Katherine glanced toward the door, clearly looking for an escape.

"Not before your aunt and I tell you something."

Aunt Letty lifted her chin. "Ah. Yes, indeed. Let's all sit down. Perhaps you'd enjoy a piece of pie, Andrew."

"No thank you. I'm not hungry."

He dropped into a chair across the table from Aunt Letty and Katherine. Her gaze darted all over the room but never lighted on him. She must feel terribly awkward after his declaration of love. He did too, but he couldn't postpone this meeting.

He leaned across the table. "Aunt Letty and I have found

two investors—friends, actually—who are very interested in the Osborne Citrus Groves. They'd like to invest some money. They're not interested in purchasing the groves, just in invest-ing." He swallowed the dryness in his throat, poured himself a glass of water from the pitcher on the table, and took a long sip. He knew he didn't sound convincing, and Katherine's suspicious eyes and tilted head confirmed it.

"How much do they wish to invest?" she asked.

"Forty thousand dollars. Your aunt and I think this is a splen-did opportunity for you to pay off your debt to the bank and—"

She stood up and pressed her fingertips against the table. "This sounds awfully coincidental to me."

"What makes you say that, Katherine dear?" Aunt Letty's eyes grew rounder as she looked at her, but then she buried her shame in her teacup.

Andrew cleared his throat. He should've thought longer and harder about a plausible story before he blurted it out. "I can assure you we can get the money together."

She shook her head and pulled in the corner of her mouth. "You two are the investors. I'm glad your lives don't depend upon it, because fibbing is not your forte."

Aunt Letty's shriveled cheeks blushed crimson while she stumbled for words. "Whatever makes you think Andrew and I are involved?"

"Let's start with the guilt written all over your faces."

Aunt Letty drew out a sigh. "We're merely trying to give you more options. If you pay off Charles's loan, then you can return to Florida to your business, with or without your parents' blessing."

"I still agreed to remain here through August in exchange for the harvest loan. And now there's the matter of the buildings . . ."

"*Pshaw*," Aunt Letty said. "As I said, your parents won't be pleased, but what could they do? They would not call your loans.

They wouldn't leave you destitute, homeless. Have some gumption, girl! Follow your heart!"

Katherine shifted her weight and wrung her hands.

Andrew stood up too. "Look, we can't let you toss away your future, Katherine, not when we can help prevent it."

"I'm grateful, and I thank you both from the bottom of my heart. But I can't take a penny from either one of you. Aunt Letty, you need all your money. And, Andrew, if you loaned me the funds, you'd be turning over all you've saved for the last few years."

"But we want to help," Andrew insisted.

Katherine shook her head vehemently. "I can't have you two paying off Charles's loan for the same reason I didn't ask Papa to help me. I married Charles, and his debts are my responsibility, no one else's."

Aunt Letty slowly rose. "Katherine, I admire your strength and determination. But you'll be forced to sell your company if you don't pay in full within a few short days. You must allow us to assist you and right away. You can't afford to dither or wring your hands. Or let your pride stand in your way."

Katherine's shoulders sagged. "I know I don't have many choices."

Aunt Letty planted her hands on her ample hips, gaining steam. "You'll lose your business and then you'll have to live with your parents until they make life so uncomfortable you'll find marriage to just about anyone an improvement. Do you think your mother will let you remain at home as a widow? Certainly not. Even if you turn Randy down, she'll throw another young man she deems suitable at you. Is that what you want?"

"No, of course not. But I won't have you two sacrificing your money for me."

"We want to," Andrew said softly. Clearly she wasn't going to accept their offer. *At least not tonight.*

The door swung open, and Mr. Wainwright and Mr. Clarke stepped through the entranceway.

Mr. Wainwright's eyes widened in shock and then displeasure, seeing the three of them together. Andrew subtly winced.

"Andrew, ladies," he said with a genteel nod.

"Mr. Wainwright," Andrew returned, refusing to back down with his gaze. If he loved Katherine, if he wanted to fight for her, he had to be able to face his boss. But he knew that his fate was now sealed. Even with Aunt Letty present, he'd gone against Mr. Wainwright's wishes and sought out his daughter.

And that won't settle well with him.

"Andrew, you're up late," Mr. Wainwright said, frowning. "Better turn in or sunrise will come earlier than you'd like."

"Agreed, sir," he said.

"Thank you for joining us, Andrew," Letty said. "I'm sorry we intruded upon the solace of your evening." She gave him a small smile that only he could see. *The old girl's a conspirator in more ways than one, God bless her . . .*

"Oh, no, Mrs. Benham. It wasn't an intrusion at all. Good evening."

Chapter Twenty-Two

Randy sat on the end of the dock, dangling his legs in the quiet water. His line didn't move. The sunshine brought out blue-black highlights in his hair. When he saw Katherine, he grinned. "Come join me. The water is warm. Relatively."

She'd changed into a pretty new lace dress made in featherweight, finely woven lawn that Mama had given her. High at the neck, it boasted ruffles and ribbons on the bodice. Her hair, secured with silver combs, was loosely piled upon her head and tendrils curled at the sides of her face. She raised a matching white parasol to shade her from the noon sunlight.

"My, you look stunning today—not that you don't every day. New dress?" His slanted eyes glinted with admiration.

"Yes, it is."

He viewed her with an appreciative gaze. "Much improved over all those prairie frocks you wore when you first came here."

Katherine blushed. "I didn't realize you noticed such things." He at least ought to keep his disparaging opinions to himself.

Since she couldn't very well sit on the rough dock in her lovely dress, she continued to stand. Reluctantly, it seemed, Randy rose, dried off his feet, and brushed off his rolled-up trousers. "Shall we sit on the bench by the boathouse?" he asked.

They strolled back to the wooden bench, partially shaded by overhanging tree branches. They took their seats close together, but she kept several inches between them. A mild breeze blew in from the lake and stirred the small birch leaves overhead. A few birds sang; a seagull dove into the water for a fish. They watched canoeists paddle by and a steam yacht pass in the distance.

Randy touched Katherine's hand lightly. "Have you thought any more about us?" He asked in an offhanded manner, but he sounded unusually tense as well.

"I have. I've given it a great deal of thought. Courting is too important to jump into headlong without praying about it first." And weighing all advantages and disadvantages carefully.

"Praying? You actually pray about courtship?" He pulled on his mustache and frowned. "I've never heard of such a thing, but I suppose it's a good idea," he murmured.

"Yes, I've come to decide I should pray about all the important decisions in my life."

"And the Lord told you I should be your suitor. I'm right, aren't I?"

Not exactly. His light tone mocked her a bit, but she ignored it. She looked deep into his dark eyes. Instead of seeing hope and affection, she found anxiety, maybe even fear. Katherine paused. Such undercurrents didn't mesh with Randy's normal lackadaisical personality. Was his love for her so strong he couldn't abide a rejection? That idea was laughable. He cared for her, but not in any deep, selfless way.

"Well, Katherine, you've kept me in suspense for weeks. It's high time you answer. May I court you?" The edge in his voice gave her pause. Why did her answer make him so tense?

She tried to add a dash of levity by smiling, but she could barely curve her lips. "Yes, you may." Horrified at the flat tone in her own voice, she broadened her grin. Her acceptance relaxed her own tight muscles, but unfortunately, not a bit of peace or joy flowed to her heart.

His frown vanished, but his emerging smile seemed almost grim. "Splendid. I'm sure we'll make an excellent couple. We'll be quite happy, I'm sure."

"Yes, of course we shall." Hadn't their mothers reminded them of their suitability often enough? But why didn't he say he loved her? Maybe the thought never occurred to him. Of course she didn't love him deeply either, so she shouldn't expect more from him. Only she did. She wanted so much more than friendship.

She yearned for love, just not the passionate, reckless kind she once felt for Charles. She wanted the sort of love that would sustain her over a lifetime. But who actually experienced such lasting joy? Aunt Letty and Uncle Norman perhaps, though they were exceptional. And maybe Mama and Papa. Who was she trying to deceive? Herself? The overwhelming feelings pushing her toward Andrew were definitely more than tame affection. They were passionate, with a force she'd never encountered before.

But this is right, she told herself. *This is what I must do. For the sake of us all . . .*

Randy leaned over and planted an unexpected kiss on Katherine's cheek and then brushed his mouth against hers. Cold and disagreeably moist, she shuddered at the feel of his lips. Gently, she moved her head away and rose.

Instinctively she knew they both felt disappointed. She'd hoped kissing him, when it happened, would kindle a fire inside her, a love she didn't expect. Even a spark would encourage her to hope that, in time, their lifelong affection would blossom into real love. But instead, nothing happened. Nor, she admitted to herself, would it ever.

Randy was still only her childhood friend. Was taking this step toward an engagement, and ultimately marriage, another disastrous mistake she'd learn to regret? But wasn't it worth sacrificing for Andrew? He'd marry her without considering all he'd lose in the bargain. She couldn't let that happen. He was much too dear to her.

Randy pressed her hand. "Shall we go inside and tell our families?"

"In a few moments. I have something I should tell you. It's a bit difficult, I'm afraid."

"Tell me about it, Katherine," he urged.

She wondered if it might be a mistake to share the secret about Harriet and Charles, but even as a suitor, he ought to know about the aspects of her marriage that still affected her life. "All right, but please don't repeat any of this because it's very personal." She took a deep breath and exhaled slowly. "While Charles and I were married, he had a love affair with a woman named Harriet. They had a son. I've heard from her recently because now she and her child are short of funds. Harriet wants me to help support the boy."

Tugging at the corner of his bristly mustache, Randy leaned back. "You don't say. I'd never have thought. My goodness, Katherine, are you sure you're right?"

She nodded. "I'm not mistaken. Anyway, I'm waiting to hear from her."

"You mean you're writing to the woman? You ought to ignore her demands. She has an unbelievable nerve asking you for money after what she did. She's getting exactly what she deserves—poverty for her sin."

Surprised to hear Randy speak of sin, she wasn't shocked that he advised her to ignore the woman's plea. "It's the boy I feel sorry for, not the mother." Maybe she should feel some compassion for Harriet, but she couldn't. Fulfilling her Christian duty was the most she could manage.

Randy sounded exasperated. "Yes, of course you feel sympathy for their plight, but he's not your responsibility. There are charities to take care of the poor and indigent. You needn't worry. Once you give her even a small amount, she'll come back and demand more. She'll drain you dry in no time."

"Maybe you're right, but I'd like to give her something to tide her over until she gets a job."

Randy touched her hand. "You're so generous and kind. Too kind, I'm afraid." His dark eyes narrowed to slits. "What do your parents suggest you do?"

She gulped. "Actually, I haven't spoken to them. I thought I'd handle this myself."

"Hmm." He frowned and squeezed her hands with too much pressure. "You should reconsider. They both have good sense. They wouldn't lead you astray."

They'd insist Papa handle the situation. He'd subtly pressure Harriet to give up her claim, or maybe he'd buy her off with a few dollars. Either way, she'd never meet the woman and her son. But for some perverse reason, she wondered if meeting them would finally end the ugly chapter of her life. Still, the idea of meeting Harriet in person was more than she wanted to face. Fortunately she didn't have to. Andrew promised to take care of it for her.

"Well, of course I'll think about telling Mama and Papa. But I have to consider how this news will upset them. I'll have to wait for the right time." Regret slithered through her. She should've solved this on her own without breathing a word to Randy.

"Shall we go tell our families the good news?" he asked. "They'll want to know we're courting."

She forced a smile. "By all means."

Taking her hand, they strolled back to the chalet without saying a word.

———

That evening at dinner the Wainwrights let it be known that Randy was courting Katherine and intimated that an engagement was in the offing. The merriment grew boisterous. From the smiles of approval all around, nobody seemed to question it.

But Andrew wanted to slip away from the celebration. He was tired of grinning and pretending good wishes to a couple with little real interest in each other—at least not the kind that sustained a lifetime together. Yet he knew he was already on tenuous ground with his boss. Mr. Wainwright would not look kindly upon any action that diminished this moment.

Both Katherine and Randy held stiff smiles throughout the meal. Andrew lost his appetite for the delicious beef Wellington, and he couldn't finish the custard tart they served for dessert, though any other time he would dig right in. When the ladies departed for the lodge, the men lingered for cigars and brandy. He didn't smoke, and the thick smell swirling toward the beamed ceiling threatened to choke him, but he stayed at the table and made an occasional comment about business matters, which normally held his attention. Tonight they seemed trivial and irritating.

As soon as the group rejoined the ladies for a few hours of entertainment, Andrew was finally able to plead a headache and excuse himself. He threaded his way through the lounge and before climbing the stairs noticed a group had gathered around Katherine and Randy at the piano. They sang with good spirit while she tapped out one popular song after another. No one seemed to take any notice of him as he climbed the stairs to the second floor.

———

Two hours later he gave up reading and tossed his book onto his bed. He hastened down the back staircase and outside into the dark night. A cool breeze blew from the lake and whistled lightly in his ears as he started across the darkened yard. He took care not to trip over branches and old pinecones that intermingled with clumps of grass.

Moonlight cast a silvery net over the water. Stars flickered like candle flames across the black sky before wispy clouds blocked them from view. The music drifting through the screened windows of the lounge faded as he drew closer to the bridge leading to the gazebo.

For a long time he sat on a bench and watched the inky waters wash toward shore, gurgling as they lapped over the gritty sand. At the sound of footsteps, Andrew turned his head. Gliding across the yard was a slender figure in white.

Katherine.

Heart pounding, he cleared away his gloomy thoughts and rose. A few seconds later she was at his side. Shivering, she wrapped her shawl tightly around her shoulders and chest.

Why was she venturing out in the night without some sort of chaperone? Surely Randy would notice her absence and come looking for her. But try as he might, Andrew couldn't find the gumption to send her away.

"I'm glad I found you." She dropped onto a bench beside him. "I wanted to ask how you're feeling." She glanced down at her hands.

He made little effort to suppress a grimace. "Obviously I'm not thrilled my cousin has won his bid to court you, but I accept your decision and wish you the best."

The temptation to reveal Randy's true reason for starting a courtship lay on the tip of Andrew's tongue. Randy didn't want to work for his father so he did what his mother urged him to do. It was as simple and as complicated as that. But he couldn't bring himself to betray his best friend and cousin.

But was he betraying Katherine by keeping silent? Maybe he shouldn't hide information that might alter her decision. He sensed it wouldn't make a difference anyway.

He reined in his feelings. "I was probably the only one in the dining hall who wasn't thrilled by the news." He couldn't help the downward twist of his mouth as he waited for her to speak. "You're doing what you think you have to do, but I can't say I understand *why* you're doing so. Not when there's another option."

Her shoulders slumped, all resistance gone. Feeling emboldened, he asked, "Why didn't you refuse your parents?"

Katherine's gaze searched his face as if she were trying to decide whether to open up to him. She sighed wearily. "It's complicated, Andrew."

"Tell me."

"I'm sorry, I can't explain, except to say the pressure is simply too great to do anything else." She paused. "But, Andrew, Randy and I are only courting. There may never be an engagement or a marriage." Her eyes slowly met his.

What was she trying to tell him? He ran his hand across his cheek. "Then why are you going through with this charade? Just tell your parents the truth. You're not interested in him. Surely your father doesn't expect you to pretend affection where there isn't any."

Katherine shook her head without hesitating. "I doubt he's

fond of the idea. But he'll go along with Mama as he always does. He'll sympathize with me. Yet in the end, he'll do her bidding."

"That's appalling," Andrew muttered. He hated to picture his mentor as a man ready to hurt his daughter rather than fight his wife's selfish agenda. "You're so courageous, Katherine. You've come through so much. But now you're bending to the pressure. I wish there was some way for me to help."

"Me too." She stared into his eyes and looked so lost, he longed to pull her into his arms. "We ought to go back," she said, glancing toward the lights burning bright in the windows. Her arm, wrapped in a soft knitted shawl, brushed his as she turned, sending a jolt through him. "I want you to know how much I appreciate what you've done for me, Andrew." Then she rose and left him, as if she were afraid of his reply.

"I tried to wait up for you last night, but sleep got the better of me." Aunt Letty glanced at her through the dressing table mirror as Katherine still snuggled in bed, groggy with sleep. The mantle clock ticked past eight o'clock.

Katherine sighed and stretched. "And I had a difficult time going to sleep. My mind was a whirlwind." The aroma of food cooking drifted from the kitchen only a few buildings away. Her mouth watered, but her stomach flipped with queasiness.

"I imagine so." Aunt Letty swallowed a sip of steaming coffee her maid had brought in from the dining hall. Deftly she fashioned her long white hair into a bun without Bridget's assistance.

Katherine lifted her head off the pillow and wiggled to an upright position. She felt rested, but no more prepared to face the day. With her future already set like a footprint in concrete, sadness threatened to overwhelm her.

"I'd like to talk to you, my dear, if you don't mind. Are you willing to listen to an old lady spout a bit of hard-won wisdom?" Letty's singsong voice and kind eyes nearly disappeared in a wry grin.

"I'm always ready to talk to you, Aunt Letty." Katherine slid her feet into slippers placed on the colorful rag rug between the twin beds. Katherine and Aunt Letty dropped onto the sofa by the fireplace.

From her box of loose photographs resting on the tea table, Letty retrieved two unframed and informal pictures. She held up the first *carte de visite*, a thin, paper photograph mounted on thicker paper card. The image was small, little more than two by three inches, and somewhat faded and unclear.

Considering how young Letty appeared in her skirt with wide hoops, it must have been taken at least forty years before. She stood beside her whiskered husband, Norman Benham, holding hands before the Roman coliseum. Her impish smile and obvious delight caught Katherine's attention. Most women looked serious and dignified in photographs, but not Letty. Then Letty handed her a second picture, taken many years later by the ocean. Her great-aunt directed the same happy look at Uncle Norman, who by then had lost most of his thick, curly hair and had gained a potbelly. Even more heartwarming, Norman's loving expression focused on his aging wife with as much fascination as he'd shown when they were still in the bloom of youth.

"These photographs bring back such happy memories." Letty gave the images one last wistful glance, tucked them back in the shiny ebony box, and let out a sigh. "Oh my, how I miss my Norman. We had a wonderful life together." Pausing, she tilted her head and gazed at Katherine. "I do hope you enjoy a happy marriage this time around. I may be a sentimental fool, but now that most of my life is behind me, I'm grateful for my memories. I hope you'll have the same. Sometimes that's all we have left at the end."

Katherine flinched, but she pasted on a smile to hide her discomfort. Aunt Letty's eyes seemed to pierce right through her facade.

"Katherine, I believe you have doubts about Randy. Grave misgivings." She leaned closer. Frown lines reappeared between Aunt Letty's eyebrows. Katherine braced herself for unpleasant advice. "Marriage without a dash of real passion won't bring you joy or even satisfaction. An arranged marriage isn't the answer. In the long run everyone needs love—an abundance of love. If you don't have it now with Randy, there's no guarantee you'll find it once you're married." She rubbed Katherine's hand. "Are you willing to take the gamble that love may never come?"

The morning chill suddenly warmed. Katherine ran her finger between her perspiring neck and the tight collar of her shirtwaist. "Yes, I'm willing to take a chance."

The blood drained from Aunt Letty's face and lips. "Was the pain you suffered so great in Act One that you're unwilling to risk it again in Act Two?"

Katherine stared at her aunt as if she'd slapped her, and she abruptly looked at her hands, twisting the folds of her skirt. Was that what drove her most of all? Fear?

"I'm so sorry things didn't work out well with Charles. But can you really live a happy, contented life without true devotion?" Aunt Letty asked in a soft but urgent tone.

Katherine forced a short laugh. "Don't most people? Very few couples experience true love, as you did." She looked to her aunt, begging her to let it go. "Randy is kind. He's fond of me. That's a form of devotion, at least." *And I've only agreed to court, not marry . . .*

She wasn't entirely convinced she could live happily, or even contentedly, without real love. Without it only family connections and family fortune would bind her to Randy—certainly not common interests. Or a shared dedication to the Lord that was even more important. But to risk her heart again . . . No, she didn't have the courage. To chase what she and Andrew were fighting would be very dangerous indeed.

"Katherine, we both know you're in love with Andrew." She reached out to hold her hands. "I can see it every time you're together. It's as plain as the blush in your cheeks."

Katherine paused for several seconds, unable to respond. Then she wrapped her arms around Aunt Letty's small but plump shoulders and hugged her tightly. "Thank you for the prayers and all your advice."

Letty pulled back and viewed her with deep affection. "You have the Lord to lead you. Consider your next steps with Randy very carefully, my dear. I'll pray even more fervently that you'll hear His voice. Will you seek His path?"

"I will."

"Good," she said, squeezing her hands. "Simply be honest and let your heart answer one question: What sort of love will bring you the most satisfaction when you're old and gray like me?" She smiled. "Then I'll be confident you'll know what to do."

Chapter Twenty-Three

Andrew bent over the billiard table, gauging his next shot, when the door to the recreation hall pushed open. Looking up, he saw Katherine scanning the grounds over her shoulder as if fearful she'd be seen, then slipping inside. She strode toward him, a letter in hand, a frown creasing her face.

He sucked in a deep breath, knowing there were likely only two reasons she'd seek him out today. And by the look on her face, it wasn't the reason he'd prayed for all night.

Katherine edged near. "I'm glad you're alone. I'd like this as private as possible."

"Of course." He placed his cue stick on the green baize table. The recreation hall was often crowded midafternoon, but today's warm, sunny weather drew most of the campers outside to the boats, tennis courts, and nature trails.

Katherine handed him the letter. "A boy from the Wayside Inn delivered this. It's from Harriet Roles. She's asking to meet with me." She pressed her palms against the rim of the table. "I both dread it and feel relieved it's finally upon us. I'd hoped to be calm and collected by the time I faced her, but I'm afraid my heart is pounding like a sledgehammer."

"I understand." He scanned the letter and returned it to Katherine. Harriet requested a meeting at four o'clock at the Wayside Inn, a modest tourist hotel on Raquette Lake.

"It's short notice, I know, but I'm anxious to get the payment settled, and I'm sure she is too," Katherine said.

"Do you still want to meet with her in person or would you like me to go in your place?" He didn't think Katherine should meet Harriet alone.

Katherine hesitated and then shook her head. "Thank you, but I should handle my own problems without help from"— pausing, Katherine's gaze locked on his—"my dearest friend."

Not the words he wished to hear, but exactly what he expected. How many times over the course of the last few weeks had she called him a friend? Too many. His colliding emotions dropped to the pit of his stomach like wooden cue balls. "All right. But let me at least row you to the inn. It's quite a distance, and you might get tired. Or the weather could turn."

She shook her head. He felt sure going alone was a mistake, yet he held back his frustration. "All right, I understand it might look inappropriate for me to accompany you. Why don't you ask Randy instead? If you explain the situation, I'm sure he'll be glad to lend you his support. Don't go through this completely alone, Katherine."

Her forehead creased. "No, I can't go to Randy. He's against me giving her anything. I'm sure he'd tell my parents, and I don't want them to know because they'd try to stop me. I'll explain everything to them later, after Harriet and I settle things."

"Maybe Randy would agree to keep this quiet for a while."

Katherine shook her head again. "No, I don't think so. Can't you understand why I need to do this by myself?" Her plaintive look tore at his heart. He wanted to sweep her into his arms and protect her from anything and anyone causing her so much anguish. But of course he couldn't. He clasped his hands behind his back and stood as stiff as a soldier.

"I want to keep this visit as discreet as possible. I'm hoping no one even notices I'm gone. If you come with me, someone might realize we were both absent. The gossips would be all abuzz, and my parents—well, they'd come after us both."

He couldn't hide his grimace. "All right. I see your point. But it's more important for me to help you than worry about the repercussions. I don't mind taking a chance."

"Your devotion to me is more than I deserve, Andrew." She smiled sadly, and for a moment he thought she'd reach up and give him an affectionate kiss on the cheek. When she didn't, disappointment pinched his chest. Why did he still covet his cousin's intended when he didn't stand a chance with her?

Katherine squeezed his arm. She stirred feelings simmering just below the surface and ready to boil over. He had no right to enjoy even her lightest touch; he wished she wouldn't tempt him in even small, innocent ways.

A few awkward seconds passed. Finally she spoke. "I must be going. It's almost time."

Andrew nodded and drummed his fingers against the polished rim of the billiard table. "Before you leave, please let me give you some advice."

"I'm listening."

"Don't make any financial arrangements until you talk them over with me. You'll need legal counsel. You're not wealthy, but your parents are. Harriet might try to acquire some of their money. So tell her you must consult with your attorney before you agree to any amount."

"Not that I even have more than a few spare dollars before

harvest," she said. "To try to wrestle more from me would be like getting blood from a turnip. But I hope . . . I hope I can come to some sort of resolution with her." She smiled gamely and left. He trailed behind her, at a respectable distance, to the boat landing, and resisted the urge to wave as she stepped into a rowboat.

The lake gleamed like the smooth sheen of satin, so at least he needn't worry a storm might brew while she was gone. He'd come back in about an hour or so and wait for her return. In the meantime, he'd try and review the information Mr. Wainwright had given him concerning the California rail line and plan his strategy. He laughed at himself under his breath. Until Katherine returned, he'd be able to think of nothing else but her.

Best to take a walk and pray for her. Please, Lord, cover Katherine . . .

Rowing eased some of Katherine's pent-up agitation. By the time she arrived at the Wayside Inn, her nerves had steadied and her mind felt clear. Over the years she'd tackled many disagreeable tasks, but this was undoubtedly the worst. *Lord, please help me to get through this with grace and charity.*

She beached the rowboat on a thin strip of sand, hauled it completely out of the water, and glanced at the small, rustic inn. The Wayside was a respectable but unfashionable establishment, catering to the middle class. It was built in the rustic style of most of the Adirondack camps. Hurrying down a path, she made her way to the back veranda. Several guests rocked rhythmically on painted rocking chairs while their knitting needles *click-clacked*; others watched the boats float by or read books and newspapers. A few gave her a disinterested glance as she approached the porch steps.

A young woman with a boy at her side stood and came forward from the opposite end of the long porch. She walked slowly, her shoulders square, her face impassive except for a kink at the corner of her wide mouth.

"Mrs. Osborne?" she called hesitantly as Katherine paused at the back door.

Katherine nodded. "Yes, I am. I presume you're Miss Roles." Raising a reserved but polite smile, Katherine's gaze swept the young woman. She looked to be about her own age, maybe a few years older. Anger, mixed with anxiety, tugged at Katherine's heart.

If she discounted the faded plaid dress and severe bun, Charles's mistress was attractive—in a washed-out sort of way. But she was hardly the beautiful vixen Katherine had imagined. Her features were sharply chiseled, and her skin so pale she seemed almost colorless. She wasn't any taller than Katherine, and so slight she looked like she could be blown away in a brisk autumn breeze.

Harriet rested her hand protectively on the boy's thin shoulders. Her dark eyes locked with Katherine's. "This is Zeke, Charles's son." Harriet glanced proudly at the boy with a mother's fierce love. When she turned back to Katherine, she held her head a bit higher. The little boy grasped his mother's hand and stared at Katherine with unabashed curiosity. The obvious bond between mother and child made Katherine cringe from sadness too deep to endure. In all fairness he should've been hers. But then she pulled herself together and smiled at Zeke.

"Hello, Zeke," Katherine said.

He responded in the childish voice of a nine-year-old. "How do you do, Mrs. Osborne?"

Even without an introduction she knew the boy belonged to Charles. The resemblance was striking: hazel eyes flecked with gold; thick, chestnut hair that curled around his square face; and a strong, prominent jaw. He seemed serious, like his mother, giving Katherine the impression he might not grow up to be a dashing scoundrel like his father.

"Why don't you go into the dining room, Zeke?" Harriet said. "The cook promised me she'd give you milk and cookies. Mrs. Osborne and I need to talk privately."

He vanished in an instant. Katherine eyed Harriet, waiting for her to begin.

The woman led her toward the deserted end of the porch where the view of the lake was obscured by clumps of white birch, hemlock, and evergreens. They settled side by side in wooden rocking chairs away from the other hotel guests.

"As I said in my letter, I'm sorry to distress you with the news of Zeke—and of Charles and me. But I lost my factory job and I haven't any prospects for employment. I'm afraid I'm not much good at sewing or any of the domestic arts."

Katherine nodded.

"I'd like to be a governess again, but I can't take a position that requires me to leave my son. None of my relatives are able or willing to bring him up." Harriet bit her lip. "And I wouldn't want them to anyway. I couldn't bear to leave him with others."

Katherine understood. If she had a child . . . "Were you a governess in Florida?"

"Yes. I used to take care of the Hall children in Brooksville. I accepted the position when I lived in New York City with my aunt and uncle. After Mr. Hall bought citrus groves in central Florida, we all moved south."

"And that's where you met my husband?" Katherine asked, her throat so constricted she sounded hoarse.

Harriet lifted her chin. "Yes, only he wasn't your husband then."

Blushing, Katherine continued, "Yes, I understand. When I married Charles I didn't know he'd had a previous relationship—

and a child." She'd never have married him if she'd learned he and his mistress had an affair, let alone one that produced a son. She wasn't at all surprised Charles hadn't bothered to tell her. "Miss Roles, I think I'd like to speak to you about Zeke's support now."

Harriet nodded, the muscles in her face tightening.

"I have no obligation to turn over any funds, as you know. Charles never made any provision for the boy's welfare. So the decision falls to me."

Harriet tensed and waited, wringing her hands. Katherine noted the desperation in her eyes and felt an unexpected surge of grudging sympathy for the woman. Taking a deep breath, Katherine cleared the emotion from her voice. "You may not know this, but Charles left me almost no money. He squandered everything we had on gambling and what I can only assume was support for you. So to help, I'd need to give you something from my own savings, which I assure you, at this point is extremely limited."

Harriet's eyes widened with disbelief. "Oh, I didn't know that. But what about your family? Surely they could help."

Katherine gave a dry laugh. "Miss Roles, if my father thought you suggested he contribute even a penny, he'd use his considerable influence against you. He'd be unhappy to know I'm here speaking with you." *Furious, in fact.*

Harriet's shoulders slumped and she seemed to wilt. "I see. I didn't mean to imply he ought to help me. But I'm down to my last few dollars, and as I said, I have no job prospects. Maybe you don't think I deserve anything, but surely you'd like Charles's son to have a roof over his head." She sighed softly. "I have no idea how much money it will take to raise Zeke, but I'm sure two thousand dollars should be enough to see us through his childhood."

Katherine gaped at the woman, dumbstruck. That wasn't a fortune for most of her contemporaries at Camp Birchwood, but for her it was totally impossible. Especially on top of meeting the bank's demand at month's end. But if she refused? "That's a large sum. But I'll consult with my attorney and get back with you as quickly as I can. I'm sure you must be eager to return to New York as soon as possible. Please excuse me, Miss Roles. I must be on my way."

Katherine rose on shaky legs and hurried to her rowboat, anxious to leave Harriet far behind. The woman had a terrible nerve asking for an enormous sum of money when she'd ruined Katherine's life. It would serve Harriet right if she didn't give her a cent. Katherine stumbled as she scrambled into her boat, her only thought that she had to talk to Andrew as soon as possible.

———

After half an hour passed, Andrew gave up his struggle to focus on his upcoming trip. What was the point of reading the same words over and over without comprehending them? He had plenty of time to go through these papers again. As far as he knew, he could still leave any day.

Finding the backyard deserted except for Aunt Letty resting in a Muskoka chair, he strolled in her direction. "May I join you, Aunt Letty?"

"Yes, yes, my dear."

He sat down beside her, pleased with the view of the wooded lawn, pier, and lake before them. They'd see Katherine as soon as she arrived.

The elderly lady chuckled. "I must have dozed off. I'm so glad you happened by. I've been meaning to speak to you."

"About Katherine? I was shocked she turned down the loan. It appears she's decided she'd rather marry Randy than return to her business."

Letty tilted her head and glanced at Andrew with questioning eyes. "She feels she must work her own way out of her mess. And I'm afraid we weren't very convincing." She shook her head dolefully and then looked out to the lake. "Tell me, Andrew. Does she confide in you?"

He nodded. For good or for ill, she told him much of what lay on her heart. More than she should, though certainly not everything. "Yes. I try to help her sort things out, but as you mentioned, for the most part, she wants to make her own decisions." He shrugged. "Maybe it's from running the citrus groves on her own these last years. She's accustomed to keeping her own counsel."

"Doesn't that strike you as odd?"

"Which part?"

Aunt Letty stared deep into his eyes, and he feared even deeper into his heart. "Don't you think she ought to confide in her fiancé? It's Randy's place to help her now, not yours, my dear friend." Aunt Letty spoke softly and gently, but her words stung because Andrew knew she was right.

It was time for him to abdicate his role as advisor. It would hurt like crazy to back away when she sought him out, but he would. And he'd try to do it with a measure of grace.

"Yes, I see she should confide in Randy, not me."

"But she doesn't wish to, does she?" Aunt Letty asked, lifting an eyebrow.

Andrew shook his head. "Apparently not."

Letty gripped his hand. "Don't you see? She's so in love with you, it never occurs to her to talk to Randy about her troubles. Katherine instinctively runs to you. Or perhaps she just won't admit to herself that you're the one who listens to her and cares for her. Admitting she relies on you would throw her life into total chaos, and she doesn't want any more turmoil after all she's endured."

Andrew didn't trust his voice. "Do you really believe she loves me?" he whispered. Just as he expected, he sounded lovelorn and pathetic. He couldn't conceal his feelings on this matter, no matter how hard he tried.

"I do, indeed. And I think you should pursue Katherine and convince her to marry you. Oh, I know you're afraid she'll turn you down. Don't look so skeptical. I can tell you're about to list all the reasons why marriage to Katherine can't work out. But I'm here to tell you, it can if you both want it enough."

Speechless at her encouragement, he sat still, mouth agape. She was the first and only one in the Wainwright family to offer any support.

Thoughts of Isabelle Wainwright and his aunt filled his head. He'd hate to cross swords with either of those formidable matrons, let alone Mr. Wainwright. He knew he was right on the verge of losing his position, given that he continued to see Katherine every time he could. A cold chill ran through his veins. He'd never been a fool, and he wasn't about to start being one now—at least not without a word of encouragement from Katherine herself.

Chapter Twenty-Four

Katherine rowed until her arms ached. Blisters rubbed between her fingers, but she kept pulling back on the oars with all the strength she had. Slowly the stress from facing Harriet eased.

Certainly Andrew would advise her about how to handle Harriet. At least he understood her predicament, when no one else did. Papa would take care of the problem in a flash and she'd never have to give Harriet another thought, but she feared he'd somehow damage her and her son in the process. None of this was Zeke's fault, and he shouldn't have to pay the price for his parents' sins. The turmoil inside her didn't reflect her charitable impulse, but she'd ignore her roiling feelings in favor of a clear conscience. She had to remember she was doing the right thing and not waver.

She found Andrew awaiting her on the pier. The knots in her heart tightened. *What does this mean, Lord? Are You trying to tell me something? Should I rely on him? He's always here when I need him.* Her head hurt from too much thinking, and her heart was crushed from colliding emotions. Yet she had to deal with this situation with Harriet, the last troubled remnant from her marriage. And then she'd be free from her past.

Andrew paced the pier as she rowed toward shore and waved. When she beached the rowboat on the rocky soil beside the dock, he rushed to help her. He pulled the craft to shore. His face looked grim, his blond hair askew. During the last few weeks he'd lost his calm, quiet demeanor and that interesting hint of sardonic amusement only somewhat concealed behind his self-assured mask. He ran his fingers through his hair, messing it up even more.

Helping her up to the pier, he asked, "Tell me, what did Harriet say? Does she still want money? Did you agree on an amount?"

Katherine gave a short, dry laugh. "She wants two thousand dollars. Of course I didn't agree to that. I said I had to speak to my attorney."

"Good. Let's take a walk, so we won't be disturbed." Glancing sideways, his smile looked crooked.

They settled onto a path that led through a thick stand of trees, affording some privacy. The light scent of Andrew's aftershave distracted her for a moment.

"Katherine, tell me—where did you envision finding any funds at all to give Miss Roles?"

Desperate, wild thoughts immediately brought her to her courtship. Randy had enough in his own right for the two of them to live comfortably. When they married, both sets of joyous and relieved parents would contribute generously to the coffers. Was God telling her to cease her resistance and find solace in financial relief, if not love?

"It will leave me with precious little, but I could give her five hundred dollars now. After the harvest, I could contribute more."

"It sounds like your harvest is getting parsed into more and more coffers," he said, giving her a rueful smile. "But five hundred would definitely keep the wolves at bay for a time. And I wouldn't offer her more than one thousand from the harvest. It's more than enough to bring up the child. Not in grand style, for certain. But not in poverty either."

She considered that. "I appreciate your advice, Andrew. But I don't want to cheat on my charity," she said. "Let's offer her five hundred now, one thousand come harvest, and another five hundred when he graduates high school. It will be meeting her wishes, in a way, but will encourage the boy to make something of himself."

He nodded, his eyes full of admiration. "That's very generous of you. I'll draw up an agreement—and stipulate that she must not request any more money from you in the future. She must leave you be, or she will not see the final payment upon Zeke's graduation."

She gave a grim smile. "I'm looking forward to it being done."

He nodded as if he understood perfectly.

"Andrew, please promise me you won't tell my father about these arrangements. I've decided what to do and I don't want my parents to consider it their obligation to counsel me. You know how distressed they get when I don't take their advice. This is a private matter, so there's no need for them to be involved."

"I wasn't planning on telling them anything. That's up to you, not me. When will you meet with Harriet again?" he asked.

"Tomorrow morning. I'll dash into town to make a withdrawal from the bank."

"Good. I'll draw up the agreement later this afternoon." He looked over his shoulder.

"Maybe we ought to go back. The mothers are probably looking for you."

"Yes, indeed. They like to keep me in their sights. Perhaps I should go alone, so no one will see us together. There's no point in asking for trouble. Thank you for everything, Andrew."

He gave a surprisingly curt nod. He looked as if he wanted to say something but couldn't find the right words. She waited for a moment.

"Katherine, there's something important I want to ask you." He sounded hesitant. "I should've spoken to you before, but I've hesitated because I don't want to disrupt your life."

"Yes?" She smiled, alternately wanting to hear the words she knew he'd wanted to say for a long time, but then knowing those words should be left unsaid. At the muffled sound of footsteps on the path, she glanced over her shoulder. "Oh no, Mama's coming and she looks out of sorts. Can our talk wait until later?"

"Of course. But look for me as soon as you can escape." He turned and strode down the trail in the opposite direction of her mother.

She closed her eyes to block out the confrontation ahead, if only for a moment.

When Mama caught up to her, she peered at her through squinted eyes. "Did I see you here with Andrew?"

"For a moment," Katherine said. "But believe me, we're both very clear about your feelings about us being together. So it was only for a moment."

"Hmph. No need to be haughty with me, young lady. Do keep in mind that we have his best interests at heart too. Leading him on shall only hurt him, in time, as well as your courtship with Randy. Please return with me. Papa and I have something to say to you." Wincing, Katherine dutifully followed her mother. She lagged a few paces behind her as they silently made their way through the woods to the lodge, and then the library.

They found Papa pacing in front of the screened windows. The plaid curtains fluttered in the mild breeze and lifted the fronds of the palms set on a nearby table. Mama crossed her arms over her chest.

Katherine braced herself. "What is it, Papa?"

His brows puckered in a frown and he glanced toward Mama. He kept his voice low.

"Now, don't get angry, princess. Randy told us about Charles's son and how the mistress wants money."

The roar in Katherine's ear nearly blocked her father's words.

"Don't blame Randy. He was reluctant to tell us," Mama said. "But he correctly decided he had a duty to explain. He's convinced you should not give money to—that woman, even for the boy's sake. He is her responsibility, certainly not yours. You were the victim in that shameful marriage."

They were right about Charles, but Mama didn't have cause to rub salt in that old, deep wound.

Mama persisted, "You must heed our judgment, Katherine. It should be clear to you that you're prone to making dreadful choices. We know what's best, so please be wise and follow our advice."

Katherine sniffed back tears of fury and betrayal and clenched her jaw. She blamed herself for the entire mess, but right now she needed support, not condemnation. "Giving the woman something for Charles's son is the Christian way. I'd be committing a sin if I refused her when she's in such need, no matter how it chafes."

Mama's mouth tightened in a grimace. "Where do you pick up such odd notions? Aunt Letty? I understand she's given nearly all her money away to foreign missions. She's sweet, but rather silly. I'm afraid she's a bad influence."

"No, I haven't spoken to her about this. But if I do, I'm sure she'll agree with me."

Mama groaned. "My point exactly. You are both so susceptible to those who prey on a kind heart." Then she stared at Katherine. "You are not to give that woman one cent. Do you understand?"

"I hear you. May I leave now, Papa?"

"In a moment. I want you to know we understand you're just trying to be generous and sympathetic. That's a wonderful trait, princess. But you mustn't give in to the woman or she'll keep demanding more."

Katherine stayed silent and looked down at the patterns of the Turkish carpet. If she explained how Andrew had solved that problem, they'd both get angry with him for interfering with family concerns.

With a weary sigh, Papa dismissed her. Before Mama could continue, Katherine rushed out of the room. There was one person she wanted to see. Randy.

She found him alone on the side porch strumming his mandolin and singing softly. "Katherine, what a pleasure to see you." He rose, but she waved him to his seat.

"I have a bone to pick with you."

A frown furrowed his brow. "What have I done to upset you?"

"You told my parents about Charles's mistress and their son. I asked you not to. I *trusted* you, Randy."

"Oh, that. I apologize for embarrassing you. But I thought they ought to know. I believe I did the right thing. Paying anything to that woman is ridiculous."

"You betrayed me, Randy. You had no right to tell my parents what I told you in confidence."

"If I'm to be your husband, I have every right to protect your interests."

She stared back at him, thinking how much she loathed those words. *If I'm to be your husband* . . . Then she turned on her heel and fled before she said something she just might regret.

———

Andrew returned to his bedroom and drew up an agreement between Katherine and Harriet. Katherine might object to him tagging along, but this time he'd try to convince her. He was afraid the woman might object to the more-than-generous terms. The trick was going with her, without being seen.

All during dinner he tried to catch her attention, but she never glanced his way. Finally after the ladies and gentlemen joined together in the recreation hall, he signaled her with one raised eyebrow. She sidestepped toward him and he passed by her to retrieve a Ping-Pong paddle, thankful for the invitation to a game by Mr. Lessman.

Under his breath he murmured, "If you can get away, meet me in the library in thirty minutes."

She gave a barely perceptible nod as she strolled off to join a group of women sitting by the fireplace gossiping. He had no trouble escaping the crowd, but he suspected Katherine might. Once in the library, with the agreement hidden in his satchel, he waited for her, anxiety mounting with every second she didn't appear. When the clock struck the half hour, fifteen minutes after he asked to meet with her, he wondered if she'd be able to come. But eventually she slipped through the door of the dimly lit room and rushed to his side, breathing heavily.

Her hand pushed against the bodice of her blue-gray silk gown. "Please pardon me for arriving so late. It couldn't be helped. Mrs. Porter kept chattering and wouldn't let me go. And Mama follows me around with those sharp eyes of hers. I only have a moment."

He handed her the agreement. "First of all, take this, read it over, and then put it in your cabin."

She scanned the paper and nodded. "Thank you, Andrew."

"You're most welcome. But before you leave, I'd like to say I'm planning to go with you tomorrow. You might find Harriet more difficult than you expect. I want to be available if I'm

needed. Don't say no, Katherine. I insist on coming. I promise
I'll stay out of your way. I won't go inside the inn while you're
speaking to Harriet. You can simply fetch me if you're in need."

She smiled and pressed his hand. "That's very kind of you,
but Papa won't allow it when you're supposed to be working. I
can handle this myself. Please don't worry about me." Katherine
shook her head. "We can't both be gone at the same time without drawing attention to ourselves. Mama is keeping such close
tabs on me—on both of us—I don't want to chance it. I don't
wish to create a scene." She glanced toward the door, her brows
drawn together. "I must be going." Grasping his hand, she
squeezed it tightly.

But he held on when she tried to leave. She paused, confused, and then turned to him, a question in her beautiful eyes.

"Wait, just a moment. I have something to say, and it can't
wait any longer."

"All right," she said slowly.

He brought his other hand up to cover hers. "Katherine, I'm
in love with you. I think I've always been in love with you. But
since we reunited"—he shook his head—"it's unavoidable. I
love you. And I believe you love me."

Her forehead creased. "I love you too," she whispered,
seeming dazed. "But it will come to nothing, so we shouldn't
speak of it. I'm so sorry, Andrew. I wish things were different,
but they aren't. We have to be realistic."

He stared at her. He loved her and she loved him, and yet
they were to turn away? The combined frustration of the last
month and a half pounded in his head. "No, Katherine! We can
overcome any barrier, as long as we tackle it together. Katherine,
listen to me. I love you with all my being and I want to be with
you. Please. Marry me." His heartbeat thundered in his ears as
he watched her expression change from fleeing joy to desolation.

"We cannot," she said, her voice echoing with ache. "You know all the reasons why. You must believe me when I say I've never been so sorry about anything in my life." She reached up and brushed her lips against his cheek. For a moment, she paused as if she'd lift her head and meet his mouth with her soft, sweet lips.

But instead she gently spun around and swept out of the library, leaving him bereft in the dark, silent room without even a fire to cheer him.

Chapter Twenty-Five

At nine o'clock the next morning, Katherine dressed in a plain cocoa brown skirt and a cream-colored shirtwaist, and donned a straw boater with a brown band around the crown. She glanced in the mirror above her dressing table. Finding a young woman staring back at her with anxious eyes, she breathed a deep sigh. She looked exhausted. All night she'd replayed Andrew's declaration in her mind. But at least she appeared presentable. It was time to go.

She opened her cabin door to find her mother striding down the walkway toward the cabin. Katherine's insides twisted. "Good morning, Mama."

Nodding a greeting, her mother halted. "I came to remind you we're all off to a short shopping trip to town." Mama's lips pursed. "You are planning on coming, aren't you?"

Katherine nodded. "Of course. I'll get my shawl." Perfect. She'd stop off at the bank and withdraw the money for Harriet.

Mama's eyes narrowed with suspicion, causing perspiration to seep through Katherine's tight collar. "Why are you carrying a satchel? Where were you planning to go?"

"There's some business I need to attend to." She angled her gaze away from Mama's probing stare.

"Oh, you mean your orange groves, don't you? I daresay you'll be so much happier with that weight off your shoulders. Now that you and Randy are keeping company, I'm sure you'll soon be ready to sell to Mr. Osborne. Have you written to him yet? Papa said he seemed anxious to hear from you. You really ought to get your business affairs settled."

"No, I haven't written, but I'm sure it will all be resolved soon." Katherine smiled sweetly and then stepped into the cabin for her shawl. Shoving the satchel into the chest of drawers, she thrust her hand over her heart and waited for it to calm. Now was not the time to tell Mama about the financial agreement with Harriet; she'd tell her later, when Mama wasn't in a contentious mood.

"Don't tarry, dear." Mama pulled open the door and poked her head inside. "It's rude to keep others waiting."

Katherine nodded. Harriet Roles would have to wait until later.

"Andrew, I have news for you." Mr. Wainwright grinned as he strode into the room, but his cheerfulness seemed forced.

"Yes, sir." A feeling of foreboding alerted him. Andrew straightened and met Mr. Wainwright's gaze directly.

He took his seat across from him on a comfortable leather chair. "I'd like you to leave for California today. I know this is short notice, and I apologize for the inconvenience. But I've heard we have some additional competition on that California trunk line. It seems the line is more popular than I'd imagined. This new group is a really aggressive bunch of investors. I'm hoping this is merely a rumor, but I need you to be there so we'll be among the first to make an offer when the owners return. We can't pass up this opportunity."

Shocked at the sudden change of plans, Andrew leaned back in his chair and tried to process the news. "When does my train leave?"

"In two hours. I'll have my valet pack for you so you'll be ready on time. How does this change of plans strike you?"

"Fine, sir," he said numbly. He'd have to say good-bye to Katherine before he left. Desolation filled him at the thought. Yet she'd turned him aside for his cousin, so there was nothing to keep him here any longer. She'd have to see through her negotiation with Harriet on her own. In fact, it might be less painful for him to leave today than to linger here and watch Randy and Katherine together, pretending a love that didn't exist.

Mr. Wainwright crossed his arms over his barrel chest and beamed. "Perhaps you should wind up what you're doing here."

Andrew nodded, excused himself, and went to his bedroom to prepare for his departure. He wished he could rewrite the ending to his summer in a much different way. But despite his hopes, winning Katherine's hand had been a futile dream, right from the start. His folly—to sweep the girl off her feet and attain the approval of her parents . . .

His mouth twisted in a grimace. He'd always known better.

When the ladies returned from town, Katherine hurried off to her cabin before Mama could bully her into an afternoon filled with social activities. She grabbed her satchel and glanced at Aunt Letty.

"In case Mama comes looking for me, I'll be back in a few hours."

Aunt Letty looked up from the album she'd just opened. "Oh, of course, dear."

She turned her attention back to the pictures with a wistful smile, and Katherine paused a moment. Would she ever have albums full of memories she could look upon fondly? "Enjoy yourself, Aunt. I'll see you at tea."

Katherine stepped outside her cabin and quickly searched the area for Mama. Finding herself alone, Katherine darted across the yard toward the boats. She tossed her satchel into the rowboat, pushed it off the shore, and boarded.

Sunshine beat down upon her, but a mild breeze kept her comfortable. A gull swooped toward the water; a family of mallards swam by; a canoe crossed her path. A lovely day, but she couldn't enjoy the outdoors when Harriet, Charles, and Zeke were on her mind. The short trip to the Wayside seemed to stretch on and on. She finally reached the beach, disembarked, and strode toward the inn, satchel in hand.

Katherine found Harriet sitting on the porch facing the lake. Anxiety distorted her sculptured features as she rose heavily from the rocker.

"Hello, Mrs. Osborne. I think we should go to my room and talk."

Katherine nodded and followed Charles's mistress inside, through a spacious center hallway with a reception desk, and up a steep flight of stairs. At the landing they turned right and strode past several closed doors before Harriet paused. "This is my room." She unlocked the door and pushed it open. "We'll be alone. Zeke is playing in the game room with another little boy."

The tiny space with its twin beds and dresser looked clean and cheerful with the early afternoon light pouring through the windows. Katherine removed the agreement from her satchel and handed it to Harriet. Taking several seconds to read the terms, Harriet finally nodded. "Thank you."

Relief flowed through Katherine, draining some of the tension that tightened her muscles and left her nauseous.

"It's not exactly what I asked for, but I'm grateful for your provision. When you left yesterday I realized I wasn't very gracious or thankful. I must've sounded dreadfully demanding. I'm sorry. I can see there are things I didn't know. Charles never told me he lost most of his fortune and yours. I thought he was still a rich man when he died, so of course I assumed you'd have plenty of money to help with his son. We're in such dire straits." Harriet's voice cracked. "All this money comes from you, doesn't it?"

"Yes."

"I'm much obliged."

Katherine cleared the emotion from her throat. "Shall we have this agreement witnessed?"

"Yes, of course. I'm sure the innkeeper and his wife will be glad to help."

Five minutes later the paper was signed and the cash exchanged.

"Thank you again, Mrs. Osborne."

Katherine strolled toward the back porch, ready to leave this behind. But at the steps leading across the lawn to the shore, she paused and met Harriet's steady gaze. Before she thought twice, Katherine drew out the question she'd locked inside ever since she learned of Charles's deceit. "Please, tell me why it happened." Her voice was so low she wondered if Harriet heard her, but the young woman startled and then nodded.

"Let's sit at the end of the porch where we won't be disturbed."

The long open veranda was empty except for an old couple bundled up near the back door and rocking gently in squeaky rocking chairs. Katherine followed Harriet. They strode to the end of the long porch and sat side by side in matching wicker chairs.

Harriet buried her head in her hands for what seemed like an eternity. When she looked up, her eyes pleaded for compassion. "I know I deceived you, but I was Charles's mistress before he met you. And also later, after your marriage. I'm so sorry, Mrs. Osborne. I didn't mean to hurt anyone. I loved Charles and he was all that mattered to me until Zeke came along. Then I fought to make us a family." Tears trailed down Harriet's cheeks. Fumbling in her pocket for a handkerchief, she sniffed back more.

Katherine felt perspiration soak the tight collar of her shirtwaist and spread into her neck and face. Her heart thumped so loudly she barely heard Harriet's words.

"I met Charles during the summer while he was home from college. We immediately fell deeply in love and he wanted to marry me. I knew his father would never allow him to marry a nanny without money or good family background. But he couldn't see why the difference in our social positions should keep us apart." Harriet sighed. "I believed Charles when he said he didn't care for society's opinions one little bit. He promised to marry me regardless of his father's objections, regardless of how his friends received me. And I trusted him. He was so sincere."

Katherine watched Harriet's wet cheeks flush with redness. Sympathy stirred at the center of Katherine's heart, despite the discomfort of hearing about Charles's hidden past and the dislike she felt toward her.

"Just before he returned to college in New York he told his father of our plans to marry. Old Mr. Osborne threatened to disinherit him if he didn't give me up. I was stunned when he caved in to his father's demands. I was so sure of Charles's love and loyalty. But at the end of the summer, he returned to Columbia and I didn't hear from him again."

"But you must have," Katherine murmured, her voice hinting at a bitterness she didn't want to feel or express. If only Charles's affair had ended at this point, their marriage might have stood at least a small chance of succeeding.

Harriet nodded. Her face blazed with what Katherine assumed was shame. "Did you tell Charles about your baby?" Katherine asked.

"Yes. Soon after he left for college I discovered I was carrying his child. I wrote to him and explained my situation, hoping he'd change his mind and marry me." Harriet took a deep breath. "Charles answered my letter several months later. He said he'd met a young lady and he hoped to marry her after graduation."

"Me," Katherine said.

Harriet nodded. "I believe so."

Katherine closed her eyes, barely able to absorb everything Harriet was saying. Charles had withheld so much. He'd never even mentioned a past relationship in Florida, let alone a child.

"Charles said our relationship was over. Of course I lost my governess position when my condition became obvious. That spring I gave birth to Zeke. Charles Ezekiel Roles. He didn't even have Charles's last name." Harriet looked down at her clasped hands. When she finally looked up, her eyes were rimmed with red. "I was alone and desperate, so I took a job as a maid at a boardinghouse in Florida. The owner let me keep Zeke. But some of the boarders complained about a baby crying all hours of the day and night, so my employer asked me to leave."

"Couldn't you have gone to your relatives in New York?" Katherine asked.

"Yes, but they didn't want me to come back with a baby. That's when I contacted Charles again. At first he refused to help, but eventually he softened. He was taken with baby Zeke, even though he fought it. He started coming around to see him. Then his visits became more frequent until—until he apologized for how dreadfully he treated me. I'm sorry to say this, but I was happy to have him in my life again. We resumed our . . . relationship." Looking down at her hands, Harriet blew out a weary sigh. "I should've tossed him out, but my anger vanished with a few kind words. I had no strength to fight my feelings. I was weak and so hopeful he'd come back to me."

Katherine's eyes widened. "But he'd married me."

"Yes, he had. Not because he—" Harriet stopped and blushed a fiery crimson. "I mean . . ."

Katherine shook her head. "I know exactly what you mean. Charles didn't love me. He only married me because his father found me acceptable. I was a suitable match and it was time for him to marry." Harriet started to disagree, but Katherine shook her head. "Please don't try to spare my feelings. My husband cared for me for only a short time. He obeyed his father and not his heart." That was the sad truth. Look what misery it had brought all of them. "Do continue."

Harriet nodded. "I had no right to love Charles, but I did, just the same. He was a weak man—an adulterer. Not that I was any different." Harriet's voice shook.

"Did he take care of you and Zeke from then on?" Katherine could hardly believe all this happened practically in front of her and she hadn't seen it.

"Yes. He rented a small place in Brooksville for Zeke and me."

"And that's where Charles spent all his time," Katherine murmured.

Harriet flinched. "Yes. I'm truly sorry, Mrs. Osborne."

Katherine met her gaze. "I can't pretend you didn't ruin my marriage, but . . . I do forgive you." She never envisioned saying those words to Harriet. But she actually meant them.

"Thank you," Harriet whispered.

"You ought to ask the Lord to forgive you as well." As she

said it, the heavy burden of grief slowly lifted from Katherine's heart. It was almost physical.

"I will. Thank you for being a true Christian. I never expected to be treated with such grace." Harriet blinked rapidly. "Perhaps I have no right to say this, but I always felt Charles and I were meant to be together—legally, as man and wife. But he feared his father would disinherit him. And in the end, Charles valued society's standards too."

Katherine nodded. It was an all-too-familiar story. Look at the misery it caused. Charles should've married Harriet and not worried about the opinions of others. Instead, he married a woman suitable to everyone but himself, and in turn, hurt them all. "Sometimes those outside forces keep us from the person we love, the one we should marry," Katherine murmured.

Her heart jolted. Only her mother's snobbish disapproval kept her from marrying Andrew. Certainly they had enough love to bring each other true happiness. Only social conventions kept them apart. God had blessed her with a second chance, one she didn't deserve. Yet she'd firmly rejected it because she hadn't understood what He was telling her.

She could follow her heart without Mama's approval. But she had to take a risk. Could she muster the courage to defy her parents?

Katherine rose from the table, her mind alive with rekindled hopes, her heart thundering. If she took a chance on love *this time*, at least she knew she'd prayed for guidance and God had answered. She knew He blessed her love for Andrew, and his for her. *It's the path I've been looking for, praying for,* she thought, eyes wide.

But was it fair to ask him to give up his job for her? He'd worked so hard, and he was in line for advancement. Papa was a kind and generous employer, probably rather rare in the business world. But Andrew had already proposed to her, so he must be willing to start over somewhere else. No one in New York City would hire him once they learned he'd married William Wainwright's daughter against his wishes. They'd have to leave the area and find someplace else.

So be it.

She'd confess her love to Andrew and allow him to decide his—their—future.

Rising on wobbly legs, Katherine smiled tentatively at Harriet. "Good day, Miss Roles. And God bless you and Zeke. Thank you for telling me your story."

Chapter Twenty-Six

Andrew searched the lodge and the grounds for Katherine, but no one had seen her since she'd returned from town earlier. He'd begun to worry by the time he ran into Aunt Letty knitting and chatting with Mrs. Lessman in the lounge.

"Excuse me, ladies. Have either of you seen Katherine lately? My train leaves in half an hour and I'd like to say good-bye. I only have a few minutes before I leave."

He'd already said his farewells to the Wainwrights and Clarkes, and with the assistance of a footman, he'd carried his luggage downstairs. Now it was time to face Katherine. Bidding her good-bye and conveying best wishes for a happy life with Randy would be most difficult. The words might snag in his throat, but he couldn't avoid saying them. And hard as it would be, he had to see her one last time before she became officially engaged to his cousin. He expected their understanding to progress to an announcement before the end of the fall. It was inevitable.

Aunt Letty placed her knitting on her lap. "I have no idea where she is. But I'd be glad to help you look for her. Where are you going in such a hurry?" She rose and stuffed the half-knitted sweater in her cloth bag.

Andrew glanced at the mantel clock. Time was quickly ticking away. "Mr. Wainwright is sending me to California earlier than I expected. He only told me a few hours ago."

She nodded knowingly. "Let's take a look in the cabin." Together they strode outside and down the covered walkway. "She'll be so disappointed if she doesn't get a chance to say good-bye. In fact, she'll be devastated you're leaving."

He glanced sideways to Aunt Letty and lowered his voice. "I proposed to her, you know, and she turned me down. I expected she would, but I had to ask anyway. If I hadn't, I would always have wondered if she might have said yes." He tried to keep the sadness from his voice, but he failed. "So maybe she won't be quite as upset as you think."

Aunt Letty touched his arm. "She will, Andrew. I'm certain she'll be heartbroken."

He shrugged, completely unconvinced. Aunt Letty's romantic inclinations had gotten the best of her, and she didn't recognize reality when it stared her right in the face. Or maybe she just refused to acknowledge it.

When they arrived at the cabin they found it empty. He looked across the lake. He knew where she was—with Harriet.

"At least put your farewell down on paper." Aunt Letty sighed as she shuffled through her bureau for stationery and a fountain pen. "Here you go, Andrew."

He scratched out his news and gave the envelope to the elderly lady. "I'm afraid I must go now or I'll miss my train. Please tell Katherine how sorry I was to leave without saying good-bye."

"I shall, indeed." Aunt Letty nodded. "Perhaps you can write to her when you get settled. She'd appreciate hearing from you. You might not think it appropriate to correspond, but it would mean so much to her. And I think you agree that's more important than propriety."

He didn't wish to disappoint dear Aunt Letty. "I'll give it serious thought." Of course, it would be better to make a clean break. In the end it might hurt less than dragging out a relationship with no future.

He kissed Aunt Letty on her cool, wrinkly cheek and took her hands in his own. "I shall miss you very much. I appreciate your advice and your wisdom."

She laughed and squeezed his fingers. "You're a dear boy to listen to a dotty old lady. Not everyone finds us old folks worth listening to." She sent him a wry smile. "I assume you'll be back in the City sometime during the fall if all goes well."

Andrew nodded. "I suppose so. But it's possible Mr. Wainwright will want me to stay on in California for a while. I suspect he won't call me back until after Katherine and Randy get engaged."

Pressing her thin lips together, Letty sighed. "You're undoubtedly right, although I'm praying the Lord will change her mind."

"Perhaps," he said doubtfully.

"Andrew, when you do return home, call upon me. I'd love to share a cup of tea and hear about your adventures in California."

"I will," he said, smiling down at her.

Aunt Letty held on to his hands for several seconds and smiled up at him. "Godspeed, Andrew."

"Take care of Katherine, all right?"

"I certainly shall."

He stepped out to the deck outside her cabin and glanced toward the pier. He spotted the footman loading his luggage onto Mr. Wainwright's steam yacht. Striding down to the dock where his boss was waiting, he steeled himself. Leaving was more difficult than he'd anticipated, and he wished he could soldier through it alone without any more farewells. When he arrived at the pier, Mr. Wainwright thumped him on the back. "Good luck in California, Andrew. I'm counting on you. I know you'll do a splendid job."

"Thank you for the opportunity, sir." He meant it, though the cost of this assignment and his future promotion seemed almost too heavy to shoulder.

Mr. Wainwright nodded. His jowly face drooped, and his mouth curved downward, as if he felt a twinge of melancholy. "Safe travels, young man," he said, giving him a firm nod.

Andrew stepped aboard and found his seat. But as they cast off and steamed down the lake, his eyes were not on his boss or Camp Birchwood, but upon the lake itself, searching for one last glimpse of Katherine.

———

Katherine saw her father's yacht steaming around the bend as she rowed toward camp. She thought she caught a glimpse of Andrew, but couldn't be sure. Frustration rose in her chest—she had to speak to him! Hopefully it hadn't been him. Where would he be going? As soon as she beached her rowboat, she returned to her cabin where she found Aunt Letty pacing on the front porch.

"Oh! Katherine dear, you're just the person I want to see."

Katherine set her satchel and reticule down. "Oh? Why is that, Aunt?"

Letty came over to her and took her hands. "Because Andrew was looking for you earlier. But I'm afraid he's gone now. He was so terribly disappointed he missed you. He wanted to say good-bye before he left. Come." She led her inside the cabin and handed Katherine an envelope.

Dropping on the bed quilt, Katherine pulled off her gloves and examined her blistered hands ruefully. "I'm eager to speak to him too. Where's he going?" She assumed her father or Randy had convinced him to head off on some afternoon foray.

"Andrew is on his way to California. Your papa advanced the date of his departure. He wanted so much to speak to you, but if he waited, he was afraid he'd miss the train."

Startled, her eyes widened. "California! Andrew wasn't supposed to leave until next week. I have so many things I need to tell him." Jumping off the bed, she paced across the room and back.

"I know, my dear. Unfortunately your papa decides these things. Andrew didn't have a choice. Read his letter," she said, nodding to the envelope in her hands.

Hesitating, Katherine noted how her aunt's normally placid gaze flashed with urgency. Slitting open the envelope, Katherine pulled out a sheet of paper and read the scribble she recognized as Andrew's. He must've hurried because she could barely decipher his scrawl.

Dear Katherine,

I haven't much time before I leave for California days earlier than I expected. I searched all over Camp Birchwood for you, but you weren't anywhere to be found. You probably were delayed by Harriet Roles. I hope your meeting went well and you had her sign the agreement.

I know you turned down the loan Aunt Letty and I mentioned to you, but please reconsider. I truly believe you'll be happiest working at your orange groves. The funds would cover your immediate needs and give you a fighting chance at turning a corner in the citrus groves, come fall. If you are interested in returning to Florida and operating your business, please tell Aunt Letty. She'll turn over the money to you. Don't let pride stand in the way of happiness. And know that we offer it freely, with no strings attached, because we only want the best for you.

May the Lord bless you and guide you in your decision.

Yours truly,

Andrew

Katherine's hand trembled. Had God's path been this clear all along? Why hadn't she seen it until now? "He wants me to use the money you two offered me. I don't know what to say."

Aunt Letty tilted her head. "Why don't you speak to him in person? If you hurry, you might get to the depot before the train leaves."

Katherine nodded as she reached for her reticule and grabbed a clean pair of gloves from her chest of drawers. "Do you think I'll make it in time?"

"Possibly. You won't know until you try." Aunt Letty clapped her hands in delight. "Go on now. Hurry!"

"I'm on my way. I have so much to tell him! Please pray I'll arrive on time."

"I shall, my dear."

Slapping on her straw hat on her way out the door, Katherine glanced back and smiled. They both understood how important it was for her to talk to Andrew before he left—and not merely because of the citrus groves. She rushed toward the pier, soon panting from the exertion.

As soon as she strode onto the dock she realized she'd have to take the rowboat once again, though she doubted her tired arms had the strength. The fastest way to the railway depot was by boat, and the steam yacht had not yet returned. If only she knew when the train was scheduled to leave the station! What were the chances Andrew would still be there? Probably small, but she had to try.

She scrambled back into the rowboat and shoved off beneath the umbrella of a cloudless blue sky and hot sun. Tilting her hat brim to shield her from the brightness, the rays still managed to create bubbles of perspiration across her forehead. She rowed as fast as she could, pushing forward and then pulling back the oars with all her strength. Even with gloves on, she rubbed her blisters raw. She bit her lip and continued to row.

Thanks to calm waters, she soon tied up among several larger boats, close to the depot and railroad tracks. A passenger train pulled in with a piercing whistle and a wheeze. From around the corner of the building, she glimpsed Andrew strolling toward the door of one of the cars behind a uniformed porter.

"Andrew!" she yelled, ignoring proper etiquette. *"Andrew!"*

But he disappeared in the crowd, apparently unable to hear her over the din.

Unless she ran, the man most important to her would board soon and vanish.

Katherine rushed down the dock and through the station, gasping for every painful breath against her restrictive corset.

She saw him again, nearing a first-class car. "Andrew! Andrew!" She cupped her hands and called in a ragged voice, nearly muffled by the sounds of the belching train and passengers strolling along the short platform, chattering like magpies. "Please, Andrew! Wait!"

Heads turned in her direction and people stared open-mouthed. Just as he stepped on board the train, she caught up to him. "Andrew, wait," she panted, tugging on his sleeve. She gulped for air and her chest heaved.

He glanced over his shoulder. When he saw it was she, his

eyes opened wide with a welcoming sparkle. "Katherine. What are you doing here?" He turned and joined her on the platform.

"Before you leave we have to talk—if you don't mind. This might be our last chance for months."

He hesitated, then led her away from the crush of passengers attempting to board, searching for a quiet place to talk.

Katherine's fingers splayed across her bodice while her heart steadied its rapid beat. Her voice exploded in breathy gasps. "Andrew, I promise not to keep you long, but I had to thank you and Aunt Letty too, of course, for offering me a loan again. I can't tell you how much I appreciate your kindness. I know you're not at all rich and this would be a sacrifice for you. Truly, I'm overwhelmed and more appreciative than you can possibly imagine."

His brows rose in surprise. "Does this mean you changed your mind about accepting the loan? Is that why you're here?"

"I haven't decided yet. But I had to tell you about my talk with Harriet."

He nodded. "Did she sign the agreement?"

"Oh, yes and without any fuss. But that's not as important as what she said about her relationship to Charles." She breathed deeply. "It was painful to listen to, but she made so much sense. She told me he wouldn't marry her because she was merely a governess and his father objected to the match. He was afraid to cross old Mr. Osborne, so he married me to please his father."

"But you already learned that from his letters, didn't you?"

"Yes, but she made me see how different things would've turned out for her and Charles and little Zeke. And also for me, if he'd followed his heart instead of his father's preferences. He and I never would have married. He would've married the woman he really cared for. His decision to follow his father's wishes instead of his own heart's desire caused all three of us so much misery."

Andrew nodded sadly. "It certainly did. But Charles was a coward."

"Indeed, he was, but no worse than I am."

His shoulders tensed and he gripped her hands. "What do you mean?"

She shivered at his touch. "It would be as wrong for me to marry Randy as it was for Charles to marry me. Neither match was right. I haven't told Randy yet, but I shall when I return to camp. I refuse to ruin his life as well as my own. He's only marrying me because his mother is pressuring him, and it's the same for me. I'm quite sure it isn't the Lord's will."

Andrew's eyes sparked. "I'm so relieved to hear you've finally come to your senses."

She nodded her head. "After a while Randy will definitely be thankful I saved him from making a dreadful mistake, but my parents and your Aunt Georgia won't be one bit happy or forgiving."

"What will you do after you refuse Randy?" His voice sounded husky.

"I'll go back to Florida and either try to make it through with the loan from you and Aunt Letty, or sell the business to Stuart Osborne. He's offered me a fair price. I have no idea what I'll do after that's settled, but I suppose with the remaining money, if there is any, I can buy a small house in New York City and design hats for a living. I won't mind leading a simple life. My parents might disown me, but it's preferable to marrying the wrong man. I never want to repeat that error."

"You'll be giving up so much, Katherine."

She shrugged as she blinked back tears. This monumental decision would change the course of her life. During the last weeks she'd struggled so hard to conform to her parents' standards and expectations, but she just couldn't measure up and still stay true to what the Lord had in mind for her. "Yes, I suppose I am sacrificing some things, but it's all right. It's better than pretending to be someone I'm not. I think, in the end, I'm simply not cut out to be a society woman."

Andrew nodded. He understood, and from his admiring smile, he approved. "I'm proud of you."

She blushed at the compliment and averted her gaze.

The train whistle blew, and she glanced past the empty platform toward the car he was late boarding. If he didn't hurry, the train would leave him behind. But he didn't seem to notice or even care. He gazed at her intently and didn't make a move.

"But, Katherine," he said, "my gut tells me you belong in Florida, not the City. I've never seen you as happy as when we were there together."

She gave him a rueful smile. Was there anything about her that he didn't understand? "I'd much rather manage the company myself than sell to Stuart, but I have to be honest with myself. I can't manage the business all alone. I need a partner to help me, and I don't know of anyone who might be interested. I hate to admit the toll the business took on me, but truly, I was exhausted and at my wit's end when you and Papa came to Florida. I can't do it again, much as I'd like to."

"What if I came with you, Katherine?" he asked. His eager expression gave her pause.

"I don't understand," she said, shaking her head in confusion. "You want to help me manage the groves? What about your position at the railroad? Papa will never allow you to take a leave of absence." She glanced toward the train. "If you don't board soon, the train will leave without you."

"I don't care," he said with a laugh. He squeezed her arms. "Listen to me. I like my job, but I love you. Marry me and we'll go to Florida. And then we'll turn the Osborne Citrus Groves around. Together we'll succeed."

Her heart fluttered and her legs weakened. "You do love me, don't you?" It was more a statement than a question. She knew she didn't really need to ask.

"Oh, Katherine. By now, you shouldn't have the slightest doubt."

"I don't." She smiled. "And I love you too, with all my being. I think I've known it for quite a while, but I never admitted it to myself. I was afraid of what our love would mean to both of us."

She reached up and stroked his face and then curled her arms around his neck and ran her fingers through the wave just above his collar. But she couldn't get carried away.

"Are you still hesitant?" he asked, apprehension reaching into his eyes.

"No, Andrew. I'm not in the least hesitant. I love you and I want to marry you more than anything in the world. And I want us to go to Florida, but only if you're sure you want to. Are you positive you won't regret quitting your job with Papa? I know you're happy working for him."

He shook his head. "It's a wonderful position, but it's only a job. You're going to be my wife." With tears in his eyes, he pulled her hands up to his mouth and kissed them. "There's nothing I want more than that." He gently drew her so close they were nearly one. She didn't care if passengers stared at them from the train windows. All she cared about was the love in her heart for Andrew and his love for her. She raised her chin, offering him a kiss, and he didn't hesitate, bending to cover her mouth with his. He pressed her tightly for several seconds before he loosened his hold.

"Let's go back to camp," Katherine said. "The sooner we're through what is to come, the better."

He nodded. "You're right. I'll see if I can summon a porter and still retrieve my luggage before the train leaves. I can store it in the depot for now."

Five minutes later Andrew helped her climb into the boat, and he followed behind. He shrugged off his suit jacket and handed it to Katherine. He pulled off his tie, rolled up the sleeves of his crisp white shirt, and started to row. She couldn't help but notice his muscular forearms.

Staying close to the shore, the boat glided through the glistening blue lake. The ride back to Birchwood seemed to take forever, shredding her already jangled nerves. Only being together and knowing they would be together, *forever*, steadied her.

Once they docked the rowboat, Andrew helped her out and wrapped his arm around her shoulder. "Don't worry. Everything will be fine." Her legs threatened to buckle now that they were back home and about to face the consequences of their decision.

"I do hope so," she murmured. She'd hate to lose her family over this. Her stomach flipped from the enormity of her decision. And Andrew's . . . Would her father fire him on the spot?

They slowly walked across the lawn and up to the veranda of the chalet where they found Aunt Letty knitting, and Mama and Mrs. Clarke doing needlework projects.

When Mama spotted her and Andrew together, she let out a gasp and her hand slammed against her mouth. "What are you doing here, Andrew? You're supposed to be on the train to California."

He kept his voice calm. "I've come back with Katherine. She has something to say to you before I explain."

Mama put up a hand. "Before you utter another word, we need William and Randy to join us." She sent a maid to fetch them.

Mama and Mrs. Clarke stared at Katherine, their mouths gaping. Clearly, they realized there'd be only one reason for Katherine and Andrew to be here, together. For the first time in

Katherine's memory, her mother was speechless. Aunt Letty cast her eyes down and bit her lip, no doubt to keep from squealing with delight. Birdsong softened the awkward silence and crickets hummed in the background. The time seemed to stand still, but finally Randy and Papa pushed through the back door.

Papa looked at them askance. "I imagine you two have something we all ought to hear."

"Yes, we do." Katherine could scarcely breathe, let alone speak coherently. "Randy, perhaps I should speak with you privately."

He shook his head. His stare slid from her to Andrew. From the look in his eyes changing from surprise to defeat, he knew exactly what they were about to admit. Sighing, he tugged on his mustache. "You're going to end our courtship, aren't you, Katherine?"

She nodded and swallowed hard. "I'm so sorry, Randy."

He half smiled and then shrugged. "Actually, I'm not as shocked as everyone else seems to be." And he didn't look as distressed either. Then he glanced at his mother with one raised eyebrow. "What now, Mother?"

"Don't worry, you needn't worry about your father," Mrs. Clarke soothed.

"Whatever do you mean?" Katherine asked, her gaze sliding from mother to son.

Mama, Georgia Clarke, and Randy exchanged quick glances and turned geranium red.

"It's unimportant, dear," Mama murmured, taking too many seconds to regain her composure.

Something was up, and Katherine was going to get to the bottom of it if she had to question them all day long. "Randy, out with it."

He shifted from one leg to another and tugged at his mustache.

"Randy, please," his mother screeched in her booming voice. "Not another word."

"What are you keeping from me?" Katherine strode closer to the veranda where Randy dropped down on a rocker, his legs sprawled in front of him, his shoulders slumped, and his chest caved in.

He straightened a bit. "I may as well tell her, Mother. She'll get it out of me eventually." He drew out a sigh as all eyes focused on him. "My parents said I had to go to work for my father in his dreadful bank unless I married you."

"*What?*" Papa sputtered, his face growing red. He cast an accusing eye toward Isabelle.

"We've always been such good friends, Katherine," Randy went on. "So I thought marriage was a good idea, although I would've preferred to wait a few more years. But nothing would stop our mothers from making plans for our future. I went along because I thought we were destined for each other."

Katherine grabbed on to Andrew's arm for support. "I knew you weren't truly in love with me, Randy."

His crestfallen face caused her a momentary twinge of sympathy for the boy slated to begin an unwanted career in his father's business. But a lot of gentlemen would jump at the opportunity. He'd be all right.

"Can you ever forgive me, Katherine?" Randy asked. "I'd hate to lose your friendship after all these years. I do apologize for my less than honorable motives. But you must know I really care for you."

"But as a friend, not as a wife."

He nodded and refused to meet his mother's glare.

Katherine shook her head. "Mama, I'm so disappointed you'd deceive me with such a horrid scheme. And you too, Mrs. Clarke."

Katherine braced herself for a confrontation with her mother, who'd no doubt lash her with cutting words. But she remained mute.

Aunt Letty clapped her hands in glee. "Don't look so glum, people. This is a grand day. An ill-advised marriage has been prevented and that's something to celebrate."

Aunt Letty glanced toward Katherine's father, who stood silently by the door. "What about you, William?"

"I love you, Isabelle," he said in a low rumble, "but you've made a terrible mistake. It's one thing to encourage two young people to consider each other, another to bully them into it. To conspire with Georgia to make marrying our Katherine the only way out from under some threat . . ." He looked over to Randy and shook his head. "If I'd known . . ." His voice cracked and he looked to Katherine, lifting his hands in surrender. "Forgive me, princess. I went along with it too long and turned a blind eye when, clearly, I should've been paying closer attention. You are free to make your own choices, with no repercussions from us."

Mama rallied. "I am dreadfully disappointed. But there are so many other suitable gentlemen! I'm sure you'll find one, Katherine. When we return to New York in September, we'll—"

Aunt Letty interrupted in an exasperated tone. "Really, Isabelle. Let the girl choose her own husband. You should understand by now that's exactly what she'll do. All your bullying won't make a wit of difference. Katherine is just as opinionated and determined as you are. And I suspect she's already made her choice anyway."

"Oh?" Papa asked, raising a brow in their direction. His eyes flicked over to Andrew.

Aunt Letty winked at her grandniece. "Am I right, dear?"

Katherine breathed deeply. "Yes, you are." Her gaze slid from Mama to Papa. "Andrew and I are going to marry and move to Florida. We're going to run the citrus groves together."

Her mother gasped. "Oh no, dear, you don't mean that. Andrew is a nice, hardworking fellow, but . . ." Her voice drifted off. "Well, you must think this over carefully. You're making another impulsive decision you'll come to regret."

"No, Mama. This feels like the least impulsive decision I've ever made," she said, smiling up at Andrew. "I'm sure we'll be happy."

"I suppose it's really up to you," Mama sputtered.

"Yes, it is, Isabelle," Papa agreed. "I had an inkling this might come about, given the opportunity. And I can't say I'm upset, although I'm sorry to lose you as an employee, Andrew." Then a wide grin spread across Papa's face as he looked toward Katherine and Andrew. "You'll make a grand couple. I imagine you'll both be quite satisfied working your groves. And your mother and I will make it a point to visit you each winter. It'll be a relief to escape the cold weather. I do hope you two will return to Camp Birchwood during the summer, given that it's a slow season and all."

Katherine's eyes widened in surprise, hope filling her heart. Could it be? Could he have just made certain that the road between them would never be blocked again?

Before she could rush to her father and wrap her arms around his ample waist, he strode over to her. He shook Andrew's hand and then hugged Katherine, nearly smothering her with his affection. When he stepped back, he said, "Don't worry. We'll all come around. Just give everyone a short time to adjust to the idea and I promise we'll all be thrilled. Isn't that right, Isabelle?"

Mama joined them on the lawn. "I'm a bit stunned, but maybe your father's right. Time will tell. Katherine dear, I don't want to lose you again."

This was probably the closest Mama would come to an actual apology, but Katherine was more than satisfied. "You won't lose me, Mama. I promise."

"Ah, Andrew," Randy said, "I wish you and Katherine much joy. I hope that we all can be friends, as time goes on."

Andrew smiled and shook his offered hand. "Forgive me for swiping your girl?"

"She never was, not really," Randy said. "I think she's always been yours." He sounded a little disappointed, but mostly relieved.

Andrew patted him on the shoulder. "Do you think your father will insist you start work?"

Randy shrugged. "I don't know. Maybe not. After all, I fulfilled my part of the bargain."

Andrew was glad Katherine had moved away to speak to her great-aunt. He'd hate for her to hear Randy's callous talk.

"But even if he doesn't insist, I'm considering going into the bank every once in a while to see if I can adapt to working. It's worked out all right for you."

Andrew smiled. "I applaud that. It'll be good for you, Randy. Work builds character."

"So you say," Randy mumbled as he ambled off toward the recreation hall, walking backward. "Are you ready for a game of billiards?"

Andrew shook his head, astounded at how quickly his cousin had recovered. "No, not today."

Randy shrugged, smiled, and pivoted on his heel, setting off alone. *He'll be fine,* Andrew thought. *Just fine.*

Katherine returned to Andrew's side and touched his arm lightly, but it felt like a jolt of electricity. "Would you take a walk with me, Andrew? I need to get away for a while."

Arms linked, they strolled across the wooded yard and down a narrow path toward the beaver pond. On the way they stopped to pick raspberries and blackberries from the brambles close to the trail. They popped the berries in each other's mouths and savored the taste. For a while they spoke of the citrus groves and building a new home on the property, of starting a life away from New York society.

"Do you think I'll ever acclimate to the Florida heat?" he asked, loosening his tie.

"In time," she said. "It's perfect in the winter. And in the summer we can vacation right here at Birchwood. How does that sound to you?"

"Perfect. When should we have the wedding?" he asked, hoping she'd agreed to an early date.

She tilted her head and looked up at him, smiling. "How about I ask the pastor of the Church of the Good Shepherd on St. Hubert's Isle? We could marry right away and have a quiet reception here at Camp Birchwood. What do you think?"

"The sooner the better." He gently spun her around until they were face-to-face. "Have I told you how much I love you?"

Katherine laughed. "Tell me again."

"I'll show you." Then he buried her in a kiss that lasted and lasted.

When they finally moved apart, Katherine couldn't stop smiling at the man she loved so dearly. The Lord had brought them together, and happily, she'd finally listened to His voice. This time she was following Him down the path He'd laid before her.

"You know, Andrew, if I hadn't opened my mind and heart to the Lord to seek His way, I never would've recognized you as the man I'm supposed to marry. I have you and Aunt Letty to thank for that."

"And in turn, He gave me new vision for a new path I never

imagined—running a business with the woman I love." He slipped his arm around her waist and drew her closer.

She couldn't stop smiling.

Together they turned, hand in hand, and ambled down the trail toward the water, secure in the knowledge they were taking the right path.

This time, a path toward love.

Reading Group Guide

1. Do you think it was unfair for Katherine's father to insist she follow her mother's agenda for the summer in exchange for a loan to save Osborne Citrus Groves? Do you think Katherine should've rebelled against her parents' manipulations and asserted her independence? Or was she merely being realistic as a woman of her times and class?

2. Andrew was caught between his love for Katherine and his loyalty to the Clarkes. Do you think he acted in the best way or could he have done something differently?

3. At first Andrew valued his job more than his love for Katherine. Was he being prudent or selfish or both? Should he have declared his love earlier? What do you think would've happened if he had?

4. Aunt Letty guided Katherine throughout the story. Could she have done something more to help?

5. Should Katherine have toyed with the idea of marrying Randy or should she have refused to even consider him as a suitor? What do you think of arranged marriages that were fairly common among the rich at that time? Could they be successful?

6. Randy wanted to marry Katherine to avoid working for his father. Should Andrew have told Katherine the truth about the situation? What might have happened if he had?

7. Should Harriet have asked for money to support her son? Would Katherine have been justified to refuse her request?

8. Do you think of Harriet as an adulteress or as a woman who succumbed because of love? Do you feel sorry for her or not? Would you forgive her easily?

Acknowledgments

I'd like to thank all the people at Thomas Nelson who have contributed so much to the publication of this novel. Your helpfulness amazes me. A special thanks goes to the art department for giving me beautiful book covers, everyone in Marketing and Promotion, Katie Bond, Eric Mullett, Ashley Schneider, and Ruthie Dean, and to my editors, Natalie Hanemann, Becky Monds, and Lisa T. Bergren. I'll always be grateful to Ami McConnell and Allen Arnold for giving me a chance to publish the stories I love to write.

My husband, Jim, is my real hero. He gives me the time I need to write while he takes care of all the countless jobs I don't have the time or energy to do. Thank you with all my heart!

"A charming peek inside life during the Gilded era.
Highly recommended."

—Colleen Coble, best-selling author of *The Lightkeeper's Daughter*

About the Author

Cara Lynn James is the author of several novels including *Love on a Dime*. She's received contest awards from Romance Writers of America and the American Christian Fiction Writers. She resides in Florida with her husband, Jim.